Ian A

The Lampmaker

Limetree Books
www.limetreebooks.net

Published by Limetree Books
www.limetreebooks.net

Copyright © 2025 Ian Assersohn

All rights reserved.

ISBN–13: 978-1-0684295-0-7

Typesetting and cover design by the author

Dedicated to the memory of
my dad, Jerrold Assersohn

CONTENTS

Author's Note	i
List of Main Characters	iii
THE LAMPMAKER	
Prologue	1
PART ONE: Tukum, Kurland, 1880	5
PART TWO: Riga, Vidzeme, 1883	77
PART THREE: Whitechapel, London, 1888	185
Acknowledgements	i
Glossary	iii

Author's Note

This is a work of fiction inspired by my paternal grandfather's life story. He died in 1937, over twenty years before I was born. I know very little about his early life and almost nothing at all about it before he came to England. That seems to be quite typical — immigrants of my grandfather's generation generally didn't talk about the lives they had fled. The little I do know is pieced together from the scanty historical records which have survived and from a few stories of his early career in London passed down by my father.

My grandfather, David Assersohn, lived in the town of Tukum in Courland, now part of Latvia (see the note about place names below). Tukum in 1880 had about 6,000 inhabitants, of whom just under half were Jews. The region had a historical association with the Teutonic order of knights and retained a strong Germanic influence, although in this period it was under Russian control. Courland's political situation was somewhat unusual because in 1829 Czar Nicholas I had removed it from the "Pale of Settlement", the territory within Czarist Russia in which Jews were allowed to live, whilst maintaining the rights of those Jews already settled and registered there.

At an early age David became, somehow, a highly skilled lamp maker and, sometime before 1891, he emigrated to London. I imagine him being thrown, as a penniless young immigrant, unable to speak English, into the maelstrom of Victorian London's notoriously overcrowded and dangerous East End and I wonder how he survived. Yet he not only survived, but thrived. In a surprisingly short time he created a successful manufacturing business. Eventually he married and moved to Ealing, West London where, among other things, he founded a synagogue.

My grandfather's life, and the host of unanswered (and, I suspect, unanswerable) questions that surround it, gave my story its starting point, but it remains, I repeat, a work of fiction.

For me, his story is as much a vehicle for thinking about the experiences of a whole generation of Russian Jewish emigrants as it is a way to explore my own family history.

I felt it was important to be faithful to the historical background, and I really have tried. I am not a historian, though, and there may be inadvertent errors and anachronisms in the book. If you know more about these places and events than I do, and you notice something wrong, then all I can say is I really did my best. I hope it doesn't spoil your enjoyment too much.

Place names

Many places in Eastern Europe have different names in different languages, and sometimes their names change over time.

The town which forms the setting for most of Part One is known in English as Tukums and in Livonian as Tukāmō, but I refer to it in the book by its Yiddish name, Tukum. For similar reasons, and to avoid anachronism, I use the names Kurland (rather than Courland or Kurzeme), Boisk (Bauska), Mitau (Jelgava) and Libau (Liepāja).

A word about language

Amongst themselves, the Jewish characters in this book would have spoken Yiddish, an Ashkenazi Jewish language derived from German but written using Hebrew characters. (They would certainly have spoken other languages as well, in order to converse with their non-Jewish neighbours.)

To help give a flavour of this, the text of The Lampmaker, especially in Parts One and Two, is sprinkled with Yiddish words and phrases (shown in *italics*). There is a glossary at the end of the book, should you need it, although in many cases it should be possible, I hope, to glean the meaning from the context.

MAIN CHARACTERS

The Yacobsohn/Gutman family

Itzhak Yacobsohn, a tailor
Scheine, his wife
Rafael ("Rafi") and Yossel ("Yoss"), their sons
Shmuel Yacobsohn, Itzhak's brother
Hirsch and Leah Yacobsohn, Itzhak's parents
Favel Gutman, a baker, Scheine's father

The Rosenberg family

Meyer Rosenberg, a shoemaker
Ester, his wife
Hannah, their daughter
Schloma and Reuben, their sons

The Gozinsky/Krupp family

Pinchus Gozinsky, a fabric dealer
Israel Gozinsky, a factory owner, Pinchus's son
Aaron Gozinsky, Pinchus's son
Sora–Roha, Pinchus's daughter
Yudel Krupp, a blacksmith, Sora–Roha's husband
David and Rosa Krupp, their children

Other Characters

In Tukum

Abram "Bushy" Leibowitz, Rafael's *melamed* (teacher)
Leib "Crutch" Lipman, an ex–soldier

In Riga

Salomon Strauss, Rafael's apprentice master
Hanna Strauss, his wife

In London

John Smart, a workshop owner
Isaac ("Ike") Klein, a worker at Smart's, Rafi's friend

(In London — continued)
    Mr. Brown, foreman at Smart's
    George Draper, a worker at Smart's
    Samuel Cohen, a factory owner
    Elizabeth Cohen, his daughter
    Jacob Rothstein, foreman at Cohen's
    Rachel Lazarus, a garment worker
    Shoshana ("Susan") Levy, an art historian

PROLOGUE

Every Friday night Ralph would take the special candlesticks from the sideboard, polish them carefully, and set them in their correct places on the starched white linen tablecloth. Their slender silver-plated columns, twisted like barley-sugar, would gleam and sparkle, so that guests, seeing them for the first time, were always entranced.

'Oh! Such beautiful *Shabbos* candlesticks,' they would enthuse, as they came into the dining-room.

Ralph would acknowledge the compliment with a graceful nod. 'Thank you,' he would reply. 'I'm very glad you like them.'

Then Lily would light the candles, and cover her eyes and say the blessing, and Ralph would watch her proudly, his heart overflowing with love and happiness.

The two candlesticks were bequeathed to Ralph by the widow of his old apprentice master, Salomon Strauss, who had made them. Hanna Strauss had no family to leave them to, and she knew Ralph would treasure them.

He did. To him they represented the things he valued most in life; love, beauty, kindness, friendship, tradition, family, and God.

Sometimes after *kiddush* the guests, their interest piqued by the unusual candlesticks, and wondering where they came from, would ask Ralph questions about his past, hoping for stories about the early days. But he would always deflect them; he didn't talk about his childhood or about how, or why, he came to England.

'No,' he would say, shaking his head. 'The past was bad. It's over. Today things are good. Please God, tomorrow they will be even better. I prefer to think about the future.'

Even now, in his mid-sixties, Ralph was still very active and showed no signs of slowing down, much less retiring. On the contrary, he was at the factory, or in the showroom, every day of the week; on the shop-floor, talking to the staff, having meetings, making deals, coming up with new ideas.

'Retire? Why should I retire?' he would ask. 'What would I do all day if I retired?'

He was joking, of course. There were plenty of other things in his life, enough to fill his time twice over. He was still a trustee of the synagogue he had founded. He and Lily were still involved in the art gallery. And there were all sorts of meetings to attend; anti-nazi meetings, and meetings of the local Labour party, and meetings of all their various charities.

But family and friends came first.

Ralph and Lily loved entertaining, especially their children, their grandchildren, their sisters and brothers and cousins. Ralph's stepmother and half-siblings came frequently, even after his father passed away. And, of course, their many, many friends.

Sometimes, quite often actually, there would be a surprise guest at the party. Someone from the factory, perhaps, or just someone from *shul* who seemed lonely, or sad. Whatever the occasion, whether an ordinary *Shabbos*, or a *Seder*, or *Rosh Hashanah*, or someone's birthday, as often as possible there would be people sitting round the Jacobsons' enormous dining-table laughing, talking, arguing, singing.

There was another important candlestick in the house, apart from the ones on the table. This one was kept on the mantlepiece in Ralph's study, not on show. It was miniature, much too small to hold a normal candle, but in form it was identical to the full-sized ones. Being smaller, it was, if anything, even more exquisitely delicate than the others.

Like its taller counterparts it was one of a pair. But its twin was missing; where the other should have been there was an empty space. Ralph felt that loss as a palpable absence. It saddened him. But the remaining one was even more precious because of it. It held a message for him. 'Don't think about what you've lost, Ralph,' said the lone candlestick. 'Think about what remains. Think about me. And be grateful.'

And he *was* grateful.

One evening, Ralph and Lily were getting ready to go out for dinner with their friends the Rosenbergs. As he trimmed his neat little moustache, Ralph glanced in the bathroom mirror and then stared at his reflection again more carefully.

It was an old man looking back at him. When had that happened?

His hair was thinning, no doubt about that. He turned his head from side to side, looking at himself out of the corners of his eyes, but couldn't make up his mind whether his ears and nose had grown larger or his face had got thinner. Perhaps a little of both? he thought.

His moustache was almost entirely white. He wondered about colouring it. Perhaps he should even grow his beard back? No, that would age him even more. Besides, he had got rid of it in the first place because it made him look too Jewish. Now was probably not the best time.

Later on, as they were getting ready for bed, he said to Lily: 'It'll be *Pesach* soon. Are any of your sisters joining us for *Seder* night this year?'

She was sitting at her dressing–table, taking off her make–up. A few years younger than him, she nevertheless had a few wrinkles now, and there were flecks of grey in her hair. But she is still so beautiful, he thought. So elegant and graceful in her movements. How lucky I am. He watched her slip off the pendant he had given her.

'I don't know yet,' she replied distractedly. 'I suppose we shall see what we shall see.' It was one of her favourite expressions, and usually passed without further comment, but this time it stirred something in him.

'Do you remember the first time you said that to me?' he asked. She smiled at the recollection.

'Of course I do. It was in 1901.'

'Over thirty years ago. Can you believe it?' Then his voice became more serious. 'Do you still love me, Lily?'

'Idiot. Of course.'

'And when I get really, really old? Will you still love me then?' She looked up at him, her eyes twinkling with mischief, and replied:

'Perhaps. Who can tell? I suppose we shall see what we shall see.'

PART ONE

Tukum, Kurland

1880

1

One Friday morning Rafael Yacobsohn, nine years old, was at the table eating his breakfast — bread and *schmaltz*. His younger brother Yossel, just woken up, came in slowly, yawning sleepily and rubbing his eyes awake.

'There you are, finally,' scolded their mother. 'I've called you twice, Yossel. Now, you boys need to hurry, or you'll be late for *heder*.'

Most of the buildings in Tukum were wooden, including the one containing the Yacobsohns' small apartment. Their home attested to the durability and adaptability of the Baltic pine, as well as that of the Baltic Jew. Floors, walls, ceilings and furniture, everything was made of wood. The place creaked almost constantly, and it reverberated with every sound made by the Wassermans upstairs, but the Yacobsohns were content with it, because they had the ground floor rooms all to themselves; not everyone was so fortunate.

The boys' mother, Scheine, was a thin young woman, with pale skin and a delicate face. When she spoke, she made quick, anxious gestures, one hand going frequently up to the small silver pendant she habitually wore. She was twenty-nine, although you might take her to be older, and had developed the habit of singing, under her breath, snatches of lullabies and other songs she had learned as a child. She was doing it now, but she broke off in mid-phrase to offer her younger son a chunk of dark bread.

'Eat! Eat!' she urged. Yossel rattled through the blessing and stuffed it into his mouth. 'Now hurry up and get dressed. And you, Rafi,' she said, 'get your coat and cap on. Come on, boys,' she commanded, clapping her hands. 'Hurry!'

Yossel went back into the other room, still chewing, and tugged on his clothes. By the time he was dressed his brother was at the door, shifting impatiently from foot to foot. Yossel grabbed his coat and cap and slipped his feet into his boots. Scheine crouched down to kiss the boys and, calling goodbye over their shoulders, they went into the outer hall and through the street door into the unpaved road.

When they were gone she threw on her shawl and went out herself, going the opposite way up the road, towards the bakery where she worked.

The boys walked through the smoky dawn light of early spring as quickly as Yossel's short legs would allow. They didn't have far to go; Tukum was a small town and the Jewish part was particularly compact, its few hundred Jewish homes and businesses huddling close, like sheep in a thunderstorm.

The town was waking, store keepers languidly opening up their tiny shops. Moishe the Pedlar was already about, one hand on the bridle of the tired old horse *schlepping* his cart, which was laden with a motley assortment of household *schlorems*. "White–hands" Yankel, the milkman, his horse waiting patiently in the traces, was flirting with Tsivja the street vendor, standing on the corner with her tray of feeble trinkets. The boys waved to "Crutch" Lipman, the ex–soldier who, having lost his foot in the Crimea, now relied on charity. They received a smart salute in response, which made them giggle.

As they went on, they passed the cobbler's shop belonging to their friend Reuben's father, Meyer Rosenberg; and the bathhouse, with its tiled walls and steamy, inviting warmth; and Rabbi Lichtenstein's sturdy, imposing house, built of actual bricks; and, next door to the Rabbi's house, the *shul* itself, with its tall windows and thick double doors.

Heder was next door to the *shul*; they were the last to arrive. They darted through the door and hurried to their respective classes.

*

Tukum, although a small town, boasted, in addition to the *Talmud Torah* school, two *heders*. The other one, which everyone called the 'Old *heder*', was favoured by the more orthodox, traditional-minded parents. The 'New *heder*', which the Yacobsohn boys attended, had been set up a few years earlier, in the teeth of some opposition, by the board of trustees responsible to the Russian authorities for the Jewish community in the town.

Despite its recent construction, it was not a particularly prepossessing or comfortable building inside. Built quickly and cheaply, using the same wooden construction as most of the town, there was an alarmingly rickety, creaky impermanence to it. In the snowy winter months it was cold, its draughty windows rattling in the wind, and in summer, when motes of dust drifted lazily in the sunbeams, it was stifling and airless. It already had the smell of a much older institution, redolent of boys, crumbling books and fungal decay. To these were added the accumulated reek of the cigarettes smoked rapidly, and in great profusion, by the *melamed*, Abram Leibowitz. *Rebe* Abram's lavish beard and luxuriant eyebrows were a source of fascination to generations of his young charges, and the source of his irreverent nickname, "Bushy".

A large, book-strewn, wooden table almost filled the room which Rafael entered. As always, the *melamed* sat upright, as if posing for his portrait, on a solid, straight-backed wooden armchair, its firmness only slightly ameliorated by an ancient, tasselled, velvet cushion. The young students were squeezed onto benches around the table.

With his imposing frame, enormous ears, nicotine-stained fingers and beard, and his thick, wire-rimmed glasses, the *melamed* might have been terrifying to his pupils. But his formidable appearance was betrayed by the slight lift at the corner of his mouth and the inveterate twinkle in his shortsighted eyes which spoke of the patient kindness and gentle humour beneath.

Clucking his tongue and shaking his head at Rafael by way of a mild rebuke for his tardiness, he gestured for him to sit down. Rafael squeezed himself between his friends, Haim the barber's son and Reuben the shoemaker's son.

'Now that we are finally all here,' said the *rebe*, emphasising the 'finally' and peering over his spectacles at Rafael, 'let us begin.'

The day, as always, started with morning prayers, followed by intensive study of the *Pentateuch*. There was also a little *Talmud*. The days were long, very long; on paper the curriculum was not dissimilar from the one at the 'Old *heder*', but the quality of the teachers made all the difference. In Rafael's case the *melamed* was a clever, well educated man and a natural and gifted educator; almost the opposite of the men who taught at the 'Old *heder*'. His aim was to provide his students with the opportunity for a reasonably rounded education; although it was true, as he often admitted, it wasn't every boy who took full advantage of that opportunity.

Late in the afternoon, just before evening prayers were due, Abram Leibowitz took off his spectacles with both hands, put them carefully down on the table, and lit another cigarette. The boys looked up at him expectantly.

'We are almost finished for today,' he began. 'But, before prayers, there is time for a short discussion. Let's see now, who shall we start with? Haim,' he said, looking over his spectacles at the boy, who jumped slightly at the sound of his name. 'What month are we in?' That was an easy start.

'Adar, Rebe,' answered the relieved Haim. He was rewarded by a reassuring, crinkly smile.

'Well done. Yes, the month of Adar. And Reuben, what festival do we celebrate in Adar?' This was another easy one.

'Purim, Rebe'.

'Yes, indeed. In fact it will be Purim in just a few days, won't it? As you all know, Purim is a joyous festival, the time when we remember the story of King Ahasuerus and Esther in the time of the Persian empire. The time when Esther saved the whole Jewish community from destruction at the hands of the wicked vizier whose name was,' he paused for dramatic effect, ' ... Haman.' The boys continued to sit quietly and he looked round at them in mock disappointment. '*Nu?*' he said with a sly smile. 'Don't you know that this evil man's name is so hateful that we make a loud noise when someone utters it, to drown out the sound?' He looked over the rim of his glasses at the class. 'Do you think you can make a loud noise, boys? *Hmm?*'

They all felt ready to take up this particular challenge.

'Very well. Let's try that again.' He repeated the last sentence and the children shouted lustily, as they had been instructed. He gave them a few moments to enjoy it and then he continued in a more solemn voice. They quietened down, listening intently. 'This wicked man wanted to destroy every single Jew. Every last one. Can you imagine such a crime? But as you know, the story ends well. Esther and Mordecai stopped him from fulfilling his wicked plans through their bravery and their cunning. The Holy One, Blessed be He, saw to it that the vizier did not succeed.' He paused again before going on. 'But boys, you see, this man, this evil man, (no, save your breath, I am not going to say his name again) was not the first person to hate the Jews. And, I'm sorry to say, also he was not the last. There are still people like him; even today. So I want you to think about this: why would someone like him want to kill all the Jewish people?'

Reuben was the first to venture an answer. 'Because Mordecai would not bow down to him?' he suggested.

'Very good, Reuben, yes that's what the *Torah* says. "Mordecai bowed not, nor did him reverence." And that is the only explanation the *Torah* seems to provide. What does it mean? Why did it matter so much if one man refused to bow?' The boys had nothing to suggest. He went on: 'Perhaps because what one man may do another may also do. It was symbolic. The Jews would not turn their backs on the Lord their God, and so the Persians wanted to destroy them. And I am afraid, boys, that this was not an isolated instance. The Purim story is about a Persian vizier, but it might have been about a Philistine king, or an Egyptian pharaoh, or a Roman emperor. They also enslaved and persecuted Jewish People. Why? Why do we find ourselves so often in history mistreated in this way?'

Again, nobody had an answer. The *melamed* let them sit in silence for a while so the question could penetrate their minds. But he saw it was too much for them; the boys were becoming fidgety and unfocused. He was cross with himself for taking them into such murky waters too soon and decided to postpone the topic to a later date.

'In the end,' he went on, 'we can do no better than to stay true to ourselves and our religion. As it is written, "You must love the Lord your God with all your hearts and with all your souls and with all your might." We must trust Him; He knows what He is doing. If there are failures, they are ours, not His; we must try to do better. But for now, it is enough that we remember the story of Purim. We should rejoice because it all ends happily. But at the same time we should remember the sufferings of our people.'

In the brief silence that followed this remark, Rafael slowly raised his hand. 'Yes, Rafael?'

'Why, Rebe?'

Abram Leibowitz smiled to himself behind his beard. 'Why what, young man?'

'Well, why do we have to remember horrible things like suffering, and slavery? Why not try to forget them? Purim is supposed to be a happy time, but it makes us feel a bit sad when we remember.'

'This is a good question. Well, for one thing, it teaches us the Lord protects those whom He loves, although not always in the way that we expect. And for another thing, it is good to honour the bravery and the suffering and sacrifices of those who came before us.'

Rafael's brow furrowed as he tried to think about this.

'But why...?'

The *melamed* held up both his palms. 'Enough for now, Rafael. Look at the sun, boys; it is time for evening prayers.'

*

When Scheine Yacobsohn smiled she was still beautiful. But life weighed heavily on her, and it showed in her troubled, haunted eyes. She felt it, too, in her chest. Often her heart would race, or miss a beat and make a sudden disconcerting thump. The singing helped her, sometimes.

She worked every day, except *Shabbos*, at her father's bakery, fetching new batches from the oven, serving customers, keeping the place clean and tidy. Once the bread was all gone and the shop was swept she closed up and went home as fast as she could; she hated for the boys to come home to an empty house.

On this Friday she was back in good time, preparing for *Shabbos*, peeling potatoes for soup, singing quietly to herself. When the boys came in, she broke off the song. '*Nu?*' she asked. 'How was *heder?*'

Yossel shrugged. 'It was all right. I'm hungry, *Mamele*'.

'You're always hungry, Yossel. There's no food just now; go outside and play. But don't get your clothes dirty. And come straight back in when *Tatty* arrives.'

Yossel ran outside, but Rafael sat down at the table, his brow furrowed in thought.

'And how was your day, Raftchik?'

'Well, *Mamale*, "Bushy"... I mean Rebe Leibowitz, told us about *Purim*. He said about how Mordecai didn't bow down, and so the man where you shout "boo", who was the viz ... viz ...'

'The vizier?'

'Yes, the vizier. He wanted to kill everyone, and it was all horrible, and ...' he stopped in mid-sentence. He had lost his thread.

'And?' she prompted, cocking her head slightly.

He picked it up again. 'Oh yes, and the Rebe said that lots of other bad things have happened and we have to remember all of them. All of the horrible things that they did to our ancestors.'

'Well? That's right, isn't it?'

'Is it? I don't know. I don't really understand it, *Mamele*,' he admitted. 'I don't like hearing about horrible things. There are so many; I can't even remember them all, and I don't *want* to remember them. I can't do anything about it. What good does it do remembering them?'

Scheine put down her knife and went over, wiping her hands on her apron. She sat on the chair next to Rafael's, taking his hand in hers. '*Oy*, Raftchik. That sounds like a very grown-up discussion for such a young head. I'm not surprised it confused you. Do you want to know something?' she leaned closer to him and lowered her voice confidentially. 'I don't like hearing about horrible things either. You know what, Rafael Yacobsohn? I think you will make a good scholar. But I never studied these things so I don't really know how to answer your questions. Why don't you ask *Tatty* and *Zeide* what they think? I expect they will be here soon. Oh! Where are the candles!' she cried, jumping up and looking around. 'Ah, there they are. Please can you get them and put them on the table for me, Rafi?'

While Rafael did as she had asked, she looked over at him. He would be ten soon. He was growing up fast. Too fast for her liking. She stroked her pendant absentmindedly and muttered '*pu, pu, pu*' to herself, to ward off the Evil Eye.

A few moments later, the door opened and Yossel reappeared. '*Tatty's* here,' he said.

A moment later Itzhak Yacobsohn came in, touching the *mezuzah* on the door post, and bending slightly to fit under the lintel. He was a tall, lean man with brown eyes set in a benevolent face. His beard was straggly and sparse and, although only 30 years old, he already walked with a slight stoop as if apologising to the world for his height.

He greeted each member of his family with a kiss and said to Scheine: '*Mm*. That soup smells really good. Is your father here yet?'

'Thank you,' replied Scheine. 'No, not yet; he should be here any minute, I hope. It's not after sunset yet, is it?'

'No. Don't worry, there's time.'

Itzhak had hardly finished speaking when the door opened again, and in came Scheine's father, Favel Gutman, reaching up to touch the *mezuzah* and kissing his fingers reverently. '*Shabbat shalom,*' he said, sitting down heavily at the table and wiping his brow. 'Candles not lit yet?'

'*Shabbat shalom, Tate,*' responded Scheine. 'No, I was just about to do it. We were waiting for you.'

'Waiting for me? So now it's my fault if you are late lighting the candles?'

'We aren't late. It's not yet dusk, Reb Favel,' put in Itzhak.

'*Hmph.* Well, don't leave it too long. Dusk doesn't wait just because you're busy, you know. What's that smell?' he asked, peering at the pan. 'Potato soup? Your *mame*, rest her soul, never made potato soup for *Shabbos*. She was a very good cook, your dear *mame*. A good hostess, too. She was not one to let her guests remain thirsty.'

'May I tempt you to a glass of something, Reb Favel?' asked Itzhak suppressing a smile and fetching down a glass and bottle for his father-in-law.

Soon it really was time to light the candles. The candlesticks which Rafael had put out earlier were made of clay; not at all grand, but functional, and the white wax candles stood upright in them well. With the family gathered round the table, Scheine lit them with a match and made the traditional movement suggestive of wafting the light towards herself. Then, covering her eyes, she recited the blessing: '*Barukh ata Adonai, Eloheinu melekh ha'olam, asher kid'shanu b'mitzvotav v'tzivanu l'hadlik ner shel Shabbat*' – Blessed are You, Lord our God, King of the universe, who has sanctified us with Your commandments, and commanded us to kindle the light of the holy Sabbath.

Itzhak blessed the children, they all sang the song *Sholom Aleichem*, and then he blessed the wine and the *challah*. They went over to the sideboard, where there stood a jug of water, a bowl, and a clean linen towel. Itzhak helped the children to wash their hands, then the adults washed theirs, and everyone sat down again.

While Scheine brought over the soup, Itzhak cut five slices from the *challah* and distributed them. Favel Gutman got down to the business of drinking the soup right away, and he took little interest in the conversation until he had partially relieved his hunger.

'How was *heder*?' Itzhak asked the children.

'*Mmmf*,' replied Yossel.

'Yossel, don't talk with your mouth full,' scolded Scheine.

'We talked about Purim,' said Rafael.

'Ah, Purim,' said Itzhak, a big smile on his face, 'Such a happy festival.'

'An expensive festival,' corrected Scheine.

'Well, my dear, God wants us to celebrate.'

'Yes, but does He insist we celebrate by attempting to drink the tavern dry, like somebody I know did last year?'

'Ah, well, perhaps I did overdo it a little last year,' admitted Itzhak with a chuckle, which he quickly turned into a cough when he caught the unamused expression on his wife's face. Then, hurriedly changing the subject, he turned to Yossel. 'And how are you getting on with your *aleph–beys*, Yoss?'

'I can't do it, *Tatty*,' replied Yossel grumpily. 'It's too hard.' Favel Gutman looked up.

'The boy still can't read?' he demanded.

'*Shh, Tate*,' urged Scheine. 'He's learning. It's just a little hard going at the moment.'

'*Pfff*! How old is he? Seven? Is he such a *schlemiel* that he can't read yet?'

'He's only six, *Tate*. Please, let's change the subject.' She gestured towards Yossel, who had reddened.

'*Hmph*. Now look at the boy,' snorted Reb Favel with derision. 'What's the matter with him? He's far too sensitive. He gets that from you. By the way,' he said, losing interest in the topic, 'this soup's watery. You should make it thicker next time. But I'll take a little more, thank you.'

'There isn't any more,' Scheine retorted, angrily clearing away the bowls.

'Reb Favel,' said Itzhak in a placatory voice. 'Would you like to *bentch*?'

'Me? Why, what's wrong with you that you need me to do it? Have you forgotten how the prayers go?'

'Not at all, Reb Favel, I just thought perhaps you might prefer …. never mind, that's quite all right, I am happy to do it.'

'Well, then, mind you do it properly. No shortcuts.'

*

On *Shabbos* mornings, the Yacobsohns, and their friends the Rosenbergs, were in the habit of walking to *shul* together. Then, in the afternoons, Rafael and Reuben usually met up again, by themselves this time; it was nice to be able to talk less guardedly than was possible in the adults' hearing. This week they were still thinking about what "Bushy" had said the day before, and they were looking forward to talking it through.

As they talked, heads together, they roamed randomly through the streets without really thinking about where they were going and noticed, to their dismay, that they had wandered into an unfamiliar part of the town, outside of the Jewish area.

They quickly turned around to retrace their steps. Alarmingly, they saw they had been spotted by a group of boys, four of them, about their own age, or a little older, who were looking at them appraisingly, arms crossed menacingly. One of the boys detached himself from the pack and advanced slowly towards them, face contorted in a smug smirk. 'Look, boys, two little Jews.' He pointed at the *tzitzit* fringes hanging down from inside their shirts. 'What are you doing here, where you aren't welcome, Yids?'

Rafael and Reuben, thoroughly scared, turned and fled, pursued by whoops and catcalls.

'Dirty Yids! Christ Killers!' The gang put up a token show of running after them, but they didn't really want to catch them, just to chase them away.

After a few hundred yards the boys, realising, with relief, that they were not being pursued, slowed to a walk and then stopped in the shelter of a narrow alleyway to catch their breath. Peering out, they assured themselves the coast was clear and then, keeping to the shadows, they made their way by a circuitous route back to more familiar and safe surroundings.

This disquieting encounter, coming on top of the discussion at *heder*, and on Shabbos too, did make it feel like God was trying to tell them something. But exactly what it was He was saying, they were unable to guess.

2

For the Jews of Tukum, poverty was everywhere, like the mud in the streets. If you were a little careless it came into the house on the soles of your boots. It needed ceaseless vigilance to keep it out. A few people, it was true, seemed to possess a gift, the ability to accumulate money, to make it stick to them. Shlaum Blechman, for example, who owned the sawmill, and whose wife wore a new winter coat every year. How they did it, nobody knew. But for most people it was impossible to hold onto money; it flowed through their fingers like sand.

Favel Gutman lacked the gift. He had taken over the bakery many years earlier, when he was a young man and his wife was alive to help him. These days he no longer took part in making or selling the bread himself, although he was always on hand if someone was needed to poke about and grumble and generally get in the way. The actual work was done by Scheine, helped by two other women. For her efforts, she received a handful of rubles (and a *challah* every Friday), hardly anything, but just enough, when combined with Itzhak's earnings, to keep them the right side of destitution.

Itzhak Yacobsohn, journeyman tailor, also lacked the gift. He worked long hours at his machine in a small, windowless room at the back of the haberdashery; sewing, pressing, cutting, altering, patching, mending, transforming. In return for the use of the space he also helped out at the front of the store whenever needed, selling pins and ribbons, just as he had when he first arrived in Tukum. He was fortunate to have this backroom to work in, though; most artisans simply used their living rooms as their workshops. He was not an ambitious man; if he could have earned enough to pay his tax and his guild membership, and put food on the table, and wood on the fire in the winter, and have a little left over for charity and religious festivals, he would have been content. But, with the children to support, however hard he worked it was never quite enough to cover all the bills, which was why the money that Scheine brought in by working at her father's bakery was so essential.

One thing that helped was that Itzhak's customers almost always paid their bills. What he never realised was how much of this was because of his wife. Scheine kept a close eye on the accounts and knew exactly who owed what.

She was sure to encounter the customer (or, more usefully, the customer's wife) in the bakery, and would say, as she handed over the bread: 'What a lovely job my husband has made of your coat, my dear. You look so stylish. Will you be passing the haberdasher's shop later? You might like to just pop in there and settle up with him while it's fresh in your mind.'

Or else: 'I noticed your husband walking past earlier, my dear. So dapper in his jacket he looks; one couldn't see where the rip had been at all. My husband's a gifted mender. You know, I was just glancing at his accounts earlier and I couldn't see any record of the payment. Just an oversight, I'm sure.'

Nobody wanted to hear that sort of thing said to them in front of the other customers, and so Itzhak found his bills paid promptly.

Itzhak's friend, Meyer Rosenberg was yet another who lacked the gift. His family were, if anything, in an even less favourable position than the Yacobsohns. Meyer, the cobbler, sat in his little shop mending boots and shoes from dawn till dusk, but many of his customers had run up large debts to him which they were unable to repay and which he, being a kind and gentle soul, was unwilling to chase.

His wife, Ester, would normally have kept on top of these things, but right now she had something else weighing on her mind. A year earlier Reuben's older brother Schloma had been listed for conscription and taken away to serve in the Czar's army. Nobody had heard from him since. Ester now spent a good deal of her time trying to find out where he was and what had happened to him. She spent whole days sitting in the outside office of some Russian official, waiting to be seen, only to be told there was no time today and she should come back tomorrow. Or, if she did manage to see the official, it would turn out he was the wrong person after all, and she should go to another office and start again. She had no time to attend to Meyer's recalcitrant customers, and so the bills remained unpaid.

Ester and Meyer's middle child, their daughter Hannah, was thirteen. Hannah was quiet, demure, overlooked, uncomplaining. She cooked and cleaned, trying to hold everything together.

*

Life was hard for many in the Russian Empire; but, for many reasons, it was always worse for Jews than for non-Jews. For example, everyone paid tax, but Jews paid double tax.

For parents of boys an even bigger worry was conscription. All Russian men were liable to be drafted into the army, but whereas for non-Jews it was from the age of eighteen, Jewish boys became liable at twelve.

Quotas for Jewish draftees were strictly enforced by the Russian authorities; every two years Rabbi Lichtenstein and the board of trustees were obliged, by law, to select thirty young men — ten for every thousand people in the community — to make up the list. Willing or unwilling, marching smartly or dragged away crying and screaming, it made no difference; the unfortunate chosen were taken away to serve in the army for a term of twenty-five years.

True, it was not as bad as it had been in earlier years; the older townsfolk remembered when they used to snatch young children off the streets and send them to 'Cantonist' schools before bundling them into the army. The current Czar, Alexander II, had ended that, thank God. But still, the fear remained, and parents could expect to find their children on the conscription list before their *bar mitzvahs*. The Russians knew what they were doing; the earlier Jewish children were removed from their homes, the easier it was to tease, tweeze or squeeze the Jewishness out of them.

The Russians also used army service as punishment, for example for Jews who fell behind in paying their taxes. The fear of such a retribution acted as a powerful deterrent.

Twenty-five years is a long time; not everyone who went away returned. But even if they did, the person who came back wasn't the same as the one who went. Anything could have happened; maybe the lad had lost a limb; or maybe he'd become a baptised *goy*. Maybe he had found himself a *shiksa* in some town or village and got her pregnant, or even married her. Maybe he would come home to find his parents were dead, or emigrated, or imprisoned or banished. Who could tell? Twenty five years is a long time. A lifetime.

So, for Rabbi Lichtenstein and the board of trustees, the responsibility of drawing up the list was a heavy, an almost insupportable burden. They tried at first to make the most of their limited freedom of choice by listing those whom they judged the community could most easily do without; men whose families didn't want them, or couldn't feed, thieves, drunkards, beggars, atheists, lazy good-for-nothings, and *meshuggeners*.

But now, as the 1870's drew to a close, the supply of such people was running short, and they had little choice but to widen the net and choose the more valuable young men.

People like Schloma Rosenberg.

*

The days lengthened. *Pesach* and *Shavuot* came and went; the summer air was hot and still, humming with flies and heavy with all the smells that arise when animals and people are crowded close together. The *hasidim* sweated in their long woollen coats and fur-lined hats, and the children in the *heder* drowsed and drooped over their books in the stifling heat.

Ester Rosenberg tirelessly *schlepped* around the Russian officials, trying to find word of Schloma, but finding only silence.

Tisha B'av came, and went; summer began to give way to autumn.

The air cooled, the wind and rains arrived, the leaves fell, and unpaved roads, trodden by many feet, and many hooves, began to turn into a stinking sludge.

Rosh Hashanah and *Yom Kippur* came, and went; the start of another year.

And all the time the air was filled with the sounds of Jewish life. The sound of praying and the sound of gossip. The sounds of singing and weeping, of laughter and anger. The chanting of the *chazzan* and the calls of traders and the whinnying of horses in the market and the lowing of cows heading to the slaughterhouse.

And the sighing of a mother looking for her son.

*

Itzhak and Scheine felt enormous pity for the Rosenbergs, because of Schloma, and were desperate not to find themselves in the same position in a few years' time.

As a precaution, Scheine carefully placed a little pyramid of salt in the corners of the rooms, as well as sprinkling some into the boys' coat pockets; everyone knew that salt could help ward off the Evil Eye. But she knew that more practical, concrete action might also be advisable. So, at her repeated urging, Itzhak agreed to talk to the rabbi, to see what he could suggest.

Rabbi Lichtenstein had set aside times for people to come to him for help or advice and, on the next such time, Itzhak made his way to the brick house next to the *shul* where he and his wife lived.

It was the rabbi's wife who opened the front door when Itzhak knocked. She greeted him politely, if without any particular enthusiasm, and led him to her husband's office, where she left him. Itzhak knocked respectfully and went in, head slightly bowed.

The rabbi ushered him to a chair then went to sit behind his desk. 'Good afternoon, Reb Itzhak. I hope you and your family are well?'

'Thank you for seeing me, Rabbi. Yes, thank you, we are all fine at the moment, thank God. And you too, I hope?'

'Indeed, thank you.' These politenesses over, the Rabbi got down to business. 'So, how can I help you?' he asked.

After a moment to gather his thoughts, Itzhak replied: 'Well, Rabbi, to get right to the point, it's about the conscription lists.'

'I see. You have two boys, of course. But, surely you have nothing to worry about — they are still too young to go on the list, are they not?'

'Yes, Rabbi, that's true. Ten and seven. But Scheine thought... I mean, *we* thought that if we did something now, if we made plans, well, ... you know,' he ended, lamely.

The rabbi looked at Itzhak with compassion and said gently: 'There is wisdom in planning ahead, Reb Itzhak. But on the other hand, who can tell what God has in store for us in two or three years' time? The Talmud says: "Do not worry thyself with the trouble of tomorrow; perhaps thou wilt have no tomorrow, and why shouldst thou trouble thyself about a world that is not thine?" I'm really not sure what you want me to say, Reb Itzhak.'

'Rabbi,' said Itzhak, laying his cards on the table, 'you help draw up the lists. Can't you see your way to saying you'll pass over their names when the time comes? My poor wife...'

'Reb Itzhak,' interrupted the rabbi firmly, 'please let me stop you there. I'm afraid it is not as simple as that. I'm sorry, but you are not the first person I have had this conversation with. You are not the only concerned parent in my congregation; there are many others in your position. You must see that it is impossible for me to give you the assurance you want; if I did, then I would have to give the same assurance to everyone. Then what? How would we fill our quotas?

And if the quotas are not met, there would be extremely serious consequences for the whole community. Reb Itzhak, as much as I would like to give you what you ask, I'm afraid I can promise you nothing.'

'Of course. Of course. I'm sorry I said anything, Rabbi. It was stupid of me,' apologised Itzhak, flustered. After a few moments he continued, tenaciously: 'But, Rabbi, are there no exceptions made? Aren't there any exemptions?'

'Well, yes,' admitted the rabbi. 'A few. If a couple have only one child, for example, then they are excused. It is also possible to buy an exemption.'

'Buy one? For how much, rabbi?'

'Five hundred rubles.' Itzhak was shocked. He shook his head sadly.

'*Oy, oy, oy*! That's an impossible sum, Rabbi. I've never even seen five hundred rubles at one time.'

'Yes, I know. I'm afraid they have made it large enough so that only the richest can afford it. I told you about it only so that you can see how hard it is to avoid the list. Let me see, what else? Well, people with certain physical disabilities are sometimes exempted, but I think that doesn't apply here?'

'No, the boys are both fit and strong, thank God.'

'I'm pleased to hear that. Well, then there are also exemptions for members of certain professions. Artisans, you know.' Itzhak looked up sharply.

'Artisans?'

'Craftsmen, if you will. Carpenters and joiners, for example, or metalworkers.' The rabbi was surprised to see a hopeful look spread across Itzhak's face.

'I see,' said Itzhak, getting to his feet. 'Well, thank you, Rabbi. You have been more help to me that you realise.' He turned to leave.

'Have I?' replied the rabbi, slightly nonplussed. 'Well, I'm very glad. Goodbye, Itzhak. I'll see you on *Shabbos*.'

'Goodbye, Rabbi! Thank you again!' Itzhak called over his shoulder as he hurried away.

Rabbi Lichtenstein looked after him bemusedly for a moment and then, with a sigh, turned to the large pile of papers awaiting his attention.

3

Itzhak and his elder brother Shmuel had grown up in Boisk, a town some sixty miles to the southeast of Tukum, in a region just outside the Pale of Settlement.

Boisk and Tukum, with their synagogues, bath houses, slaughterhouses, and market squares, were quite similar towns, of a similar size. The rabbi in Boisk when Itzhak and Shmuel were young was a man by the name of Mordekhai Eliasberg, a reformer steeped in the *Haskalah*, the Jewish enlightenment movement.

Shmuel and Itzhak's father, Hirsch Yacobsohn, did not approve of Rabbi Eliasberg and his ideas. Hirsch was orthodox in outlook, a patriarch in the traditional mould; a man with inflexible notions and a domineering will, who issued instructions to his family and expected them to be obeyed. They generally were.

Hirsch spent his days in study and prayer. His work was the *Torah*, *Talmud* and *Mishnah* and he devoted himself to them fully. The boys' mother, Leah, was the breadwinner; she did whatever she could to bring in money, provided it was on the list of employments her husband deemed appropriate.

When Itzhak was ten years old, Hirsch decided that his younger son was no scholar and had better get an apprenticeship. So, one day in 1860, a bewildered Itzhak found himself deposited at the door of Tsalel the Tailor.

So began a miserable seven years. By the end of it Itzhak would know enough to join the tailors' guild and earn a living, but the skills he acquired would be hard-earned. When he fell, exhausted, onto his bed at the end of a long, long day, it was onto a hard pallet, thinly covered with straw, in the corner of the tailor's living room–cum–

workshop. When he wasn't asleep, he worked; fetching, carrying, sweeping, cleaning, sharpening tools, washing dishes, rocking the baby, throwing out the slops. He was housekeeper, baby-sitter, cook and drudge. Berated for his youth and stupidity, and beaten for his slowness, it was a time of toil and tears. In other words, a normal apprenticeship.

Hirsch Yacobsohn's closest friend, and sometime business partner, was Pinchus Gozinsky, the owner of a small fabric business. He was a man after Reb Hirsch's own heart; the two thought alike, dressed alike, enjoyed the same food and drink, and sat next to each other in *shul*.

The Gozinskys had three children; the eldest was a son, Israel, the next a daughter, Sora-Roha, and their youngest another boy, Aaron.

As Aaron was about the same age as Itzhak, the two spent a lot of time together in the days before the apprenticeship, and in fact were firm friends.

Israel, being older, was rather aloof from the other children; when the families met up he seemed always to be busy elsewhere. But Sora-Roha often played with the boys when they were children, and eventually became the unwitting cause of much trouble.

The two patriarchs decided to cement their friendship and form a lasting bond between their families, by arranging a marriage. In their view a union between Hirsch's eldest boy, Shmuel, and Sora-Roha was highly desirable. So, accompanied by much hand-clasping, back-slapping and drinking of toasts, a deal was struck.

Accordingly, when the children attained an appropriate age, they instructed them to prepare for the wedding.

But Shmuel, having formed the opinion that he wanted a say in the question of who he would marry, astonished the patriarchs by refusing. It turned out that he had plans of his own, and was intending to marry the schoolteacher's daughter, a girl by the name of Sara Rosental.

Hirsch raged and stormed and took the case to the rabbi. Much to his amazement and disgust, Rabbi Eliasberg, with his extraordinary reformist views, took Shmuel and Sara's side. Before the furious fathers could find a legal way to stop it, Shmuel and Sara were married.

If he was powerless to prevent the match, Hirsch nevertheless refused to take his son's betrayal lying down. Shmuel was promptly disowned and disinherited and he and Sara bundled up their possessions and moved away.

They travelled first northwest, to Kurland and to its capital, Mitau, then west to Libau on the Baltic coast where they boarded a passenger ship. Arriving in the Port of London some days later they gravitated, almost inevitably, to the East End, and there they set up home.

The baffled fathers' focus now turned to the other Yacobsohn boy, the newly qualified tailor Itzhak, and the astonished lad duly received the information that he was engaged to marry Sora-Roha Gozinsky.

Itzhak considered. It would have been the easiest thing in the world to comply, for Sora-Roha was a beauty. She had jet black hair, a lovely smile and eyes that sparkled with life. True, she was at present somewhat cowed by her tyrannical father, and was therefore quieter and more subdued than Itzhak would have liked his wife to be. But he had known her since childhood, and he knew there was more to Sora-Roha than that; there was a spark within her which needed only a little kindling to burst into flame. A big part of him longed to be the one to provide the kindling.

But it was not to be. Sora-Roha made it clear to Itzhak that, although she was fond of him, and knew he would make somebody a good husband, she did not want to be his wife. She went on to confide that, during the years he had been toiling in the tailor's workshop, she had fallen head-over-heels in love with the blacksmith's burly, handsome son, Yudel.

For Itzhak, that was the end of the matter. He did not intend to be married to someone whose affections lay elsewhere. Besides, after years of being browbeaten by his father, and by the tailor and his wife, he was getting tired of it. So, like his brother, he refused to comply with Hirsch's plan.

The two fathers raged and stormed for a second time. But Itzhak was adamant; he would not do it. So, disowned and disinherited like his brother before him, the seventeen-year old Itzhak left Boisk bound for Mitau. He hoped he might find Shmuel and Sara there, but they had already moved on, he knew not where.

Since Mitau was crowded and uncomfortable, and he couldn't find work there, he kept moving. He headed to Tukum where he sought, and gained, permission from the authorities to settle, and there he made his life.

*

When Pinchus Gozinsky died of heart failure at the age of forty-nine, it was assumed that his elder son Israel would inherit his fabric business. However, it turned out Israel didn't want it, so it had gone instead to his younger brother, Aaron.

Israel moved to Riga, armed with a small sum of money inherited from his father, to which he added a larger one he had made for himself, nobody was quite sure how. Since then, he had prospered by investing in a small metalworks and transforming it, by slow degrees, into a large and thriving modern factory. Gozinsky Metalworks was now an important business, and Israel Gozinsky was a wealthy businessman whose money brought him influence in Riga and beyond.

A man of the modern age, Israel Gozinsky was an enlightened factory owner and a social reformer. But he was under no illusions; he knew that most factory owners ran things differently. In their hands men, women and even children worked eleven or twelve hour shifts for poor wages in unsafe, unsanitary conditions. His own vision of the way to run a factory was different, and so it was little wonder that he had no trouble attracting staff; in fact workers queued up to be hired at Gozinsky Metalworks.

Israel frequently warned his fellow tycoons that their workers would not stand it for ever; he could see there was a witches' brew of anger and discontent bubbling away in Russia's factories. He worried very much about what would happen to him, and to everybody, when the lid blew off the cauldron. But prophets are seldom listened to, and his warnings went unheeded.

Following his discussion with the rabbi, Itzhak knew that if he could enrol the boys as apprentices in Gozinsky's factory, then they had a route by which they could escape the fearful disaster of military service and gain a measure of financial security at the same time. It became a fixed idea in his mind that this was the solution to their problems and it must be made to happen.

He discussed it with Scheine. She thought the idea was sound in theory, but she was anxious about sending the boys away to Riga. What would happen to them there? Wasn't it a dangerous place, this big city? Were there no workshops here in Tukum they could go to?

Yes there were. But Itzhak knew those workshops. They were replicas of the one he had sweated in for seven long years back in Boisk. Itzhak was not like his father; he was not going to subject his own sons to what he had endured.

Aaron was proud of his brother's achievements, and in his letters had described the factory in glowing terms. So Itzhak knew it was not a sweatshop but a modern factory with a proper apprenticeship scheme. There, he was sure, the boys would not be mistreated. He showed Scheine the letters, and eventually she was satisfied. Yes, she thought, he was right. If they could get apprenticeships there, then everything might indeed be fine.

But unfortunately, Itzhak hadn't seen or spoken to Israel Gozinsky for years. He was a big important man now; why should he say 'Yes' to this request? How, in fact, was it to be done?

*

All through the winter Itzhak and Scheine talked about what they should do. Itzhak's idea was to send Israel a letter or even go to Riga and try to speak to him in person, but Scheine counselled against a direct approach. She reminded him that Israel was now a man of some standing and importance and that Itzhak hadn't spoken to him since they were children. Her suggestion was to get in touch with Aaron in the first instance, in the hope that he might have some sway with his elder brother, or at least some advice on the best way to go about things.

This conceded, the discussion then switched to the question of how to contact Aaron. Scheine thought a personal visit was better than a letter, and so it was decided; Itzhak would go to Boisk. It would mean losing income while he was away, but Scheine thought they could manage for a few days.

So, one day in early Spring, he began asking around and soon found a trader willing, for a few kopeks, to take him on his cart as far as Mitau, where Itzhak felt sure he would be able to pick up another lift to Boisk.

When it was time to leave, Scheine carefully attached a pin to the inside of his lapel for protection against the Evil Eye on the road. She begged him to agree everything with Isaac, to be careful, to come back quickly and safely, and not to sit on the parcel of food she had put in his bag for the journey.

He kissed her cheek, promising he would remember everything and do just as she said and, waving goodbye, went to catch his lift.

The first part of the road wound through a region of flat wetlands, low–flying birds skimming across the surface of the marshes in the morning sunshine. It was a long time since he had been on a journey, and the anticipation had been exciting, but once on the road the taciturnity of his companion and the monotony of the

Kurland countryside induced in him a state of torpor, and he drifted into a reverie.

'This horse is walking unevenly,' he thought. 'I hope it's not lame. Perhaps it just needs a new shoe. Maybe there's a farrier in the next village. I wonder how Sora–Roha is doing with her blacksmith. I hope they are happy together, after all that. She's a fine woman. I wonder if I should have ... no, no, I definitely did the right thing; she wouldn't have been happy with me, or with Shmuel either.'

'Scheine's a fine woman too, of course. No regrets, I'm very lucky. I wonder what she's given me to eat. I hope I haven't sat on it after all. Maybe I'll take a look. No, if I've sat on it, I've sat on it, it won't make any difference looking. And once I see it, I'll probably want to eat it, and it's too soon, I should definitely save it until we stop. Yes, she's a fine woman. A good mother. I wish she wouldn't get so anxious, though; I'm sure it unsettles the boys. It makes them feel uncomfortable. Talking of which, *oy!* this seat is hard. How does he bear it, this carter? He must have a *tush* like leather ...'

As the sun neared the horizon the carter pulled off the road; the horse could go no further that day. Once it was unhitched and stood nibbling the grass at the side of the road, they sat down with their backs to the cart and ate their meals.

Itzhak's food had got a little squashed, after all, but fortunately it was still edible. The two men sat silently for a while, eating their food and sharing the carter's flask of whisky, until it was time to lie down in the meadow next to the cart.

That night, for the first time in many years, Itzhak slept under the eyes of the seven heavens.

The second leg of the journey was much like the first, except the country was more fertile here, and increasingly there was farmland on either side of them instead of marsh. In the afternoon, as they neared Mitau, they passed out of the sunlight into a forested region. The tall straight pines on either side of the road made Itzhak think of ships and their masts. He'd never actually seen a ship in real life, but he'd seen them in pictures and he knew people valued these particular trees because their height and straightness made them particularly suitable for hanging sails on. 'Shmuel and Sara must have been on a ship,' he thought, 'when they went to London. I wonder how they managed when they got there, and what their apartment is like.'

He reflected how easy it would have been for he and Shmuel to lose touch forever. By the time Shmuel had arrived in London, Itzhak had left home and was on his way to Tukum. It was Isaac Gozinsky who saved the day, simply by staying where he was. Shmuel had written to him with his address, and Isaac had forwarded it to Itzhak.

'Good old Isaac,' he thought, grinning to himself. 'I'm looking forward so much to seeing him again. Please God he can help.'

In Mitau, Itzhak paid the carter and found a meal and a bed in a tavern. There was plenty of trade between Mitau and Boisk and it wasn't difficult the following day to find someone to take him on the second leg of the journey.

This carter was as talkative as the other had been silent, so the hours passed quickly, with little time for more introspection. The horse was young and fresh, and covered the distance in a single day. Nevertheless, after three days Itzhak had had enough of bumping up and down on a cart, looking at the back end of a horse, and he felt considerable relief when they reached the familiar bridge over the Memel which marked the entrance to Boisk.

It was early evening when he found himself in his birth town, a place he had never expected to see again, and he made his way, with renewed excitement, straight to Aaron's house. He knocked jauntily on the door and stepped back a pace in happy anticipation.

But after a few moments it dawned on him, with a great sense of anti–climax, that there was nobody home.

While he was standing there, wondering what to do next, an elderly lady appeared, shuffling slowly out of the house next door.

'Good evening, madam,' he said, touching his cap politely.

The lady peered at him suspiciously, but made no reply. He went on hurriedly 'I am here looking for my friend, Aaron Gozinsky. I don't suppose you know where he is?'

'What was that? Speak up,' she said sharply, cupping her ear with a gnarled hand.

'Aaron. GOZINSKY,' he roared.

'*Oy vey!*' she cried, covering her ears. 'Too loud! There's no need to shout. Just speak clearly, that's all. You want Gozinsky, do you? And who are you?'

'My name is Yacobsohn, madam. Itzhak Yacobsohn.'

The old lady looked a little startled. 'Itzhak Yacobsohn? No, you're dead,' she said, shaking her head.

'No. madam. I only went to Tukum.'

'No, that's not right. I distinctly remember. I'm sure you're dead. Your brother too, God rest your souls. You've made a mistake.' She turned away.

'Wait, madam! Please tell me; does Reb Aaron still live here?'

'Yes, yes, I imagine he'll be back presently. Well, well. Back from the dead, he says? The man's crazy.'

She turned away and Itzhak watched her make her slow, arthritic way up the road until she turned the corner.

Feeling more hopeful that Aaron would come if he waited long enough, he sat down on the doorstep and, leaning against the doorframe, closed his eyes. It was so strange to be back in Boisk after all this time. He thought about his childhood. He wondered if he would ever see his parents again, or his brother. Should he have gone to London like Shmuel, instead of stopping in Tukum? If he had, what would his life have been like?

His thoughts drifted off into speculation and he dozed off. The next thing he knew he was being shaken awake, and opening his eyes he looked up into the beaming face of his old friend. He scrambled hastily to his feet and they shook hands warmly.

'Itzhak!' cried Aaron, delightedly pumping his arm. 'Can it be you? Well, well, I was certainly not expecting to see you when I got home today. How wonderful this is! Come in, come in! This calls for a drink! How wonderful!' he repeated, beaming.

Aaron was a widower, and the evidence that he now lived alone was everywhere to be seen in the cluttered, untidy room they now entered. His wife Etta had passed away seven years earlier, hours after giving birth to their first baby, a boy, who also had not survived.

Seeing the mess, Itzhak felt a little embarrassed on his friend's behalf, but Aaron seemed hardly aware of it. He moved piles of clothes off the chairs so they could sit down and he piled up the dirty plates littering the table and put them on the floor. Then he fetched a couple of glasses, wiped them quickly with a corner of his shirt, and poured them each a drink from a half-empty bottle of whisky.

The two drank each other's health and began the process of catching up, talking of the old times, of mutual acquaintances, of politics and of families. When they got hungry they decided, as it was a special occasion, that they would go to the local tavern to eat..

Later that evening, as the two friends sat contentedly together after a meal of fried fish at the inn, Itzhak judged the time was right, and began to talk about the conscription lists. Aaron listened with interest and concern, and eventually Itzhak came to the point.

'So there we are, that's the problem,' he concluded. 'Now, Aaron, as you've probably guessed, I have a favour to ask you. I hope you don't mind?'

'Of course not, Itzhak, I'll certainly do whatever I can. But what is it you want me to do?'

'Well, we want the boys to be trained as metalworkers.'

'Really? Not tailors?'

Itzhak shook his head regretfully. 'Sadly no, it won't do; it's not an exempt job. But metalworking is; a member of a metalworking guild will not be put on the list.'

'Now I understand. So, you want me to ask Israel if your boys can train in his factory?'

'Yes, yes, exactly!' cried Itzhak, delighted at his friend's ready understanding. 'Would you do that?'

'Of course, yes, for you I'll certainly do it. But why don't you ask him yourself?'

'Well, I was going to but, look Aaron, I don't really know him. He probably doesn't even remember me; he's a big-shot factory owner now. Scheine says… I mean, I would feel much happier if you could ask him for me. Please.'

'I see how it is. Of course. But you are being too modest; he definitely will remember you. You made a big impression on this family, you know, you and Shmuel. You stood up to our father; not many people did that.' They both sat a moment, remembering.

After a while Itzhak said: 'I wanted to ask you, Isaac; how is Sora-Roha? I mean, is she happy?'

'Oh, yes, she's fine, thank you; I still sometimes wish she'd married you, but Yudel the Blacksmith is a good man, a kind man; she could have done a lot worse. They have four children now. Did you know?'

'Four? That's wonderful. I'm pleased, truly. Please remember me to her the next time you see her.'

'I will. But look, Itzhak, going back to your boys; they're very young, aren't they? What are they, twelve and nine?'

'Almost. Rafael is not quite twelve and Yossel is still eight. Yossel's too young to go to work, I agree, but his brother? I was only ten when I was apprenticed. And twelve is old enough for the army, apparently.'

'Yes, I know. But things have changed since you went to slave for that awful tailor, thank God. Israel won't take children away from their families. Maybe if you wait for a few years …?' Itzhak raised his hands in horror.

'No, no! Don't say that! There are fresh conscriptions every two years. Scheine feels every day of delay as a torment. Please, Aaron.'

'All right, all right! Calm yourself, Itzhak. Of course I will do what I can to help. As a matter of fact I am going to Riga in a few weeks and

I'm planning to stay with Israel. I'll put the whole thing to him and then, when I get back I will write to you and let you know what he says.'

'Oh thank you, Aaron! Thank you! I can't tell you what this means to me,' said Itzhak fervently. His eyes were moist with emotion. He leaned across the table and grabbed his friend's hands. 'You are a *mensch*.'

'Thank you, but don't go too far,' replied Aaron, embarrassed. 'I haven't done anything yet.'

'It's nothing but the truth.'

'Well, if I can help you then it's my pleasure. Now, I think perhaps it's time we went home, don't you? You'll stay with me tonight, of course. Let me just settle up with them here — no, please keep your money; you're my guest.'

The next day was Friday. Aaron went to work and Itzhak spent much of the day wandering the streets in a kind of daze, reacquainting himself with the town he hadn't seen for so many years.

His memories of Boisk were badly tainted by his experience in the tailor's workshop, and the subsequent rows with his father. He tried to remember the earlier days, when Aaron, Sora-Roha, Shmuel and he were children. It was such a long time ago.

A sense of obligation made him walk out to the cemetery at the edge of town. He found his mother's grave, said a prayer and placed a small stone on the headstone. Strolling among the rows of graves, he came across the resting places of several others whose names he recognised, including, in a prominent and shady spot, that of Pinchus Gozinsky.

His thoughts turned to the future he was trying to make for his boys. What did people actually do in a metalworks? What kind of items did they make? He tried to think of things made of metal; parts of carts, candle holders, street lamps. Was it dangerous? Noisy? Were there huge furnaces? Did you need strong arms like a blacksmith, or did they have machinery these days that did the hard work for you? He really had no idea.

As the evening approached, the friends reconvened at Aaron's house to welcome in *Shabbos*. During the meal, Aaron said to Itzhak: 'Will you come to *shul* with me in the morning?'

'Of course. It will be wonderful to attend the *shul* I went to as a boy again.'

'Good. It's just that I thought …'

'What? Oh, I see, you thought I might not want to risk running into my father.'

'Well, I wasn't sure. He is likely to be there.'

'Do you know what, Aaron? If we meet, and he acknowledges me, then I'm happy to talk to him. And if he ignores me, then, well at least I know where I stand.'

'Good for you, Itzhak. Good for you.'

The Boisk synagogue was a nondescript brick building, nothing to look at on the outside; if it hadn't been for the star of David picked out in lead on each of the arched windows it might have been a small warehouse.

But for Itzhak the inside was full of resonance and he was flooded with memories. Here were the all things he remembered from his childhood, just as they had been. The thick, heavy pillars, painted to resemble marble; the imposing flight of steps leading up to the *bimah*; the *ner tamid*, the eternal flame hanging in front of the *ark*; the embroidered heavy blue curtain at the back of the *bimah* which could be drawn aside to reveal the *Sifrei Torah*. The familiar surroundings and smells made him almost giddy with nostalgia.

He couldn't help looking around at first, to see if he could spot his father. But the *shul* was packed, the lighting was dim and the pillars restricted his view, so he soon gave that up and tried to focus his attention on the service. He was amazed to find that Rabbi Eliasberg was still there; older, of course, but hardly changed. Essentially nothing about the *shul* seemed to have changed at all since the last time he had been there.

As he and Aaron were leaving he glimpsed a familiar–looking figure behind one of the pillars. He thought at first the man was too old to be his father, but then realised he was probably about the right age. Itzhak was taken aback by the sudden tide of emotion that washed over him. Shaking, he closed his eyes for a long moment, breathing deeply and when he opened his eyes the man was gone.

When it was time to go he bade an emotional farewell to his friend and began the journey back to Tukum on the back of yet another cart. Aaron gave him food for the journey and promised not to forget to do what he had been asked.

Scheine breathed a deep sigh of relief when she came home from the bakery and found her husband sitting comfortably at the table one evening.

After they embraced, and Itzhak had succeeded in reassuring his wife that he was quite well, and nothing terrible had befallen him on his journeys, she asked: '*Nu*? How did it go?' although she could tell by his beaming smile that it was good news.

'Just as you predicted. He understood immediately, and he promised to speak to Israel. He's going to Riga in a few weeks and said he would let us know what he says when he gets back. I think it's going to be all right.'

Scheine felt a momentary dizziness as she took in the hoped–for news. She sat down heavily, clasped her pendant tightly and closed her eyes. 'Thank God,' she said. 'Well done, husband.'

Itzhak waved away the compliment. 'So, how was everything here while I was gone? Did your father come for *Shabbos*?'

'Yes, of course. Naturally, he demanded to know where you were.'

'Did you tell him?'

'I had to. Otherwise I think he would have told everyone you were with your mistress.'

Itzhak laughed. 'No, that's next week.'

'*Hmm*, very funny. Actually, do you know, I think he was impressed. He was quite complimentary about people who take action to prevent disaster instead of just waiting for it to overtake them. He rather surprised me.'

'Your father was complimentary? It must have made a nice change to hear him say something nice.'

'It was. But, you know, it's all an act, that *kvetching* he does. I don't really know why he does it; that's not really him.'

'Well, if you say so. But it's a good act.'

'Well, it should be, by now. He's had a lot of practice. But, believe me, Itzhak, it's an act all the same.'

4

It was 1881 and another recruitment list was published. The Yacobsohn boys themselves were still too young to be called, although Rafael was not that far off, but one of the names on the list belonged to a friend of his from *heder*, a bright twelve-year-old boy who had been looking forward excitedly to his *bar mitzvah*. Many of the other names were also of people known to the Yacobsohns.

This was just the normal sort of disaster. But not long after the list was published, a few weeks before *Pesach*, there was some truly shocking, shattering news.

The Czar, Alexander II, was dead. It was said that he had been assassinated.

Rumour, counter-rumour, conjecture and wild speculation whirled through the air like leaves in a gale. But the basic facts were confirmed a day or two later when a notice was posted in the town square. Everyone crowded round to read it. Czar Alexander, they read, had been travelling in a closed two-seater carriage to the Winter Palace in Saint Petersburg when a bomb had detonated, damaging the carriage and forcing it to stop. The Czar had climbed out just as another bomb went off, fatally wounding him.

Everyone realised immediately that this was a catastrophe. Alexander had been a moderate man and, on the whole, his reign had represented something of a relative respite for them. The throne would now pass to his son, and nobody in Tukum thought this would be good news. But that wasn't the really disastrous part.

Whoever was responsible for the assassination, which for the moment was unclear, it didn't really matter. Everybody knew who would get the blame. This was going to mean big trouble for the Jews.

Even in a normal year Easter, which the Jews called Cross Day, was a dangerous time. Religious fervour, heightened by the retelling of the Passion story, had been known to boil over into violence many times. When Easter and *Pesach* coincided, as it did this year, there was a heightening of tension even as families sat down to their *Seder* meals. With the Czar's assassination at the front of everyone's mind, nobody felt the slightest bit safe.

It was traditional to invite a guest to share the *Seder* meal, and this year Itzhak and Scheine had invited Leib Lipman, the ex-soldier, whose nickname was "Crutch".

Leib Lipman had marched off on two feet to take his place in the Czar's army as a young man, and limped home ten years later with only one. Since his return he had not found work and survived mostly on the kindness and generosity of the community.

The old soldier had some unusual ways, such as saluting passers by and addressing people, without irony, as 'your honour' or 'your ladyship'. But he was scrupulously clean; he kept himself decent through regular visits to the bath house and the barbers, who offered their services gratis. Itzhak helped him by mending his clothes when they were mendable, and sourcing replacements when they finally fell apart, and Meyer Rosenberg did the same for his single boot. Reb Leib had taken particular care to smarten himself up for *Seder* night, and the Yacobsohns wanted to make him feel welcome.

Due to an incident involving a perceived act of minor impertinence on Scheine's part the previous week, her father had decided not to favour them with his presence this year; instead the privilege had fallen on Isaac the miller, who had failed to think up a way to evade the honour before it was too late. Isaac was one of the more well-to-do citizens and a generous host, so Favel Gutman was sure of a good meal.

Scheine and Itzhak had been planning and saving for weeks, and had managed to ensure that everything was in its proper place as described in the *Haggadah*: the *matzos*, the wine, the sweet apple and raisin mixture known as *charoset*, the parsley, the shank bone, the roasted egg, and finally the *maror*, the bitter herb, the symbol of slavery.

When the family and guest had assembled around the table, Itzhak lifted the cloth covering the *matzos* and raised the plate, reciting the ancient formula:

'This is the bread of affliction that our ancestors ate in the land of Egypt. Let all who are hungry come and eat.'

Then followed the breaking of the *matzo* and the hiding of a portion of it, followed by the 'Four Questions' traditionally posed by the youngest child and recited, painfully slowly and with much stumbling and prompting, by Yossel. Then, more explanations and stories, more hand washing, more blessings, after which they ate the *maror*, dipping it into the *charoset* to make it a little more palatable.

Itzhak, following tradition, broke off a piece of the *matzo*, and made his sons close their eyes while he hid it for them to search for later. Then, at last, it was time for the meal itself, beginning with hard-boiled eggs in salt water.

This was the first time Reb Leib had sat down at the Yacobsohns' table, and the conversation was rather stiff and formal to begin with. The children were also unusually quiet, being rather awestruck by their guest.

After the eggs had been dealt with, Leib Lipman turned to his hostess and said, politely: 'If I may say so, your ladyship, that is a striking necklace you have on.' He was referring to the small silver pendant which Scheine touched so frequently.

'Thank you, Reb Leib. It belonged to my *mame*, and my *bubbe* before her. It's my most precious possession.'

'She wears it all the time,' put in Yossel, pleased to be able to contribute to this adult conversation.

'I think it has some writing on it, your ladyship, but I am unable to read it.'

'Yes, it does. The writing is a charm against the demon Lilith. The women in my family wear it to protect their children, or when they are expecting a baby. In my case, I'm sorry to say, it hasn't always worked.'

'What do you mean, it hasn't always worked, *Mamele?*' asked Yossel.

Ignoring him, she continued: 'But still, I like to wear it. I think it holds some protection. I expect you will laugh, like my husband, at such superstitious nonsense.'

'Oh no, I don't laugh,' Itzhak protested.

Reb Leib shook his head. 'Not me, either, your ladyship. You won't find an old soldier scoffing at such things,' he said. 'There's nobody who believes in the power of amulets and the like more than we soldiers; you should have seen the rituals and superstitions we went through to keep us safe in battle.' He stared over Scheine's shoulder, as if looking at something a great distance away which the others could not see. Then, shaking away the vision, he heaved a deep sigh. 'But you are quite right, your ladyship. Unfortunately they don't always work.'

At this point, Yossel, who had lost the thread of the conversation, turned to their guest and asked: 'Reb Leib? What happened to your foot?'

'Yossel!' cried his parents together, glaring at him. Yossel turned bright red.

'*Oy, oy*, I'm so sorry, Reb Leib,' scolded Scheine. 'Yossel, don't be so rude. You can't ask things like that.'

But Leib Lipman raised his hand, unembarrassed. 'It's all right, your ladyship,' he said, 'please don't chastise the lad on my behalf; I don't mind at all. Young people are naturally curious, and soldiers aren't easily offended. Well, your honour,' he continued, addressing Yossel directly, 'it was like this. A long time ago, more than twenty years, when I was a soldier, I rode a horse. He was a beautiful beast and I cut quite a dash on him in my day, I can tell you. But we got caught up in a big battle and he was mortally wounded. He went right down — crash, like that — my foot got caught in the stirrup, and he landed right on top of me. They're very heavy, you know, horses. He crushed my poor foot in his dying, and later, when they pulled me out, it was all…' Scheine's alarmed cough reminded him that he was talking to a child and should spare the details, '… well, er, it was no good any more. I was of no use to the army any more after that, so they sent me home.'

There was a silence around the table. Yossel's eyes had widened at this exciting tale. It was Rafael who broke the silence. 'Reb Leib,' he said, frowning. 'That must have been really awful for you. A tragedy.'

'A tragedy?' echoed Leib Lipman, turning to face Rafael. 'No, I wouldn't say that, your honour. I seem to remember it hurt rather a lot at the time, but, do you know, I consider it the luckiest thing that ever happened to me.'

'Lucky?'

'Oh yes, very lucky. It got me out of the war, and out of the army fifteen years ahead of time. I'll be quite honest with you,' he went on, leaning towards Rafael conspiratorially, 'if I had thought of it, I would have asked someone to chop my foot off ten years earlier and spared myself a lot of *tsuris*.'

Scheine stood up quickly, and said: 'Rafi and Yoss, please clear away the bowls. I'll get the next course. Itzhak, perhaps Reb Leib is thirsty.'

'Oh yes, yes, Reb Leib, your glass is empty, how rude of me,' said Itzhak. 'Please allow me to pour you some more.'

'Well, that's very kind of you, your honour. As a matter of fact I think I will accept your offer,' replied the guest, with a small bow.

At the end of the meal, Yossel and Rafael were sent to hunt for the *afikomen*, the piece of *matzo* which Itzhak had hidden earlier. It didn't take them very long, as he hid it in the same place every year, but they dutifully spun it out by looking in a few wrong places first.

They ate the *afikomen*, and then Itzhak recited the grace, and there were traditional songs and everyone joined in with the final line of the ceremony: 'Next year in Jerusalem!' Then, when it was time to go, Leib Lipman got up, with some reluctance, to leave, and saluted his host and hostess smartly.

'I'm very grateful to you, your honour, and you, your ladyship, for your kind hospitality to me this evening. It was a privilege and a joy to celebrate *Seder* with you and your lovely family. *Gut yomtov*, your honour, *gut yomtov*, your ladyship. Young your honours, you too.'

'It was our pleasure, Reb Leib. *Gut yomtov*,' they replied, and then off he went into the cool evening, his crutches echoing in the empty streets. Where he spent his nights, nobody knew.

'I'm rather anxious about him out there on the street, with Cross Day so near,' said Scheine. 'Do you think he'll be all right? Shouldn't we have asked him to stay?'

'Where?' Itzhak replied, looking round the tiny apartment.

A few days later, a wave of savage anti-Jewish attacks began spreading through towns and cities in the Pale of Settlement. Men were killed, pregnant women had their bellies cut open and the babies ripped out, and children were butchered indiscriminately.

To the appalled Jews of Tukum the few hundred miles that separated these horrific, terrifying incidents from their town did not feel anything like enough.

*

At last, Itzhak received a letter from Aaron. Everything was all right. As he had predicted, his brother had not forgotten how Itzhak had stood up to their father, and was glad to have a chance to do something in return. Israel himself, or his factory manager, would write later, explaining all the details.

But, as Aaron had warned, Israel refused absolutely to take on children younger than thirteen. It was a rule of his and he was quite resolved on that point. The boys would have to wait until after their *bar mitzvahs*.

This was a disappointment, but Itzhak and Scheine still felt a huge sense of relief. The plan was in place.

Well, almost; all they had to do now was tell the boys.

*

The first shock of the Czar's assassination began to fade and, although there were more vicious anti-Jewish attacks in the Pale, so far there were no such disturbances in Kurland. So, life continued; after all, what else could it do?

Then, the following spring, there was yet more bad news. The new Czar, Alexander III, had passed a set of laws which further restricted Jewish freedoms in the Pale.

Jews were no longer allowed to live in villages; only in settlements officially designated as towns. This caused considerable confusion and alarm, especially in larger villages and smaller towns, because often nobody was really sure in which category their place fell. Jewish families who had lived quiet, peaceful lives for generations became homeless overnight. Another one of the laws forbade Jews from working on the Christian Sabbath, Sunday, reducing the days on which work was possible and squeezing peoples' finances even further.

Although Kurland was outside the Pale, and not directly impacted by the new laws, these restrictions, indicating as they did the start of a new wave of repression, were still very alarming.

Attacks on Jewish homes and settlements in the Pale were also spreading, and who knew when they would reach Kurland? So far in Tukum there had been only minor skirmishes — smashed windows and the like — nothing to equal the horrific, lurid stories one heard from the Pale. Nevertheless, it was enough to drive away some families, who fled abroad. Others stayed, but kept their bags packed and ready, watching and waiting.

Some people started talking about the idea of building a new home for the Jews; a place where they would be safe from attacks and allowed to live in peace. But people had been saying that for centuries; it was just talk, everyone knew nothing would ever come of it.

Scheine touched her amulet more and more frequently. She suffered from insomnia and was not really eating enough; Itzhak noticed how thin she was getting.

5

MEANWHILE, RAFAEL HAD developed an entirely new interest; an enthusiasm which, in the way of youngsters, was quite an obsession while it lasted.

In 1877 Tukum had acquired something absolutely novel; a railway station. The smart two-storey brick building on Dzelzceļa street was at one end of the line; at the other end was the city of Riga.

The station had brought new wealth into the town, and created new possibilities, at least for the *goyim*; Jewish adults were more suspicious, though. Change, which so often heralded bad news, made them anxious.

But for Rafael the station was a wonder, a fascination, a magnet. He loved everything about it – the noise, the smells, the bustle, and especially the trains themselves. They fascinated him and he quickly developed an ambition to work with trains one day. He wanted to be like the men he saw walking up and down checking the wheels and couplings, or squirting oil, or rubbing grease, into the trains' mysterious moving parts. He hardly dared think about the thrill of actually driving one. At the very least, he longed to ride in one of the carriages, and be like the important-looking people he saw showing their tickets, and climbing up the steps and disappearing inside, to be whisked away to who-knew-what adventures.

He was not the only boy to be drawn to the station; there was quite a large group of young railway enthusiasts. On *Shabbos* afternoons they would meet up at the station to watch the goings-on, and swap stories and information. Reuben sometimes came along with Rafael out of friendship, but he did not really share his enthusiasm. Not all of the boys in the train enthusiasts' group were

Jewish, and some of the *goyim* were risking a severe talking to by their parents for fraternising with 'those people', but the shared fascination with the trains was too strong to be resisted. Rafael formed a particular friendship with one boy in particular, whose name was Ēriks, and the two of them spent many happy hours together.

The station master tolerated the group hanging around the station, on the condition that they didn't annoy the passengers. Rafael got to see the trains up close, which was good, but he often got scolded by his mother for getting dirty, which was less good.

The boys even helped out from time to time, a well-intentioned activity which nevertheless led to an unfortunate incident.

On the day in question, the boys were at the station waiting for the second of the two daily trains to arrive. When it had drawn to a halt, the doors swung open and Rafael saw a smartly dressed young woman backing awkwardly down the steps, trying to bring down a large, unwieldy pram. It seemed likely she would tip it over, so Rafael darted forward to help, and grabbed hold of it.

The woman, perceiving a dirty Jewish urchin making a sudden grab for her baby, let out a piercing scream and aimed a kick at him. Her husband who, unseen by Rafael, was inside the train carriage, thrust his head out of the door shouting angrily. Rafael jumped back. The couple got the pram safely down the steps, and the man hopped quickly down from the train and grabbed the bewildered Rafael by the arm.

Hearing a commotion, the station master hurried up. The man was shaking Rafael by the arm and berating him furiously. 'What do you think you are doing?' he shouted. 'Are you trying to steal our baby?'

The station-master attempted to calm the situation, which had already drawn a small crowd. 'What is the matter, sir?' he asked the man.

'This dirty Jew-boy tried to steal our baby, right from under our noses,' replied the enraged passenger. 'I've heard about this. They try to steal Christian children for their vile purposes. But we've got him. (Stop wriggling, you). Fetch a policeman! Quickly, man!'

The baby had been woken by the noise and was now screaming and the woman had snatched it up into her arms and was rocking it, sobbing quietly. Rafael was speechless with shock. How could things have gone so badly so quickly?

His friend Ēriks, who had edged closer to the scene, tried to say something in Rafael's support but the man, by now quite red in the face, turned his fury on the newcomer. 'Jew–lover, eh? Helping him, are you?' he shouted. Then, turning back to the station–master, he said: 'You see? It's a conspiracy; there's a gang of them. Well? Why are you still here? Where is that policeman?'

The station–master found himself in a difficult position. He knew the situation had the potential to get really serious. He himself had no doubt that it was all a ridiculous misunderstanding, but the growing crowd was showing signs of agitation. It was time to end the scene. He drew himself up. 'There is no need for the police as yet, sir,' he said pompously. 'I have full authority to deal with incidents taking place on the railway's premises. I thank you for your prompt action in apprehending the, er, accused. I will now take him to my office for questioning. Come along with me, young man,' he concluded.

Before the angry passengers or crowd of onlookers had time to react, he took Rafael by the arm and marched him off in the direction of the station office. Realising the excitement was over, the crowd dispersed and the two passengers, finding themselves alone on the platform with their baby, eventually departed, the man still muttering darkly, the baby still wailing and the woman still snuffling miserably.

In the office the station–master wiped his brow with a large handkerchief and, offering Rafael a chair, said sadly: 'What a time we live in, eh? What a time. Don't worry, lad, I know perfectly well you meant no harm. *Phew*. What a time,' he repeated. 'Honestly, you just can't help some people. Best wait here for a few minutes until everyone's dispersed and then go straight home, lad. You know, it might be best to keep away from the station for a bit. They'll forget all about it in a few days. Then you can come back. But I wouldn't try helping the passengers off the train again, eh? Just in case. You never know who you're dealing with. What a time,' he concluded.

Then, still shaking his head, he went back to his duties and Rafael was left alone in the office.

He sat there for another fifteen or so minutes, as the man had advised, and then, still shaken, ran home, keeping to the side streets as much as he could. He didn't say anything to his parents when he got back, in case they forbade him to go to the station again.

The story of the 'attempted abduction' circulated briefly in the town, but it failed to gain much traction — there had been many such tales before which had, rather disappointingly to some, turned out to have no substance behind them — and the couple, who it turned out were spending some of the summer with relatives in the area, proved themselves so difficult and unpleasant to everyone that the whole story quickly lost credibility, and with their departure in August it evaporated.

It was a long time before Rafael dared to return to his train-watching activities. When he did, he found the group of boys much reduced from before and Ēriks was nowhere to be seen. The glory days of the railway enthusiasts were gone, and the boys moved on to other interests.

*

Unfortunately the incident at the station was not the only disquieting thing to happen to Rafael around that time.

Now that he was older, he sometimes helped his father out by delivering finished items of clothing, expertly wrapped in brown paper tied with strong cord, to his customers.

On this particular day, he took a pair of mended trousers to a man who lived a few streets away. The man gave him a small tip and, delighted, he went in search of somewhere to spend it.

Venturing into the non-Jewish part of town, he passed by a butcher's shop which was run by an unpleasant character called Boris.

Boris was busy inside his shop serving customers, which was lucky. Unfortunately though, his son, Bruno, was hanging around at the corner of the road with a group of friends. As he always did when in the non-Jewish part of town, Rafael had taken the precaution of making sure his *tzitzit* fringes were tucked inside the top of his trousers. He hoped there was nothing else immediately marking him out as a Jew and thought perhaps he could slide by without interference.

But as he approached the group, Bruno called out to him, his tone inquisitive rather than threatening: 'Hey! Who are you?'

'Me?' said Rafael innocently. He gave the first name that came into his head. 'My name's Ēriks'. This seemed to satisfy them, and Rafael began to feel more relaxed.

'Wait a minute,' said one of the other boys. 'I've seen you before. Aren't you a Yid?' This roused the interest of the others.

'No,' said Rafael scornfully. 'Of course not.'

'Prove it then,' said Bruno, jutting out his chin.

'How can I prove it? I tell you I'm not one.' And then, for added effect, he added, with as much bravado as he could muster, 'I hate those filthy Yids.'

Bruno fished into his pocket and pulled out a greasy-looking length of pork salami his father had given him for his lunch. 'Jews don't eat pork, do they? All right, then. If you're not a Jew you won't mind eating some of this.'

Rafael was in trouble, and he knew it. Eating non-kosher meat, let alone pork, would be a terrible thing to do, and in any case he didn't think he could actually physically do it — his gorge revolted at the thought. But hesitating now could prove disastrous.

'Sure. Thanks,' he said, with a smile. He took the sausage, lifted it to his mouth and breathed in deeply.

The sausage reeked of garlic, which gave him a sudden inspiration. He turned his head away, held his nose and grimaced. 'Aw no! *Phoo*! It stinks! I'm not eating that! It'll make my breath smell. That wouldn't do; I'm just on my way to meet my girlfriend.'

The gales of laughter and sniggering innuendos which followed this remark broke the tension completely. Rafael handed the meat back to Bruno and waving goodbye to his new 'friends', sauntered as nonchalantly as he could manage to the next corner and disappeared from sight.

He was pleased to have escaped so lightly but the words that he had said — 'I hate those filthy Yids' — echoed painfully in his memory. He never told anyone that he had said it, but as long as he lived he never forgot it, or ever quite forgave himself.

*

Over the summer and into the autumn, stories of anti-Jewish attacks in the south kept the Jews of Kurland in a state of constant alert. They heard of trouble from Podolia, Volyn, Chernigov, Ekaterinoslav and many other places. People with relatives or friends in Kiev started getting letters containing hair-raising details of what had been happening there. Yiddish newspapers which made their way to Kurland, although subject to heavy censorship which made them unable to refer to the attacks openly, began referring to 'storms' in the south, references which everyone understood.

Everyone else used the newly-coined word 'pogroms'.

When the talk wasn't about pogroms, it was about conscriptions; they were coming round again next year. The Rosenbergs, still unable to get any news of Schloma, knew that, with aggressive anti-Jewish sentiment being whipped up everywhere, things must be bad for Jewish conscripts. The rabbi's wife confided in a whisper to Scheine, when they happened to meet at the market, that her husband was feeling even more anxious than usual about the next list.

September came, Rafael turned twelve, and there was still no letter from Israel Gozinsky about the boys' apprenticeships.

Yitzhak decided that if he had not heard from him before *Yom Kippur* he would himself make a visit to Riga. Yes, even if it meant braving the railway. But, fortunately this proved unnecessary, as a letter arrived at last, bearing the emblem of Gozinsky Metalworks; a lantern with rays of light radiating outwards.

It was a businesslike document, signed by the foreman, and set out clearly the terms of the contract into which Rafael, and later Yossel, would be entering. There was nothing now to be done except to write back expressing their gratitude and accepting the deal, and then, at some point, informing the boys.

There was still a possibility that one of the boys would be drafted before they finished their apprenticeship, or possibly before they even got to Riga, and then the plan would have failed. Itzhak and Scheine prayed that God would see they had done all they could and would also do His bit to keep them safe.

*

Rosh Hashanah was a happy, hopeful day. The meal, which included, by ancient tradition, the eating of apple and honey to symbolise the sweetness of the year to come; the blowing of the *shofar* and the familiar rituals of the services in *shul* — all of these brought comfort and a sense of order and stability. This year the Yacobsohns and the Rosenbergs — Meyer, Ester, Hannah and Reuben — were together for the meal to welcome in the new year. Beer and whisky had been consumed and almost everyone was in a playful mood, particularly Itzhak and Meyer, who had drunk a little more than they were used to. Even Ester was able to smile, putting the grinding worry about Schloma to the back of her mind for a while. The exception to the general gaiety was Scheine's father, Favel Gutman, who was behaving as miserably and cantankerously as ever.

'Isn't this nice, Scheine?' slurred Itzhak, casting a benevolent smile around the room. 'Our family and friends all here to welcome in the new year. What could be nicer?'

Scheine and Ester exchanged glances. It was fortunate their husbands became playful and sentimental when they had been drinking, rather than malicious and violent like some men, but it was still rather tiresome, and a bad influence on the children.

'Please tell us the story, Reb Itzhak,' said Meyer, 'of how the two of you first met. It's a good story,' he said to the children.

'The two of who?' asked Itzhak, puzzled.

'The two of you two. You and your beautiful wife.'

'Ah, what a lucky day that was!' said Itzhak, sitting back in his chair. 'Do you know this story, children? Should I tell it?' Itzhak asked Scheine. 'Or not?'

'Not,' interrupted her father. 'But you can pass the drink this way. If you're quite sure you can spare a little.'

'I beg your pardon, Reb Favel,' said Itzhak, spilling some on the table. '*Oops*. Here it is.'

Meyer Rosenberg and the children assured him they wanted to hear the story, and so, after closing his eyes, and gathering his thoughts, he began.

'I had not been long in this beautiful town, and I was wondering to myself how I was ever going to find myself a wife when I didn't know anyone. And then, this wonderful lady,' he said, indicating the smiling Scheine, 'happened to come into the store one day.'

'Which store?' asked Reuben.

'Which store young man? Well, when I first came to Tukum I had some skills, but no job. Nothing. So I asked in all the stores around the market place if they would have me, and nobody would. Not until I reached the hasherbashers, pardon me I mean the haberdashers, which at that time was run by "Threadneedle" Gitelson. That's what we called her. She was old even then and she's long passed away, may her soul rest in peace. Maybe she wasn't that old. She seemed old to me, though. How old was I then, Scheine? Eighteen?'

'*Oy oy oy*, will you get to the point, husband!' complained Scheine. 'These children will need to go to bed sometime tonight!'

'Sorry, sorry. Where was I?'

'In the hasherbashers,' reminded Meyer. '*Oy*, you've got me doing it now. *Ha ha!*'

'Yes, yes. The same store where I work to this very day. So, when I told old "Threadneedle" I was a tailor by training, she gave me a job selling pins and needles and ribbons and whatever else she kept in her store. And then one day a young lady comes in. Well! She was the most beautiful girl I had ever seen up until then, and still, up until this very day, I have never seen a more beautiful one.'

'Yes, but when did you meet Scheine?' put in Meyer, roaring with laughter at his witticism. Ester slapped him on the arm.

'Be quiet you fool. Of course he meant the young lady was Scheine. Don't embarrass yourself.'

'Quite right,' put in Favel Gutman. 'For once, by some miracle, my son-in-law has spoken wisely, despite the drink. Or because of it. All three of my daughters are beauties, you know,' he said, addressing the Rosenbergs. 'But Scheine here is the loveliest one of the three. She is the one most like her dear late mother, my poor Yente.' Everyone was rather taken aback by this speech; it was a long time since Favel Gutman had been heard to say something heartfelt and complimentary. Nobody said anything for a few moments, as they digested what had just happened. Scheine reddened and Itzhak continued the story.

'Thank you, Reb Favel, for calling me wise. Unfortunately I did not have the honour of meeting your late wife, but if my own wife resembles her, then she must indeed have been a beauty, because...'

'Oh stop it,' said Scheine. 'For goodness sake, if you must tell this endless story, get on with it.'

'Where was I? Oh yes, she came into the store. Well, anyhow, she made an order for a few small things, and she told me where she wanted them sent, which was the bakery. So then I knew she was the baker's daughter, do you see? Because she said she lived in the bakery. Then, that very same evening, after I finished work I went straight round to your house, Reb Favel, and I asked your permission to court my wife. I beg your pardon, *ha ha*, I mean your wife, or rather I should say your daughter. And, well here we are,' he concluded lamely, spreading his arms wide.

'That's it?' said Ester, scornfully. 'Here we are? You kept in all those boring details and missed out all the interesting parts? Just like you men.'

Scheine came to Itzhak's defence. Indicating the children, she said: 'Well, Ester, Itzhak can't really go into details of our courtship in our present company. But I will say that I remember that visit to the haberdashers very well. I rather liked the young man behind the counter and hoped to see him again, so I was very happy with how things turned out. Of course,' she continued, changing her tone, 'I didn't know then that thirteen years later he was going to get drunk on *Rosh Hashanah* and embarrass himself in front of his family and friends.'

Meyer, deciding that now was a good time to change the subject, before his own wife started making awkward reference to getting drunk on *Rosh Hashanah*, turned quickly to Rafael and said: 'Well, young man, this will be the year in which you celebrate your *bar mitzvah*. And then what, *eh*? How do you plan to bring riches to the family?'

'What are you asking *him* for?' interposed Favel. 'He's a child. What does he know from jobs?' Scheine and Itzhak exchanged anxious glances; was Reb Favel about to discuss the plan in front of the boys? But to their relief, he concluded by saying 'He'll do whatever he's told to do.'

Rafael, who had given almost no thought to his future since the evaporation of his engine driver ambitions, replied 'I don't know, Reb

Meyer, I'm not really sure what jobs there are. What about you, Reuben? Have you got any ideas?'

No, Reuben had no ideas apart from following his father into the shoemaking business which, it so happened, was his father's idea too, so that was settled.

Nobody asked Hannah what her plans were.

Itzhak and Scheine, by a small exchange of glances, silently agreed that it was high time for the conversation about the apprenticeship at Gozinsky's, which had perhaps been put off for too long already. As soon as *Rosh Hashanah* was over, they decided, they would tell the boys.

*

One midweek evening during the ten days between *Rosh Hashanah* and *Yom Kippur*, when the family were sitting quietly at home, Scheine decided the moment had come. She caught Itzhak's eye and twitched her head in the direction of Rafael and Yossel.

'Are you all right, my dear?' said Itzhak, concerned.

Scheine sighed at his obtuseness. 'I'm trying to suggest that now would be a good time to have *that conversation*,' she whispered.

'Which one? *Oh*! Yes I suppose so,' he replied quietly. Then in a louder voice he said 'Boys, please come over here; your mother and I have something we would like to discuss with you.'

The brothers came over obediently, if a little suspiciously, and sat down on the floor near their parents. Itzhak looked hopefully at his wife, lifting his eyebrows, and said nothing, waiting. He was right, she realised; maybe it was better if she started.

'Boys,' she said. 'You remember the other night, when Reb Meyer was asking you, Rafi, what you were planning to do when you grew up? Well, you are twelve now, and it's really time to think hard about it. Yossel, you've got a little more time, but we should also think about your future.'

'Rafi wants to drive trains,' said Yossel.

'No I don't. *Shush*,' responded Rafael furiously.

'And I want to be a soldier,' went on Yossel, undaunted. The adults stared at him, aghast.

'Well,' said Itzhak, picking his words carefully, 'those both sound exciting. But we have another suggestion for you. Do you know what a factory is?' They nodded warily. 'Well, I know a man, a very nice man, actually, who owns a factory in Riga where they make things out of metal. I've spoken to him and — what do you think of this? — he has agreed that after your *bar mitzvahs* you can both go and work in his factory and learn to be metalworkers.' There was no immediate response.

'Isn't that wonderful, boys?' said Scheine enthusiastically. 'Isn't *Tatty* clever to have organised that for you?'

Rafael was the first to respond. 'What do they make out of metal, *Tatty*?'

'Well, all sorts of things. You know, um, metal things. Well to tell you the truth, I'm not really sure, not exactly.'

'And will we still have to go to the army when we're older, like Reuben's brother?'

'No,' Itzhak said, emphatically. 'If you become a metal worker you will never have to do that.'

'And… did you say the factory is in Riga?'

'Yes.'

'So, would we go there on the train?'

'Er… well, I hadn't really thought about it. But yes, I suppose so.'

Rafael pondered all this information for a few moments, his brow furrowed, while his parents glanced anxiously at each other. Then his face cleared and he said: 'All right. Thank you, *Tatty*. I want to go.' And that was settled.

But Yossel, pouting his lips and jutting out his jaw declared: 'No. I don't want to go. I don't want to work in a factory. I want to be a soldier.'

'Well, my dear,' said Scheine hurriedly, 'you don't need to choose right now. It's not yet, not for you. You're only ten, so you will stay here with us for another three years, and then you'll go.'

'No. I'm not going in three years. Never,' he declared loudly before jumping up and stomping into the other room.

'Don't worry,' said Rafael, in a reassuring voice that suddenly sounded very like his father's. 'He'll go. We both will.'

The more he thought about it, the more happy Rafael was with the plan; he didn't really understand what conscription entailed, but he knew it was something to be avoided if possible, and so that part of the plan was good. He was also quite intrigued by the prospect of learning how to work in metal, the material used to make the trains that still fascinated him.

The idea of living away from home for the first time, which Itzhak had thought would be the biggest stumbling block, Rafael also took in his stride. Itzhak realised he should be pleased about this, because it was an integral part of the whole idea, but he found it also saddened him.

He wondered whether they would ever see the boys once they left home. He and Scheine had the fixed idea that Riga was two or three days' travel away and kept forgetting what Rafael knew; that the journey could now be accomplished in under three hours. If you had the fare money, Rafael said, you could go and come back in the same day. Once this astonishing fact was clearly understood the whole idea of the boys going away seemed somehow less daunting.

But Yossel continued to say he would refuse to go when the time came. Blinded by the glamour of the soldier's uniform, he remained, for now, implacably against the entire plan.

*

On *Kol Nidre* the Jews of Tukum, freshly cleaned and deloused at the bathhouse, gathered in *shul* just before sunset. They were there to participate in the solemn, immemorial ritual which signals the start of *Yom Kippur*, the holiest day of the Jewish calendar.

The *Sifrei Torah* were brought out of the *ark* and the *chazzan* chanted the service's opening words, using the traditional, richly figured, poignant melody. As Rafael listened, he looked around at the other members of the congregation. In years gone by they had towered over him and if he looked to the side when they were all standing his eyes would be level with the black stripes of his father's *tallis*. This year, he realised with surprise, the stripes were level with his shoulders. When had that happened? His father had his eyes closed and his lips were moving silently in time with the *chazzan's*. Rafael looked down at his feet and remembered, with a burning sense of shame, how he had denied his Jewishness to Boris the butcher's son. He had denied all this, everything he saw and heard around him now. He had denied himself. He felt bitterly ashamed and hoped, if he atoned with all his heart, as he intended to do, that God would forgive him. He doubted if he would forgive himself.

Soon after *Sukkos*, as the temperature fell, the Yacobsohns hunkered down for the Kurland winter for the last time before Rafael's departure for Riga. The midwinter *Hanukkah* lights that year seemed especially significant and, on the last night of the festival, the singing of *Maoz Tzur* felt more than normally poignant.

*

One evening in the spring of 1883 there was a knock at the door. When Itzhak opened it he was astonished to see the boys' *melamed*, Abram Leibowitz, outside.

'Good evening, Reb Itzhak,' he said. 'I'm sorry to disturb you. May I come in?'

'Yes, of course, good evening Rebe, come in. Something to drink?'

'No, thank you.'

After greeting Scheine, he turned to the boys who were staring at him in open–mouthed astonishment. What was he doing here?

'Good evening, Rafael and Yossel,' he said. 'I wonder if I might talk to your parents for a moment?'

'Go outside for a few minutes, boys,' said Itzhak. 'But don't go too far away.' They obeyed, worried looks on their faces.

Itzhak indicated a chair to their visitor and the three adults sat around the table. Itzhak and Scheine were unsure what to expect, and were only slightly reassured by Abram Leibowitz's kindly expression.

'I apologise again for disturbing your evening,' said the *melamed*, 'but I'm afraid I need to talk to you about Yossel.'

'About Yossel?' repeated Scheine.

'Yes. As you know, he has recently joined my class. Were you aware that he is unable to read properly?'

'Yossel can't read?' exclaimed Itzhak, shocked.

'Did you not know?'

'Well, we know he found it hard at first but, these days he doesn't really tell us anything about *heder*. The other *melamed* didn't mention it.'

'I see. Well, I suppose it's unfair to say he can't read at all; he does know the *aleph–beys* and given enough time he can puzzle out some words, but it's very slow and I'm afraid it gives him a lot of trouble.'

Scheine asked 'Rebe, do you think he's stupid?'

'No, I do not.'

'Lazy, then?'

'Not really, no. At least, no more than the other children. I can't explain it to you. I have seen it before, once or twice, but I'm afraid I don't really understand it. Some people just seem to find reading very difficult.' They sat for a few moments in silence until Scheine asked:

'Are you saying that you can't teach him?'

'I'm sorry, yes that is what I am saying. He is slow, and also disruptive to the class; it really isn't fair to the other children. There are really two options; the first is to send him back to learn with the younger children and hope that he picks it up second time around.'

'No,' said Itzhak firmly, 'I don't think we can do that. It would be humiliating for the boy. What is the second option?'

'The second option, I'm afraid is for him to leave *heder*.'

This was a blow. Yossel was just ten, and it would be three years before he could go to Riga. What could they do with him in the meanwhile?

Itzhak was the first to speak again. 'We understand. Thank you for coming to talk to us, Rebe. We won't send him any more.'

'Thank you. And again, I am sorry. Do you have any thoughts about what you'll do with him?'

'Yes,' said Itzhak decisively. 'He will come to work with me until his *bar mitzvah*.'

The 1883 conscription list was published. Everyone could see it had been prepared with great care and attention, but inevitably there was heartache for some. The list included people known to the Yacobsohns: Mottel, the son of Hirsch the Atheist; Samuel Sherman, known as "Sam the slow"; Itze, whose parents had four other children, more than they could really feed; and a number of other young men whose names the Yacobsohns recognised but whom they did not really know.

Thank God, Rafael's name was not on the list.

There was one particularly nasty shock, though; this was seeing the name of his friend Haim, the son of Abraham Peletz the barber, listed. Haim had been one of the railway enthusiasts.

When Rafael saw Haim at *heder* he was at a loss to know what to say to him. He noticed that the others also avoided talking to him, and at break time Haim sat by himself, crying softly.

Itzhak wrote directly to Gozinsky's to make sure everything was still set for Rafael's arrival, and to finalise a few details. He received a short, impersonal reply from the secretary to the effect that he was expected shortly after *Sukkos*.

*

One *Shabbos* evening during the meal, Favel Gutman turned to Yossel. 'Well, young man,' he said. 'Lots of changes, eh? I hear you're working with your father now. Do you like that?'

'Yes, it's all right, *Zeide*.'

'And your brother will be going to Riga soon to take up his apprenticeship. What do you think of that?'

'I don't mind, if he wants to go.'

'But you're not going to follow him when the time comes, eh?'

'No,' replied Yossel, defiantly, jutting out his jaw.

'Quite right. It's a stupid idea,' exclaimed the old man, clapping his grandson on the back. Scheine dropped her fork in surprise.

'*Tate*!' she cried.

'Oh, don't shout at me. If the older one wants to go and twist metal, that's fine. Let him. But for Yossel, no. He's going be a soldier and march away to war, isn't that right, young man?'

'Er... well,' said Yossel, suddenly uncertain.

'A much better life. Fresh air! Discipline! The thrill of the battle. Danger. Blood! Death and glory! What's not to like?'

'Blood?'

'Oh, yes. Lots of blood. Hopefully not your own, eh?'

Yossel's face went a little green. 'Actually I'm not quite sure about it. I think perhaps I'd rather stay and learn to be a tailor, *Zeide*.'

'Well maybe you would, but the Czar has other ideas, young man. He's going to gather you up into his army, like Schloma Rosenberg and Haim Peletz and everyone. If they are still alive you might even see them when you get to the war.'

'I don't think I really want to go to war, *Zeide*.'

'Nonsense. Don't you want to be in a big battle, like your friend Leib Lipman? And you never know, you might be luckier than him — you might get to keep all your arms and legs. It's unlikely but it's certainly possible. And when you come back, if you do, then think what exciting tales you will have to tell. Now then, Reb Itzhak, pass me over that other piece of fish, would you? Perhaps it's not as badly overcooked as the first one.'

Yossel stared frowningly at his plate while Itzhak looked questioningly at his father-in-law, who gave him a furtive wink.

6

On a day in early spring, when it was still cold enough for light flakes of snow to drift onto the roofs and cover the cart-tracks on the road, a dishevelled, exhausted figure in worn military boots was seen limping into town. He was soon identified as Schloma Rosenberg.

Someone flew off to tell his parents and they hurried out to meet him. There was an emotional reunion on the road and the boy, faint from hunger and exhaustion, was quickly taken home.

News of this sensational reappearance spread fast, reaching the ears of the community chairman. He was gripped by the suspicion that Schloma had deserted, which would be a disaster for them all. He paid the Rosenbergs an urgent visit. No, it was not like that, Schloma had official leave. Well then, where were the papers? Here they were. Everything was all right.

He had been stationed in Windau some 80 miles away and, for lack of transport, had walked the whole way home. He was weak with exhaustion, and half starved, and it was several days before his strength started to return.

One day, about a week later, Schloma was sitting at the kitchen table sipping at some chicken soup made for him by his mother as she looked on adoringly. Hannah was out, running errands.

Ester decided it was time to ask Schloma the question that had been on her mind almost since the day he arrived. 'So, my dear one, how long are you able to stay with us before you go back?'

Without looking up from the bowl, he said quietly: 'I'm not going back.'

Ester stared at him blankly for a moment. 'I don't understand, dear. I... I think you are meant to go back, aren't you?'

'Yes. Of course I'm meant to. But I can't. I won't.' At which he abruptly pushed his chair back, stood up and went back into the bedroom, closing the door on his astonished, frightened mother.

When Meyer came back home after work, he and Ester talked quietly together in the front room, after which Meyer went into the bedroom. Ester could hear the murmur of conversation through the closed door.

When he came out a few minutes later there was a concerned look on his face. 'It's just as you said. He says he's not going back. I couldn't get anything else out of him. Ester, this is really serious. I'm not sure he understands what will happen if he doesn't go back.'

'Of course he does, Meyer, he's not a *schlemiel*. But he's scared. What have they been doing to him, the poor child? *Oy, oy. oy!*' She began to weep.

A desertion would be a catastrophe, not just for Schloma and for the family, but the whole community. If Schloma did not return to his post by the prescribed time, there would be a fine of three hundred rubles, an impossible sum. Furthermore, the community, in the shape of the board of trustees, would be required to replace him with, not one, but two other young men. The family's reputation would be in tatters. This was a very serious situation.

On the other hand, having just got their beloved son home at last how could they beg him to go back, to force him to return to a situation he found unendurable? What were they to do? It was an impossible dilemma and try as they might they could think of no way out. Nor did they dare to tell anyone about it.

Schloma took to spending days sitting, or strolling, by the lake.

Reuben asked him once, when they were walking together: 'What is it like, Schloma? In the army?'

After a long pause Schloma replied quietly: 'I think it's better if you don't know, Reuben. God forbid you ever find out.'

He would not be drawn further. After a few moments, Reuben asked: 'So are you staying here, Schloma?'

'No, Reuben. Actually, I'm not.'

'Oh. I thought perhaps you had come home to live?'

'No,' he replied, giving a short laugh in which there was no mirth. 'That isn't why I've come home.'

*

On Saturday evening, after *Shabbos* ended, Schloma kissed his parents, his brother and his sister goodnight, and went to bed.

On Sunday morning he was nowhere to be found, and they realised that, at some point in the night, he must have got dressed again and slipped out. Hannah and Reuben were told to wait at home while Ester and Meyer looked for him. They spent two hours searching high and low around the town until they discovered his body in the undergrowth near the lake, an ugly gunshot wound disfiguring his temple, and his army gun lying on the ground a few feet away.

They looked at the scene. It was what they had half expected to see, but still they were not able to understand what they were seeing.

They didn't move.

A white stork lifted off from the lake with a clatter of its enormous wings and flew lazily away overhead. The noise jolted them and they rushed over to the body of their son.

Ester knelt down beside him and, with trembling hands, tenderly attempted to smooth his hair, which was matted with dried blood and damp with dew. She took off her scarf, tore it into strips, and rubbed at a stain on the sleeve of Schloma's jacket.

Meyer was still standing, looking down at the body. Whispering to himself dazedly, he kept repeating: 'His days are as grass. His days are as grass. His days are ....'

Then, aloud, he said: 'Ester. I don't know what to do.'

'Go and get help,' she replied, quietly. 'I'll watch him. He mustn't be alone.'

Meyer hurried back to town in a state of shocked bewilderment. When he returned some time later with two other men, they found Ester still kneeling beside the body of her son, still cleaning it. The men lifted Schloma onto a wooden board they had brought with them, and carried him home, Ester walking beside the body.

When they got near the apartment, Ester said: 'Please can you wait here a moment? I have to tell Reuben and Hannah before we take him in.' Her voice was calm but her hands were shaking.

She went in and closed the door behind her. A few minutes later she came back to where the others were waiting and said: 'All right. We can go in now.'

The procession went into the building, and the door closed behind them.

Rabbi Lichtenstein was informed, and was presented with an immediate difficulty. On the face of it the boy, by taking his own life, had committed a grave sin, and could not therefore be buried in the Jewish cemetery.

However, after careful consideration, Rabbi Lichtenstein ruled that the death was an unfortunate accident, occurring while the boy's mind was disturbed and confused, and that moreover circumstances beyond his control had driven him beyond his endurance and so he was not accountable for his actions. Therefore the suicide was, in this case, forgivable.

This meant, among other things, that his family would be allowed to mourn and to bury him in accordance with tradition.

On the following day Itzhak and Scheine went to pay their condolences to the Rosenbergs. They didn't know what to expect when they knocked on the door, but the family appeared strangely calm, almost cold, as if drained of all emotion. They welcomed the visitors politely, however, and Itzhak, taking Meyer's hand, recited a sentence he had prepared. 'All that the Lord does, he does for the good,' he said.

To which Meyer Rosenberg replied quietly, in a toneless voice, which made it somehow even more shocking: 'Thank you, Reb Itzhak. But I would rather leave the Lord out of it. He does not appear to me to be on our side. Hannah, please can you make some tea for our guests?'

The funeral took place the next day, Tuesday, and it was attended by a large number of mourners. After that, there were some pressing legal concerns to worry about. Was Schloma's death the factor that prevented him reporting back to his post after his leave, leaving him blameless? Or was he a deserter? Would the family be made to pay a ruinous fine? Would the entire community be punished by having to provide two replacements?

The Russian authorities took some time to decide. Fortunately, the rabbi's ruling that the death was accidental was very helpful and, in the end, wishing to avoid the publicity of a court case, the authorities agreed, and no fine was levied. But the army was still a soldier short, and the community was ordered to provide a replacement. A young Jewish orphan of Lithuanian parentage, who had just turned twelve, was duly selected and dispatched.

The day after the funeral, Yossel told his parents he had changed his mind; when the time came he would go to Riga.

*

In the summer, as the day approached for the new set of conscripts to leave, Tukum started filling up with *goyim* from nearby towns and villages. This was not surprising or unexpected, because they would be using the train to travel to the barracks in Riga, but it did feel a little menacing.

Then, on the day before they were due to leave, fuelled perhaps by a mixture of despair, anger and alcohol, the conscripts ran amok, hurling stones through the windows of Jewish businesses. They trampled in the mud any meat, bread or other food they could find. Terrified Jewish citizens cowered inside their homes while the storm raged outside, but some were caught in the open and beaten, or raped. They caught Leib Lipman and beat him over the head and shoulders with his crutches.

Cowering inside their homes or workplaces, the Jews listened in terror to the shouting and crashing outside. Itzhak, who had been alone in the haberdashery when it started, hastily retreated to his back room and barricaded the door as best he could. The boys in the *heder* were bundled into the *shul* by their *melamdin* who shut and bolted the big doors behind them. The tables and benches in the market place were overturned and broken up to be used as makeshift weapons, and a group of rioters made the remainder into a bonfire.

The sight of the fire gave them the murderous idea of burning down the *shul* with the Jews inside. Alarming curls of acrid smoke began drifting in from beneath the doors. But to the Jews' intense relief the tough old wood wouldn't catch, and after a while the rioters gave it up.

Ultimately, as dark began to descend, the police moved in to restore order. As pogroms went, it did not approach the scale of the worst, but for the Jews of Tukum it felt terrifying enough. The whole thing lasted only a few hours, and early the next day the rioters were gone, taken away on the first train to serve their time in the Czar's army. With them went the Jewish draftees, among them Haim Peletz, looking very young, and very scared.

A few families, those who could afford it, left Kurland for good; some ended up in New York or London, or Palestine. But most stayed put, swept up, mended or replaced as many of the damaged things as they could, and tried to carry on. But they were badly shaken.

*

As his thirteenth birthday approached, Rafael made final preparations for his *bar mitzvah*. He received a number of appropriate gifts; Abram Leibowitz presented him with a set of *tefillin* and taught him the correct method of using them (Itzhak made a small leather pouch for him to keep them in). The Wassermans gave him a *siddur*, and his parents presented him with a *tallis*. His grandfather gave him a silver coin and a lecture about the superiority of spiritual riches over earthly possessions.

Thus equipped, Rafael celebrated his *bar mitzvah*. In *shul* he read aloud, in an uncertain voice, his allotted portion from the *Torah*. His parents watched proudly, and when he finished there were encouraging cries of *Yashar koach!* from the congregation.

After the service he smiled shyly as members of the congregation gathered, shaking his hand or slapping his back, and wishing him *Mazel tov*.

Following the service there was a small party in the tavern. As well as his grandfather, those present included the Wassermans and Abram and Mirjam Leibowitz, but the Rosenbergs, still in mourning, were absent.

When they finally got home and closed the door on the excitement of the day, the Yacobsohn family sat companionably around the fire until Yossel, blinking sleepily, was sent to bed.

Scheine looked over at Rafael; a man now, according to the Law, but still her little boy, her *kaddishel*. It was a pity that there weren't more family members around to help him celebrate his *bar mitzvah*, she thought.

She tried to remember her own *mame*, who passed away before she really knew her, so long ago that her face was hard to picture; she was barely even a memory now, hardly more than an empty feeling and a memorial candle. She also thought about her two elder sisters,

Feige and Blume, married and gone away, the one to Palestine and the other to America. Would she ever see them again?

The *bar mitzvah* boy, in all the activity and excitement of preparing for this one occasion, had not given much thought to preparing for his future. But, now it was all over, he realised the future was coming, whether he was prepared for it or not.

In a few days he would be in Riga, and his Tukum childhood would be in the past.

PART TWO

Riga, Vidzeme

1883

7

It was the end of October, and the day of his departure, and Rafael went around saying his goodbyes. He went to see his grandfather, who warned him to behave himself and do what he was told, and his old *melamed*, Abram Leibowitz, who shook his hand solemnly and advised him to remember what he had been taught. He bade an emotional farewell to the bereaved Reuben and his parents, and he even sought out Leib Lipman, still recovering from the injuries sustained in the pogrom; he was rewarded with a smart salute.

He knew he would be allowed to make annual visits home, and in any case his apprenticeship would be over in five years, but he couldn't shake the feeling that he was leaving something precious behind forever.

His father was coming with him to Riga, but Scheine was to stay at home with Yossel, so she said her goodbyes at home. Now that the moment had arrived, it was much more difficult than she had expected, and the tears flowed freely down her face as she embraced her son.

'How tall and strong he's growing,' she thought. 'Each time I see him from now on he will be even taller and stronger.' She touched her pendant, felt to make sure the pin she had put in Rafael's lapel was still there, and said: 'Write often, Raftchik. Work hard and learn quickly. Above all, remember how we've brought you up. Never forget you are a Jew. Come home to see us when you can. We will always be here.'

Rafael did not want to cry, so he adopted a breezy attitude. 'I'm not going very far away, *Mamele*. I'll be fine. I'll see you soon. Please don't worry. Goodbye, Yoss. Don't get into trouble while I'm gone.' He embraced his younger brother, who held on to him tightly for a moment before turning away.

'Come, on, Rafi,' Itzhak urged. 'The train.' He had the tickets in his pocket and there was plenty of time, but he had never been on a train before and was feeling more anxious than he pretended. 'I'll be back tomorrow, Scheine. *Tsum gezunt*'. He picked up Rafi's bag, kissed his wife, and they walked off towards the station.

Itzhak showed the tickets to the station-master with an air of self-importance which was somewhat punctured when the station-master greeted his son as an old friend. They were early, and there was hardly anyone there to begin with, but soon the platform began to fill up with other passengers — mostly *goyim*. After a while, the rails began to hum, a black plume of smoke appeared in the distance, and then the train itself appeared, looking powerful and monstrous. Itzhak suppressed the urge to step back in alarm, and watched, open-mouthed, as it drew up beside the platform; he had never been so close to such an enormous machine. It was strange and unnatural, too loud, too powerful, and it made him nervous and uncomfortable. He looked at Rafael to see if he was afraid, but on the contrary, he seemed beguiled, spellbound.

The train belched another cloud of steam and drew to a clanking halt. Doors flew open along its length and the machine began to disgorge its passengers; Itzhak was amazed by how many it held.

After a while the stream of people stopped, and the station-master blew a whistle to indicate that it was time for the new passengers to board. Itzhak and Rafael found a compartment, put their bags on the rack, and sat down opposite each other on either side of the window.

Rafael was entranced with everything. At first Itzhak was too tense to enjoy it, and when the train began to jolt, and then to move, the colour drained from his face. However, after a while the rhythmic clacking of the wheels and puffing of the engine soothed him and he began to relax a little. The sight of the countryside sliding so quickly past the window was astonishing to him.

The journey took them through the coastal town of Jurmala, where Itzhak and Rafael glimpsed the ocean for the first time (Itzhak muttered the special blessing for that) and then, after a lazy bend in the track, over the Daugava River bridge and into the city of Riga.

Barely three hours after it had left Tukum, the train slowed for its arrival in Riga, finally coming to a halt in a vast cloud of smoke and steam.

Itzhak, still utterly amazed at how quickly they had made the journey, pulled down the bags. They stepped down onto the busy, noisy platform and stood for a few moments, trying to get their bearings in all the hubbub. Then, absorbing themselves into the stream of disembarking passengers, they made their way along the platform and out of the station.

*

They found themselves in an area of cobbled streets, imposing yellow-brick warehouses and jostling crowds. Asking directions was a wearisome business as many people they stopped were strangers from out of town, or spoke a language Itzhak could not understand, or were simply in too much of a hurry to stop. They carried on walking though, and after a short while found themselves at the edge of the city's broad river, the Daugava, almost as congested with traffic as the roads. Slow-moving barges laden with timber vied for space with passenger ships and ships carrying goods.

Turning left, and following the river bank south, they started to hear more Yiddish-speaking voices, and eventually Itzhak found someone with whom he could converse, a middle-aged man who stopped when addressed and waited politely to see what Itzhak wanted. Yes, the man said, nodding and pointing, he knew Elijas Street; it was in the Latgale neighbourhood, just a little further south.

Relieved to find themselves on the right track, they followed the man's directions, heading away from the river now, until they came at last to Elijas Street. Here they found the object of their search; yet another yellow–brick building, distinguishable from the others by the brass plaque on the wall next to the entrance which bore the lantern emblem and the name 'Gozinsky Metalworks'.

Going inside, they found themselves in a broad space full of workbenches, machines, men, bustle and noise.

They approached one of the men operating a machine and, shouting above the din, asked him where they could find the owner. Without taking his eyes off his work, the man pointed to a wrought iron spiral staircase at the far end of the building and they made their way towards it. Half way there they were startled by a sudden crash; the thunderous cacophony of a stack of metal sheets falling from a trolley. It gave them quite a jolt, but nobody else seemed even to register the noise and so, taking a moment to regain their composure, Itzhak and Rafael continued towards the staircase. Reaching the top, Itzhak gave Rafael an encouraging smile and knocked on the door.

It was opened by a smartly–dressed lady who eyed them enquiringly. 'Yes?' she said. 'Can I help you?'

Itzhak introduced himself and explained that Rafael had come to enrol as an apprentice. 'Wait here, please,' she replied brusquely, and closed the door.

There was a short delay and then the door opened again to reveal Israel Gozinsky himself. Itzhak, seeing him for the first time in so many years, saw before him a fatter, balder version of the man he had last seen as a very young man.

Israel greeted them affably, with just a slight trace of condescension. 'Ah, Itzhak,' he said, 'It's been a long time. So this must be Rafael. It's good to meet you, young man. Come in.'

He led them through the secretary's small office into his own, much larger one.

THE LAMPMAKER — PART TWO

Israel Gozinsky's office was sparsely furnished. There was a padded chair behind a polished wooden desk on which stood nothing but a pen, a glass inkwell and a blotting pad. Some hard-backed chairs, a wooden filing cabinet and an imposing and secure-looking metal safe were the only other items of furniture. Large windows along one side allowed a view of the factory floor, and a small fire glowing in a small fireplace gave off a little warmth. Another door led, Itzhak presumed, into some other office.

'Please, take a seat,' Israel said, indicating the hard-backed chairs in front of the desk.

He was polite, but businesslike and formal. At his request the secretary produced two sheets of paper which she placed on the table in front of Rafael. 'This is your contract, Rafael' said Israel, 'Two identical copies. Please write your name at the bottom of each one where there is a space, then I will sign them. You will keep one and we will keep the other. Then you will be an apprentice.'

Rafael nodded, but did not make a move to pick up the pen.

'If you can't write, just put a cross' Israel said, showing the first, slight sign of impatience.

'Oh no, I can write, sir,' said Rafael, as politely as he could. 'I'm just reading it first to make sure I understand what it says.' Israel was slightly surprised — few apprentices took the time to read the contract before signing. He leant back in his chair, interlaced his fingers, and tapped his forefingers together while he waited.

Itzhak leaned over and read it too. He already knew most of the details of the arrangement, but now, seeing it written down formally, it suddenly seemed more real.

Rafael would work for a master craftsman, learning the skills he would need to join the guild and make a living in the profession. The hours would be long, the work would be tiring and to begin with he would be given menial tasks. At the end of one year, if his work was not up to scratch, he would be sent away, and the contract would be terminated. If he was kept on, though, he would be bound for a further four years. If he tried to leave during that time he would be brought back and punished. He would receive board and lodging, and a small stipend, and at the end of his term he would receive a certificate and a set of tools.

'Five years,' muttered Itzhak, half to himself.

'It used to be seven,' said Israel.

'What if he's conscripted to the army in that time?'

Israel leaned forward and smiled. 'Oh, don't worry about that, Itzhak. I have a special arrangement with the authorities. They don't take my apprentices.' Itzhak leaned back in his chair, too relieved to speak. He shut his eyes for a moment, and by the time he opened them the document was signed and Rafael's future path was set.

He was to start work the following morning.

Armed with his copy of the contract, Rafael went next with his father to the police station to register his residency. After examining the document carefully, the official on duty took down his details and stamped his papers. He was now a legal resident of Riga.

Itzhak planned to spend the night at an inn and take the train back to Tukum the following day, whilst Rafael would lodge in the Apprentice House just down the road from the factory.

The Apprentice House, on the corner of Elijas Street, near the imposing wooden Church of Jesus, was maintained jointly by a group of factory owners and housed both Jewish and non-Jewish apprentices in an attempt to foster and encourage mutual understanding and tolerance. The secretary had given them a key which she said would get them into the building, after which Frau Pucher, the housekeeper would tell them where to go.

Before going to the Apprentice House, Itzhak took Rafael to explore the immediate area. They located the nearest synagogue and Itzhak pointed out the shops, the police station and various other landmarks. It was all rather unnecessary; he was just trying to postpone the inevitable moment of parting.

Returning to Elijas Street by this circuitous route, they finally came to the Apprentice House. Itzhak noticed with pleasure that there was a *mezuzah* on the doorpost. He touched it reflexively and Rafael did the same. Then they unlocked the door and went in.

Despite its grand-sounding title, the Apprentice House was not a particularly grand building; it reminded Rafael of his old *heder*, with its dark corridors and creaking floorboards. They stood for a moment in the entrance hall, wondering where to go; there didn't seem to be anybody around. They walked along the corridor until they found a door under which a light was shining. Putting down his bag, Itzhak knocked gently. A woman's voice called out: 'Go away.'

Puzzled, he knocked again 'Excuse me,' he called through the door. 'We need some help.'

From inside the room came a groan followed by the sound of footsteps. The door was opened by a large, middle-aged woman dressed in a pinafore, holding a half-smoked cigarette. 'Can't a woman sit down for five minutes? What do you want?' she demanded.

'I'm sorry to disturb you, Madam,' Itzhak said politely. 'Are you Frau Pucher?'

The woman gave the smallest of nods. 'Maybe. Who are you?'

'My name is Yacobsohn and this is my son Rafael. He's the new apprentice at Gozin ...'

'Room two. Bed three,' interrupted the woman. 'Dinner at eight. House rules are up on the wall. Read them.'

She closed the door abruptly and the footsteps retreated.

'What a rude woman,' said Itzhak, more puzzled than angry.

As they started to walk away, the door opened again and the woman called after them. 'Normal or Jew?'

'Pardon me?'

'For the food. Normal or Jewish?'

'Oh, I see. My son needs food that conforms with the laws of *kashrut*, madam.'

'Well we only do normal or Jewish.'

'Well then, Jewish, please.'

'Right. Well, say so then,' she said, rolling her eyes and shutting the door for a second time.

They walked back along the corridor until they came to a door bearing a brass "2", and went in. There were just three beds in the room, which was a relief to Rafael; he had been worried that he would be in an enormous dormitory. Two of the beds had clearly been slept in but the third seemed unused. 'Bed three,' he thought, putting down his bag. He turned to look at his father, who gave him an encouraging, if rather forced, smile.

'Well, here we are,' Itzhak said. 'This is a nice room, isn't it? Quite clean, I think.' He tested the mattress with his hand. 'Ah, good. The bed feels quite comfortable.' He was starting to feel unequal to the situation, but tried hard not to let it show. He noticed that Rafael had gone rather pale. He thought: 'Perhaps it's best if I just go.' Then he said, as breezily as he could: 'The other boys will be back from work soon, and you won't want me to be here then.' He rubbed his hands together. 'I think I'll leave you to it. Work hard, Rafi. Do as you're told, and try to stay out of trouble. Don't forget your religion. And don't forget to write. You remember where the shul is? Good. And you know how to get back to the factory in the morning, don't you? Don't be late, especially on your first day. Have you still got the key?'

Rafael wished his father would stop fussing. Now that the moment for parting had arrived, he wanted it to be over quickly. 'Don't worry, *Tatty*,' he said, 'I'll be fine. I remember everything. Really. You can go. Look, here's the key. I haven't lost it.'

'Good. Keep it safe.' What he really meant was: 'Keep yourself safe.'

They embraced, and Itzhak, with an aching heart, reluctantly left. Half-way down the corridor he suddenly remembered something, and rushed back to press a ruble into Rafael's hand. Then he was really gone.

Rafael stood in the centre of the room, which was suddenly very quiet and empty, and looked around again. Next to his bed was a chair with a wicker seat, and a small cupboard which he assumed was where he was meant to keep his clothes. There was a small washstand in the corner of the room on which stood a chipped tin water jug. He emptied his bag, tucked it under the bed and sat down on the chair.

He felt very young, very lost and very alone. After a while he got up again and wandered through the building's empty corridors. He wondered what the time was, how long it would be before the other apprentices came back from work, and what they would think of him.

There didn't seem to be anything else to do, so he went back to the room, unpacked his few possessions, and sat on his bed.

Eventually he started to hear noises in the corridor; footsteps, voices, the banging of doors. His own dormitory door flew open and two boys came in, evidently his roommates. He stood up, expecting them to say something to him, but they hardly seemed to notice him. They were older than he was, and appeared to treat him as an interloper, resenting his presence in the room they had previously had to themselves. They dumped a few things on their beds, carrying on the conversation they had been having, gave their hands a superficial rinse at the washstand, and went back out into the corridor just as a gong began sounding from somewhere. It was dinner time.

Rafael joined a stream of boys of varying ages heading to the communal dining room. Inside the room was a large wooden table, surrounded on each side by benches, laid with forks, spoons and bowls. The boys, none of whom seemed particularly interested in the new arrival, took their seats. Rafael squeezed onto the end of one of the benches.

The housekeeper, Frau Pucher, was the only person employed in the house and she was responsible for providing the apprentices with an evening meal, a task she approached with a sense of resentment which somehow found its way into the food she prepared. The requirement to cater for the Jewish boys was one she seemed to find particularly irksome.

She came in carrying a steaming pot of mutton stew, dropped it heavily on the table and called out 'Normal!' The first group of boys grabbed their bowls, clambered off the benches and lined up to receive their food. Sloppily, she ladled a portion into each bowl. Once they had their food the boys went back to their places and tucked in hungrily.

When the first group had been fed, Frau Pucher took the pot away, to return a few moments later with another one. She called out 'Jewish,' and the rest of the boys grabbed their bowls and went up in turn. Rafael copied them. It was a meatless broth, a few roughly chopped vegetables floating miserably in a greasy-looking liquid. But Rafael was hungry and took his portion gladly enough to the table. He quickly said the blessing under his breath and, using his spoon, began eating, or rather drinking, the disappointing meal.

After dinner there seemed to be little else to do, so he went to bed early; there was no sign of his two roommates. He lay awake, listening to all the strange, unfamiliar sounds of his new home. When his roommates came in at last, making no effort to be quiet for his benefit, he pretended to be asleep. Eventually, they stopped talking and started snoring. As he lay on his back, staring into the darkness, listening to the snores of the two boys, he tried to pretend he was at home, that it was Yossel's snores he could hear, that tomorrow he would wake up in his own bed and his mother would be singing while she prepared his breakfast. He blinked away hot, stinging tears, feeling utterly miserable.

At some point, without realising it, he fell asleep.

Early in the morning Rafael presented himself at the factory for the first time as an apprentice.

The first person he met was the foreman, a stern-looking man known, because of his military bearing, as 'the Captain', a nickname he bore with pride. The Captain took Rafael to meet the master, Herr Salomon Strauss, a short, stocky German Jew who carried himself

THE LAMPMAKER — PART TWO

with a confident bearing which inspired immediate respect. He welcomed his new apprentice warmly. His kind, intelligent face reminded Rafael of Abram Leibowitz, although with less exuberance to his beard and eyebrows, and he felt at once that this was an ally, a feeling that was only slightly diminished when Herr Strauss handed him a broom and told him to start sweeping.

Despite Israel Gozinsky's zeal for social reform the factory was no earthly paradise; the hours were long, and in the first few weeks Rafael found there was a great deal of sweeping to be done. Also carrying, lifting, stacking and packing. There was sheet metal to be fetched, tools to be tidied and sharpened, machinery maintained and finished items to be packed and loaded. But, although his arms and legs ached and his hair became plastered to his forehead with sweat, he did what he was told uncomplainingly.

Over time he came to understand how the factory worked and realised that all the seemingly chaotic activity had a carefully designed rhythm and structure. The process started when Natalia Ivanovna received a customer's order. She passed it to the Captain, who co-ordinated all the activities required to complete it. Apart from the people involved in making the products, there were other men whose job it was to make sure raw materials were in stock, and in the right place, when needed, and still others who were responsible for packing and shipping finished goods.

Some of the men were semi-skilled and their job was solely to work with the machines. Others were entrusted with more delicate tasks. Herr Strauss was the only master craftsman employed by the firm and was accorded the greatest respect, even by the Captain. The book-keeper scratching away in his huge books in the little room next to the main office and Natalia Ivanovna completed the workforce.

Israel Gozinsky himself rarely visited the factory floor although he could be glimpsed from time to time as he moved past his office window. Occasionally he could be seen standing at it, looking keenly at the activity below. He worked as long hours as anyone else, arriving early and leaving late and Rafael had very little idea what it was that he actually did. Whatever it was, he obviously did it well because the factory was thriving and Gozinsky himself was clearly doing very well from it.

Salomon Strauss was a patient teacher who found in Rafael a willing and capable student. He began to teach him the names of the tools and how to use them, demonstrating each technique and gently correcting Rafael's faltering attempts. Under his guidance Rafael made quick progress and the two began to develop an understanding, a bond which deepened with each passing day.

*

Each evening Rafael came back to the Apprentice House with a sinking feeling. Nobody befriended him and he ate his meals in a solitary bubble, listening to the chatter of voices around him but never spoken to. It was not that the other apprentices were actively hostile; they were all at different factories and seemed to be, at best, only dimly aware of his existence. He began to feel like a ghost walking among the living.

His roommates never included him in their conversation either. One evening they were sitting on their beds, talking animatedly to each other, and during a brief lull in their conversation he tried to interject. They simply waited until he stopped talking, as they might have waited for a donkey to finish braying, and then carried on with their conversation. He felt deeply humiliated and never tried it again.

So it was a particular thrill when, at the end of his second week, Herr Strauss invited Rafael to his home to meet his wife and welcome *Shabbos* in with them. Rafael felt honoured, and also a little apprehensive.

Salomon and Hanna Strauss lived in the heart of the mainly-Jewish Latgale neighbourhood, a little way south of the metalworks.

Rafael left the factory with his master, who led the way, striding down Latgales Street with his confident, erect bearing while Rafael trotted along a respectful half–step behind. Turning off Latgales Street, they passed through an area of cobbled streets lined with neat, low wooden buildings until Herr Strauss stopped outside one of the buildings, and said: 'Well, here we are!'

He ushered Rafael inside. The living space was compact, but comfortably furnished, and a delightful cooking smell hung in the air. An inner door opened and, accompanied by a waft of steam, Hanna Strauss appeared from the kitchen, wiped her hands on her apron and looked appraisingly at Rafael.

'So, this is the new apprentice? A bit shorter than the last one, I think,' she said, her eyes twinkling. 'But he has a nice face. Welcome, young man. *Shabbat shalom.*'

'*Shabbat shalom,*' replied Rafael. 'Thank you for having me.'

Hanna Strauss was strikingly similar in looks to her husband; the same height, and almost the same build. She had a similar bearing, the same kindly eyes and the same perpetually amused expression. Rafael had felt quite anxious about coming to his master's home but he immediately felt more relaxed.

Hanna went back into the kitchen and Herr Strauss disappeared into the bedroom to change, leaving Rafael alone for a few minutes. He looked around the room, taking in the upright piano, the lid covered with an embroidered cloth on which stood a portrait of an elderly woman, and the large tasselled rug covering much of the floor. It seemed like a very homely room.

He turned to look at the dining table and it was then that he noticed for the first time the pair of *Shabbos* candlesticks which stood on it.

He gasped and widened his eyes. They were far and away the most beautiful candlesticks he had ever seen. Tall and slender, plated with silver polished to a bright sheen, they seemed to glow from within. Their columns were twisting spirals that grew out of stepped bases like graceful climbing plants and ended in flowing sconces with delicate, tapered edges.

Herr Strauss returned a few minutes later in his *Shabbos* clothes, clapping a *koppel* on his head.

'There,' he said happily. 'Now I'm properly dressed to receive our guest.'

Rafael suddenly became conscious of his own soiled work clothes and wished he something to change into. The Strausses, however, appeared not to notice. Hanna kept popping in and out of the kitchen and Salomon bustled around, putting things on the table and occasionally asking Rafael to move something for him.

Salomon noticed that Rafael couldn't take his eyes off the candlesticks. He smiled and said: 'Do you know what this type of column is called, Rafael?'

'No, sir.'

'They are known as Solomonic columns; perhaps that's why I like them so much. Columns like these once supported the roof of Solomon's Temple, you know.'

'They are so beautiful. Where did they come from?'

'I'm glad you like them. Actually, I made them myself, many years ago. They were my 'masterpiece' — the piece I made to gain my master's status.'

'They are really wonderful.'

Rafael tried to imagine himself making things of such delicacy and perfection of form. Having seen his master working only on more mundane items so far — lanterns, parts for machinery, trays, nameplates and so on — he only now realised the level of craftsmanship and creativity the man possessed. It took his breath away.

Herr Strauss started to explain how they were made, but just then Hanna returned. 'Now, now, Salomon,' she chided. Don't bore the poor lad on his first visit.' She placed a new white candle in each of the candlesticks and Rafael noticed with admiration how precisely they fitted, standing completely perpendicular.

Salomon, going to the window and peering out at the darkening sky, said: 'Yes, I think it's time,' and he joined Hanna and Rafael at the table.

Striking a match, Hanna reverently lit the candles and then, just as Rafael's mother always did, made the traditional wafting movement. Then, covering her eyes, she recited the blessing:

'*Barukh ata Adonai, Eloheinu melekh ha'olam, asher kid'shanu b'mitzvotav v'tzivanu l'hadlik ner shel Shabbat*'.

A single tear slid down Rafael's cheek. The Strausses exchanged quick glances, but said nothing. They all washed their hands from the pitcher on the sideboard, Salomon blessed the *challah* and the wine and Hanna brought out steaming bowls of chicken soup and *lokshen* noodles.

Hanna was a good cook and the food would have been delicious at any time; after two weeks of meals at the Apprentice House it was ambrosial. After their first hunger had been assuaged, Hanna turned to Rafael and said: 'So, Rafael, tell me about yourself.'

Thus encouraged, Rafael began to tell them about his home, his parents, and his brother. It was the first time he had talked about his family to people who didn't know them and it felt strange, as if he was seeing his own life from the outside, but it eased his homesickness a little, as they had hoped it would.

At the end of the meal Salomon performed the *bentching* in a strong and tuneful voice, and afterwards Rafael thanked them earnestly and prepared to leave.

They wouldn't hear of his walking back to the house on his own at such a late hour, and gently insisted that he stay the night. Hanna Strauss produced blankets and pillows and, with experienced deftness, turned their sofa into a comfortable bed.

After the Strausses had wished him good night and retired to their room, and he was lying comfortably on the sofa–bed, he unexpectedly felt a great churning bubble of emotions rising up from somewhere deep inside him.

Tears began to spill and he tried to wipe them away with his hands to stop them drenching the blankets. 'What's all this about?' he thought. He wasn't sure what it meant, or what it was he was feeling.

But he closed his eyes and let the tears flow freely.

In the morning the Strausses gave him a good breakfast and offered to take him to their *shul*, which was none other than Riga's famous Great Choral Synagogue on Gogol Street, an offer which he gratefully accepted; he had been eager to attend a service in the famous house of prayer since he arrived.

He ran back to the Apprentice House to change into his *Shabbos* clothes and then walked as quickly as he could to Gogol Street where he was to meet them. His first view of the building did not disappoint him; the colossal synagogue was easily the most magnificent he had ever seen. People were already streaming in but the Strausses were waiting patiently for him outside. Hanna climbed the stairs to the women's gallery while Salomon ushered Rafael into the downstairs area. The space was vast and airy, the light streaming through the coloured glass of the windows tinting everything with blues and reds.

Rafael was mesmerised by the sight of the huge congregation; so many men wrapped in their black and white striped *tallitot* muttering prayers, swaying forwards and backwards over their prayer books. Everything about the place was impressive; the powerful chanting of the *chazan*, the gorgeously decorated covers of the *Sifrei Torah* with their silver finials, and the intense fervour of the prayers. It was almost overwhelming.

Herr Strauss smiled to himself when he saw Rafael's reaction to the building. His eyes were shining the way his own had the first time he came here. He was receptive to beauty and to atmosphere, that was plain. He had intelligence, imagination, perception.

'He is good,' he said to Hanna later. 'Very good. You know, if he continues as he has started, I think I might be able to make something of young Yacobsohn.'

8

WITHIN SIX MONTHS Rafael had learned the basic techniques of working with sheet metal; cutting, bending, forming, soldering, joining with rivets. He learned curling, spinning, hemming and seaming. He began to appreciate the properties of different materials and which thickness to use for different applications. He watched, absorbed, as Herr Strauss showed him how to make items in which form and function were harmoniously combined; ornate lamps, architectural decorations, parts for vehicles and more. Under the watchful eye of his master he attempted items of his own – boxes, trays, candle-holders and eventually lanterns – and began to develop a feeling for how the materials behaved. He found it satisfying work and the time went quickly.

Israel Gozinsky was enthusiastic about innovation, and the factory owned some of the latest types of equipment and machines. The men grumbled each time a new piece of kit appeared, because then they needed training and had to change the way they worked. But when they discovered that it improved their safety, or efficiency, they would quietly drop their opposition. Rafael loved all the machines, and was always keen to find out how they worked. The men started to get into the habit of calling him over whenever there was a mechanical problem, and often he was able to fix it.

On one occasion, Rafael happened to look up at the office window and he saw Israel Gozinsky holding an oddly-shaped black object to his ear. 'What on earth is that?' he asked one of the men.

The man looked up at the window and grinned, 'It's a telephone. It lets you talk to people at a distance.'

Rafael nodded sagely, as if he understood. He was not entirely sure whether or not he was being teased. 'So, could I use it to talk to my parents?'

'Only if they've got one too,' laughed the man.

'Oh,' said Rafael, feeling foolish and confused. 'Of course.'

*

As time went on, the transformative power of adolescence began to work its magic on Rafael's body, mind and emotions. He had only the vaguest notions about what was going on, and unfortunately there was nobody he could ask. He felt bewildered, and at times ashamed, but strangely exhilarated.

He was shooting up in height. By late spring he found the arms of his shirts and the legs of his trousers were far too short for his newly lanky limbs. Lacking his father's tailoring skills he had no option but to spend his stipend on replacement clothes.

With the exception of Natalia Ivanovna, Gozinsky's was entirely staffed by men, but outside, in the larger world, there were suddenly girls. Rafael was delighted, entranced, intrigued and curious.

On *Shabbos* afternoons in the summer he took to strolling northwards out of the Latgale neighbourhood to a place where the canal twisted through a pleasant park. Girls promenaded there with their families.

He enjoyed these outings very much, but they were solitary. He had little social life beyond occasional visits to the Strausses and the odd inconsequential conversations with other boys at the Apprentice House, and he worked longer at the factory than strictly required, partly to stave off the pangs of loneliness.

When autumn came he was given leave to go home for the High Holy Days, his first opportunity since he started, almost a year before, to see his parents and brother. He begrudged the train fare, but time was of the essence if he was going to get home in time for *Rosh Hashanah*, so he had little choice but to pay it. In truth, he was also quite excited at the prospect of his first independent train ride.

When the train pulled up in Tukum, he climbed down onto the platform, and there was his father waiting for him. They embraced warmly. 'Look at you!' said Itzhak, shaking his head in wonder, 'So big. A man already.' They began to walk home.

'How is *Mamele*?' asked Rafael after a while. Itzhak didn't answer immediately.

'Well, to be honest with you, Rafi, she's a little down. She'll be so happy to see you, though. It will lift her spirits.'

'A little down? But why? She knows I'm not in danger from the draft any more. Is it Yossel?'

'No, no, it's not about you or Yossel. First of all, she's distressed about the pogroms; well, of course we all are. And on top of that there's this latest business with poor Getta and her baby …'

'Sorry, who is Getta?'

'You remember your mother's friend, Leah who is married to "White–hands" Yankel? Well, her daughter Getta had a baby girl. Yankel and Leah's first grandchild.'

'What happened to the baby? Did it die?' Rafael's assumption was a natural one; many infants died. 'I'm so sorry to hear that.'

'Oh no, the baby is alive. A lovely little girl; although she is subject to fits.'

'But then, what's happened?'

Itzhak let out a long sigh before continuing. 'Getta made a terrible mistake. One day in the middle of winter her father asked her to help him on his milk round, and as it was so cold she thought it best not to take the baby with her. She couldn't find anyone to leave it with — none of the usual people could take it for some reason — so, as a last resort, she asked a woman she barely knew to look after her. A *goy*.'

He paused again and shook his head before continuing.

'Well, it seems that, while Getta was out, the baby had one of its fits. The woman panicked. She said she thought the child was going to die. So she blessed some water and gave it a Christian baptism; so it wouldn't die a heathen, she said. The baby got over its fit and when Getta got back the woman told her, quite proudly, what she'd done. Getta was a little cross but didn't think much of it — until a few days later when the police came, with people from the church. They told her it was against the law for a Christian child to live with a Jewish family and as the baby was now a Catholic they had come to take it away.'

'*Oy gevalt!*' cried Rafael in horror. 'But how can that turn it into a Christian? Don't you have to be a priest to conduct a baptism?'

'Apparently, in an emergency anyone can do it. That's the law.'

'So they took the baby away?'

'Thank God, no. At least, not yet. There was a big tussle, all the neighbours heard. Getta was screaming, and the men were shouting and trying to grab the child. At last, someone fetched the rabbi, and he managed to quieten things down and make the men leave. They'll come back again, though. So now Getta can't leave the house, or let the baby out of her sight.

'What about her husband?'

'He's not here; he was conscripted. He hasn't even seen his baby yet. Leah and *Mame* have been sitting with Getta, trying to comfort her. Everyone is very upset. I'm sorry to tell you about all this, but it's best you know.'

They had reached the apartment and the last few words were said standing outside. Then Itzhak opened the door and called: 'Scheine! Yossel! Look who we have here!'

Yossel was sitting at the table but jumped up when he saw his brother. 'You're so big!' he said.

Scheine came up, smiling broadly. 'Raftchik. You look good,' she said, hugging him tightly.

'She looks really tired,' thought Rafael.

'Come on,' his father said, bustling around breezily, 'put your things down and wash your hands, Rafi. You can help us get things ready for tonight, then it'll be time to go to *shul*. When we get back we'll celebrate your return properly and you can tell us all about it!'

'Is *Zeide* coming?'

'Of course. He'll be here any minute.'

Scheine had prepared a special meal for the twin celebrations of *Rosh Hashanah* and Rafael's homecoming which included chicken soup, gefilte fish and fresh fruits. When Favel Gutman arrived he brought with him a *challah* studded with raisins which they dipped in honey. There were no other guests this *Rosh Hashanah*, the Yacobsohns wanted Rafael all to themselves for the short time they had with him.

The family peppered Rafael with questions; about the work, the place, the people. 'Is the master kind?' 'Yes, *Tatty*.' 'Do you enjoy the work?' 'Actually, yes, *Zeide*.' 'What's Riga like?' 'It's big, Yoss.' 'Have you made any friends?' 'Yes, *Tatty*.' 'Are you looking after yourself?' 'What do you mean, *Mamele*?' 'Well, are you eating properly?' 'No, not really.' 'What do you mean "Not really?"' 'Well …'

And on and on.

At *shul* the next day he had to go through it all again with everyone he knew. Going away for a year seemed to have turned him into a minor celebrity.

After *Yom Kippur* it was time to return to Riga. Scheine insisted on loading his bag up with as much food as he could carry to take back with him.

9

THE YEAR 1885 was yet another conscription year in Kurland, and it followed the usual pattern. Yossel was still eleven, just, so he was safe this time. But one of his old friends from *heder,* a few weeks older, had turned twelve and was on the list. The boy's parents went to desperate lengths to have him declared unfit; they actually cut off one of his fingers. But it was a wasted sacrifice; he was bandaged up and marched off to the army just the same.

Meanwhile, in Riga, Rafael made a very successful ornate water jug, earning him praise from Herr Strauss. There was less sweeping and fetching for him now; he felt he was on his way to becoming a proper craftsman.

One big event at Gozinsky's that spring was the installation of electric lights. It was not the very first factory in Riga to have electricity installed, but it was still an exciting, almost astonishing innovation.

The older workers were wary. Why was it necessary? What was wrong with the old lights? Was it safe? What if a bulb exploded or the switches caught fire? In the end, though, despite the grumbling, everyone realised there was no going back, and the men had to admit that the light was actually much better.

As the youngest person in the factory, Rafael was fascinated and enchanted by electricity and the promise it seemed to carry for the future. He loved to trace with his eyes the path of the cables through the rafters and down the wall to the switches, and he loved the glow of the bulbs, so strong and steady compared with the flickering gas lamps he was used to. He wanted to find out how it all worked; he asked his workmates, but nobody knew. He resolved to find out for himself, one day.

He could see, too, that it was all part of a process, Riga was changing; the world was changing. First trains, then telephones, now electricity. Horse–drawn trams plied the streets and new buildings were shooting up. For an older generation this relentless change was bewildering; for the young like Rafael it was exciting, intoxicating, ripe with possibilities.

*

He found living in Riga more and more comfortable and although he missed his family and friends he no longer felt homesick in the way he had in the early days. The scale of the place no longer daunted him and, although he still had huge gaps in his geographical knowledge, within his limits he could find his way round confidently.

Riga was more cosmopolitan and tolerant than Tukum, even if he was occasionally jostled, or sworn at, or spat at, or instructed to 'go home'. But, there could still be serious trouble on occasion.

In 1885 the timings of Easter and *Pesach* coincided exactly and, since the Great Choral Synagogue was separated from The Church of Jesus only by the short length of Jesusabaznicas Street, it was inevitable that the two groups of worshippers would meet at some point. Rafael and the Strausses left *shul* after the morning service, and were walking down Jesusabaznicas Street as part of a large crowd of Jews when they encountered the congregation streaming out of church.

It was a tense moment. Nevertheless, the chanting, name–calling and scuffling that ensued might have passed off without too many problems, if it hadn't been for a detachment of police stationed in the area to prevent trouble who, through a combination of heavy–handedness, aggression and stupidity, succeeded in turning what would have been at most a minor fracas into an angry riot. Soon stones, bottles and sticks were flying through the air. People ran in every direction, trying either to flee the riot or, in a few cases, to inflame it.

Keeping their heads down, and staying in a tight group, Rafael and the Strausses struggled to get away. In their haste, Hanna stumbled on the kerb, falling heavily and Rafael was forced to hunch over her to act as a shield while Salomon helped her to her feet. A stone struck him with some force between the shoulder blades, causing him to yell out in pain, but he kept his balance somehow and the three of them were able to move on, and out of the danger area, shaken but highly relieved to have escaped so lightly.

A number of more serious injuries were reported and a number of 'Jewish trouble-makers' arrested but the whole incident was soon forgotten by everyone — except for those caught up in it.

*

In the summer Rafael's two taciturn roommates completed their apprenticeships, collected their tools from their masters and set out into the world as journeymen. He breathed a sigh of relief and, for a few weeks, he had the dormitory to himself; it was almost the first time he had slept in a room on his own.

But one day in the early autumn he returned to the house at the end of the day to find that someone else had moved in; there were clothes and other personal items lying on one of the beds. Whoever it was had clearly dumped his stuff and gone out again, so Rafael would have to wait to find out who it was. He came in at last, just as Rafael was thinking of getting into bed, and apologised politely for his lateness.

The newcomer introduced himself as David Krupp, a reassuringly Jewish name. David was seventeen, with a lean, athletic frame, an unruly shock of dark hair and keen, twinkling, brown eyes. He was not an apprentice, he said, but a student at Riga Polytechnic, studying architecture. Rafael wondered why a student had been allocated a bed in the Apprentice House. But as David himself offered no explanation, and it seemed rude to question him about it when they'd only just met, that question remained, for the moment, unanswered. Rafael supposed that, since the Apprentice House had empty beds at the moment, they could accommodate students if they wanted to.

In any case, David was an engaging companion and the two became friends almost at once. On weekend afternoons, while the weather remained fine, they took to strolling together through the elegant streets and parks of Riga. When they got tired, they would sit on a bench watching the world go by, chatting amicably.

One autumn evening, soon after he turned fifteen, Rafael got back to the Apprentice House after work to find David lying on his bed, reading. This was unusual enough to invite comment. 'Not going out, David?' he asked.

'No, not tonight.'

'I hope you don't mind me asking, but where is it that you go most evenings?'

David grinned. 'I wondered when you would get round to asking. It's no big secret; mostly, I go to the tavern to drink beer with my Polytechnic friends. What about you? What do you do in the evenings?'

Rafael looked thoughtful for a moment. 'Well, actually I come back here and lie on my bed reading until it's time to go to sleep. Occasionally, I go to the Strausses.'

'Sounds thrilling. Poor Rafi. You haven't met many people in Riga, have you?'

'No, I suppose not.'

'Then come with me tomorrow night. You can meet my friends.'

The next evening, after they had eaten, they walked away from the river into the heart of the city's famous beer district. There was a strong smell of fermentation coming from the group of breweries clustered round Aristida Briāna Street.

'This is it,' announced David suddenly, diving down a steep flight of steps into the cellar of one of the buildings. A metal sign hanging above the entrance announced the place's name: *Das Goldene Kalb* — The Golden Calf. After hesitating for a moment, Rafael followed.

David was waiting for him inside the door of a cheerful, if dimly lit, German-style tavern filled with the sound of chatter and laughter, and delicious smells. Aproned waitresses bustled around with trays of whisky, or foaming beer, and somewhere in the gloom an accordion was playing. David laughed at Rafael's open-mouthed expression. He'd never been anywhere like it before and he was thrilled.

'Come on,' he said, slapping him on the back, 'come and meet everyone.' He led his friend between the tables to one of the groups sitting in a cosy corner near the bar. They let out a cheer when they saw David, and another one when he announced: 'Everyone. This is my friend Rafi.'

'Hello Rafi,' they chorused happily.

Rafael took a place at the end of the bench, against the wall, and looked round the table. Apart from him and David, there were seven young people there, boys and girls, and they were some of the noisiest and happiest people he had ever met. They were speaking German, all talking at once, gesticulating wildly, laughing, drinking, and slapping the table. It couldn't have been more different from his usual quiet evening in the Apprentice House, and he couldn't have been more delighted. David, sitting a few seats away from him, was immediately swept up in the conversation and, having introduced Rafael, had just left him to it.

Someone presented Rafael with a beer. He thanked them and took it tentatively; he didn't want the others to realise it, but he had never drunk full-strength beer before. He tried to remember if there was a special blessing, decided there wasn't, and quietly muttered an all-purpose one. He took an experimental sip, decided he liked it very much, and took a much bigger one.

Wiping the foam from his mouth, he realised that the girl sitting next to him was addressing him. He turned politely and looked at her properly for the first time.

His eyes widened and his heart beat faster as he realised two things in quick succession. The first was that the girl, with her luxurious black hair, piercing eyes, dimpled chin and amused expression, was astonishingly pretty. The second thing, almost inevitably given the first thing, was that he desperately wanted her to like him.

'I'm sorry,' he stuttered, 'what did you say?'

The girl laughed and leaned closer to his ear. 'I said "Hello Rafi, my name's Rosa".' The feeling of her warm breath in his ear made him feel dizzy. She was smiling at him, and it was almost more than he could bear. His mouth was dry and he took another sip of beer before replying

'Hello Rosa. It's nice to meet you.' He lapsed into silence, staring desperately at his beer and completely unable to think of anything else to say.

The girl sitting on the other side of the table leaned over. 'What have you done, Rosa? I think you've broken him,' she said, laughing.

Rafael reddened with embarrassment, but to his surprise Rosa didn't join in with the laughter She put her finger to her lips ('Oh my God,' he thought. 'Those lips!') and said: 'Shush, Inge. Be nice.'

'Are you studying at the Polytechnic, Rosa?' he asked her.

'They don't let girls in, silly,' she replied teasingly, 'Don't you know anything? Inge and I are art students.'

'Oh, I see. Art students. That's wonderful.' And with that, Rafael found he had run out of things to say again. To cover his confusion, and give him time to think of another question, he took another large swig of beer. But, to his dismay, Rosa quickly became engaged in a conversation with her other neighbour and Rafael was left to stare moodily into his glass and berate himself for being an idiot and missing his chance. He decided to finish his beer as quickly as he could, say goodbye, and leave.

He sat, wrapped in his own thoughts, when he became aware of his name being spoken. He looked up and realised that the table had gone quiet and everyone (including Rosa) was looking at him. He had no idea why.

'Rafi!' said David. 'Didn't you hear? I asked you what you thought.'

'About what?'

'There you are. Completely broken,' said Inge, and then '*Ow!*' as Rosa's shoe collided sharply with her ankle.

'Haven't you been listening to anything? We want to know what you think about socialism. Unions, workers' rights, strikes. All of that.'

'Well, I'm afraid I don't really…' He had heard some of the men in the factory discussing the topic but had paid little attention. He racked his brains to think of something intelligent to say until he suddenly remembered something he had read at *heder*.

'In the *Torah* it says: You shall not oppress a hired servant who is poor and needy, whether one of your brethren or one of the aliens who is in your land within your gates. Each day you shall give him his wages, and not let the sun go down on it, for he is poor and has set his heart on it; lest he cry out against you to the Lord, and it be sin to you.'

There was a moment's silence following this recitation, broken by the sound of David slapping the table in delight.

'Brilliant!' he cried. 'Word perfect! I knew you were a scholar! Bravo, Rafi!' Rafael saw Rosa flash a triumphant look at Inge, who reddened. 'You're like that commentator … oh, what's the name of that mediaeval rabbi?' David asked, searching his memory. 'It sounds a bit like your name…'

'Do you mean Rashi?' asked Rafael.

'That's him! You're like our very own Rashi!'

This exchange broke the ice, and Rafael found himself at last drawn into the general conversation.

As students will, they discussed animatedly the politics of the day; Czarist repression, socialism and workers' rights. Although there was much he was unable to follow, Rafael found it intoxicating just to be with people of roughly his own age.

Rafael was so engrossed in the conversation, and so delighted with the company, that it took him completely by surprise when Rosa leaned across the table and tapped David on the arm. 'Come on David, it's time for you to escort Inge and me home, please. We have our classes in the morning.'

Rafael stood up to let her out, looking so crestfallen that she laughed. 'Oh don't look so miserable, *Rashi*. You can come too.'

Emerging into the cool air and walking through the quiet of the night time streets, Rafael found he felt a little giddy. When he found himself next to Rosa, with David walking a few steps behind with Inge, he felt even giddier.

'So,' she said. 'What do you think of my brother?'

'Your brother? Which one was he?'

'What do you mean "which one?"' She stopped, turned sharply round and pointed at David who was grinning. 'That one right there. Oh David, honestly! Haven't you told him anything?'

'David? He's your brother?'

'Of course. We're twins.' Rafael looked from one to the other and wondered how he could possibly have missed something so obvious.

They started walking again.'You do know who we are, right?' she said.

'As you can tell, David's told me next to nothing about himself. What do you mean by "who we are"?'

'Oh David!' she repeated over her shoulder. 'For goodness sake, what's the matter with you? Look, Rafi, Israel Gozinsky, your boss, and Aaron Gozinsky, your *tate*'s friend, are our uncles, our *mame's* brothers.'

'What? So you know who I am?'

'Who you are? ' laughed David. 'We know a lot about you, my friend! When we left home our *mame* said we were to look out for you. That's why I asked Uncle Israel to get me a bed in your dormitory in the Apprentice House. *Mamele* also said something else. "If he is anything like his father," she said, "he'll be shy, kind and intelligent." Well, she was partially right. You are quite shy.'

'You've remembered it wrong, David. She said shy, kind, intelligent and good–looking,' corrected Rosa. 'So, it's one out of four,' she concluded, laughing.

'That's right,' agreed David.

'So, hang on a minute, why didn't you tell me any of this?' demanded Rafael, turning on David.

'All right, calm down. I don't know why I didn't, really. Just because it seemed quite amusing, I suppose.'

'This is fascinating,' said Inge to Rosa. 'Your mother thinks his father is kind and good–looking and all of that, does she? It sounds like she knew him rather well. I definitely want to know more about that.'

'Me too,' said Rosa. 'You should ask him next time you see him, Rafi.'

'Oh, don't worry, I will.'

'Well, here we are, boys,' said Rosa. 'Thank you for escorting us. Good night, Rafi.' She took her right glove off, so she could shake his hand. 'It was very nice to meet you.'

As their hands touched, it seemed to Rafael as if his heart started beating more strongly. 'And it was very nice to meet you, Rosa,' he said with sincerity. 'Goodbye. Until next time.'

'Who says there'll be a next time?' said Rosa, lightly.

Inge laughed. 'Good night, *Rashi*. Sweet dreams,' she said. And they disappeared through the door.

'Quite an evening,' said David as the two young men walked back to the Apprentice House together.

'Yes,' agreed Rafael. 'It certainly was.'

The next day, his attention was not fully on his work; he kept drifting off into delicious daydreams of Rosa. Herr Strauss became rather exasperated and snappy. It brought Rafael up sharply; he was glad he hadn't seen much of this side of his master before.

As in the previous year, Rafael obtained leave to go home for the High Holy Days.

After being reunited with his family, he next went to the Rosenbergs, to pay his respects to Reuben and his parents. Itzhak warned him that he would find them changed, and it was true; they were in a sorry state. It had been three years since Schloma's death, but it was clear the wound was still raw.

Reuben and Rafael went for a walk and, while they were out, Reuben confided that his father was in very low spirits. Following his son's death Meyer Rosenberg had simply lost the will to work, and his shop was failing.

Reuben had tried to keep the business going, but he didn't have his father's skills and the customers were drifting away. Hannah and Ester had started weaving baskets to sell for a few kopeks, but it wasn't enough. Debts were mounting; they had needed to make another plan, quickly.

Reuben had approached Leiser the *shochet*, an influential and important man in the town. He knew of the Rosenbergs, partly because he supplied animal skins to the tanners from whom Meyer bought leather, and was sympathetic. The cobbler's shop was closed and Reuben now worked at the slaughterhouse. It was unpleasant and poorly paid, but much better than nothing. He had become the family's main breadwinner.

Rafael left the Rosenbergs feeling dismayed, and wondering what, if anything, he could do now to help.

10

I**T WAS A** long, hard winter. Snow lay thickly on the ground and people shivered in their homes. Stores of grain and potatoes, particularly in the small towns and villages, began to run low.

But, as if in compensation, the spring weather, when it finally arrived in late March, was warm and delightful. Rosa and Inge announced one evening at Das Goldene Kalb that they had been given a new assignment at college. They were to paint a landscape from life.

'We need to find some place we can paint. Somewhere beautiful. Where can we go? Any ideas?' asked Inge.

'How about Lucavsala?' suggested David.

'That's actually a great idea,' said Rosa.

'Where?' asked Rafael. The others stared at him.

'Wow, you really don't get out much, do you, *Rashi*?' said Inge. 'Lucavsala is an island in the river. A little patch of countryside — people go there on picnics all the time.'

'Would you laugh at me if I said I'd never had a picnic?'

'Of course I would.'

'Then I won't say it. But in fact, I haven't.'

'Well, that settles it,' said Rosa, slapping the table with the flat of her hand. 'A painting picnic on Lucavsala it is. It'll have to be on Saturday; I don't suppose you'd consider bunking off *shul* for once, Rafi?' She caught sight of his startled face. 'All right, forget I said that. You pick David up after *shul* and then you boys come and find us and we'll walk over the bridge to the island. Inge and I will make the picnic but you're going to have to carry it David, because we'll have our painting stuff.'

'What's Rafi carrying on this expedition?' asked David

'On the Holy Sabbath?' asked Inge. 'I'm guessing nothing. Right, *Rashi?*'

'Right,' confirmed Rafael, grinning. 'Sorry David. No carrying on *Shabbos*. Don't look at me like that; I don't make the rules.'

It took the four friends half an hour to walk over the bridge to the picnic spot they had selected on Lucavsala and when they got there they dropped their burdens gratefully, spread out the picnic rug and threw themselves to the ground.

'My arms!' complained David. 'What have you got in this basket?' Inge and Rosa exchanged grins.

'Just a few lunch essentials,' said Rosa, massaging her brother's arm. 'Don't worry, Hercules, it'll be nice and light on the way back.'

'This is so lovely,' said Rafael, staring at the view across the river and back to the city. 'I can't believe I haven't been here before.'

'Yes it is lovely,' agreed Rosa. Right, you boys, go to sleep or something and let the artists work. We'll stop for lunch in an hour or so.'

'An hour!' groaned David. 'Come on Rafi, let's go for a walk to take our mind off our hunger.' The boys sprang to their feet and trotted through the meadow, delighting in the unfolding views, ceaseless birdsong and intoxicatingly fragrant and colourful carpets of spring flowers. Meanwhile, the girls set up their easels, took out their prepared canvases, opened their paints and started work.

When David and Rafael returned they found Rosa still hard at work, while Inge had succumbed to hunger and was sitting on the ground gnawing at a chicken leg, which she hurriedly attempted to hide.

'Too late,' said David, 'we saw you.' He went over to look at Rosa's painting. 'Hey, good work, Sis,' he said enthusiastically. 'Come and look at this, Rafi.'

Rafael went over and stared admiringly at the painting.

'Oh, don't look,' grumbled Rosa. 'It's nowhere near finished.'

'But it's amazing, he said earnestly. 'I can't believe what you've done while we've just been strolling around. It's absolutely lovely.' He switched from looking with delight at the half-finished painting to gazing adoringly at the artist. She looked up at him smiling and their eyes connected. An electric shiver went down Rafael's spine as he became fully conscious of the depth of his feelings for Rosa. The birdsong, which had been a persistent backdrop since they arrived on the island, faded into the background. For Rafael there was no sound except the beating of his heart.

Suddenly the spell was broken by a piercing whistle from Inge.

'Hey, you two. Are we eating, or what?' she demanded. Rafael felt like strangling her, but contented himself with a filthy look to which, however, she appeared oblivious.

'Here you go, Rafi,' said David, with his mouth partially full of chicken. 'Have a leg, quick before Inge eats them all.'

'Doesn't anyone want to admire my painting?' asked Inge.

'What painting?' said David, waving a chicken leg towards Inge's canvas. ' It's a couple of lines and a blob.

'Yes, you're right,' she admitted. 'I got hungry. I think I've got a bit of catching up to do.'

'Aha!' cried David, triumphantly holding up two bottles of wine. 'So that's why the basket was so heavy. Well done, girls! Now, where's the corkscrew?'

David and Inge carried on the chatter, pretending not to notice that Rosa was sitting, knees drawn up to her chest, biting her lip and staring across the river, while Rafael, facing resolutely the other way, was gazing into the distance, floating helplessly in a whirlpool of emotions.

They stayed on the island for hours, the girls struggling with their assignments and the boys chatting, walking or dozing until the light started to fade and the evening became chilly. Then they packed everything up and started to trek home.

'*Shabbos* has finished,' said Rafael, 'Here, let me carry something.' Rosa and Inge unhesitatingly loaded him up with their easels, under the weight of which he staggered back across the bridge. Inge kept up a relentless chatter to Rafael the whole way.

When they got back to the Apprentice House, David asked 'Did you enjoy your first picnic, Rafi?'

'Yes, thank you. Actually, it was amazing.'

'Well, about that...'

'I don't know what you're about to say,' he interrupted, 'but please don't say anything to spoil it, David. Let me just enjoy the way I'm feeling right now.' David nodded.

'Sure thing,' he said.

*

In May, Yossel turned thirteen, and, as planned, Rafael went home to attend his *bar mitzvah*, and to accompany him back to Riga afterwards.

During the service Yossel had to recite, like every *bar mitzvah* boy, a portion from the *Torah*. He still had a treble voice, which he controlled well in the chanting — when he remembered the words. But sometimes he forgot them and then, red in the face and perspiring with the effort of reading, he stumbled over the text, and Rabbi Lichtenstein had to prompt him, which he did rather impatiently.

After the ceremony and the celebrations were over, and the family had retired for the night, the two brothers lay in their beds talking quietly together for a long time, enjoying the nostalgic feeling of being in the same bedroom again.

'You did well today, Yoss,' said Rafael.

'Thanks, Rafi. I suppose it might have been worse. I had memorised it. Or thought I had. Anyhow, I'm very glad it's over.'

'So, now it's time to think about Riga!'

'Believe me, I've been thinking about it for weeks.'

'Aren't you looking forward to it?'

Yossel didn't answer straight away. After a while he said: 'You know, Rafi, I'm different from you. You love making things, and learning stuff, and all that sort of thing. To be completely honest with you, I still don't really want to go. But I will go; I know I have to.'

'I expect it will be hard at first; it was for me,' admitted Rafael. 'But, you know, Herr Strauss is very kind and patient and I'm sure you'll be fine. And I'll be there to help you.'

'Thank you Rafi.' Through a yawn he said: 'I expect you're right.'

'I am. Well, I think it's exciting; it's going be nice to have you in Riga with me. I can introduce you to my... to my friends. it's going to be a new phase in our lives. But I wonder — what do you think *Mamele* and *Tatty* will feel when we're both gone? It's going to be strange for them, don't you think?'

There was no response, except the sound of slow, rhythmic breathing. Yossel was asleep.

*

Before departing for Riga, Rafael said he was going to visit the Rosenbergs. Unexpectedly, his father replied 'Good idea. I'll come with you.'

On the way there, Itzhak asked him something he had been wondering about. 'Well, Rafi,' he began, 'how is your social life? Have you made friends in Riga? Is there anyone special there?'

Rafael, who had at that very moment been daydreaming about the person in question was startled. 'Well, actually, *Tatty*, yes, there is.'

'I knew it,' thought Itzhak. '*Nu?* Who is she?'

'Her name is Rosa Krupp, from Boisk. Oddly enough, I think you know her *mame*.'

'Krupp? Well, yes, she must be the daughter of Sora–Roha Gozinsky. How wonderful!'

'So you did know her mother?'

'Indeed. I'd better tell you the whole story. But this is just between us, Rafi. Don't look shocked, it's nothing bad. My *tate* and Sora-Roha's *tate* were best friends, and they ordered your Uncle Shmuel to marry her in order to cement their friendship. He wouldn't do it, so they ordered me to marry her instead; but I wouldn't do it either. I would have done, mind you; she was a lovely girl. Probably still is. But she loved Yudel Krupp.' A far away look came into his eyes and he paused before continuing.

'Anyhow, Shmuel and I both disobeyed our father. We wanted to marry for love and in my day, Rafi, people didn't do that. *Tate* was furious and he disowned us, which is why you have never met him and, I'm sorry to say, probably never will. Shmuel went away to England, and I came here, to Tukum. It was a terrible time, terrible. *Tate's* rage! Listen, I want you to know, Rafi, that I will never do anything like that to you. You are a man now, you're independent and sensible and I trust you to make your own decisions. I married for love and, as long as she is Jewish, you can marry anyone you want. I mean it. Marry for love, Rafi. Do you hear me?' he concluded in a mock-authoritarian voice.

Rafael was grinning from ear to ear, and his heart was singing. 'I hear you, father,' he replied.

'So what is she doing in Riga, your Rosa Krupp?'

'She's an art student. There's a lady in Riga called Elise von Jung-Stilling who runs an art academy. I've seen some of Rosa's work; she's amazing. Amazing at painting, I mean. But, actually, also amazing in every other way you can imagine.'

'Oh, I see you have it bad' he said, smiling. 'Well, well. Another Gozinsky, eh? Perhaps it's fate. But wait a minute, this art teacher takes Jewish students, you say? And girls too? That's something new.'

'Is it? Yes, I suppose it is. The world is changing, *Tatty*. You don't see it here, in this town, not yet. But Riga is not like Tukum.'

'I suppose not. Good, I'm pleased. Things need to change; they can't always stay the same. Right, here we are.'

The scene at the Rosenbergs was much worse than either Rafael or Itzhak had expected. Ester was sitting at the table sobbing, a handkerchief pressed to her eyes, and Hannah was trying in vain to comfort her. Mrs. Yakubovich from upstairs was also there, fussing around with the samovar.

Reuben stood up when Itzhak and Rafael came in.

'What's happened?' asked Itzhak. 'Where's your father, Reuben?'

'He's gone,' replied Reuben. 'He's been taken.'

'Taken? What do you mean?'

'The police came. They've taken him to the army. He's been conscripted.'

'What are you talking about? How can that be?'

Reuben went to the front door and beckoned them to follow him outside. Once outside he closed the door gently and said: 'As you know, my *tate* hasn't worked since Schloma died. It turns out he also hasn't been paying his tax. He's two years behind. Do you know what they do to Jews who fall behind on their tax?'

'No,' said Rafael, 'what?'

'They send them to the army as a punishment. Even if they are *Tatty's* age. It doesn't matter how old they are, or what the reason is.'

'*Oy vey!*' said Itzhak, clutching at his beard in his distress. 'How terrible! Oh, Reuben, I'm so sorry. But what's going to happen now'

'I really don't know, Reb Itzhak. We've lost everything. I've been giving my parents almost all my earnings since I've worked for Reb Leiser, but it's not been enough. And that's not all; the rent's not been paid, either. Tomorrow we will lose the apartment.'

'Oh, no! Where will you go?' asked Rafael, appalled.

'Reb Leiser says I can bed down at the slaughterhouse. But where *Mame* and Hannah will live, I don't know.'

Rafael looked at his father. Itzhak hesitated, but only for a moment.

'The boys' room is empty. Of course they must come to stay with us. Until you get things sorted out.'

To Itzhak's intense embarrassment, Reuben burst into tears, fell to his knees and flung his arms round his legs, murmuring blessings. Itzhak pulled him to his feet.

'Please, Reuben, enough. Come on, we need to talk to your mother. I can't bear to see her like this.'

As Reuben had suggested, Ester was distraught, and it wasn't easy for Itzhak to get her to listen to him, but eventually she calmed down sufficiently to take in what he was saying and thanked him brokenly. Meanwhile, Reuben and Rafael discussed what should happen to the furniture and other possessions they would be unable to take with them.

It was decided the quickest and best thing was to sell the furniture to Moishe the Pedlar for whatever he would give them; the money could be used to pay off some of the family's debts. Rafael went off to fetch Moishe, while Itzhak went home to tell Scheine what had happened and about the invitation. Had he done the right thing? What else could he have done? he asked himself. What else could anyone have done? And above all — what would Scheine say?

He needn't have worried. Scheine agreed completely and immediately began making the room ready to receive their unexpected guests.

Ester, with Reuben and Hannah, spent a final, sleepless night in the apartment where she and her husband had brought the children up with such hopes for the future.

Moishe came along first thing in the morning. He drove a hard bargain, and the Rosenbergs, looking at the empty room and the small pile of coins they had received in return for everything, wept again. Then Ester tied her shawl round her head, Reuben and Rafael loaded the bags onto Meyer's hand cart, which Reuben pushed, and the four of them walked slowly to the Yacobsohns, trying to ignore the stares of the people they passed.

As they walked, Rafael quietly asked Reuben: 'Will you be OK?'

'Yes, I'll be all right.'

'I don't really know; what exactly do you do at Reb Leiser's slaughterhouse?'

'Honestly, Rafi, I'd rather not tell you. I don't think you want to know.'

'I see. Do you like it?'

'Well, what do you think? Would you?'

'No. So, what about money, now?'

'Well, the money we got from Moishe will get some of our creditors off our backs, and with my wages I'll probably be able to pay off the others eventually. *Mamele* and Hannah can still make a little with their baskets. We'll manage, somehow. It's *Tatty* I really feel sorry for. He is strong, or at least he was, but I don't know how he's going to survive this. Even Schloma couldn't do it, and he was young.'

'Oh Reuben. I'm so sorry about all this.'

'Thank you, Rafi. I can't tell you what it means to us that *Mame* and Hannah have somewhere to live. Your parents are really kind people, Rafi.'

'Thank you, Reuben. Yes, I know.'

*

The next day Yossel bade an emotional farewell to his parents and the two brothers boarded the train for Riga.

When they got to Gozinsky's, Rafael took Yossel to the office, and watched as he put his mark on the contract (without reading it). Then he took him to register at the police station, after which they walked to the Apprentice House together, Rafael pointing out places of interest along the way. Yossel looked obediently in the direction he was pointing, but without really seeing. It was too much for him to take in.

Rafael took him to meet Frau Pucher, the housekeeper, and showed him his bed in the dormitory, Yossel following his brother around dazedly as if the whole thing was a dream from which he was trying to wake up. Later he had his first experience of Frau Pucher's cooking, which did nothing to improve his mood.

In the morning, as they walked to work together for the first time, Rafael turned to Yossel, grabbed his shoulders and said sternly: 'Look, Yoss; you will only get one chance at this. Herr Strauss is a kind man and will help you, but he'll expect you to listen, so remember what he says, and do what you're told. They won't keep you on if they don't think you're up to it, you know.' Yossel looked up at his brother.

'Yes, I know that, Rafi,' he said. 'Come on, let's get this over with.'

Rafael introduced Yossel to the Captain, and to Herr Strauss, who eyed his new apprentice shrewdly. He set him to work sweeping the floor and Rafael went to the workbench to continue working on the piece he had started before he went home.

Rafael didn't see Yossel again until the end of the day. His brother had a sullen expression on his face.

'Well, how did you get on?' he asked breezily.

'Terrible,' said Yossel. 'It's even worse than *heder*. I'm not doing that again.' Rafael looked at him pityingly.

'What one earth do you mean?'

'I mean I spent the entire day sweeping and carrying. That's not metalwork. I thought this was about making stuff, not sweeping.'

'Yoss, that's not how it works. You do whatever the master tells you. You knew it would be like that; I warned you. You don't just make things right at the start. You have to learn it gradually.'

'Well how's that going to happen if I'm sweeping the floor? It's all right for you. You spent the whole day sitting on your *tush* making a jug or something.' Rafael was becoming exasperated.

'You're being ridiculous. I've been here almost three years! I swept the floor too, when I started.'

'Well, more fool you. I tell you, I'm not doing it.'

'Fine. Forget it. I give up,' concluded Rafael angrily.

Each day, Yossel seemed to be involved in some sort of trouble, and on the first day of the following week the master took Rafael to one side. 'Rafael, are you close to your brother?' he asked.

'Well, sort of, I suppose. Why do you ask, sir?'

'I was hoping you could have a word with him about his attitude.'

'I have tried sir, but he doesn't listen to me.'

'Does he even want to be here?'

'I think he's just finding his feet, sir. Please give him a chance; I'm sure he'll improve.'

'*Hmph.*' The master's face darkened. 'I hope you're right. All right, Rafael, get on with your work now. I'll come along later and see how you are getting on.'

Rafael bent to his work obediently, but kept his eyes surreptitiously on the master as he strode determinedly across the factory floor to where Yossel was standing, half–heartedly poking at some detritus with his broom. There was a brief angry confrontation, which Rafael was much too far away to hear and then, to his intense shock, he saw the master raise his hand and give Yossel a thundering clout. Yossel's hand flew up to his ear, which had turned bright red. Everybody in the factory was watching to see what would happen next.

For a moment Rafael considered going over, but thinking better of it, turned and continued with this work. He had no doubt that Yossel had deserved the slap – although he was astonished that it was the master who had delivered it. The rest of the men stopped watching and went back to their tasks. Yossel began sweeping the floor in earnest and Herr Strauss walked swiftly over to the Captain. They exchanged a few words and the Captain climbed the stairs to the office. Rafael saw him knock on the door and disappear inside.

A short while later Natalia Ivanovna the secretary went down the stairs and said something to Yossel, who put down the broom and followed her back to the office. When he came out a few moments later, he looked chastened. He walked back to his station grimly, picked up the broom with a fixed, fierce expression, and swept.

That evening, after work, Rafael asked him what had happened. Reluctantly at first, and then with increasing fluency, Yossel told him. They had made it clear to him that he had to mend his ways or there would be big trouble. They had also docked his first month's wages; this was what he was most upset about.

'I've got no money now,' he groaned, 'You must have some money saved up, Rafi. Lend us some, will you?'

'What for?'

'Something. Will you lend me some or not?'

'No. Not unless you tell me what it's for.'

'Well if you must know, it's for the train. I'm going home.'

'What are you talking about?'

'You saw what happened. It's awful here. I can't do this; I'm leaving. I'm going to work with *Tatty* and take my chances with the draft.'

Rafael looked at his brother in frank amazement. 'Yoss, you've signed a contract.'

'So what?'

'Listen, you stupid fool, get this into your head. That is a contract in law. You cannot break it. If you go home without permission the police will arrest you and bring you back here to be punished. Do you understand?'

Yossel turned white. 'The police! Would I go to prison?'

'To be perfectly honest, I don't know. Maybe. But I do know you'd be in a lot worse trouble than you are now.'

'Then, what can I do?' wailed Yossel, starting to sob.

'You can try doing what you're told, for a start.'

Yossel continued snivelling for a while and then seemed to reach a conclusion. 'I didn't know it would be like this,' he said, shaking his head. 'All right. I'll try.'

'Good.' Then in a gentler tone, and with more optimism than he actually felt, Rafael said: 'You'll see; it'll be fine. I'm sure it will.'

He put his arm round Yossel's shoulder and the two brothers sat companionably together as the daylight slowly drained from the sky.

*

Meanwhile, the Czar and his ever-busy advisors and administrators were hard at work finding new ways to harass Russia's Jews and in the summer of 1886 they passed yet another restrictive law, forbidding Jews from moving from one drafting district to another. Rafael and Yossel weren't entirely sure what this meant for them; they thought they would be allowed to visit Tukum, provided they got permission first, but they weren't sure if they would be allowed to go back there to live.

They felt more cut off from home than ever.

But, on a more positive note, Yossel seemed at last to have buckled down to work. He was meek and obedient, and seemed to be trying to remember what he was taught. There was no more shouting and there were no more slaps. Rafael, who felt keenly the responsibility of being the elder brother, started to feel more hopeful about his prospects.

The warm weather had arrived at last, and with it Rafael felt a renewed longing to be outside, preferably with Rosa. He spent many *Shabbos* afternoons strolling with her and David by the canal, or through the park, and enjoying the tranquility to be found there. Sometimes Yossel came with them, although more often than not he stayed at the Apprentice House and slept.

Rafael admired David in so many ways, and wished he was more like him; confident, worldly. But he wished he and Rosa were observant Jews. Perhaps secularism was the price of worldliness, he thought. He tried, once or twice, to bring the conversation round to the topic, but it seemed to be a touchy one, and he learned to steer clear of it.

When he had first arrived in Riga he was shocked at the new type of Jew he found; Jews who went bare-headed, shaved their beards, ate anything they liked, kosher or not, and attended *shul* only on High Holy days, if at all. He understood what they were trying to do; they were trying to blend in, to integrate. But was such a thing even possible? Or were Jews always destined to be outsiders, however hard they tried?

Perhaps it was a good thing, he thought, that this type of Jew existed; perhaps they could help the *goyim* understand that Jews were normal people and not, as they seemed to think, horned devils who drank the blood of Christian children. But what would God think of Jews who turned their back on His commandments? Would He forgive His people for abandoning His laws in exchange for comfort and security? Or did He expect them to suffer at the hands of the *goyim* until the coming of the Messiah?

Could he become more like David and Rosa? Forget about *shul?* Forget about *kashrut?* Shave his beard? Go bare headed? Carry things on *Shabbos?* No. It would be a lie, a denial of himself, of his family, of God. He couldn't change who he was, or abandon everything he had grown up with and been taught.

But what if that meant losing Rosa? Could two people be happy together if one was an observant Jew and the other not? Or, given the right encouragement, could she come back to the laws and traditions of her people?

It wouldn't matter at all, none of it would matter, if only he didn't love her quite so much.

That problem aside, Rafael realised, looking back on it later, that the summer of 1886 was one of the happiest and most carefree times of his life.

He was young, fit, strong and in love. He was growing in confidence and skill at work and was making real products now, for real customers, requiring only minimal supervision from his master.

There were more weekend outings and expeditions. The four friends took the train to Dubbeln, sat on the beach, paddled in the sea and strolled beside the river.

They explored Riga's Old Town, attempting unsuccessfully to prevent David expounding on points of architectural interest as they went.

There were evenings featuring discussions and arguments in Das Goldene Kalb covering every topic under the sun; politics, religion, history, the future. Although he was younger than most of them, Rafael felt fully accepted by David's friends, and he revelled in the sense of belonging it gave him.

And all the time he was falling deeper and deeper in love with Rosa. It was a delightful, painful sensation. And yet. There was something not quite right; not a coolness, exactly, but a distance.

He couldn't quite account for it, and it troubled him.

*

The following year would be a conscription year back home. Rafael felt confident that he and Yossel were protected by Gozinsky's 'special arrangement' with the authorities, but he felt the familiar tightening in his gut when he thought about his old friends who might be taken.

That started him wondering about David and the other students; they didn't seem particularly concerned. One evening in early Autumn, as he and David were strolling to Das Goldene Kalb, he brought the topic up.

'When it comes to conscription, Polytechnic students are different,' explained David. 'We just have to do six months in the army when we reach twenty–one. That's it.'

'Really? That's amazing. I wish we'd thought of that! I could have gone to the Polytechnic.'

David looked embarrassed. 'No, I'm afraid you couldn't have,' he said. 'They don't accept Jews.'

'Well, how did you get in, then? Oh, wait, don't tell me; Uncle Israel fixed it?' David grinned sheepishly.

'Yes. Well, sort of. What happened was…'

'Yes?'

'Actually, no, some other time.'

'You and your secrets. Well, it doesn't matter, I'm pleased you got in. But I'm worried about my friends back home; I wonder who I know who is going to be on the list.'

'I don't blame you. It's a nightmare. With that and the pogroms, more and more Jews are leaving.'

'Yes, I know. If you had to leave, David, where would you go?'

Without hesitation, David replied 'The Land of Opportunity, of course. America. They definitely need architects there, they're building like crazy. What about you?'

'I don't know, really. England maybe? I've got an uncle and an aunt in London.'

'Ah yes. The other brother.'

'That's right. Uncle Shmuel.'

11

ONE BITTERLY COLD winter's day an unfamiliar noise from outside penetrated the factory's din and the men stopped what they were doing to listen. As it grew in volume and intensity, it revealed itself as the sound of marching feet and the chanting of angry voices. For the Jews, especially for those who had witnessed pogroms, it was a terrifying sound.

The Captain strode to the door and looked out. 'It's all right,' he said. 'Get back to work.' Relieved, the men did as they were told, but Rafael couldn't restrain his curiosity. Pretending to need the privy he went out of the back door and doubled round to the front, where the noise was loudest.

It was a march, albeit a rather disorderly one. A chaotic procession of men and women, clearly factory workers were shouting, chanting, banging pots with sticks, anything to make a noise. A number of passers-by had stopped to watch, their faces registering either sympathy or disapproval. Rafael was mystified.

'What do you think it was?' he asked David that evening.

'It sounds like a workers' protest,' David said.

'What do you mean? Protesting against what?'

David looked at his friend in surprise. 'Do you really not have any idea what's going on in the world?' he asked.

'Not much,' Rafael admitted. 'I know quite a lot about ancient Babylon, if that's any help?'

'Maybe you should read something more modern than the Talmud occasionally. Look, Rafi, I don't think you have any idea how good the conditions in your factory are compared with others; not just in Riga, but everywhere. I know you work hard, but, honestly, you've got it really easy compared with most. Gozinsky's is justly famous because it's completely different from most places.'

'In what way?'

'In almost every way. Other factories are dirty, unsanitary, disease-ridden death traps. Men, women and even quite young children spend their lives in mindless, repetitive, back-breaking tasks. The pay is terrible. If they make a mistake, or work too slowly, or break some other rule they're shouted at, or fined, or even beaten. They can be thrown out of work at any moment. The machines are often totally unsafe — people get injured or maimed or killed at work all the time, and there's no compensation.'

Rafael was appalled. 'You're right, David, it's not like that at all where I work. I thought most factories were like Gozinsky's.'

'Like I say, you don't appreciate how lucky and privileged you are, Rafi. Your father did very well by you when he got you an apprenticeship with my uncle.' Rafael thought about this for a moment. Yes, he undoubtedly owed his father a huge debt.

'No wonder people protest,' he said.

'Yes. But they're being extraordinarily brave; they're taking a terrible risk. The Government is furious and they are cracking down on protest. I don't think anyone knows where this is going to end.'

'It just seems stupid to treat people so badly. What's the matter with these factory owners?'

'It's greed; they are driven by profit. Labour is cheap, people are expendable.'

Something Rafael had read at *heder* came back to him. 'It is written; "He that oppresses the poor reproaches his Maker: but he that honours Him has mercy on the poor." Perhaps it's not just me that needs to widen his reading; those factory owners ought to spend a bit more time reading the *Torah*.'

*

On a chilly day in the early spring, Salomon Strauss stopped Rafael as he was settling down to work on an intricate lantern.

'Good morning, Rafael. Actually, leave the lantern for now, please. There's a change of plan for today.' Rafael stood and looked at him quizzically. 'I'd like you to go and help Yossel this morning.'

This was something new, so he was intrigued, and also happy to have an opportunity to judge Yossel's progress for himself and to help him, as his father had requested.

'Yes, sir.' He walked over to where Yossel was standing, staring gloomily at a misshapen object on the bench. Rafael looked at it in dismay.

'Hi,' he said, as breezily as he could. 'I've been sent to help you.'

'Good, I need it. Look at this. I can't make the stupid thing come out right. Look at it! Why has it done that?'

'I don't know. What is it meant to be?'

'Very funny. As you can perfectly well see, it's a candle holder thing for a wall.'

'You mean a sconce?'

'Do I? Probably.'

'Well, er, how can I put this? It's not quite right, is it?'

'I know it's not quite right, genius,' he snapped.

'All right, calm down, I'll help you sort it out. How long have you been working on it?'

'Since yesterday morning.'

Rafael tried to disguise his shock; a sconce should not take that long.

'And how many are you supposed to make?'

'Three. By the end of today. It's ridiculous! I can't even do one!'

'Right. Well, look, I think we might be able to save this one. Where's your design?'

Yossel showed him a scrawl which was no help at all. 'Right, well, it doesn't matter. I know what they should look like. I'll make the first one and then you can copy it for the others. OK, then, let's organise the tools,' he said, scanning the workbench. 'Where's your nibbler?'

'Which one is that?'

'Yoss! Look I know you've only been here a few months but, honestly, you should at least know the names of the tools. And look at this bench; it's completely disorganised.'

'Oh, don't you start! I get enough of that from Herr Strauss. Go on then,' he said, 'you show me how it's done.'

Rafael sighed but made no other reply. He took up position at the workbench, organised the tools methodically and started to work on the misshapen sconce. Almost immediately the familiar pleasure of the work soothed his irritated nerves and he began to feel the correct form of the piece take shape in his hands. After a while he remembered that he was supposed to be teaching his brother and looked round to explain what he was doing. Yossel wasn't really watching, but staring in the opposite direction with a vacant expression.

Rafael realised, with a sinking heart, why Herr Strauss had asked him to come over.

That afternoon, Rafael was back at his own workbench working on the lantern. Herr Strauss came and looked at it approvingly. 'That is progressing well. Excellent work, Rafael. Well done.' He pointed out a couple of minor imperfections, but really, he thought, his training was almost complete.

Rafael turned to the master and said earnestly: 'Herr Strauss. I... I think I know why you sent me to work with Yossel.'

'I thought it was better to show you than to try and tell you; I didn't want you to be taken by surprise. I'm really sorry, Rafael, but he's been here almost a year. We can't keep him on.'

'No, I see that. Thank you for warning me. Does he know?'

'We haven't told him, but I think he must know, really. He knows this is not the right place for him. May I ask you; what do you think he will do?'

'I don't know, sir. I really don't know. I don't think he can go home to Tukum. He's going to need to stay in Riga, try to find a job, and hope he doesn't get enlisted.'

'Well, he's got a few weeks to make a plan, but I think he may need your help with that.'

'Yes, sir. Thank you.' A plan? What plan? he thought. This *was* the plan; and it had failed.

When Yossel learned the news shortly after his fourteenth birthday, he was at first relieved rather than anything else. His contract was ended and he no longer had to pretend to be interested in metalwork. As usual, it was up to Rafael to point out to him some of the problems.

'You do realise, after this month there's no more stipend? Have you managed to save much?'

'Not much, no. Nothing, basically.'

'I thought so. And you won't be able to stay at the Apprentice House. You're no longer an apprentice.'

'That's OK. I'm going home.'

'No you're not. You can't.' Yossel looked startled.

'What do you mean I can't? Why not?' he demanded.

'Two reasons. First, the Rosenbergs are in our room.'

'Well, they'll have to move out. Go somewhere else.'

'Go where?'

'I don't know. That's not my problem is it?'

'Yossel Yacobsohn! How could you be so heartless? They've lost everything!'

'Sorry. You're right.'

'Anyhow, it's not up to you. But in any case, there's a second reason. Have you forgotten that Jews are not allowed to move from one conscription area to another? We're allowed to go home on short visits, but that's it; we even need permission for that, and if we didn't come back we'd be arrested. You are registered in Riga; you live in Riga now, not Tukum.'

'But that's ridiculous!' he shouted. 'What am I supposed to do?'

'It's no good shouting, that's just how it is. Look, don't worry. I will pay for you to rent a room somewhere.' Yossel looked at his brother with respect and gratitude.

'Would you really do that for me? Could you afford to do that?'

'Yes, you're my brother, of course I would. And yes, I think I can afford it, just about, anyhow. All the while I get my room and board provided for me, I can afford to pay your rent. But that's all; there won't be anything left over for food or clothes. You still need to find work.'

Rafael was not being entirely open with his brother; in actual fact he had already found him a room. But he didn't want him to know that he had been planning for this moment, or to make it look too easy.

In fact, it hadn't been hard at all; he had had a stroke of luck. He simply asked the students at Das Goldene Kalb, and one of them knew of an attic room which had become available in the house they rented. He had already visited the room, which was small and poky, and up two dingy flights of stairs, but in a safe part of the city, and had put down a deposit to secure it.

Two days later, Yossel was installed in the attic, feeling very lonely and very sorry for himself. Rafael, suspecting that his brother would need help landing a job, had been asking around on his behalf, with increasing desperation. So far, he had come up with nothing.

To his surprise, it was Yossel himself who found the solution. It happened this way; a day or two after moving into the attic room, hungry and worried, he went out. After wandering more or less at random for a long while, he found himself in Latgales Street. Despondent and weary, he sat down, leaned his back against a building and closed his eyes.

Unbidden, a vision of his childhood came into his mind; *Shabbos* evening, his mother lighting the candles, his father saying the blessings. He began to sing to himself one of the songs he remembered:

Shabbos lights and Shabbos lamps,
O, how sweetly do you glow,
Shabbos, O Shabbos, O holy Shabbos!

Bringing comfort to the Jew
In his loneliness and pain,
Shabbos, O Shabbos, O holy Shabbos!

As the verses went by, his voice, without him realising, became stronger and louder. He still sang in a treble voice of great purity. At length he reached the end of the song and, feeling somewhat calmed, opened his eyes. There was a scattering of coins on the ground around his legs that hadn't been there before. He stared at them in a confused manner for a few moments before it dawned on him that people passing by must have dropped them, mistaking him for a beggar, a *luftmensch*, a person of the air, singing for coins.

He smiled at their error but, gathering up the coins gratefully, realised that it was he who was mistaken. They had thought of him as a *luftmensch* and that was exactly what he was. A *schnorrer*.

'Very well, so be it,' he thought. There was nothing dishonourable in begging. He would sit and sing, and people would give him money.

He closed his eyes again and tried to recall another song. This time he went even further back, to a lullaby he remembered his mother singing:

Sleep, my child, sleep,
I will sing you a song,
And when you grow older
Then you'll understand.

*And when you grow older
Then you'll be like us,
You will know what it means
To be rich, to be poor...*

Again, a smattering of coins appeared and once more he quickly gathered them up. He felt rather proud of himself. He had solved his problem, without any help.

All the same, he wondered what his parents would think, and what Rafael would say.

*

Every two years the population of Riga became swollen with army draftees. Frequently there was small-scale trouble, fuelled by a heady mixture of alcohol and desperation.

Rafael, his head full of love for Rosa and concern about Yossel, decided to visit Das Goldene Kalb for an evening of drink and lively conversation to take his mind off things.

He found the usual crowd in their normal place. David was there, although Rosa and Inge were not because they were both working late at the art school adding the finishing touches to their final examination pieces.

The trouble began when one of the students, happening to throw his arm out in a wild gesticulation, knocked over a beer glass on a tray carried by one of the waitresses. The beer flooded the tray and spilled over, some of it falling onto the head of one of the draftees.

Getting unsteadily to his feet, the man looked round ferociously and roared 'Who did that?' The students assumed expressions of perfect innocence and waited for it to blow over. 'Look at these poncey fuckers, sitting there all innocent,' shouted the man. 'It was one of you wasn't it? Must have been.' He stared glassily around the group and his gaze fell upon Rafael. 'You. You're a Jew, aren't you?

Look at your little Jew hat. Want a fight, do you, Jew?' He moved menacingly towards Rafael, who froze, bracing himself for the attack.

David had been sitting unnoticed, with his back to the man, but now he stood up, turned and squared up to the man, preventing him from reaching Rafael.

'Well, well. What do we have here?' sneered the man leaning close to David, flecks of spittle spattering his face. 'You another Jew? Or just a Jew–lover?'

'Jews have long tails,' yelled another of the draftees drunkenly. 'See if he's got a tail.'

'That's right, so they do. Come on then,' said the man, making a sudden lunge at David. 'Show us yer tail!'

Without warning a furious David butted the man hard in the face with his head, breaking his nose. The man stepped back with a cry of pain, and David hooked his foot round his ankle, sending him crashing heavily against the table.

The other draftees and the students all jumped up and from that point on there was pandemonium. David was in the centre of a maddened group of draftees all trying to get at him and bring him down. So far he had fended them off successfully, but his opponents had the advantage of superior numbers and unless something changed it could only be a matter of time before they got the better of him.

Rafael had never been a fighter; he had avoided head–on confrontation all his life so far, but this time he was at the centre of a brawl. And he found, to his astonishment, that he didn't feel like escaping from it; he wanted to fight. All the suppressed frustration and anger of years of petty mistreatment suddenly boiled over. He had no experience, but he was young, agile, sober and very angry. He vaulted over the table and landed heavily on a draftee who was trying to hit David with a chair leg. The man collapsed with a grunt, hitting his head on the floor, and was out cold.

Ignoring him, Rafael turned to find another target. He spotted one, but this man was ready for him, and slashed out with a broken bottle. Rafael just about managed to dodge it and, before his assailant recovered his balance, smashed a fist into the side of his head, dazing him. A further blow from David put him out of the fight.

Rafael was beginning to find an unexpected confidence, but someone punched him in the face, confusing him, and he started lashing out indiscriminately, landing a few blows and taking others, David and the other students protecting him as best they could

At the very first sign of trouble someone on the tavern staff had run to fetch the police, and now they arrived in force, laying about themselves indiscriminately with their heavy sticks, and hauling off anyone they could lay their hands on.

David, Rafael and the students, being far less drunk than the draftees, and with better knowledge of the building, were quicker than them to respond, and they disengaged and disappeared through a door at the rear of the bar and up the back stairway. They emerged into the night and ran away from the area until they felt they were sufficiently distant to avoid being picked up. Then they halted, their hands on their knees while they regained their breath. Their clothes were torn and they had scratches, cuts and bruises, but none of them had sustained serious injuries.

Rafael and David limped home. Rafael's hand was swollen and painful. He said to David: 'You didn't need to do that; it was me they were after. But I'm really grateful. How on earth did you learn to fight like that?'

'Practice. It's not my first fight, unfortunately. You did really well, Rafi. You came to my rescue too; I thought they had me at one point.'

'It's a new experience for me. I'm shaking now but I'm ashamed to say at the time it felt really good.'

'I know. It does feel good — when you win,' grinned David.

There was no disguising Rafael's injuries; his face was swollen, he had a black eye and his right hand was a mass of bruises.

The Captain called him into a quiet corner of the factory to talk to him. 'You do realise,' he growled, 'that your contract forbids you from brawling in public?'

'Yes, Captain.'

'And that if you are found to have broken your contract, then you're out?'

'Yes, Captain.'

'Right. Then think very carefully before you answer my next question. How did you get those injuries?'

'I fell down some stairs, Captain.'

'Down the stairs. I see. And why did you fall downstairs? Were you drunk?'

'No, Captain. I tripped over a cat.'

'A cat? What cat?'

'I don't know, Captain. It was an unexpected cat.'

'I see. And you definitely weren't involved in any kind of drunken tavern brawl with a group of draftees last night?'

'Good gracious, no, Captain.'

'All right. You tripped over a cat and you fell downstairs. That's all right then. We'll say no more about it. Get back to work.'

'Yes, Captain.'

'But Rafael. I warn you to be careful of those cats in future,' he said, and then continued, in a whisper 'Some of them are hiding sharp claws.' He made a stabbing motion with his right hand as he said this, then turned and marched smartly off.

Happy the grilling was over, and relieved that he still had his job, Rafael breathed out heavily and went back quickly to his place.

When he left the factory after work, Rosa was waiting for him, accompanied, as usual, by Inge. It was too dark to see her expression. Did she know about the fight? 'Hello,' he said tentatively.

'Idiot,' hissed Rosa.

'I thought you were going to say "Stupid idiot",' corrected Inge.

'Oh, be quiet, Inge,' she snapped.

'Yes, be quiet, Inge,' agreed Rafael. 'You heard about it, then?'

'Of course I heard about it. Everybody's heard about it. Oh, you idiots. Honestly, what's the matter with you boys?'

'It's not our fault. They were determined to start something, we had no choice. I actually think we did quite well. Your brother's an excellent fighter, you know. "For You have girded me with strength for battle; You have subdued under me those who rose up against me."'

'Again with the *Torah* quotes. My God, I believe you're actually pleased with yourself! Don't you realise you could have been arrested? You could have been killed! What if they find out about this at work; you could be fired!'

'They already know, but it's fine. I told them I fell down the stairs.'

'Why did you feel the need to tell them anything?'

'Well, because they wanted to know how I got all the cuts and bruises, of course.'

'What cuts and bruises?' Rosa stopped under a street light so she could get a better look at him. He turned his face to the light.

'These ones,' he said, pointing them out. She gave a little cry.

'Oh my God! Your poor face! You look terrible! Does it hurt?'

'Yes, quite a lot actually'.

'Serves you right,' put in Inge, disappointed that sympathy seemed to be gaining ascendancy over annoyance in Rosa's demeanour.

'Inge, will you please shut up!' demanded Rosa. 'You poor thing,' she said soothingly to Rafael. 'That looks awful. I'm sorry I was angry just now. I was worried.' She stood on tiptoe and kissed Rafael on his cheek.'

'Ow.'

'Oh, sorry.'

'Try kissing the other side; it's less painful.'

'Oh, for God's sake,' said Inge.

That evening David stayed in, but Rafael and some of the students who had been involved in the fight met up at again at Das Goldene Kalb to compare notes.

They had only been there a few minutes when the proprietor swept up to the table and, pointing to Rafael, said 'You. You're not welcome in here any more. You need to leave.'

'What?' cried Rafael. 'Because of the fight? But we didn't start it. You saw what happened; they were drunk and picked on us.'

'It doesn't matter who started it. You're a provocation.'

'Why? Because I'm Jewish?'

'Yes. Exactly that. We don't want any trouble here, and apparently Jews attract trouble. The rest of you can stay, but not you. Go on. Out.'

Humiliated and angry, Rafael obeyed. The rest of the group, after a very brief discussion, followed. It seemed that the evenings of fun at Das Goldene Kalb were over.

*

One day, about a year after Meyer Rosenberg was sent to the army as punishment for falling behind on his taxes, a young man in a soldier's uniform appeared in Tukum. It was Haim, the son of Abraham Peletz the barber, who had been conscripted four years before, home on leave.

After seeing his family he told them he needed to go to see the Rosenbergs. 'You won't find them in their old apartment,' said his mother, shaking her head sadly. 'They lost it. Ester and Hannah live at the Yacobsohns now.'

He went to the Yacobsohns' apartment and knocked. Scheine opened the door and was startled to see a soldier standing there. She didn't recognise him at first, but when he introduced himself she remembered. 'Little Haim? From *heder*?' she exclaimed, 'Look at you! Are you looking for Rafi?'

Then she saw how grim his face was. He asked if he could come in and speak to Ester and Hannah. Realising then why he had come, she let him in and, going over to the bedroom door, tapped gently.

'Ester! Hannah!' she called softly. 'Haim Peletz is here. He would like to talk to you.'

When they heard the news of Meyer's death Ester and Hannah hugged each other. Hannah was sobbing but Ester became very calm and still, as she had on the day that she and Meyer had found Schloma's body.

Scheine went out into the street with Haim and then, out of the Rosenbergs' hearing, asked him for the details. He told her what he knew.

Meyer had been endlessly bullied by his fellow conscripts, and also by the officers, who picked on him because he was a 'tax-dodger', because he was a rather unfit, slightly overweight middle-aged man, but most of all because he was a Jew. One night he was set upon and kicked by a group of drunken squaddies. It had happened many times before but on this occasion he failed to get up.

He died the following day.

Then Haim went to the slaughterhouse to deliver his sombre message to Reuben Rosenberg.

*

One dark morning in the autumn, as Rafael was arriving for work, he spotted a figure in a long coat, his cap pulled down to hide his face. He held a sheaf of papers and was handing one to each man as he arrived. Rafael went up to the man and took one of the sheets, tucked it into his coat pocket and soon forgot all about it. But at the end of the day, walking home, he put his hands into his pockets against the cold and found it again.

When he got back to the Apprentice House he looked at it properly for the first time. The message on it was written in an untidy hand, with numerous spelling mistakes, but the meaning was clear; it was a call to factory workers to attend a meeting to discuss strike action. The meeting was to be held in front of the Cathedral that same night.

Although the spelling mistakes had made him smile, Rafael knew this was a deadly serious matter. Anyone involved in a strike could face severe punishment, ranging from a birching to imprisonment or even banishment. Those found guilty of instigating it were the most harshly treated of all; it was no wonder the man handing out the leaflets hid his identity.

He threw the paper onto the fire.

His initial reaction was to ignore it. He had no personal reason to risk anything by going on strike, other than to show solidarity with his fellow workers. He was so near to the end of his apprenticeship; why jeopardise all of that for a cause that was not really his?

But on the other hand, going to the meeting wasn't the same as going on strike. He felt he ought to hear what people had to say, to educate himself, to understand their grievances. He admired those with the courage to stand up against the avarice of the factory owners; those the students had taught him to call the 'bourgeoisie'. He wanted to stand with them. What harm could come from at least just going to listen?

When David came in, he told him about the meeting. 'Are you going?' asked David.

'I think I am. Yes.'

'Good for you! Then I'm coming with you.' Rafael was delighted; it would be reassuring to have some support. 'That would be great. But listen, David, you don't have to.'

'Of course I do. You don't know it, but you are way out of your depth.'

When they arrived at the large open space in front of the Dome Cathedral it was clear that the meeting had already started. It was not yet a big crowd, just a few dozen people, both men and women, but more were arriving all the time.

A man standing on a makeshift platform was feverishly haranguing the crowd, trying to work them up into a state of anger and indignation, urging them to put their fears aside and demand better pay and conditions.

'Look at that guy; he's really working the crowd,' said David thoughtfully.

'I suppose he's just saying what he thinks.'

'Maybe. I wonder, though. Look at his boots.'

'Oh yes. They look quite new, and expensive.'

'They sure do. Who can afford to wear boots like that?'

'I don't know. Not me. Nor most factory workers, that's for sure. What are you saying?'

'I think he's Okhrana.'

'What's Okhrana?'

'Russian Secret Police. Or working for them, at any rate.'

'What? He's demanding a strike; why would he do that?'

'I've heard about this; we talk about Okhrana's tactics a lot at the Polytechnic. I actually expected them to be here. This is exactly what they do. Infiltrate the crowd, provoke them. They want to see who bites. Then they report them, and let the local police do the rest.'

'The sneaky *momzer*. Incidentally, where are the police? I really thought they'd be here.'

'Oh they're here all right, Rafi, just hidden somewhere.' David scanned the surroundings. 'There! Look.' He pointed to the buildings lining the square.

Following the direction of his finger, Rafael could make out a slight movement in the shadows.

'I see him. So, what now?'

'We listen to the speeches. But if that police lookout makes a move, or disappears suddenly, we run, OK? In that direction.' he pointed to a narrow alleyway on the opposite side of the square to the one where the shadowy figure lurked.

'OK. Got it.'

After a while the original speaker came to the end of his peroration and stepped down from the podium. They watched him moving slowly through the crowd, shaking hands and engaging people in brief conversations.

Another speaker stepped up. He was less rousing and less fluent than the first man, but somehow more sincere and convincing. He and his wife worked in a cotton mill, he said. He described the terrible conditions there, and the devastating effects on their health. Like the first man he was asking the crowd to join together to strike.

'They can arrest me, or you, or you,' he was saying, pointing to people in the front ranks of the crowd. 'But they can't arrest all of us if we stand together. Our father, the Czar, is a long way away, it's true, but he cares for all his people. If we make enough noise he will hear us, and he will come to our aid.'

'He's delusional,' whispered David. 'The Czar's on the side of the factory owners. They're the only people he's going to listen to.'

A voice somewhere in the crowd shouted out 'Nothing will change round here until we get rid of the Jews.' A murmur, either of assent or disagreement, it wasn't clear, rippled round the crowd.

'It's the Okhrana man again,' David whispered.

The speaker at the podium paused, his flow momentarily disturbed, and he blinked uncertainly. This was not the direction he intended his speech to take.

The heckler continued. 'It's the rich Jews who own all the factories. Squeezing the poor, like they always do. The Rothschilds and the Gozinskys and the rest of those rich, powerful bastards.' The crowd began to grow uneasy; they had heard this sort of talk often and knew where it could lead. But this wasn't what they were here for; they wanted higher wages, not a pogrom.

A few people shouted back: 'Shut it,' 'Quiet,' 'Let him speak.'

The speaker at the podium regained his composure.

'I don't know anything about Rothschild, but I do know about Gozinsky', he said. 'It's nothing to do with him. Truth be told, I wish

I worked for Gozinsky. I'd give anything to work for him, we all would, you know that. I don't care if he is a Jew, he's a good man. He runs a good factory and treats his men well. You leave Gozinsky out of it.'

The crowd was divided in their reaction to these impassioned remarks. Some cheered and applauded. Others booed vigorously. Small scuffles broke out between the two sides.

That was what the police had been waiting for. There was a shrill blast on a whistle, and a squad of men appeared from the side street where they had been hiding, and fanned out quickly to round up as many of the crowd as possible.

Rafael and David were too quick for them. They were sprinting away even before the whistle had finished blowing and they disappeared into the alley just as the police started pouring into the square from the other side. But they weren't the fastest; the man David had identified as the Okhrana agent was ahead of them, vanishing into the shadows just as they cleared the square.

Afterwards, they felt exhilarated, and glad to have escaped. They knew things would go particularly badly for the man who had been on the platform when the police arrived, and also for anyone naive enough to give their names to the Okhrana agent.

'It's so unfair,' Rafael said to David as they walked through the quiet streets of the Latgale neighbourhood. 'Your uncle is a reformer. He's doing his best. I bet he's as frustrated as anyone with the conditions in the other factories. And still people blame him for their misfortunes, because he's a Jew. When Jews are poor everyone says they're a drain on society. And when they're successful, they're evil scavengers. We can't win.'

'They need someone to blame. They can't blame the Czar, or the state, whose fault it really is, because they'd be arrested. So they blame the Jews. It's how it's always been.'

'Well I know one thing. If I owned a factory, I'd model it on your uncle's.'

'That's good to hear, Rafi. If you owned a factory I'd come and work for you.'

'Well, thank you,' said Rafael, smiling. 'As soon as my metalworks needs an architect I'll call you on the … what's-it-called again?'

'The telephone?'

'Yes. On the telephone.'

*

Rafael and David met up with Rosa and Inge one day in their new regular tavern, the Bishop Albert, near the Cathedral. They were celebrating. David had passed his final examinations at the Polytechnic and was now a qualified architect, and Rosa and Inge were getting close to concluding their time at Elise von Jung-Stilling's academy.

'Well done, David,' said Rafael, after they had drunk a toast to his success. 'It sounds like you passed with flying colours. So, what now?' he asked.

'Oh, that's all settled,' replied David. 'I've already got a job lined up with a practice here in Riga.'

'Marvellous! That was quick work — I wouldn't have thought it was that easy.'

'Well, for a man of my abilities, you know….'

'Don't tell me; Uncle Israel fixed it, right?'

'Well, possibly,' grinned David. 'And?'

'And nothing,' admitted Rafael. 'I'm really pleased. And what about you girls, everything ready for your final exhibition?

'Yes. Well, as ready as it can be,' replied Rosa. 'The pictures are all hung; it opens to the public tomorrow morning.'

'I wish I could come, but it's only open when I'm at work,' said Rafael. Rosa and Inge exchanged looks.

'Who says it needs to be open?' said Inge, mysteriously.

'What do you mean?'

'I think what she's trying to say,' said Rosa, 'without actually, you know, saying it, is that we could take you there right now. We can get in.'

'Really? You've got keys?'

'Um, well, no, not exactly. But we know a window we can climb through.'

'Amazing. Well, what are we waiting for? Drink up and let's go. Coming, David?'

'Oh, yes. I'm not going to miss this!'

After stopping off at the girls' dormitory to get some candles and matches the four made their way to the exhibition hall. Rosa led them into a narrow alleyway down the side of the building and stopped under a small window set into the wall a little above their heads.

'Give me a leg up, David,' she whispered. David crouched down, clasping his hands together, and boosted her up to reach the window ledge. Pulling herself up, she levered the window open and clambered in. Reaching her arm down, she pulled Inge up, and together they helped the boys scramble up until all four were safely through the window.

It was pitch dark inside. They lit their candles and the shadows lurched into life, swaying around the room. They were in a small storeroom lined with shelves.

'Follow me,' said Rosa, and led them out of the storeroom, along a corridor, and through a set of double doors which opened into the exhibition hall itself.

The flickering, dancing candlelight threw glowing circles onto the wooden floor and, as the four young people approached the walls, the nearest paintings became visible. They were looking for Rosa and Inge's pictures but the walls were covered with works of art, and Rafael didn't know what he was looking for.

Suddenly, Rosa exclaimed: 'Ah! Here we are. Here's mine. Have you found yours, Inge?'

'No, I don't think mine's here. It must be in the other room. Come on David, let's see if we can find it.' David and Inge went through a set of glass-panelled double doors. Through the glass, Rafael could see the light of their candles flickering as they moved around in the other room.

He walked over to where Rosa was holding her candle aloft and looked at her painting, illuminated now by both trembling flames. It was a portrait of a young Jewish man, wearing a *koppel* and a *tallis*. He was holding a book, but looking directly at the observer with haunting brown eyes, as if just disturbed whilst reading.

Rafael had no difficulty in recognising it as a portrait of himself. He gasped. The expression on the face of the man in the picture was captivating, mysterious, hypnotic. Is that what he looked like to her?

After a moment Rosa whispered, shyly, 'What do you think?'

'I ... it's me.'

'Yes, obviously.'

'I don't ... I don't know what to say.'

'Are you cross? Don't you like it?' He turned to her.

'Rosa, I think it's completely wonderful. I'm speechless. I had no idea you were so amazing.' She wore a broad smile, but then she became suddenly serious.

'So now you know why I was so keen to show it to you. You don't mind that I did it?'

'Of course not. I'm thrilled. Honoured. I love it. And Rosa,' he moved closer to her, 'I love you.'

She made no reply, but did not move away. They put their candles down on the floor and clasped hands. She looked up into his face, her eyes shining. They held each other's gaze for a long moment.

Her voice dropped to a whisper as she said: 'Rafi. I...'

'We found it!' interrupted Inge loudly, bursting through the doors with a clatter. 'They've put it right at the back, next to some stupid picture of the canal.' She caught sight of Rosa and Rafael, frozen as if in a tableau, lit from below by their guttering candles. 'Hello! I'm not disturbing anything am I?' she said breezily.

'Rosa!' called David, following Inge into the room. 'I think it's time we left. Come on. Where are those doors?'

Without speaking further, Rafael and Rosa bent down to pick up their candles, and, following Inge, the little group made their way out of the hall and back to the storeroom.

They climbed back out of the window, and jumped lightly down to the pavement. Finally, David lifted Rosa up again and she pulled the sash closed.

'Come on, then,' said David briskly. 'It's getting late.' He looked at Rosa meaningfully. 'Very late.'

A few days later David, no longer a student, moved out of the Apprentice House into an apartment of his own. Rafael was once more alone in the dormitory.

*

Around the time of his seventeenth birthday, Rafael arrived at the Apprentice House after work to find a letter from his father waiting for him. It was unusual to get a message from home, and he opened it as soon as he got to the dormitory.

My dear sons, it said.

It is my sad and painful duty to write to you with some awful news. I must ask you to bear it with as much fortitude as possible.

I am very sorry to have to tell you that your dear mame is no more. She passed away in the night and has been called to her eternal rest.

Rafael sat down heavily on the bed. He closed his eyes. Something seemed to have happened in his head; the words swirled around in his mind; he couldn't seem to make sense of what he had just read.

He read the second paragraph again, and this time the words started, slowly, to gather some meaning. He began to comprehend that his mother was dead.

He read on.

> *Thanks be to God, it was very quick; she did not suffer. It happened like this. Yesterday, she looked a little pale and was somewhat short of breath. It did not seem serious and she did not want me to call a doctor. We went to bed as normal, but when I woke up this morning, she was already gone.*
>
> *I am sorry that there was no time to fetch you and your brother, and that you were unable to be here to bid her farewell.*
>
> *My boys, I assure you that everything will be done correctly. Rabbi Lichtenstein has done us the honour of visiting the house today and has instructed me about what to do. As you know, the funeral must be held before Shabbos. Zeide and I will sit shiva, and there will be prayers every day.*
>
> *I do not know how long it will take for this letter to reach you but if you can receive permission to return, so that we can be together in our grief, it would be a great comfort to me, and I'm sure to you also.*
>
> *This is a heavy thing to bear, but remember that all that the Lord does, he does for the good.*
>
> *I assure you of my deep love for you both.*
>   *Tatty.*
>
> *P.S. Rafi, I have not written separately to your brother, for reasons you both know, so I must ask you, please, to be my mouthpiece and read the letter to him.*

Rafael sat numbly for a while. Then he grabbed his shirt in each hand, pulling it apart, harder and harder, until it tore, and in a voice shaking with misery he recited the blessing appropriate for hearing of the death of a loved one.

He found Yossel at his spot in Latgales Street and went with him back to his attic room. There, as his father had requested, he read the letter to him.

*

The following day they were numb with grief. They did not know when the letter had been posted, their father had not dated it, but it was *Shabbos* the next day, so either the funeral had already taken place, or it was about to.

They were desperate to get home, but there were administrative hoops to jump through before that would be possible. Rafael required permission from Herr Strauss and the Captain, both of which were obtained without fuss, and then it was necessary for both boys to go to the police station and obtain temporary travel permits. By the time all that was accomplished, they had missed the first train and would certainly miss their mother's funeral.

They arrived in Tukum by the second, and last, train, and went straight to the apartment. Their father and grandfather were there, together with a large number of friends and neighbours, enough to make a *minyan*, and prayers were said.

In accordance with tradition, the boys, their father and grandfather sat on low chairs — somebody had fetched children's chairs from the *heder* for the purpose. Something about the ritual helped a little but the boys were still dazed; nothing felt real any more.

Scheine's father stayed for the meal, but he said little, and ate nothing, which in itself was a sign of his great grief.

Finally, towards the end of the meal he said, as if to himself: 'Just like her dear *mame*.'

'What was that, *Zeide*?' asked Yossel.

Favel looked at him as if seeing him for the first time. 'Your *bubbe* passed away at about the same age as your *mame*, you know. She was just like her. Just the same. *Oy, oy, oy*, it's a terrible thing for a man to bury his daughter.'

Turning to Itzhak he said, tears running down his cheeks and into his grizzled beard, 'I loved her so much, you know. I love all three of my daughters. The others, Feige and Bluma, I drove away by my rudeness and bad temper. Yes, yes, it's the truth. But she stayed with me, right to the end. Next to my dear Yente I loved my little Scheine the most of all.'

'You know, Reb Favel,' replied Itzhak, 'since you loved her so much, it is strange that you were not always kind to her.' Itzhak was surprised to hear himself rebuking his father–in–law, a thing he would never have done in normal times. But to his surprise his father–in–law meekly accepted the criticism.

'Yes, Reb Itzhak, I know. You are right. I *kvetched* to her all the time. I don't know why. I wasn't like that when I was a young man, you know. I've somehow become a person I myself hate. Take warning; don't end up like me, Reb Itzhak. I wish I could take it all back. *Oy, oy, oy*.' Itzhak laid a hand gently on his arm. The old man looked into Itzhak's kind eyes. 'Do you think she knew I loved her?'

Without hesitation, Itzhak replied 'Yes, Reb Favel. She knew. Please don't distress yourself. She knew. And she loved you back.'

Scheine's father left to go back to his own apartment and Ester and Hannah retired to their room. Itzhak, Rafael and Yossel were sharing the other bedroom and they talked quietly together for a long time until they dozed off.

The next day Itzhak, searching for something to talk about with his sons other than the death of their mother, asked them how they were getting on at Gozinsky's. It came as a shock to Rafael that Yossel hadn't told him he had lost his apprenticeship, and he looked at his brother to see what he would do next. Yossel turned white.

'Rafi,' he said. 'Please will you tell *Tatty*? I'm just... going out.'

Ignoring Rafael's glowering expression, Yossel scooted out of the door.

'*Nu*? What's this all about, Rafi?' growled Itzhak. 'Tell me what?'

Sighing, Rafael told him about Yossel's failure at the factory. He stopped short of mentioning the begging. He assured Itzhak that he was looking after his brother, that he had money and a roof over his head and that everything was all right.

On any other day this bombshell would have been Itzhak's main concern, but on this day he was so distracted with exhaustion and grief that he just looked at his son with red-rimmed eyes and said: 'Then the whole plan is ruined. Thank God she didn't know.'

Later on, Itzhak took the boys to the cemetery and they prayed beside the mound of fresh earth under which lay their mother's coffin.

On the way home, he said to Yossel: 'Your brother told me you lost your apprenticeship. I don't think there's anything we... anything I can do for you now to ensure you aren't conscripted, except pray.'

'I'm sorry, *Tatty*. I've failed you and *Mamele*.'

'No. Please don't think like that, Yoss. I know you never wanted to do it; you did it to please us. I realise now, it was a bad plan. It was never going to work. You can only be who you are. I did what I swore I would never do; try to force you to be something you aren't. Just like my father did to me.' They walked on silently for a few moments and then he continued 'Remember all those years ago when you said you wanted to be a soldier? God forbid you get your wish.'

After walking on a little in silence, Rafael said: 'So, *Tatty*, what about Ester and Hannah?'

'What about them?'

'Well, are they going to stay now that *Mamele* has... isn't here any more?'

'I don't see why not. I can't think about that now, Rafi.'

The three Yacobsohns and Reb Favel sat *shiva* for seven days after the funeral, as required, and then it was time to return.

'You know, Yoss,' said his father as the boys bade farewell, 'You don't need to go back to Riga with Rafi. You can always stay and work with me, like before.'

'I'm not allowed to stay here any longer, *Tatty*; I have to go back. I only have a temporary permit.'

'Well, I'm worried about you. What are you doing for money? Do you have a job?'

'Oh, don't worry, *Tatty*, I'm managing.'

'You're being very mysterious.' Then he turned to Rafael. 'Tell me the truth, Rafi, is it all right?'

'Yes, *Tatty*, please don't worry. I'm taking care of him.'

'All right. Well, now, look boys, before you go, I have some things to give you. Rafi, I want you to take this; it's your mother's amulet. You remember? She would have wanted one of you to have it. Perhaps one day your own wife…,' he didn't finish the sentence. Rafael took the necklace with moist eyes and placed it carefully in his pocket.

'Thank you, *Tatty*,' he said.

'And this is for you, Yoss. This is a bracelet I gave to your mother when you were born, to celebrate your arrival. It's not an expensive thing, I'm afraid. She wore it all the time after you went away; I think it calmed her. I know she would have wanted you to have it.'

'Thank you, *Tatty*.' Yossel took the bracelet and turned away, felled by the depth of loss and grief he felt at that moment.

The three of them embraced each other. Then it was time for the boys to catch the train. Ester and Hannah, who had tactfully stayed in their room until this moment came out to say goodbye.

'Don't worry about your father,' said Ester to the boys 'We'll look after him.'

One day about two weeks later, Rafael received a letter from his father enclosing an additional sheet of paper; it was a letter of condolence to him from his Uncle Shmuel.

He was touched to be remembered in this way by someone who had emigrated two years before he was born.

Dear Rafael,

Your father has informed us of the sad passing of your dear mother. We wanted to let you know that we are thinking about you and your brother, and of course your father. He tells us that you are doing well in your apprenticeship, which must be a great blessing to him in his grief.

Your cousins, Mala, Sorre and little Hirsch, who of course you have never met, are doing well. They speak English fluently, as we are also trying to do.

We pray you stay well. Look after your father and brother.
Uncle Shmuel and Aunty Sara

His father's letter was full of sorrow, of course, but it also included some other news from home, including an update on the story of poor Getta, the girl whose baby had been baptised.

For three years, she and her parents had, with the rabbi's help, been fending off the authorities' tireless attempts to remove the child by legal means or by force. Getta's husband was still in the army, but the next time he came home on leave the entire family, worn out by the never-ending fight for custody of the child, had fled. Until now, nobody knew where they had gone. But Getta's mother, Leah, had sent a letter to her friend Scheine, unaware that she had passed away, and Itzhak had opened it. In the letter, Leah described how the family had made their way to the port of Windau and smuggled themselves aboard a cargo ship. After a long and arduous journey they were now in the city of Lübeck, where they felt they would be safe.

Rafael shook his head sadly but he hoped that poor Getta and her family would now be allowed to live in peace.

Rafael had his work to help take his mind away from grief for his mother. But Yossel, alone in his draughty attic room, was struggling. Some days he was able to beg, but on the very coldest days of the year he was unable to face going out on the streets to sing. On those days he sat in his room, wearing as many clothes as he could, wrapped in a blanket and staring out at the snow–swollen sky through the grimy skylight.

*

Eventually winter gave way to spring and Rafael began to reflect on the fact that he was in the final few months of his apprenticeship.

Uncharacteristically, he had no plan in his mind for what he was going to do when it finished. He knew he should make one, but somehow he couldn't focus his mind on it. He was just going to have to wait and see what happened.

One day Herr Strauss came over to his bench. 'Well, young man,' he said, 'it's time to demonstrate your skills.'

'What do you mean, sir?'

'I'm talking about your final pieces; the pieces that will mark the conclusion of your apprenticeship. Before you leave I want you to make two special items. One of them must be a lantern; the emblem of Gozinsky Metalworks. It's a tradition here.'

'I've made several lanterns, sir.'

'Indeed you have, but those were all to the standard design. This one must be original — to your own design.'

'Oh, I see. That's a challenge. And the other?'

'The other will be something for you to keep. An item of your own choosing. Useful or decorative or both, it's up to you. But make it portable; this is to be something to really show off your skill and creativity. Something you can show to prospective employers.'

'That's exciting. This will need a lot of thought, Herr Strauss.'

'Well, don't spend too long thinking about it. The autumn will be here sooner than you think.'

These final projects helped to focus his mind on the future. The key to the future was Rosa; of that he was sure. His imagination flew ahead through the years; he pictured her wearing his mother's amulet.

He smiled to himself as he suddenly knew what he was going to make for his showcase piece. That one would come first. He saw the design vividly in his mind in all its detail; he only hoped he could do it justice.

The other one, the lantern, would have to wait.

12

He worked on his showcase piece obsessively; it was a labour of love. His idea was to use two different metals entwined together to form a single, harmonious item. He had never made anything quite like it before, and there were a number of failed experiments and false starts to begin with. But eventually he worked out how to do it, and he spent long hours and days cutting, folding and shaping.

He finished it on a Friday, and since he was invited to the Strausses for *Shabbos* he decided to take it to show Herr Strauss at home, rather than at the factory.

Herr Strauss examined it carefully, nodded and said: 'Oh, yes. Yes. This is excellent. A real showcase for your skills. It is beautiful work. Well done, Rafael.'

Rafael glowed with pleasure and pride.

He wasn't going to keep it to show prospective employers, though.

It was a present.

When he got back to the Apprentice House, David was there.

'Hi, David,' he said cheerfully, '*Shabbat shalom.*'

'Hello Rafi. You look cheerful.'

'Well, so I am. You're not, though. What's up?'

'Oh, nothing.'

'All right, if you say so.'

'Rafi, I saw Rosa earlier. She wanted me to ask you to meet her by the canal tomorrow afternoon.'

'Of course. That's perfect. Actually I wanted to see her too.'

So, after *shul,* he walked briskly to their usual meeting place. Rosa was sitting on a bench, looking lovely, but downcast. He noticed with a pang of disappointment that Inge was with her, but when she saw him coming she whispered something to Rosa, squeezed her hand, stood up and walked briskly away in the opposite direction.

'That was strange,' said Rafael airily when he sat down. Then Rosa looked up at him and he saw she had been crying. A damp handkerchief lay crumpled in her lap.

'What is it?' he said, his voice full of concern. 'What's happened?'

She looked down at her lap again. Her voice was quiet and shaky and he could barely make out what she was saying.

'I'm so sorry.' His heart lurched. He waited. After what seemed a very long time she continued.

'I asked you to come because I … I want … because I need … to say goodbye.' She lapsed into silence and Rafael made no immediate reply. He reached out to take her hand, but she pulled it away. 'Please don't,' she said.

There was a shocked silence. 'I don't understand what's going on,' said Rafael at last. 'What do you mean, goodbye? What have I done?'

She looked up at him again through red-rimmed eyes from which tears were falling freely. 'Oh my dear. Nothing. You've done nothing. It's all my fault.'

'All your fault? Rosa, I'm sure that whatever it is you've done, it doesn't matter. Rosa, you know how I feel about you. I meant what I said that night; I love you. And even though you didn't say anything in reply, I know you feel the same. I know you do.'

'Listen to me, Rafi. You are a wonderful person. You deserve someone wonderful. You'll find her.'

'But I already have; it's you. Rosa, listen, I ….'

'Stop! Stop! I'll tell you everything, and then it will be over.' She heaved an enormous sigh and then said: 'There is something about me you need to know. I am not a Jew.'

'What are you talking about? Of course you are. Your whole family's Jewish …'

'Our parents are Jewish. But we're not, David and me. We're baptised Christians. Russian Orthodox. We've converted.'

'What?' He was shocked into silence. At last he said: 'I don't understand. I mean ... why?'

'David did it because his plan to avoid the army draft was to become a student, and the Polytechnic doesn't take Jews. It was as simple as that.'

'But I thought your Uncle Israel got him into the Polytechnic?'

'Yes, sort of. They wouldn't let in a Jew, not even for him, so he arranged for a Russian priest to train us in the Christian faith and perform the baptism. That was all it took; then the doors to the Polytechnic opened.'

'All right, but that's David. Why did *you* convert?'

'When David converted it just felt like the right thing to do. It made it easier to get into the Academy, of course, although, to be honest, I think Elise might still have allowed me in, Jewish or not.

'I still don't understand. That's not enough.'

'No, you're right. The real reason was that I was just tired. I was tired of struggling to be accepted. Tired of wrestling with all the legal restrictions. Tired of always having to explain myself. I was tired of trying to eat Kosher in a world of pork. I've never been really devout, or anything. I just wanted to paint and to be like everyone else.'

'So you're not a true believer? In Jesus as the Son of God, all of that?'

'I told the priest I was, of course, but truthfully, I don't know. Actually, I worry about that a lot.'

'And what do your family think?'

'They're disappointed, I know they are, but they are reconciled to it; they haven't disowned us. I think our family has always been quite secular–minded. Do you despise me?'

'Despise you? Of course not. But, Rosa, so what? What does it matter? It's nothing compared with how I feel about you. It doesn't mean we have to part.'

'I knew you'd say that, Rafi. But you're not talking sense. Think about it. Believe me, I have, over and over. It's no good really, is it? How could we marry? No rabbi would perform the ceremony and no priest either. But even if we did somehow find a way; you'd be marrying out of your faith. Think what that would mean. If we had children they wouldn't count as Jewish; the church would claim them. They'd have to be baptised. You're a good Jew, Rafi, an observant Jew. You're a *heder* boy. You need to live a Jewish life with a proper Jewish wife. You know what I'm saying is true.'

'All right, maybe that's all true. But why can't you just switch back? Un-convert?'

'It's not like that, Rafi. It's not so easy to go back. I've been baptised. I've sworn to embrace Christ; that's kind of a big deal. And, if I'm really, really honest, I don't want to go back. I like my life. I'm not an outsider any more; I'm just an ordinary Christian girl. It's comfortable. I blend in. I know I seem like a free spirit, but deep down I desperately need that. I know I still look Jewish and I've still got a Jewish-sounding name. But there are doors which are open to me now that just weren't before. It shouldn't be that way but it just is. I am really not cut out to be a Jew, not the way things are.'

'Why didn't you tell me?' he said quietly.

'I did try a few times, but ... I couldn't do it. I kept thinking "I'll do it tomorrow", but tomorrow never came. I'm so, so sorry.'

Rafael looked away, his sight blurred. 'Just tell me one thing,' he said.

'Anything.'

'Do you love me?'

'Oh, Rafi, it's not as simple as that.'

'Just answer. Do you love me?'

She hesitated for a long time before answering. 'Yes. But not enough.'

He closed his eyes, releasing a tear which rolled down his cheek. He wiped it away and stood up.

'I'm glad you didn't tell me sooner. I would have missed out on a lot of joyful moments. Anyhow, I'd still like you to have this,' he said, handing her the long, heavy, brown paper parcel he had brought. 'I made it for you. Goodbye, Rosa.'

She stood up too, and took the parcel. 'I'll never forget you, Rafi,' she said. She held out her hand and he pressed it one last time. Then he turned on his heel and walked briskly away.

There were ducks on the canal, quacking hungrily. A young couple walked along the path, arm in arm, with a tiny dog trotting along beside them on a lead, its short legs shooting forward and back comically.

Rafael saw and heard none of it.

When he had gone, Rosa sat on the bench alone with her thoughts for some time. When Inge returned, she asked 'How did it go?' Rosa shrugged miserably by way of response.

'He gave me a present,' she said.

'Really? Are you going to open it?'

'I suppose so.'

She unwrapped the parcel. Inside it was the piece which Rafael had laboured over with such joy and hope. It was a perfect replica, made of copper and tin entwined together, of a long–stemmed rosebud, just coming into bloom. There was a small rectangular card placed loosely on the flower, on which Rafael had written:

'A rose for my Rosa.'

When her tears fell onto the burnished metal leaves they formed dew–like beads.

*

It was a year since Scheine's death, and the boys said prayers and lit a candle in her memory. Rafael was numb with sadness. He felt his mother's absence as a deep emptiness, a nagging ache. And the loss of

Rosa was a raw wound, very hard to bear. He found it a struggle to muster the energy to work. Even the fine late summer weather and the approaching conclusion of his time as an apprentice did nothing to alleviate his despondency.

He met up with Yossel one evening after work and they went together to the tavern. 'How was your day, Yoss?' he asked.

'Not bad, actually. This nice weather makes people more willing to stand and listen, and then they give more. I sang *"Papir iz dokh vays"* — remember that one? — and it pulled quite a big crowd. What about you?'

'Not so great. I just don't seem to have any enthusiasm for the work at the moment.'

'Poor Rafi.'

They sat on for a few moments, absorbed in their thoughts.

'Any news from home?' Yossel asked, changing the subject.

'Yes, actually, there is, I was coming to that. There was a letter from *Tatty* today.'

'*Nu?*'

'Well, the big news is that the Rosenbergs are moving out. Ester is getting re-married.'

'Oh, that's nice. Who to?'

'You'll never guess. Isaac the miller. *Zeide's* friend.'

'What? Isn't he a bit old for her? How did that come about?'

'He's not that old, he's quite a bit younger than *Zeide*, I think. Apparently, she's been helping out at the baker's since *Mame* died, and that's how she met Isaac. I think it's all rather sweet. And he's quite well off so she will be comfortable at last. But apparently she's had a big row with Hannah.'

'With Hannah? But Hannah never makes a fuss about anything.'

'I know. But she's decided she doesn't want to move, for some reason, and for the first time in her life she's putting her foot down.'

'Well, she'll have to move, when her mother goes to live with Isaac, won't she? She can't just live with *Tatty* on her own. That wouldn't be right.'

'No, exactly. I don't know what she's thinking.'

*

Rafael went for a walk by the canal to clear his mind and try to order his thoughts. He still didn't know what he was going to do when his apprenticeship ended and he was running out of time. His options were limited but, such as they were, he ran through them in his mind.

The obvious thing was to stay where he was; he thought Israel Gozinsky would almost certainly give him a job if he applied. He would receive a proper wage instead of an apprentice's stipend, which would mean he could rent a decent apartment, big enough for him and Yossel to share. Then they could focus on getting Yossel a proper job; he obviously couldn't beg on the streets for the rest of his life.

But now that his dream of a future with Rosa had evaporated he had a strong desire to get out of Riga and make a fresh start somewhere else. Also, it wasn't a complete plan; it didn't solve the problem of Yossel being in danger of conscription, and it would leave their father living all alone, which Rafael knew he would hate.

So the next option was for him and Yossel to move back to Tukum. But could they get permission? And could he settle comfortably back into small town life after living in Riga? There were no big metalworks there; where would he work?

There was one further option, and this was the only one that really excited him. To apply for passports and visas, and emigrate. Not just him and Yossel, but also their father if he would come — he was on his own now, so why not him too? They could go to Germany or America or England. Somewhere new, where they would be free. He felt sure his skills would be in demand in one of their big cities.

It seemed like a good plan. He would discuss it with Yossel and then, when his apprenticeship ended, they would go home and put it to their father. Rafael had enough money saved up for the fares, and they could live cheaply at home while they waited for their passports to arrive.

He spent many hours working on his final piece, the lantern. When it was completed at last he showed it proudly to Herr Strauss, who examined it minutely.

Herr Strauss nodded. 'Very good. This is an imaginative design, Rafael,' he said, smiling broadly. 'Eminently functional and a very pleasing shape. These details here are very cleverly executed. I am impressed. Well done, young man.'

Rafael glowed with pride.

During the last few days of his apprenticeship another letter arrived from his father. He read it in open-mouthed amazement.

My dear Rafi,

I hope you are keeping well and the two of you are looking after yourselves. I have some wonderful news to share with you.

As you know, Hannah Rosenberg and her mother Ester have been living in the apartment for the last two years. In that time, and especially since your dear mame passed away, I have come to feel very comforted by their presence. As I told you in my recent letter, Ester is shortly going to be moving out. But not Hannah. You probably thought that was strange, but I can now explain.

Hannah has blossomed into a charming and beautiful young woman. She has her mother's kindness, but with a gentle calmness all of her own. Well, to 'cut a long story short', as they say, I have asked her to marry me, and she has done me the honour of saying 'yes'. We are planning to hold the wedding very soon, so that when you next see us we may already be married.

> *It is not always in life that one gets a second chance. This news may be unexpected, perhaps even shocking, to you, but I hope that you will rejoice in my great good fortune. Of course there is an age difference between us, but after all, it's not so very great and Hannah is kind enough to say that she doesn't consider it of importance. I will write again later but I wanted to tell you the good news straight away.*
>
> *With love from*
> *Tatty*

As soon as he could, he went to find Yossel. 'Come and have a coffee, Yoss. I've got something to tell you,' he said, taking his arm.

Yossel blanched. 'The last time you said that was when *Mamele* died,' he said. 'What's happened?'

'Nobody's died. But it is unexpected news from home. You're going to want to be sitting down when I tell you, believe me.'

'What is it?'

'Not here. If you want me to tell you, come to the coffee shop.'

'All right,' he agreed. 'But it better be important. I was doing rather well here today.'

In the coffee shop, Rafael ordered two cups from the waitress and waited until she brought them before he read the letter out to Yossel, keeping his voice down so the other customers wouldn't hear the embarrassing contents.

When he'd finished he said: 'Well? What do you think of that?'

'What do I think? I don't know what to think! It's completely out of the blue. How did this happen?'

'I don't know.'

'He must be twice her age.'

'Well, no, not quite that. I've been working it out; I think *Tatty's* about thirty-eight and Hannah must be about twenty-one or twenty-two.'

'It's still a big difference.'

'Yes. But you know, it does sort of make sense for both of them. He was facing the prospect of being completely on his own, which he would hate, and she saw an opportunity to become independent from her mother.'

'Yes, I know. But… Oh, my God! It's going to be so odd. Do you think they love each other?'

'Even older people can fall in love, Yoss. Maybe they really do.'

'You do realise they could easily have children together, don't you? *Tatty* could start a whole new family with Hannah.'

'*Oy, oy oy*. What a thought. Well,' said Rafael, half to himself, 'this certainly complicates the plan.'

'There's a plan? Care to share it?'

'Oh yes, sorry, I was coming to that.' He explained his idea to Yossel, who loved it.

On the day his apprenticeship came to an end, Rafael climbed the wrought-iron stairs for the final time. Natalia Ivanovna showed him into the inner office.

'Ah, Rafael,' said Israel Gozinsky looking up from his desk. 'So you're leaving us today?'

'Yes, sir.'

'I hear from Herr Strauss that you have done very well. He seems very impressed with you. I hope that you have enjoyed your apprenticeship here?' He pressed a button on his desk connected to an electric wire, ('That's new,' thought Rafael,) and the secretary came in.

'Natalia, do you have Rafael's certificate?' said Gozinsky. She disappeared back into her office for a moment and reappeared with the document. He took it and passed it to Rafael. 'Well, here you are, young man. Your first step to joining the guild.'

'Thank you, sir.'

'Before you go, tell me, how is your father? Is it a year since your mother passed away yet?'

'A little over a year, sir. He's getting remarried.'

'Is he? And how do you feel about that?'

'Um. Well …'

'I see. It must be difficult for you. In any case, please wish him *mazel tov* from me when you next see him. He's a good man. An honourable man. I hope they will be happy together. And how is your brother getting on?'

'He's … currently working as a musician, sir. A singer.'

'Well, well. I'm sorry things didn't work out for him here, but it sounds like his calling lies elsewhere.'

'Yes, sir. Before I leave I wanted to thank you for everything you've done for me.'

'I'm just glad I could help you.' He stood up and showed Rafael to the door. 'I'm sorry we can't persuade you to stay, but I know your mind's made up. I hope it all works out for you, and for your brother too. *Zay gezunt*, Rafael.'

'Thank you, sir. Goodbye.'

They shook hands solemnly, and Rafael went out through the small office and down the stairs for the final time.

Salomon Strauss was waiting for him. He shook Rafael's hand warmly and presented him with a canvas bag containing a complete set of brand new tools. 'Well done, Rafael,' he said. 'It has been a great pleasure to teach you, young man. You are a quick learner, intelligent, hard–working, and good with the tools. And, even more importantly, you know how to behave. I'm sure you will do very well for yourself.'

'Thank you, Herr. Strauss. I feel sad that my time here has come to an end. I am so grateful to you for everything.'

'I'm sorry it didn't work out for your brother.'

'Thank you. But it was never going to. He knows it himself. I'm not sure what he's going to do in the end, but he'll be all right.'

'You do know, Rafael, don't you, that there will always be a job for you here?'

'Thank you, sir. But my mind is made up. Yossel and I are leaving Riga.'

'Do you have permission from the authorities to go elsewhere?'

'No, not yet. We're going home to Tukum this afternoon, just for a while, and then we plan to go abroad.'

'I see. Well, if you want my advice,' said Herr Strauss, 'go to my country, Germany. They have many metalworks where your skills will be in high demand, and just as importantly they treat Jews decently there.'

'Thank you for the advice, sir. I will certainly think about that.'

'Good. Well, whatever you decide, I wish you the very best of luck. But, before you go, I have something else for you. A small gift to remind you of your time with me.'

He put his hand into a bag and pulled out a pair of small, exquisitely made, silver-plated candlesticks. Their columns were delicately twisted into Solomonic spirals. They were exact replicas, in miniature, of the Shabbos candlesticks which Rafael had so much admired the first time he had visited the Strausses five years before.

Rafael turned them round in his hand. The workmanship was astonishing. They must have taken Herr Strauss a long time to make. He was moved beyond words.

'They are... so beautiful. I really don't know what to say, Herr Strauss. Thank you so much.'

'They are only decorative of course, too small to be used. But I thought they would fit in your bag and remind you of me. They're only plated of course, but in an emergency they might also turn out to be quite valuable, should you ever find yourself short ... well, you know.'

He left the thought hanging in the air. They said their final goodbyes, Rafael picked up his new tools and left Gozinsky's for the last time.

At the Apprentice House he collected his bag, already packed, took a last look around, said goodbye to Frau Pucher, and left. Outside the House, he was surprised to find David waiting for him. 'Shouldn't you be at work?' he asked.

'Yes. I bunked off. I couldn't let you leave without saying goodbye. I was afraid I'd already missed you.'

'Thank you. I'm touched.'

'I wish you'd change your mind and stay in Riga, Rafi.'

'I can't. I need a fresh start, David. You know why.'

'Yes, I know.'

'I wish you'd told me, David. About the whole Christian conversion thing, you know. I wish you'd said something right at the beginning.'

'Believe me, so do I. I'm so sorry, Rafi. At first it wasn't relevant. And then, it became more and more difficult. I know what she meant to you …'

Rafael interrupted. 'Thank you, but don't say any more. I know you mean well, but I don't want to talk about it. It's all over.' He put out his hand. 'Goodbye, David.'

'We're still friends, I hope?'

'Of course. I wish nothing but the best for you. For both of you.' David looked relieved.

'That means a lot to me, Rafi. Let's try and stay in touch.' They shook hands rather formally, but then Rafael changed his mind and enfolded David in a bear hug.

He turned, picked up his bags, and walked off towards Latgales Street. He needed to find his brother.

*

He expected to find Yossel at his usual spot in Latgales Street, but he wasn't there. He looked around for a moment, baffled, and then spotted a newspaper seller on the other side of the road. He crossed over to talk to him.

'Excuse me, sir,' he said politely, 'I don't suppose you know what happened to the young man who usually sits over there and sings?'

'The famous "Singing *Schnorrer*"? Yes. He's been arrested.'

Rafael froze. 'Arrested? Why?'

The man shrugged. 'It happens. Every so often they choose to round up a bunch of beggars. Get them off the street. Maybe someone complained. Who knows? I'm not too sorry myself, to be honest; he's a good singer but I was getting tired of listening to those depressing melodies.'

'Where did they take him?'

'I've no idea. Look, are you going to buy a paper, or not?'

Rafael ran to the police station and approached the desk. He recognised the policeman on duty; he was the same man who had signed the boys' permission to travel to Tukum for their mother's funeral. Yes, he confirmed, they had arrested Yossel for begging, and he was here, in the cells. He had to pay a fine, and if he didn't, or couldn't, then he'd likely be sent off to the army.

Rafael clutched his brow at this disastrous news, but he said, as calmly as he could, 'How much is the fine?'

The policeman mentioned a distressingly large sum. It was almost all the money Rafael had. Fishing in his bag, he found his purse and all but emptied it on the counter. The policeman counted the pile carefully and grunted.

'Right. Wait here.'

A few minutes later, a dishevelled, shaken Yossel appeared from a back room. When he saw Rafael he burst into tears.

'It's all right, Yoss,' said Rafael. 'It's sorted. They're letting you go.'

'Oh, thank God! But the fine?'

'It's all right, I tell you. It's paid. Come on, let's get out of here.'

Outside the police station, Yossel embraced his brother. 'Thank you Rafi. Thank you. I was so scared,' he sobbed. 'I thought I was for it.'

'Shh.' Rafael tried to comfort him as their mother used to do. 'It's all right, Yoss.'

'But the money!'

'I know. That actually is a bit of a problem. Look, your place is paid for until the end of the week. Let's go back there.'

'But you can't sleep in my room, Rafi. There's only one bed, and in any case we're not supposed to have visitors.'

'I'm not a visitor — it's me who's paid the rent. Anyhow, it's only for a couple of nights. I'll sleep on the floor. No, wait!' He clicked his fingers. 'I've got a better idea.'

'Great. What?'

'*You* can sleep on the floor.'

When they got back to the apartment Yossel found a letter waiting for him. 'That's unusual. I never get letters,' he said absent-mindedly, tucking it into his pocket.

Upstairs in the attic, the two brothers sat on the bed. 'I'm so sorry about what happened, Yoss,' said Rafael. 'It must have been really horrible.'

'It was,' Yossel replied, shakily. 'I knew you'd try to rescue me, but I didn't know if you'd be able to find me, or if you'd be able to get me out of there, even if you did.' He was shivering with the reaction from the tension he had been under. 'I didn't know if I'd ever see you again. I don't mind admitting, Rafi, I was terrified.'

Rafael put his arm round him, stroking his back and making soothing sounds, until his brother's shivering began to subside. 'I wonder what's in that letter of yours,' he mused.

'Oh, the letter. I forgot all about it'. Yossel fished it out of his pocket and handed it over. 'Please can you read it to me?'

Rafael opened the envelope, took out the letter, and began silently to read it. As soon as he did so, the colour drained from his face. 'Oh, no! Oh, my God, no,' he groaned.

'What is it?'

'It's happened, Yoss. It's happened. You've been conscripted.'

Speechless with horror, Yossel buried his head in his hands. They sat in silent despair trying to reckon with this new calamity. 'Wait a minute,' Yossel cried. 'It's not the right time. The recruitment was last year.'

'I know. You must be a late replacement for someone who absconded, or didn't show up.'

'Oh, my God. What do I do, Rafi? I can't go into the army. Not after everything we've been through.'

'No, you can't,' Rafael agreed.'

'Does it say when I'm meant to report?'

'Let's see.' He examined the letter again and, in a leaden voice, said. 'Yes it does. Two days from now.'

'Two days! What are we going to do? Rafi, help me.'

'Wait a minute. Let me think.' Feverishly, he paced the floor while Yossel felt a sort of cold horror creeping over him. 'Right, that's it,' Rafael announced decisively. 'We're going to get you out of here. We've got to leave the country. Right now.'

'But I've only got two days. There's no way I can get a passport in that time.'

'It doesn't matter. They aren't going to give you a passport anyhow.'

'What, then?'

'Remember Getta?' said Rafael, sitting on the edge of the bed. 'She needed to leave in a hurry because of the baptism thing, so they went to Windau and smuggled themselves aboard a cargo ship. We can do the same.'

'How do we get to Windau?'

'We don't have to go to Windau, schlemiel. We're already in one of the biggest ports in the country. I just mean we can escape on a cargo ship.'

'Oh yes, sorry, I'm not thinking. But we'll obviously have to go back to Tukum first, to see *Tatty* and *Zeide* to explain everything and say goodbye.'

'No. I'm afraid we can't do that. We'd need permission, and we'd never get it, not now that you've had this letter. In any case, we don't have the time. We've got to get out of the country as fast as possible. Within the next two days, anyhow.'

Yossel looked at Rafael in horror. 'Are you seriously talking about leaving the country without seeing *Tatty* before we go? What if we never see him again?'

Gently, Rafael took Yossel's hand and said: 'Yes, Yoss. That is what I'm saying. I'm so sorry. We really have no choice. But we will see him again, I know it. One day, when we're properly settled, he'll come and stay with us.'

Yossel wept. After a few moments, he sobbed: 'Where will we go?'

Rafael's brain was whirling. The situation made him feel both angry and desperate. He had just paid over almost his entire savings to prevent his brother being conscripted for an unpaid fine, only for him to be conscripted anyhow. 'There's really only one place that makes sense, now that we have no money, and no time to make any,' he said. 'London, where Uncle Shmuel and Aunty Sara live. We can stay with them for a time, I'm sure, until we get on our feet. What do say, Yoss? Shall we do it?'

After a long pause, Yossel wiped his eyes and said: 'All right. I trust you Rafi. You know what's best; you always have. If you say that's what we should do, that's what we should do.' Rafael patted him on the back. They looked at each other in trepidation at the enormous step they were about to take. 'But we still have to find a way to tell Tatty what we're doing, somehow,' he said, desperately.

'Yes, of course we do. Don't worry, I'll send him a letter before we go. And while I'm at it, I'll write to Uncle Shmuel and Aunty Sara so they know we're coming.'

'How can you do that, though? We don't know their address.'

'Good point.' He thought a moment and then clicked his fingers. 'Hang on. Actually, yes we do. I kept the letter they sent us after Mamele died; the address is written at the top.' He rummaged in his bag for a while before triumphantly extracting the letter. 'Aha. Here it is. See it? "48, Brick Lane, London E1." So, I can write to tell them to expect us, and we'll know exactly where to go when we get to London.'

He expected this news to elicit a cheer from Yossel, but he didn't appear to have even heard. He had a thoughtful look on his face and had gone very quiet.

'Wait a minute, Rafi,' he said at length. 'This isn't right. You haven't been drafted, only me. I should go on my own and you should stay here while you wait for your passport and follow me on a proper passenger ship later.'

'No. Absolutely not. I promised Mamele I'd take care of you, and I will. We're doing it together.'

Yossel heaved a huge sigh. 'Thank God. I had to say it, but I really don't fancy making my way to London on my own. I know I'm a bit useless without you. Thank you, Rafi.' He hugged his brother tightly. The brothers clung together in their misery.

'We still need to think about money, Yoss. The ship's captain will demand a payment and We're almost penniless. What do you have?'

'Only this.' He fetched a small tin from the mantlepiece and emptied it into his palm. It made a depressingly small pile.

'Well, I suppose it's a start,' Rafael said, trying to sound more optimistic than he felt. 'But it definitely won't be enough. It'll get us food for the journey, that's all. We need to make some more, and fast.'

'How do we do that?'

'I can only think of one way. I'm so sorry, Yoss.'

'What do you mean? Sorry about what?... Oh no! No, no, no!' he protested, jumping to his feet and crossing his hands on top of his head. 'You must be joking. I'm not singing on the streets again. No way. They'll arrest me again, for sure.'

'No, they won't,' Rafael said soothingly. 'I'll keep lookout. It'll be fine. Calm down.'

Yossel sighed and tugged at his hair, but eventually resigned himself to the inevitable. 'Oy! Well, you better be good at keeping lookout, Rafi, that's all I can say. I really don't think I'm the army type.' He pointed at the draft notice lying on the bed. 'What shall we do with this letter?'

'Burn it.'

*

The boys left the room early the next day, to make sure they had as much time as possible to scrape together the money they needed. Rafael got the two letters written and sent, then they went to the market to lay in provisions for the journey. They only had the haziest idea how long the journey would take, but Rafael guessed it would be three or four days. They realised bread would spoil too quickly, so they bought biscuits, hard cheese, and some dates. They wondered what to do about water, but decided they couldn't carry it and would have to trust being able to get it on the ship.

By the time they were done shopping, they had a pitifully tiny collection of coins remaining.

They left the provisions in Yossel's attic room, and then came the part of the plan they were most anxious about. They made their way to Latgales Street and Yossel took up position in his familiar place, his cap on the ground in front of him. Rafael stationed himself at what he judged to be the best vantage point so that he could keep a lookout; close enough to be able to alert Yossel if he saw a policeman coming, but, he judged, far enough away that a casual observer wouldn't think he and Yossel were connected in any way.

Yossel closed his eyes and began to sing. Rafael had to admit to himself that his brother had a sweet voice, strong and resonant. It was no longer the treble he had heard chanting the *Torah* at his *bar mitzvah*; Yossel now possessed a rich baritone.

There was a lot of passing foot-traffic and the hat began to fill with coins. Yossel had a big repertoire; he sang on and on, song after song — lullabies, songs of poverty, songs of toil and heartbreak, religious songs.

A small knot of people began gathering round him, listening, and even sometimes applauding at the end of a song. Little by little the crowd swelled until it threatened to block the pavement, and Rafael began to sense danger. A crowd that size could definitely attract unwanted attention.

He could no longer see Yossel through the crowd and, more importantly, Yossel would not be able to see him if he signalled for him to stop. It was time to draw the performance to a close. Rafael prayed that Yossel had made enough for them to bribe their way onto the ship.

He had begun to make his way surreptitiously towards the crowd when he spotted two policemen strolling round the corner on the opposite side. They were relaxed, merely sauntering along, but as soon as they saw the crowd which had gathered round Yossel they became alert, quickening their pace.

There was not a moment to lose. If they reached Yossel at the centre of the ring of onlookers, all would be lost.

Elbowing his way energetically through the crowd, ignoring their irritated protests, Rafael reached the open space in the centre and shouted:

'Police! Run!'

Yossel wasted no time. He grabbed the hat, now heavy with coins, and clutched it tightly to his chest. The brothers pushed through the crowd on the side furthest from the police, and took off.

Taken aback by the sudden disappearance of the performer, the disappointed crowd started milling around, momentarily obstructing the policemen and gaining the fleeing boys a few precious seconds. But the policemen, well used to dealing with crowds, quickly forced their way through and set off in pursuit.

Rafael and Yossel were fast, but so were the policemen, and Yossel was encumbered by the hat full of coins. As they hared down the street they realised the policemen were steadily gaining on them. Rafael desperately wanted to get off the main street and was searching for a side road.

Suddenly he saw a narrow passageway just up ahead. 'In here,' he hissed, grabbing Yossel's arm. They darted into the passage, closely followed by their pursuers, and emerged at the other end to find themselves, by a stroke of luck, plunging straight into a busy and chaotic market, thronged with people and tightly packed with rows of stalls.

They zigzagged between the rows, stooping as low as they could, and after a few minutes felt certain that the policemen had lost them.

They stood gasping for breath and, when they had recovered, set off back to the attic room, keeping to the back streets as much as they could and keeping careful watch for the policemen as they went.

*

Early next morning, well before sunrise, they went down to the port. Even though it was still very early, and not yet light, there was plenty of activity and noise; horse drawn carts were lined up on the dockside, being loaded or unloaded, or just waiting their turn. Men were toiling up the ships' gangplanks with barrels on their shoulders, or carrying crates between them. Mechanical cranes were picking up huge tree trunks from piles on the quay and dropping them onto barges or into holds. The boys crouched behind a barrel and peered out. Yossel was wide-eyed and open-mouthed, trying to take it all in, but Rafael was looking for something very specific.

At last, he spotted it. 'There!' he hissed. 'That ship with the black hull. "*Kristaps*".'

As they watched, a small family group, carrying bags and peering around furtively, scuttled up the gangplank and, moments later, disappeared into the recesses of the ship.

'See that? That's the one. Come on,' whispered Rafael. 'I'll do the talking.'

They ran over, hurried up the gangplank and stepped onto the deck, to be confronted by a large man wearing a grimy black jacket and a weatherbeaten cap. 'Where do you think you're going?' he growled.

'London, we hope,' said Rafael.

'Not on my boat, you ain't. Hop it. This ain't a cruise ship.'

'Really? Well, you seem to have some passengers on board already. Can't you manage another two? We can pay.'

'*Hmph*,' replied the man, noncommittally. He looked at them closely again, and spat onto the deck out of the corner of his mouth. 'How much?' They showed him what they had and he looked at them contemptuously.

'Is that it? You're having a laugh. Go on, clear off.'

'But…'

'Clear off, I say,' he shouted, raising the flat of his hand in a threatening gesture.

'Wait', said Rafael, diving into his bag. 'Wait. That's not all. Also this.'

In his hand was one of the two miniature candlesticks, the polished surface of its twisted column twinkling alluringly in the pale light of the rising sun. The man's expression softened. 'Well, that is quite pretty,' he said, his eyes narrowing with a mixture of suspicion and greed. 'Where'd you get a thing like that?'

'It's mine. It was given to me.'

'Yeah, yeah, if you say so. All right, let's see it.'

Rafael handed it over, and the man turned it around in his hands, feeling its weight and holding it up to the light. He looked narrowly at Rafael. 'Is there a pair of these?'

'No,' lied Rafael. 'Just the one. That's all I've got. So, is it enough? Will you take us or not?'

'Oh, go on then,' the man replied, with a jerk of his head. 'Hurry up and get below with the others before someone sees you. And don't come up again until we're out to sea. Understand?'

They grabbed their bags and moved quickly in the direction he had pointed, passing a number of other crewmen, who looked past them as if they were invisible. They went through a hatch, and down a ladder into the ship's gloomy interior. There they stood for a moment, unsure of themselves, waiting for their eyes to adjust to the darkness.

Then they realised they were not alone.

They were in a hold full of people. Elderly couples; parents with gaggles of small children; gaunt men with tangled beards and grimy long overcoats, their haunted eyes peering out of pinched faces; young women with exhausted, defeated expressions cradling a moaning infant, or holding the hand of a listless toddler; and old women with dirty shawls draped over bony shoulders, bonnets that may once have been white perched on their lank, grey locks.

The boys gawped in amazement. They knew they were not the only ones needing to take an unofficial route out of the country, but they had not realised how many others there were. This was just one ship and there were maybe dozens of people here. How many people had made this same trip before, or would do soon? Was the whole country emptying itself?

The hold was so crowded there was hardly anywhere to sit, but the boys managed to find a space. Although they could see a little, now that their eyes had adjusted, it was still, by any measure, a dark and gloomy place. What little light there was came in through a small, round, grimy porthole or through the hatch above; it must be getting light outside, they realised.

Soon, though, the hatch was closed and that source of light, and fresh air, was shut off. The air quickly became dank and stifling, the walls dripped with condensation and it became more difficult to breathe.

Eerily, there was almost no talking. But the noise of softly moaning infants and the coughs and groans of the adults created a sort of desperate background music.

'I'm sorry, Yoss,' whispered Rafael. 'I didn't know it would be like this.'

'Don't worry, Rafi' replied Yossel as cheerfully as he could. 'It's not for long. You did really well to get us on board. Soon we'll be in

London. We'll go to Uncle Shmuel and Aunty Sara's house, and everything will be fine.'

'Sure. That's right.'

*

Seasickness took hold of many of the passengers almost as soon as the ship sailed. The boys had anticipated a voyage of three or four days, but *"Kristaps"*, although powered by a combination of steam and sail, took over a week to make the trip. Three days were taken up going through the Eider canal alone. Although the calm waters of the canal helped to ease the symptoms of seasickness, the days spent going through the Eider were the worst of the entire journey, even worse than the open ocean, because the hatch had to be kept shut, and the air became so foetid that some people passed out.

But the Captain was not wantonly cruel, just cautious, and once back on the open sea the hatch was opened again and people were allowed on deck in small groups to get some air and stretch their legs. Thankfully, water was provided and gratefully received, and people shared their food around so, although the boys suffered great hunger on the journey, they survived.

On a day when they were allowed on deck, and Yossel judged he couldn't be overheard, he said to Rafael 'I wonder what happened when I didn't report for duty?'

'I don't know. Try not to think about it. There's nothing you can do.'

'They'll have to pick another replacement, won't they?'

'I'm afraid so, yes.'

'I've done a terrible thing, Rafi. I should have stayed.' Rafael didn't know what to say. There really was nothing he *could* say. The brothers stared out at the waves, lost in their tangled thoughts.

Changing the subject, Yossel turned to Rafael. 'About that candlestick,' he said, 'I'd never seen that before. It was beautiful. Did you make it?'

'No — Herr Strauss did. He gave it to me when I left. It broke my heart to give it away but it's the only valuable thing I had, apart from the tools, and I'll need them when we get to London.'

Leaning closer, and talking more quietly, Yossel asked: 'Was it true, what you told the Captain? Did you really only have one candlestick?'

Rafael put a finger to his lips, said 'Shh,' and gave a little smile. Yossel understood.

To while away some time, and take their minds off their seasickness and discomfort, the boys did their best to engage their companions in conversation.

A sweet, inoffensive, older couple, the Shusters, seemed an unlikely pair to find travelling in this furtive manner, so out of curiosity Rafael asked them their story. They had made their way to Riga surreptitiously from Yekaterinoslav. It was a now-familiar story; He was an artisan who had lost his home and workshop at a stroke in one of the pogroms, and been unable to pay his taxes. Wanted by the authorities, they had spent months moving from place to place until, finding themselves in the port of Riga, they decided almost on a whim to bribe their way onto the ship, using the last of the coins which the husband had carried sewn into the lining of his jacket.

Of the others, not all were approachable; some were too forbidding in their aspect or too withdrawn into themselves. But some were happy, indeed eager, to share their stories and their dreams.

One of the passengers had recently arrived in Riga after a long and arduous journey from Rostov, where his shtetl had been razed in a pogrom; another had lived peacefully in a village until exiled overnight by the change in the law seven years earlier, and had been wandering from town to town ever since before coming, almost accidentally, to Riga and on to the ship; a third, like Yossel, had been drafted and had run away; a fourth was fleeing his debts; a fifth was wanted by the police.

One old man seemed to be quite insane, insisting, despite all attempts to correct him, that the ship was going to New York.

Each story was unique. Yet, in a way, each story was the same.

*

After a week, it was hard for Rafael and Yossel to remember a time when they weren't on the ship, with these sad people and these awful smells.

It was hard, too, to imagine there would be a time in the future when things would be different, when their world would not consist of this filthy, dank, heaving ship.

But all journeys come to an end eventually. The ship reached the Thames estuary, the hatch was closed again, and they began to steam up the river. Finally the ship docked, the engine was stilled, the vibrations stopped at last, and all that could be heard inside was the breathing and coughing of the passengers, the crying and snuffling of the children, and some faint sounds of shouting and banging from outside the ship as it was unloaded.

They waited quietly for a long time, listening as the noises died away and there was no more sound coming from outside the ship. Then the hatch was opened, and a voice hissed 'All right. Come on, then. Quietly, now.'

The people gathered their meagre possessions, helping older ones to stand, and one by one they climbed the ladder. The air outside was fresh and cool and the sky was dark; it was the dead of night.

They stepped off the ship, finding themselves unsteady on land at first. They were in a large dock surrounded on three sides by enormous warehouses.

'So, this is London,' breathed Rafael. 'We did it, Yoss. We made it. Our troubles are almost over.'

They followed the line of passengers through the maze of warehouses until they came to a wide, cobbled street which eventually opened up into an irregular shaped square dominated by an enormous, ancient–looking structure which looked like a fortress, or a prison. The passengers looked up at the high, forbidding stone walls and shuddered. The cobbled streets were glistening and wet, and there was a thick, greenish–tinged mist hanging in the air, glowing wherever the flickering yellow beams of the gas lamps penetrated.

The immigrants peered round them uncertainly. Then, out of the murky night, a short, thin, rat–faced man appeared, almost at Rafael's elbow. He was wearing a patched tweed jacket, with a filthy flat cap perched on the back of his head.

'*Shalom*,' he said, grabbing Rafael's hand and shaking it. Then in Yiddish, heavily tinged with an unfamiliar accent, he went on. 'Welcome to London, lads. Just arrived?'

'*Um*. Thank you. Yes, just arrived,' said Rafael, glad to hear a language he could, just about, understand. 'And to be honest we're not exactly sure where we are.'

'Tower Hill,' said the man. 'You're right in the City, you are. You were lucky, you lot, you came right into the Western Dock. Saved you a long walk, that did. Here, let me help you with that.' He reached out to try and grab one of Rafael's bags. Rafael snatched it quickly away.

'Oh no, it's all right. I'll think I'll carry them, thank you,' he said suspiciously.

'All right, all right,' said the man, holding his hands up in mock surrender. 'Have it your own way. You're lucky you met me, you are. There's some dodgy people about. Look, I feel sorry for you, you seem a bit lost. Don't worry, I'll look after you. All right, follow me; I'll show you where you can get a bed for the night. Very cheap. Comfortable. Nice and clean.'

Yossel picked up his bag and began to follow the man, but Rafael pulled him back and looked round uncertainly. He saw others from the boat being led off in various directions by similar–looking men.

He hesitated and then announced firmly 'It's all right. I was confused for a moment but actually, I know where we are now. We're fine. Thank you.' The man looked at him appraisingly for only a moment before darting off.

'Why did you say that?' asked Yossel crossly. 'You don't know where we are at all. We haven't got a clue. He said he was going to help us. At least, I think that's what he said,' he concluded, uncertainly.

'I know,' replied his brother. 'But look, Yoss, we don't know who we can trust. Honestly, I don't think we should trust anyone until we get to Uncle Shmuel's house, OK? Once we're there, then everything will be easier. They can help us figure out what to do next.'

'OK, you're the boss,' said Yossel sulkily.

They watched as the man approached the elderly couple they had befriended on the boat, the Shusters, who were still looking around them in a bewildered manner. He inserted himself between them, put his arms round their shoulders and went into his patter.

'*Shalom*. Welcome to London. Just arrived? Ah, well, you're lucky you met me, you are, there's some dodgy people about. Don't worry, I'll look after you. Here, let me help you with that.'

He grabbed their bags and they followed him meekly into the night. The boys watched them go until they were swallowed by the darkness and the fog.

One by one, the other passengers also disappeared into the surrounding roads. The brothers stood on the deserted, damp, cobbled street, in the shadow of the brooding stone tower, cold, lost and alone.

'What have we done?' thought Rafael. 'What have we done?'

PART THREE

Whitechapel, London

1888

13

'I'M COLD,' SAID Yossel. 'Can't we get moving?'

'So am I,' agreed Rafael. 'It must be morning soon, surely. Yes, let's start moving. I think if we head away from the river we should start to meet more people.'

They picked up their bags and, keeping the Tower and the river behind them, walked through the quiet, cobbled streets and alleys, trying to find something that would help them get their bearings.

'Look, there's a sign on the wall over there,' Rafael said, pointing. 'It's in the same sort of writing as German, that's good; it says 'Leman Street E1.' The E1 is encouraging, that's the same as on the address we're looking for. That must mean we're close.'

'I can see a building with Hebrew writing on it,' said Yossel excitedly. 'What does it say?'

'Where? Oh, I see it. It's a shelter for Jews.'

'Well we don't need that. But maybe they can direct us?'

'It looks like it's all locked up. But well done for spotting it. Let's remember where it is in case we can't find Brick Lane. We could come back later on, when it's open, and ask them for directions if we get stuck.'

They kept walking and at length came to a wide, cobbled thoroughfare lined with tall buildings, many of which had shops at street level. In the first, grey light of dawn it was getting easier to make things out.

'Look!' said Rafael, pointing at a spot on the opposite wall. 'Another street name at last. "Whitechapel High Street E1".'

'This road is so wide! Do you think it's the main street in London?'

'I don't know. Maybe. And there's a few people around now, too. Look, there's a horse and cart. Oh, it's a milkman. Let's see if he speaks Yiddish.' They walked over to the cart and waited by the horse until the man came back from making a delivery.

'Excuse me, sir,' said Rafael deferentially, 'Do you speak Yiddish?'

'Does Simon Schwartz speak Yiddish, he asks! Does my horse have four legs? Well, well, look at you two lads! Where have you come from?'

'Riga. We've just arrived,' replied Rafael, relieved and surprised to have found a Yiddish-speaker so easily. 'We're looking for a street called 'Brick Lane', but we have no idea where it is. To be honest, we've no idea where anything is.'

'Riga! Well that's a long old journey. You want Brick Lane? Well, if you didn't know the way, then you've done very well by accident, you're nearly there. It's that way,' he said, pointing. 'Over the main road and the second on the left. It's quite a long road, mind; what number do you want?'

'Forty-eight.'

'That'll be about half way up. Ten minutes walk.'

'Thank you, sir, you've really helped us. We were lucky to find someone who speaks Yiddish.' The milkman roared with laughter.

'In Whitechapel? That's a good one. You try finding someone round here who *doesn't* speak Yiddish! Ha ha! You really have just arrived, haven't you! Right well I better get on. Good luck to you. And remember, if you want milk, Simon Schwartz, Fournier Street.'

'We'll remember. Thank you!' Waving goodbye, the boys hurried off, following his directions. As they went, they encountered more and more people until the pavements became so congested they sometimes had to step into the road to get by.

'I hope they're in,' said Yossel. 'I'm starving. I could do with a big breakfast.'

'Me too,' agreed Rafael. 'Look! It says "Brick Lane". We're here. This is only number six, so it's a way to go yet. Half way up the road, he said.'

The street they were on was lined with shops, each one bearing its name in both English and Yiddish. It felt almost like being at home, and they wondered if the whole of London was like this. There were poulterers, bakers, chandlers, butchers, boot shops, glass cutters, egg merchants, pickle merchants, chemists, every conceivable type of store. But looking above the shops to the rows of lifeless, grimy windows, Rafael wondered if the people who lived in those rooms could actually afford to visit the shops below. He was disappointed; he had hoped that his aunt and uncle might live in more affluent surroundings.

Finally they reached their goal; forty-eight Brick Lane. Rafael closed his eyes and silently said a blessing appropriate to the significance of the moment. He had done it; he had got them safely out of harm's way, travelled the ocean and found his way to this sanctuary, this haven. There would be a warm welcome, a bed, and food.

'I hope your letter got here before us,' said Yossel, chuckling, 'or they're going to get a surprise.'

Rafael pushed open the door.

*

The tenement building they entered had three more floors above the shops, linked by a rickety, dangerous-looking wooden staircase. Not knowing which floor they wanted, they would have to try each in turn. There was nothing on the ground floor except a cupboard, some rank, overflowing bins, and a strong stench of cabbage and of damp, so they climbed, with some trepidation, up the rotten stairs to the tiny first floor landing. There was just one door on this floor and, with barely suppressed excitement, Rafael knocked on it.

After a few moments it was opened by a child, a young girl of about eight. She looked careworn and exhausted, with lank, dirty hair framing her thin, grimy face. Behind her was a chaotic scene, a large, bare room seemingly teeming with small children and toddlers.

'*Du redst eydish?*' asked Rafael — 'Do you speak Yiddish?' The girl just stared at him. '*Mamele? Tatty?*' he asked. She shook her head. He tried a different tack. 'Yacobsohn?' She shook her head again and closed the door.

'Did you see any adults in there?' asked Yossel.

'No. It looks like that little girl is in charge of the whole family. The poor thing; how could that happen? Well, anyhow that's clearly not the right place,' he said. 'Come on, let's try upstairs. They climbed up to the next floor, noticing with dismay the peeling paint, crumbling plasterwork, and black mould stains. Rafael knocked on the door. It opened a crack and a suspicious pair of eyes peered out, about level with Rafael's chest.

'Yes?' said a woman's voice, sharply. Rafael bent down so as to address the eyes directly.

'Excuse me. We're looking for Shmuel and Sara Yacobsohn.'

'Yacobsohn? Top floor.' Rafael breathed a heavy sigh of relief. 'Who are you?'

'We're their nephews. My name is Rafael Yacobsohn, and this is my brother Yossel. We've just arrived. Thank you madam. Sorry to have disturbed you.' The door opened fully and the boys saw that the eyes belonged to a very short, grandmotherly woman dressed in a patched smock and scarf in the Russian style. She looked at the boys carefully.

'Yes. You look like him. Talk the same too. You better come in.'

'Thank you, madam, but we're anxious to see them.'

'I think you had better come in, all the same.' Unsure what to do, but not wishing to appear rude, the boys stepped into the apartment. The woman closed the door carefully behind them and turned round.

'When did you last eat?' she asked.

'Eat? I'm not sure. Yesterday morning I think. Or the day before. Why?'

'Your brother's about to faint.' Rafael turned and saw that Yossel's face had turned white and he was tottering unsteadily. Rafael caught him just in time as he pitched forward. The woman fetched a chair and, with her help, Rafael manoeuvred Yossel onto it just as he began to come round.

'Sit there. You sit down too, whats–your–name elder brother. I'll get you some bread,' said the woman, starting to cut thick slices from a loaf, leaving just a thin crust, which she eyed sadly.

'I'm all right now,' said Yossel. 'Thank you. I'm sure that our uncle...'

'Eat,' interrupted the woman. They obeyed her greedily. 'Slowly,' she urged. 'It's better.' She gave each of them a tin mug of tea taken from a samovar, then watched them as they downed the drink and finished the bread. The colour started to return to Yossel's face.

'Look boys,' she said, at length. 'I'm sorry to have to give you bad news, but your uncle and aunt are not there.'

'Oh. Do you know when they'll be back?' asked Rafael, disappointed.

'I mean, they don't live here any more. They've moved.' Rafael momentarily felt a surge of hope; perhaps they had moved somewhere a little more upmarket.

'Do you know where they've moved to, madam?'

'Yes. New York.' The boys stared at her in horror. 'They left about a week ago.' She went over to the fireplace and took down an envelope from the mantlepiece. 'I think you might recognise this,' she said, holding it out. It was the letter Rafael had written on their last day in Riga. He stared at it numbly. 'Is this from you?' He nodded. 'It arrived the day after they left. I'm sorry, boys.'

'Is their apartment still empty?' asked Rafael, with a last flicker of hope. She shook her head.

'Nothing stays empty around here for long. A new family moved in the same day.' The boys looked at each other, each reading dismay in the other's face. 'I'm sorry.'

Rafael said: 'We passed a building on the way here that said it was a shelter. In Leman Street. Have you heard of it?'

'Everybody knows the Poor Jews' Temporary Shelter. Yes, that's the first place to try. They'll help you if they can.' She looked sadly at her empty shelves. 'You still look hungry. I wish I could give you more, but I'm afraid I have nothing to offer.'

'We'll be all right now. Bless you madam, for your generosity and kindness. We're very grateful.' The boys stood up, shook her hand warmly and went back down to the street.

'The shelter in Leman Street it is, then,' Yossel said dismally.

*

They retraced their steps to the shelter and went in. There was a determinedly severe austerity about the interior, but it was scrupulously clean, and smelled strongly of carbolic. They stood in the entrance hall for a few moments wondering where to go, and were approached by a matronly woman in a long, dark dress with puffed sleeves. She was brisk and efficient, but her expression was kindly. 'Hello, boys. Are you new?'

'Yes, Miss.'

'It's Mrs. Levy. Any money?'

'No, madam.'

'Well, then you're eligible. There's space in the dormitories. Two weeks maximum stay. Had breakfast?'

'No, madam.'

'Go and get some breakfast and then come back here and go through that door — see the sign? — so my husband can register you. Off you go, then. Leave your bags here, they'll be quite safe.' She pointed the way and the boys went gratefully through to the communal dining area, where the delicious smell of fresh bread, coffee and fried potatoes enveloped them like a warm blanket. They stood breathing in the delicious aroma, allowing themselves for the first time to feel their hunger properly, and dived in.

After breakfast, they went as instructed to the office. A man was sitting behind a desk on which lay a large hardback ledger, opened to a blank page. 'You're the new arrivals?' he asked. 'My wife said you'd be along. Take a seat.'

'Thank you, sir,' said Rafael.

'No need to 'sir' me. Mister Levy will do just fine. What's your name, young man?'

'Rafael Yacobsohn.'

'And who is this?'

'My younger brother, Yossel.'

'Ages?

'Eighteen and fifteen.'

'Trade?'

'I'm a metalworker. Yossel is, um…'

'I'm a tailor,' put in Yossel, firmly.

'Where are you from?'

'Russia. Riga.'

'And where are you heading to?'

'Well, we were planning to stay in London, Mister Levy.'

'Oh dear. No, we don't encourage that. There's terrible poverty in the East End. Too many people, overcrowding, not enough work. You'd be well advised to move on. Still, tailor and metalworker, I suppose you may find something. Any relatives in London?'

'No. We thought our uncle and aunt lived here, but they've gone.'

'So you don't know anyone in London?'

'No.'

'*Oy.* Well, look, it's a two week maximum stay here, you know.'

'Yes, Mrs. Levy told us that.'

'All right. One last thing, when did you arrive in England?'

'Late last night. Or early this morning.'

'That's strange. We try to send people out to meet the ships; we weren't expecting one last night. What was the name of the vessel?'

Rafael felt the interview was taking an ominous turn and thought it best not to name the *Kristaps*. 'I don't remember.'

'Oh? Well, what shipping agent did you book the tickets with?'

'*Er...*' Rafael sat in confused silence.

'Oh, I see how it is now,' said Mr. Levy, sitting back in his chair and stroking his chin. 'Unofficial trip, was it? No passports either?' Rafael shook his head. 'I thought not. You do know, don't you, that it's not just illegal, but it's a very dangerous thing you've done? You're fortunate to have made it here safely; those ships are not designed for passengers and some of the captains are real devils. What are you boys running away from?'

'I don't know where to start, Mr. Levy. Yossel was conscripted and it was the only way I could think of to save him. And, there were other things too, I don't really want to say. We've done nothing bad, I swear to you. What are you going to do?' Rafael said in alarm.

'Me?' replied Mr. Levy, holding up his hands. 'Nothing. I'm not here to judge you. I'm here to give you a bed, and help you if I can, that's all.'

Rafael sighed with relief. 'Thank you.'

'All right, here are your dockets. Dormitory four; any beds you like, they're all free. You can leave your bags under your beds, they won't get stolen. But you can't stay here during the day; come back at dusk if you want some supper. We lock the doors at ten.'

Back outside, they decided to explore their new environment. Heading back to Whitechapel High Street they crossed over the now-busy road, dodging the omnibuses, cabs and carts, and made their way into an equally crowded thoroughfare which the sign told them was called Commercial Street. Peering down the narrow side roads, lined with slum lodging houses, the poverty Mr. Levy had mentioned was evident; amid the greengrocers, chemists and other respectable shops, there were pawn shops and beer houses, dark courtyards alive with rats, and littered, sloppy, urine-soaked passageways, their gutters overflowing with sewage. Slimy stone steps led down to dank basements that looked, and smelled, abominable.

Halfway up Commercial Street they were surprised to find, amidst all the squalor, a fine-looking old church standing in a large grassy open space. It was the first bit of greenery they had seen and they wandered in, hoping to find somewhere to rest; a bench, or just some dry grass. They found a bench, but it was occupied by an elderly couple. They seemed to be in distress; the woman was sobbing, her face buried in her hands, and the man appeared to be on the verge of tears.

'Look!' whispered Rafael to Yossel. 'It's the Shusters, from the ship.' They went up to them and Rafael touched the man lightly on the arm. 'Hello,' he said, gently. 'Remember us? What's happened? What's the matter?' Mrs. Shuster didn't react; she seemed not to hear at all.

But her husband, who had one arm round her shoulder, looked up and said: 'Yes. I remember you. *Oy, oy oy*! It was that awful man, that *ganef*. He popped up, out of nowhere, just when we didn't know where to go, and he promised he would help us.'

'The rat-faced man. Yes, we saw you go with him.'

'He said he would help us,' he repeated. 'Show us where to go. But he didn't help us. Instead of that, he robbed us. He stole everything. We've got nothing left. Everything, all gone. Oh! I trusted him. How could I be such a fool?' Tears rolled down his cheek.

'I'm so sorry. How terrible. But look, we know where there's a Jewish shelter. I'm sure they will help you; they're good people. Kind people. Come on, it's not far. We'll take you.'

The grateful couple followed the boys back to Leman Street and, after a brief explanation from Rafael, were delivered into the care of Mr. and Mrs. Levy.

'Bless you, lads,' said Mr. Shuster. 'Thank you for your help.'

'It's nothing, really. I hope everything works out for you. Goodbye.'

*

Back on the street again, the boys walked almost at random around the teeming neighbourhoods of Whitechapel and Spitalfields until the short winter day began to fade into evening and the lamplighters began their rounds.

They made their way back to the hostel through the darkening streets. From the many pubs and beerhouses they passed on the way came shouting, laughter and the sound of piano playing. Women with heavily painted faces stood on the street corners and beckoned to them as they hurried past and strange-looking men peered furtively at them from alleyways, cigarettes dangling from their lips. It was a relief to reach the warmth and security of the hostel.

When they got there, Mr. Levy was walking through the hallway. They stopped him and asked after the Shusters.

'Poor things,' he said. 'It happens all the time, unfortunately; that's why we always try to meet people off the boats. Thank you for bringing them here. We can't accommodate married couples in this building, but we've found them a temporary lodging and we've given them a ticket so they can get food at the soup kitchen. They have a son living somewhere or other in London, so once they find him, if they can, I think they'll be all right.'

Inside the hostel there was a large communal dining-room with a long thin table in the centre, covered with a white, starched, cotton cloth. Around the table sat eighteen or nineteen men of different ages wearing dark jackets and a varied assortment of hats; cloth caps, battered bowlers, Polish *shtreimels*. There were bearded and clean-shaven men; men with lined, impassive faces and men with youthful, worried faces. All were waiting eagerly for something to line their empty bellies.

Rafael and Yossel found spaces on the bench. A hunk of bread, a mug of tea and a bowl of soup was put in front of each man by a small team of young volunteers. Nobody started until Mr. Levy came in and pronounced the blessings. Then every man said 'Amen' and instantly began to devour the supper. There was little chatter. The food was gone in almost no time at all, the bowls were passed up to the end of the table and taken away and, one by one, the men got up and left the room.

'I'm looking forward to sleeping in a bed,' said Yossel, standing up and swaying with tiredness.

'Oh my God, yes,' replied Rafael.

They tumbled straight into bed immediately after supper and were asleep within moments.

*

In the morning, after breakfast, the residents were again turned out until the evening. Now rested and fed, the boys felt more optimistic and were determined not to waste the day. They went out looking for work, Rafael taking his bag of tools.

'I suppose I can always go back to singing,' said Yossel, without enthusiasm.

'No,' replied his brother, firmly. 'No begging. Not if I can help it. You told Mister Levy you were a tailor, and a tailor you shall be. All right?'

'Fine with me.'

'How much can you remember of what *Tatty* taught you?'

'Quite a lot, I think. But it has been three years since I stopped working for him.'

'All right, then, that's a good start. Right. Let's see what we can find.'

They spent the morning methodically working the streets, examining nameplates outside likely–looking buildings, listening for the sound of sewing machines, or peering in through grimy windows. They walked miles, and found several tailoring workshops, but none of them had any vacancies.

'I'm sure we've been down this street before,' moaned Yossel.

'*Hmm.* I think you might be right. It does look sort of familiar.'

'Come on, Rafi, we've been *schlepping* for hours. It's hopeless.'

'No it isn't. It can't be. We've just to keep looking. Come on.'

They traipsed on a little further until Rafael stopped by the entrance to a cellar. 'Wait a minute, Yoss, there's definitely one down there, in the cellar. I can hear the machines, and look, you can see them working, through that grating. We definitely haven't tried this one before. Come on, down you go.'

Yossel went down the steep stone steps and vanished through the door at the bottom. After a few moments he popped his head out of the door and called up the stairs.

'Found a job! They're taking me!'

'*Mazel tov!* What's it like?'

'The same as all the others.'

'You mean crowded, airless, damp and smelly?'

'That's it.'

'Sounds great. When do you start?'

'Right now, this minute. I've just come to tell you. I'll see you at the hostel this evening.' He disappeared once more into the cellar.

'Well, he seems happy enough,' thought Rafael. 'Thank God we found something. Now, what about me?'

He spent the rest of the day looking for a job which would make use of the skills he had laboured for so long to acquire. 'Surely that'll be easy,' he thought. 'How many metalworkers can there be in London?' He pictured himself proudly showing off his certificate and being welcomed with open arms.

But he found nothing.

It wasn't just that there were no vacancies — there didn't seem to be any firms doing metalwork at all.

'There have to be some,' he thought. 'I must just be looking in the wrong place.'

When it got dark he admitted defeat for the day and went back to the hostel. Yossel wasn't there, and when, uncharacteristically, he hadn't turned up by supper time he started to get worried. He wondered whether he should go and look for him but realised it would be a hopeless task, especially in the dark, and he risked being locked out of the hostel, so decided he had no option but to wait.

To his intense relief Yossel appeared in the dormitory shortly before ten o'clock. 'Thank God,' said Rafael. 'Where have you been?'

'What do you mean where have I been? I've been at work. I've only just finished; I came straight back.'

'Oh, I see. That's a really long day. Have you eaten this evening?'

'Never mind this evening, I haven't eaten all day.'

'Poor you. Here, I saved you some bread and cheese.'

'I hoped you would. You're a good brother, Rafi. Here, pass it over, quick.' Yossel grabbed the food and ate hungrily.

'What's the pay?

'Fourpence an hour.'

'Well, I don't really know what that means, so I'm not sure if that's good or bad, but it's definitely something, and it's more than I'm earning. Well done, Yoss, you're the family breadwinner. I'm proud of you.'

'Thank you. So you haven't found a job yet, then?'

'No. But don't worry,' he said brightly, 'Tomorrow is another day. I'll find something.'

'Of course you will,' said Yossel with an encouraging smile. 'You're Rafael Yacobsohn. You always find something.'

It was still pitch dark when Yossel set out for work early the next day. Rafael waited until first light and then set out again with his bag of tools.

This time he ventured further up Commercial Street than he had the previous day, and was relieved to find an area where there were buildings housing a number of small industrial–type workshops. From one of the larger ones he heard the familiar, distinctive sound of metalworking, so he went in.

Men were standing at benches making household goods; pots, pans, kettles, pails, and other items. He watched them for a few minutes until a portly, red-faced man noticed him and came over. He was wearing a waistcoat a size too small for him. Across its straining buttons stretched a thick silver chain. He was evidently the foreman.

'Can I help you?' he demanded in English.

Rafael had a sinking feeling. He had no idea what the man had said. 'Good morning,' he replied deferentially, in Yiddish. 'I am looking for a job.'

'Oh, blimey,' said the portly foreman. 'Another one. Here we go again.' Then, raising his voice, shaking his head and pointing to his ears, he said 'Sorry mate. I can't understand a dicky bird.'

Stymied, Rafael turned to leave. But one of the workers, as thin as the foreman was plump, called out in Yiddish. 'Wait a minute, my friend.' Then he spoke to the foreman in English. 'This young man needs a job, Mister Brown. We are a man short; can't he talk to the boss?'

The foreman scratched his chin, and indicating a door at the back of the workshop, said with a shrug, 'Oh, go on then.'

Rafael nodded gratefully to the worker. '*A groisen dank*,' he said. Then, in a whisper: 'How would you say that in English?'

'You'd say "thank you very much",' the man whispered back.

Rafael repeated the phrase loudly to the foreman, which seemed to please him.

The thin man grinned at Rafael and wished him good luck: '*Heyl zikh arayn.*'

Rafael returned the smile, walked to the rear of the workshop, and knocked firmly on the door.

'Come in,' said a voice in English. Rafael walked in, closing the door behind him. Having no choice, he copied the words he had heard the thin man use, hoping they would convey the correct meaning.

'This young man needs a job,' he said. 'Thank you very much.'

The manager stared at him and laughed. 'Look, mate,' he said, shaking his head. 'If you're going to come over here, you could at least take the trouble to learn the language. Maybe come back when you can speak English, eh?' He waved him out of the room dismissively and turned his attention back to the papers on his desk.

Rafael didn't know what the man had said, but clearly he had been told to go away and there didn't seem to be anything to be gained by staying. Frustrated, he left the office.

When he came out he saw the men in the workshop were looking at him inquisitively and he made an unpremeditated, and reckless, decision. Instead of looking downcast, he arranged his features into a broad smile, and nodded. As he had intended, the others believed he had been taken on. Then he looked for an empty place at the workbench.

He saw a place and started towards it, but the person next to the space, a short man with grey hair and bad teeth, shifted across to block him. 'Piss off,' he growled.

Rafael didn't understand the words, but the man's tone and gesture were unmistakably hostile, so he quickly moved on. To his relief, the man who had helped him earlier waved him over and moved over to make room. Gratefully, Rafael took the place next to him and began to set out his tools.

'Welcome to Smart's,' said the man. 'Isaac Klein. Ike.'

'Hello Ike. I'm Rafael Yacobsohn. Rafi.'

'Have you been in London long, Rafi?'

'Two days.'

'Oh, well that certainly explains why you can't speak the language.'

Mr. Brown, the portly foreman, bustled up.

'Stop talking, you two,' he said. 'You, new bloke, what's your name?'

'He's asking what your name is,' whispered Ike.

Rafael told him. 'All right, Jacobson,' said the foreman. 'Come on, then, let's see if you can make a kettle.' Ostentatiously, he yanked on the silver chain, pulled out a large pocket watch and, holding it lovingly in his podgy hand, looked expectantly at Rafael.

'He wants you to make one of these,' said Ike, holding up a completed kettle. 'Can you do that, Rafi?'

Rafael grinned and nodded. He picked up the materials he needed, selected his tools, and within a short time he had made an almost identical copy of Ike's kettle. Ike looked at it in admiration.

'That's really good work. Mister Brown,' he called, 'please come and take a look at this.'

The foreman examined the kettle and nodded approvingly. 'Not bad. It'll do. Now make a pitcher.' Ike explained to Rafael what was wanted, and he started working on it.

'Careful, Rafi,' said Ike. 'You're going wrong. That's not how we make them.'

'I'm not going wrong, Ike, this is how I was taught. Wait and see.' He worked away confidently for some time and then showed the finished jug to Ike.

'Oh!' said Ike. 'You were right. That's a beautiful job. Where did you learn how to do that?'

'In my apprenticeship,' said Rafael. Just then the manager came out of his office. He strode through the workshop, stopped dead in his tracks and waved Mr. Brown over. 'What's that man doing here, Brown?' he demanded, pointing to Rafael. 'I distinctly told him to go away.' Rafael reddened but said nothing and made no move, waiting to see what would happen.

'I'm terribly sorry, Mister Smart,' said the flustered foreman. 'I thought you'd taken him on.'

'Why on earth did you think that?'

'Because ... I'm not sure, really. He just sort of gave the impression he'd been taken on.'

'Well he hasn't, the cheeky bugger. Get rid of him.'

Ike intervened. 'Mister Smart,' he said, 'He's a really good craftsman. Before you send him away, please take a look at what he's made.'

Smart glanced quickly at Rafael's pitcher. Then he looked at it again, more closely. 'Give it here,' he demanded. '*Huh,*' he grunted, turning it around in his hands thoughtfully. 'Not bad at all. All right. Let him stay. But be more careful in future, Brown. And you, no more tricks.' With that, he jammed on his bowler hat and left the workshop.

'What did he say?' Rafael asked Ike.

'He says you've got a job.'

'Phew! Thank you, again, Ike,' Rafael said. 'I think you must have done that. Thank you so much.'

'You did it yourself. I'm happy if I helped,' said Ike, grinning. 'We've got to look out for each other. But I have to say, with your skills and your *chutzpah,* I think you're going to be fine!'

By the end of the day Rafael knew he had made a good friend in Ike. As the men were putting their coats on, the one who had told him to piss off barged past him. 'Who is that man?' he asked Ike.

'George Draper,' replied Ike. 'Don't mind him. It's nothing personal.'

'It feels a bit personal.'

'If it's any consolation, he doesn't particularly like me either.'

14

Now they had found work, the Yacobsohns' next priority was to find a more permanent place to stay. Because Rafael was earning a skilled worker's wage they were now able to afford a room, and with help from the shelter and its information network, they found one, by coincidence on Brick Lane, close to the house their uncle and aunt had lived in.

The room was on the top floor of number fifty-two, a four-storey brick tenement identical in plan to number forty-eight. Number fifty-two was directly opposite Fashion Street, gateway to a notorious East End slum filled with filthy, stinking courts and passages. The entrance of Fashion Street was flanked by two pubs, the 'George and Guy' on one corner and the 'Three Cranes' on the other. This part of Brick Lane could be a rowdy, threatening place, especially on pay day when the pubs filled with drunks. The noise of drunken singing, shouting and fighting, combined with the lamp outside the George and Guy shining through their window, made it hard to sleep. But the room was definitely a step up from the filthy and overcrowded common lodging houses in which the very poorest immigrants slept, and they were more than happy to have it.

They were sub-letting from a young Jewish family called Goldstein, refugees from the Pale, who had already been in London for several years. Technically the Goldsteins' lease prevented them from taking in lodgers, but it was a common enough arrangement, and for the Goldsteins it was a financial necessity. Rafael and Yossel slept in the one and only bedroom, and Mr. and Mrs. Goldstein and their young son slept in the living-room, on a bed which they were able to put away during the day.

Finally, now the boys were a bit more settled, Rafael felt able to send a letter to their father.

Dear Tatty, he wrote,

I'm sorry it has taken me so long to write. Yoss and I are safe and well. We have secured jobs and lodging; Yoss is doing tailoring and I am working in a tinsmiths. You would be proud of Yoss — he is working hard, and coping well. We have had a lot of adventures which we can tell you all about sometime but the biggest shock was to discover that Uncle Shmuel and Aunt Sara are no longer in London.

We are staying in a house almost next door to where they used to live, which feels very strange. The old lady who lives in the flat below theirs said they've gone to America, but the Goldsteins, the family we rent our room from, think it's South Africa. We don't know which one it is. I have written our address at the top of this letter in case you would like to write to us here.

Tatty, I'm sorry we had to leave in such a rush, without seeing you and saying goodbye properly. I hope you are not angry. As I said in my letter, it was necessary, otherwise Yoss would by now have suffered the fate which you and Mamele have done so much to try to avoid. I hope his disappearance hasn't caused you any trouble with the authorities.

You and Hannah must be married by now. We are sorry we were not able to attend your wedding but we pray that you and she make a happy life together. Please send our best wishes to Ester and Reuben.

It is my dearest wish that we will all be together again one day, somehow. Until that happy day arrives, we send you all our love.

Rafi and Yoss

Every morning, the boys set off for work before dawn and got home well after dark, and by the weekend Rafael was exhausted, although Yossel seemed tireless. Early on Friday evening they went with Hyman Goldstein to Schewzik's Russian Vapour Baths along with, it seemed, half the Jewish men in the East End, and on *Shabbos* morning they took the short walk with the whole Goldstein family to the newly built *shul* at the back of 19 Princes Street; Rafael looked carefully at Yossel as they walked to *shul*; he felt proud of his younger brother. He had obviously grown a lot in the last couple of years, not just in height, although that was impressive enough, but in character. He remembered how much fuss he had made about being told to sweep the floor on his first day at Gozinsky's, and here he was, at the end of a week toiling in a sweatshop in London and he hadn't complained at all. What a difference.

Unless…

There was no time to finish the thought because they had already arrived at the synagogue. It was tiny, built into the back garden of a terraced house, but it had a small ark, three ornate candelabras hanging from the ceiling and even a women's gallery built around three sides of the narrow room and supported, Rafael smiled to see, by slender Solomonic columns.

After *shul*, the Goldsteins went home but Rafael asked Yossel to walk with him a while. He needed to talk to him, he said. They walked a few yards side by side and, glancing at his brother, Rafael could tell that Yossel looked shifty. He knew immediately his suspicion was correct.

'How long did you last?' he asked, in as neutral a tone as he could manage.

'What do you mean?'

'You know exactly what I mean,' he snapped. 'At the tailors. Did they fire you, or did you quit?'

'I quit at the end of the second day.'

'Oh, my God.'

Yossel stopped and turned to face his brother. 'Rafi, you've no idea how bad it is in there. It's a filthy, airless sweatshop.'

'Of course it's a sweatshop, Yossel. I know that. But it's work. Work, don't you understand? Work means food, and clothes, and somewhere to sleep.'

'And it means a sore back, sore eyes and sore fingers. It means people shouting at you, telling you what to do, to hurry up, to stop talking. It means no time to drink, or eat, or pee. It means you never see the sun and you never breathe fresh air.'

'A day and a half! You did a day and a half!' Rafael could no longer keep the anger out of his voice. 'People round here do it for years, decades, and they're glad to have it. You quit after a day and a half!'

'All right, stop shouting. I'm not going back, that's it.'

'So what have you been doing the last two days when I thought you were at the tailors?' Yossel jutted out his jaw and clamped his mouth tightly shut. 'You've been begging, haven't you? What did I say? I won't have my brother begging!'

'You don't get to decide. You're not my father!'

Rafael made no immediate reply to this; he was too angry to speak. At last, he said 'Fine,' and walked away, leaving Yossel standing.

*

The following day the tension between the brothers had hardly lessened. Rafael felt he needed to be by himself, so announced he was going to take a look at the market and left quickly, in case Yossel offered to come with him.

He elbowed his way slowly through the teeming, jostling crowds in the market, letting the vendors' cries and the shoppers' chatter wash over him. There were voices talking in Yiddish, German, Russian, English, shouting, bargaining, *kvetching*, wheedling. There were smells too; animal smells and the smell of frying, onions, fish, potatoes, meat. Every conceivable type of stall was there; *schmutter*, trinkets, food, pots, pans, ornaments, books. He bought nothing, lingered nowhere, kept moving through the crowd. As he did so he felt the tightly-wound spring of anger inside him begin to uncoil, to be replaced with a feeling of intense sadness. He allowed himself to stray wherever the crowd carried him and felt himself drifting, directionless, without aim or purpose, alone, friendless, betrayed. Bitter tears ran down his cheeks, and he let them flow.

After some time of this, he found he began to feel a little better. He made his way hastily back to the room and was pleased to find his brother still there. Yossel looked up when he came in and went to turn away but Rafael caught hold of his arm.

'Yoss. Stop. There's something I want to say.'

'I don't want to hear it.' Shaking off his brother's hand Yossel abruptly left the room. Moving to the window Rafael could see him hurrying angrily along Brick Lane and disappearing into the crowd. He returned late at night and went straight to bed.

In the morning, the first working day of his second week at Smart's, Rafael shook Yossel awake early.

'Go away,' he grumbled, turning over in bed.

'I'm going. But I have to talk to you first. Wake up. Look at me, Yoss. I apologise. I'm sorry. Can you hear me? I'm sorry. You were right; I'm not your father. I can't tell you what to do. You're old enough to make your own decisions. You're all I have, and I'm all you have, and neither of us is going to get very far without the other. We can't afford to fall out. That's it. That's what I wanted to say.'

Yossel sat up. 'Thank you for apologising Rafi. I forgive you,' he said, magnanimously. Rafael waited, arms crossed. There was a long pause.

'All right,' Yossel said at last. 'Yes. Of course, I'm sorry too.' Rafael smiled and they shook hands. But now that he had started Yossel had more to say. 'I don't know what's the matter with me, Rafi. Why do I get so angry? Of course you're only looking out for me, I know that. I hate to admit it but you're doing a good job too.'

'Thank you Yoss. That means a lot to me,' Rafael said, with sincerity.

'Look, I have actually been thinking about this, believe it or not. I'm going to get up in a minute and look for a job and by the time you come back tonight, with any luck I'll have found one. And, this time, when I do find one I'm going to do everything I can to keep it. I promise.'

'That's great, Yoss. I can't ask for more than that. So, are we still friends?'

Yossel grinned. 'I'm not sure I'd go that far. We're still brothers, anyhow. I can't seem to do anything about that.'

'Then that'll have to do. Right, I'd better go. I'm going to be late.'

Hurrying through the streets Rafael suddenly had a vision of himself as a nine-year old hurrying to *heder*. He wished it was "Bushy" Leibowitz waiting for him now instead of Mr. Brown and his infernal watch. He arrived at the workshop just in time; the foreman was standing in the doorway, clipboard in one hand and pocket-watch in the other. Brown glared at Rafael, looked at the watch, and made a note on the clipboard. Rafael slid into his place.

'Well done' said Ike, grinning. 'Just in time, by the look of it.'

'Phew. What is it with Brown and that wretched watch?'

'I know. How he loves that watch. He's had it ever since I've worked here, and probably a lot longer than that. Apparently it was passed down to him by his grandfather.'

He was interrupted by a shout from the other end of the workshop. 'Stop talking, you two.'

At the end of the day Ike said to Rafael, in English, 'Fancy a pint?'

'What does that mean?'

'That's one of the first phrases you should learn in English. It means would you like to come to the pub with me and drink some beer?'

'You said all that in three words? Yes, I've been looking forward to trying a pub, but I didn't want to go by myself.'

'Don't blame you. Come on, I usually go to the Ten Bells.'

The Ten Bells at the end of Fournier Street was heaving with customers in various stages of inebriation but Ike, navigating the throng with polished expertise, installed Rafael in a corner, instructed him not to move, and headed to the bar. He returned a few minutes later carrying two foaming pint glasses.

'Trumans,' he said. 'Made in Brick Lane.'

'I know, I can smell the brewery from our room, even in my sleep. Thank you, Ike. I'm excited; my first taste of English beer. *L'chaim!*'

'*L'chaim*! Or, as they say here, cheers!'

Rafael took a swig of the beer and looked at Ike in perplexity.

'I thought you said this was beer, Ike?'

Ike laughed. 'It is beer, I'm afraid, Rafi. English beer. Don't worry, you'll get used to it. At least it's safer than the water. Tastes better too.'

Rafael took another cautious sip and hoped Ike was right about getting used to it. Putting the strange taste of the beer to the back of his mind, he realised this was his opportunity to ask Ike the thing that had been bothering him since his first day at Smart's.

'Ike, I wanted to ask you about George Draper. Why does he have such a problem with me?'

'Like I said, it's not personal. He's lived round here his whole life, and his father before him, and he's worked with John Smart since he was a young man. He's one of the old East End types; he doesn't like immigrants, especially Jews. He says they've turned his home into a foreign country. There are lots of people who feel like him, I'm afraid. It's actually difficult to blame them — so many Jews have poured in from Russia since the pogroms started that it's forced a lot of the old Londoners out. We speak a language they don't understand, eat different food, wear different clothes. It's tough for them.'

'Thanks for explaining that, Ike. It may sound stupid, but I hadn't really looked at it like that before.'

'Of course, we're not the first immigrants in the East End; the Huguenots and the Irish were here before us. But nobody worries about people who were already here before they were born; it's only the new ones they object to. And by the way, it's not just the English who dislike new arrivals; in some ways the Jews who have been here for a while are even more hostile. They've tried so hard to integrate and when people like you come along — no offence — you remind everyone that Jews are different. Talking of which, have you seen the three men over there who keep looking at us? Come on, drink up, I think it's probably time we left. Nope, it's too late; here they come.'

Looking up Rafael now also saw the small group Ike had drawn his attention to. The three men elbowed their way through the crowd and stood in a small ring, blocking Rafael and Ike into the corner.

'Oy! You two,' said one of the men. 'If you come into a London pub, then you talk English, all right? We don't like that foreign jabber round here.'

'My friend and I we were just going,' replied Ike in English.

'Oh, so you do speak English!' said the second. 'Then why were you talking in foreign?'

'I speak English but my friend hasn't had time to learn it; he's only been in London two weeks. I'm sorry if it bothered you. He is trying.'

'Well tell him to get on with it,' said the third, and the three truculent men moved away to get another drink.

'I'm sorry about that, Rafi,' said Ike as they walked hurriedly away. 'Don't let those three men, or people like Draper, make you think badly of England and the English. This really is not like Russia; they're decent, tolerant people once they get to know you. They're definitely terrible with languages though. I think once you learn English you'll find things go much better.'

'Well, I'm trying. How's this: *Fancy a beer?*'

'Not bad,' laughed Ike. 'Well remembered. Good start. That will get you a long way.'

*

Rafael got back to the room about nine, but there was no sign of Yossel; he shambled in well after ten o'clock, took off his boots, collapsed on the bed without saying anything other than 'Hi,' and was asleep in seconds.

A few hours later he was awake again. Wearily he got up, put on his boots and headed straight for the door.

'Hang on,' said Rafael. 'Before you go, tell me what happened. You obviously found a job, then?'

'Yes. Another sweatshop. Almost as bad as the first one. Wonderful girl there, though. I think she likes me.' He shut the door and Rafael could hear him wearily descending the rickety staircase.

It was a cold morning and the fog was almost impenetrable as Rafael made his way to work. He was just one of thousands of men and women shuffling through the East End, hands thrust in pockets, shoulders up and scarves pulled tightly round their raw, red faces.

He realised that, yet again, he had it better than many; true, his work was repetitive and not exactly fulfilling, and the foreman with his damned watch could be tyrannical, but he was doing something he enjoyed, that took some skill, and he liked the company of the other men. It was all thanks to their father. Had he thanked him properly? He wasn't sure he had.

His father was much on his mind; they hadn't yet received a reply to the letter he had sent him, but a few days later it arrived, and he opened it eagerly.

> *My dear Rafi,*
>
> *I cannot tell you how relieved I was to get your letter and to learn that you are safe and well. I imagined all sorts of things. It feels very strange to me that you are there, not only in the same city but actually the same street where Shmuel and his family*

have been living. I wonder what Brick Lane is like? I am imagining a broad, leafy boulevard lined with stately brick houses.

'Is that what Uncle Shmuel told you?' wondered Rafael, smiling at the contrast between the description and the reality.

I am so very sorry they were not there when you arrived; that must have been a terrible shock and disappointment to you. I have now received a letter from them in New York, (so the old lady in the flat below was right). I think they must have left only a very short while before you got there.

There was some trouble when Yossel failed to report for duty. As there was no record of him leaving the country the authorities believed he was hiding somewhere, either in Riga or Tukum. Fortunately your letter, and especially the envelope with its English stamp and all the different postmarks, helped us to convince them that he was out of their reach, and they have finally left us alone.

Things have changed a lot since you left. Zeide no longer comes round for Shabbos — you can see it would be rather awkward — but I hear that he is all right, so that is good.

I miss you both so much, Look after each other, and do write again when you can.
With love from
Tatty

Time went by, and still Yossel went out early and came back late. At the end of each week he put a pitifully small pile of coins on the table but, together with Rafael's wage, it was enough for the rent, food, and coal for the fire when it got cold later in the year.

The question was, though, how long could he keep it up? He was young, and he was fit and strong, for now, but he was almost past the point of exhaustion; he worked, he ate and he slept. Nothing else.

Because he heard English spoken at work Rafael was beginning to recognise words and phrases and, occasionally, to try speaking a little English. The sounds felt strange in his mouth and he knew he would never sound like an Englishman, but he was determined to get to grips with the language as quickly as he could because he knew it was a crucial part of the key to escaping the East End Jewish ghetto.

He noticed that Jewish children playing in the street called to each other not in Yiddish but in English; he supposed that they were encouraged, or even forced, to speak it at school. He understood why that would be, but he wondered what their parents felt about it.

Ike was a popular and respected worker, and his friendship made it easier to build relationships with the other workers at Smart's. It was a small but motley group, all men, mostly Jews and mostly from an earlier wave of immigration. As Ike had warned him, these people were generally wary and suspicious of new arrivals.

But they recognised something in Rafael; not just his skill with metal, but something about his cleverness, his vitality, his kindness and decency which endeared him to them all, or at least all except George Draper. He remembered their names and stories and asked after their families. And he crafted metal into items of such quality that they could not help but be impressed.

One Friday in early spring Ike and Rafael were chatting together during the lunch break,

'Your brother's a garment worker, isn't he?' asked Ike. 'Is he going on the march tomorrow?'

'What march?'

'Hasn't he talked to you about it?'

'We almost never get a chance to talk. When he's not at work, he's asleep. What is this march?'

'The union is organising a march of garment workers through Whitechapel to demand shorter working days.'

'But tomorrow's *Shabbos*.'

'When else are they going to do it?'

'Good point. Well it's understandable they would want to march; everyone can see how inhuman the sweatshop conditions are.'

'You would think so, wouldn't you? But the problem is, the bosses won't change anything until they're forced to. Just like Bryant and May.'

'What do you mean?'

'Oh, I keep forgetting you've not been here long. The girls at the match factory in Bow went on strike last year.'

'Girls?'

'Yes, the match workers are mostly girls and young women. It was about the fourth or fifth time they'd held a strike, but this time was different; to everyone's surprise they won, although not before they had some nasty run-ins with the police. Still, their victory has put heart into workers all over.'

'This all sounds very familiar. It sounds like the sort of thing I saw in Riga; I wonder how it will end.'

'God knows. Listen, if Yossel does go, tell him to be careful, all right?'

'I will. But careful of what?'

But there was no time for Ike to reply, because Mr. Brown the foreman, glaring at his watch, shouted 'Lunch break's over. Back to work.'

*

The following morning as he was getting ready for *shul,* Rafael said, innocently, 'Not coming today, Yoss?'

'No, I think I'll give it a miss this week, Rafi. I'll just stay home quietly.'

'I see. You're not going on the march, then?'

'Oh. You heard about that.' He looked at his brother warily, tensing for an argument.

'Don't worry, I'm not going to lecture you. As a matter of fact, I'm proud of you. Did you join the union?'

'Yes. Of course.'

'That's good. Hopefully the union can achieve something; a march sounds like a good place to start. So what's the plan?'

'I'm not really sure. We're meeting in Berner Street, that's all I know. God knows how many people are going to turn up, but most of the people where I work said they were going, so if that's any guide it could be hundreds.' He looked at Rafael. 'Want to come with me?'

'I'm tempted but, no, I don't think so, actually. This is your fight.'

'Well, thank you for not trying to talk me out of it.'

'Like I said, I'm proud of you. Keep your eyes out, though; trust me, I know how these things can go wrong. I know England is not Russia, but police are police. Stay near the back, and at the first sign of trouble, get out of there, all right?'

'Relax, Rafi. There won't be any trouble.'

When Yossel arrived at the rallying point outside the International Workers Education Club he was astonished at what he saw. There were thousands of people — over three thousand, he was told later — many with banners or flags; there was even a brass band. The marchers listened to a rousing, anarchic speech from the organiser, a Lithuanian Jew called William Wess. He told them they were marching to Duke's Place, to the Great Synagogue, where Hermann Adler, the Chief Rabbi of the British Empire, was conducting the service, to pressure him to support their demand for an eight-hour working day.

There was a holiday atmosphere. The crowd was good-humoured on the surface, but there was a grim determination underneath. Yossel felt the exhilaration of action, of being part of something that felt powerful, unstoppable. All the same, he wished Rafael was there.

The head of the procession moved off, and slowly the amorphous group started to form itself into a line. It was an astonishing sight, the downtrodden poor parading through the streets of Whitechapel and Aldgate. They drew some cheers, but also received disapproving stares and boos, especially from orthodox Jews angry at what they considered the desecration of the Sabbath.

The marchers walked along in buoyant mood until they got to Duke's Place. The Rabbi, they were told, had refused to meet them, or preach on their behalf, and their mood soured. There were angry shouts and chants, at which point the police moved in.

Neither police nor marchers wanted trouble and there were only minor scuffles, but it was enough for Yossel who, feeling suddenly vulnerable, terrified and alone, ran back the way he had come, dodging through the alleys and narrow streets until he reached the safety of Brick Lane. Shivering, he put his hands in his coat pockets for warmth, and was surprised to find something grainy in the bottom of each one.

He took some out, looked at it and smiled. It was salt.

'Thanks, Rafi,' he murmured.

15

Rafael had been working at Smart's for about six months. He was very glad to have a job, but he couldn't help admitting to himself that it wasn't what he really wanted to do. The items Smart's made were simple functional pieces, required little skill to make and offered almost no room for creativity.

He thought about the ornate candelabras hanging from the synagogue roof and how satisfying they must have been to make. Even the lantern on the wall outside the George and Guy had a complexity that made it interesting to look at; those were the type of things he longed to work on, but there was simply no opportunity for that sort of thing where he was.

One Monday morning he arrived to find some of the men standing on the pavement outside the premises. The door was locked. This had never happened before; the foreman, Mr. Brown, was always the first one there. He would open up and stand by the door with his watch and clipboard, checking off each man's name as he arrived. But not today.

As the minutes went by, and the rest of the workforce arrived, the men became more and more puzzled and concerned. Had the firm gone out of business? Were they all out of a job? It was very worrying.

After they had been waiting outside for about half an hour, John Smart arrived.

'What are you men doing standing around?' he demanded.

'The door's locked, Mister Smart. We can't get in.'

'What? Well, where's Mister Brown?'

'We don't know, sir.'

'Has anyone been to his house?'

'No, sir. Nobody knows where he lives.'

'Well this is very inconvenient. One of you had better go and see what's happened. No, wait, I'll let you in and you can start work; I'll go myself.' He fished out his key and, after fumbling with the lock, managed to get the door open. 'Right in you go. You can make up the time at the end of the day.'

He ushered them in and marched off angrily. When he returned some time later he looked even grimmer. He stood inside the door and clapped his hands to get the men's attention.

'Listen here,' he called. 'Mister Brown has been the victim of a vicious attack. He was set upon in the street on his way home from work on Friday and beaten unconscious. He is not expected to recover fully. The motive for the attack appears to have been theft; his valuable watch and chain are missing.'

He moved towards his office through a shocked silence. As he reached the door he turned and said: 'I trust that none of you men were involved. Draper — in here, if you please.'

Draper followed Mr. Smart into the office. The two men came back out a few moments later. Draper was smirking from ear to ear.

'Men,' announced Mr. Smart. 'Mister Draper is the new foreman.'

*

Draper embraced the foreman's role with relish; having worked at the firm for so long he felt it was no more than his due.

Unfortunately, though, he was utterly unsuited to it. He was chaotic and disorganised, gave contradictory or confusing orders and roundly berated the workers for his own mistakes. He refused to speak directly to Rafael, steadfastly maintaining the fiction that Rafael, despite his increasing fluency in English, still could not understand a word. He issued instructions to Rafael only through Ike. 'Klein,' he would say, 'tell Jacobson he needs to make three more like that before he goes home.'

Or perhaps:

'Here's a new order just come in, Klein. Jacobson's to do it. Tell him what's wanted, will you?'

If Rafael answered him directly he affected not to be able to hear or understand him, and in the end it was easier to go along with it. But it affronted and irritated both him and Ike, as it was meant to.

By the end of the first week with Draper in his new role as foreman, Rafael was fed up, and decided it was high time he found a way out. He knew he wanted to work for a firm that made lamps, so decided to approach the problem methodically.

He needed to find out what firms there were, and started making a note of names and addresses he found in newspaper advertisements. This proved to be a tedious task; he found a few companies that way but, he thought, there must be many more than this.

Eventually he realised that a better method was simply to go round the streets examining the lanterns he found and locate the manufacturers' marks set into each one. This way, he could make a list of their names and appraise their quality at the same time.

He spent much of his precious free time peering at lamp posts or squinting up at wall lanterns, and in this way he compiled what he thought must be a pretty comprehensive list of local companies.

In the new library in Whitechapel High Street he found a reference book which told him the addresses of each of the firms, and this helped him to compile a shortlist of three local companies which seemed to produce the right type of product.

'So far, so good,' he thought. But now what? How could he interview for another job when he was working every day? Did he have the nerve to leave Smart's without a guarantee of finding something else?

No, he didn't. So, for a time, nothing changed.

*

The following Monday, Ike came to work in a state of great excitement.

'You'll never guess what I saw when I was in the pawnbroker's yesterday,' he whispered to Rafael.

'Why were you in the pawnbroker's?'

'Never mind, that's not the point. Guess what I saw?'

'I don't know, what did you see?'

'Brown's watch!'

'What? How do you know it was his?'

'I've seen it often enough, I should know what it looks like. Same case, same chain, same dents and scratches, everything. It was definitely his.'

'Well, well. I wonder if it was the thief that pawned it, or someone he passed it on to.'

'That's still not the point. The point is this — whoever it was can't have got much for it.'

'Why do you say that?'

'Because it's broken. I don't mean it just got broken in the attack or something; the pawnbroker said it clearly hasn't worked for years; it's all rusted up inside. All those years he terrorised us with that watch, and it was all an act. It didn't even go!'

Rafael said nothing for a long time, so Ike prompted him. 'Well say something, then. What do you think of that?'

Rafael seemed to come out of a trance. He turned to Ike and said: 'I should be furious but, do you know? I'm actually rather impressed. It was so convincing. He had everyone believing in that watch. He was much cleverer than I thought he was. Poor man, though — flashing his silver watch everywhere has cost him dearly. Look, Ike, I don't think you should tell the others about this.'

Draper came bustling over, scowling.

'Oy, Klein, tell your pal to get a move on. I ain't seen him do a stroke of work yet.'

'Yes, Mister Draper.' But Draper wasn't finished.

'Just because Smart's not here today, he thinks he can get away with bloody murder. Typical bloody foreigner. The place is swarming with them. He tricked his way into the job, and now look at him.' Raising his voice and waving his arms to include the rest of the workforce, he went on. 'You're all the same. Bone idle, the lot of you. You're all a bloody useless bloody waste of space. Cockroaches. You need to go back to Russia and let some proper English people have these jobs.'

It was nothing, really. They'd all heard it a thousand times before. But it was the final straw. Rafael took off his apron, laid it, neatly folded, on the workbench, and packed away his tools. George Draper and the others watched, open-mouthed, waiting to see what would happen.

'Mister Klein,' Rafael said to Ike, in the best English he could manage. 'To Mister Draper a message please give. Please say him he is very rude man and so Mister Yacobsohn is his job now quitted.'

'Mister Draper,' said Ike, 'Mister Yacobsohn says…'

'I heard him,' growled Draper.

Rafael addressed Draper directly. 'Ah, Mister Draper, it is good you can now hear me. Just in time. Goodbye.'

He shook hands with a flabbergasted Ike, who asked him, in Yiddish: 'Are you absolutely sure about this, Rafi?'

'Oh yes, quite sure. I've been through too much and come too far to put up with this shit. Don't worry about me. Good luck, Ike. I'll miss you. Thank you for everything.'

'I'll miss you too. Good luck, Rafi.'

With that, Rafael picked up his bag of tools, turned on his heel, and, to the applause of his fellow workers, left the works for the last time.

*

THE LAMPMAKER — PART THREE

He went back to the rented room in Brick Lane feeling rather sick. A gesture of defiance is all very well, he reflected, but how long would it be before he came to regret it?

He didn't let himself think too hard about it. Instead, he changed out of his work clothes, put on his *Shabbos* suit and, armed with his bag of tools and his list of manufacturers, went out to find another job.

The first factory on the shortlist turned out to be quite a long way away, the furthest west he had ventured. He thought about paying for a ride on an omnibus, or trying the Metropolitan Railway, but he had no idea how long it would be before he was earning again, so he decided to save his pennies and walk. By the time he got to the factory his feet were sore.

This was a very different part of London to the one he was used to; the air smelled different and there were no Yiddish signs on the shops here. At the factory gate he was faced immediately by a large sign on which was written, in English and Yiddish: 'No Jews.'

He turned and retraced his steps.

The second factory was in Bow and looked more promising at first. Here he did manage to speak to the foreman, but was told firmly that they were not hiring.

There was only one factory left on his shortlist. He found it at the top of Commercial Street, near Shoreditch station. This was the only one of the three with a Jewish–sounding name, Cohen & Company, and the one he felt most hopeful about.

Entering the main door, Rafael found himself in a familiar world; it felt so much like Gozinsky's he half expected to see Salomon Strauss greeting him with his twinkling smile.

Recollecting himself, he walked purposefully across the floor. Nobody questioned him as he headed toward the door at the end of the workshop that clearly held the offices. He turned the handle and found himself in a small room containing a desk with a typewriter, an old wooden filing cabinet and a few chairs. There was nobody in the room. Another door led through to an inner office. The name Samuel Cohen was picked out in gold lettering.

Rafael knocked and after a moment the door was opened by a middle-aged man dressed in an expensive-looking suit. He was rather under average height and sported a small, rather dapper, moustache. 'Mister Cohen?' asked Rafael.

'Yes. What do you want?'

'I'm sorry to knock.' He indicated the empty room. 'Your secretary is not here.'

'She's ill, blast her. I wasn't expecting anyone. Do you have an appointment?'

'Yes, Mister Cohen.'

'Really? Well in that case I suppose you had better come in.' He escorted Rafael into his large, comfortable office, motioned to one of a pair of leather-covered, wing-backed chairs and sat in the other one, facing him. 'Well then, Mister, er...?'

'Yacobsohn. Rafael Yacobsohn.'

'Ah. You'll think me rude, Mister Yacobsohn, but I can't at this moment recall what our appointment was about.'

'I come to help you, Mister Cohen,' said Rafael in his halting, heavily accented English. 'There is a master craftsman working in the city of Riga called Salomon Strauss. You have heard of him?'

'Strauss? No, I don't believe so. German, is he?'

'Yes, exactly.'

'Ah, very good with metal, the Germans. We can't match their workmanship here.'

'Indeed. He has very good craftsman. I have been since many years in Riga to study the working ways of Herr Strauss, and I come now here, in London, to show it to you.'

'To me? Why me?'

'I examine your lamps, Mister Cohen. You are already very good lampmaker. So I come here.'

'I see. I only have one question.'

'Yes?'

'What the devil are you talking about?'

'Er...'

Mr. Cohen stood up. Looking down at Rafael, and switching to Yiddish, he began to speak more rapidly and with none of his earlier reserve. 'You didn't have an appointment with me today. What is all this nonsense? Who are you?'

Rafael blushed deeply and dropped his head. 'I'm sorry, Mr. Cohen,' he said, switching back to Yiddish with relief. 'I didn't know how else to get into see you, so I lied about the appointment. Everything else really is the truth. I really have completed an apprenticeship with Salomon Strauss. At Gozinsky's in Riga.'

Mr. Cohen sat down again, somewhat mollified. The mention of Gozinsky seemed to have eased the strain somewhat. 'Gozinsky's? You should have said that sooner. Of course I know of Gozinsky's. It has a very fine reputation.'

'My younger brother and I have been in England for about six months. I really am a good craftsman, sir, fully trained in the German method. I have a certificate if you would like to see it.'

'*Hmm.* Show me.' He examined the certificate and handed it back. 'Well, it looks real enough. If it's all true, then you could actually be the very man we're looking for to give us an edge over our rivals, despite all that balderdash you started off with. How old are you?'

'Eighteen, sir.'

'Still very young. You're obviously Jewish. Single?'

'Yes, sir.'

'Well, look here, I don't condone the way you sneaked in at the start. But you've got pluck, I'll say that for you. And you're a quick thinker. You're a fast learner too, if you've only been here six months.'

He paused to think for a moment, and went on. 'All right. You know what I'll do? I'll give you a trial until the end of the week. If you're as good as you say I'll give you a job. But if you haven't proved yourself by then, you're out. You'll start tomorrow morning. But no more lying, all right? Off you go, then, I've got work to do.'

'Yes sir. Thank you, Mr. Cohen.'

*

Rafael was delighted to have found work, even though he felt intensely embarrassed that his naive, improvised *spiel* had been so easily picked apart. He wasn't quite sure why it had landed him a job instead of getting him thrown out on his ear, but he was happy to accept the outcome nonetheless.

Early in the morning, he took the short walk up Brick Lane, past the Truman's Brewery and along Quaker Street to the factory. This time the secretary was at her desk in the outer office. She looked up when he came in.

'Can I help you?'

'Good morning. Yes please. My name is Yacobsohn. I am new.'

'You want the foreman, Mister Rothstein.'

'Where can I find him?' he started to say, but the secretary, losing interest in him, went into the inner office leaving him alone. He shrugged and went back to the factory floor. He looked around as other workers arrived and went to their workplaces. Then he spotted someone he thought must be the foreman, and went over to him.

'Mister Rothstein?'

'Yes.'

Whereas Samuel Cohen was about the same age as Rafael's father, Jacob Rothstein seemed to be almost as old as his grandfather. He was a wiry man, still full of energy despite his age and bubbling over with humour. As Rafael was to discover, he had been with Cohen since the factory's early days and had been foreman for most of that time.

'I'm Rafael Yacobsohn. I am here to start today.'

'Ah yes! The man who's come to teach us how to make lamps,' teased Rothstein. 'You're rather young to be such a master.'

Rafael looked shamefaced.

'I'm only teasing,' said Rothstein, slapping Rafael on the back. 'I heard all about your interview with Cohen. He thought it was hilarious. One word of advice for you, though. Don't try to get one over on Cohen. Don't let that 'fluffy old man' act fool you; he's as sharp as a razor.'

'Yes. I found that out.'

'Right, well, stay there. I'll get you an apron and set you to work.'

Rafael's first day at Cohen's caused a sensation. He was set to make a lantern to one of the factory's patterns and he did it with such precision, and such effortless skill and affinity with the material, that it was clear he had an exceptional talent. Jacob Rothstein clapped him on the back and, in his report to Samuel Cohen at the end of the day, expressed himself more than satisfied. At the end of the week Rafael received his pay and the offer of a permanent job which he enthusiastically accepted. He was delighted to see that the pay was quite a bit higher than he was getting at Smart's. At last, he felt, his apprenticeship was really beginning to pay off.

Ever since he had watched electric lighting being installed at Gozinsky's, Rafael had wanted to find out more about electricity and how it could be used. He applied himself to the task of finding out everything he could, by seeking out those in the factory who had knowledge supplemented by research in the books at Whitechapel library. He asked Mr. Rothstein if he could work on the electrical side of the business, and soon he had a good working understanding of it. Within a fairly short time he knew as much about electrical engineering as most of the others and was able to work on any of the factory's projects.

At the same time as he was studying electricity, he was also studying Jacob Rothstein. He liked him and admired his skill as a foreman. He was calm and well organised and he had the trick of being friendly with the workers, able to share a cup of tea and a joke, and at the same time to command discipline and respect. He was not condescending to those beneath him in the factory hierarchy, and he was respectful, but not subservient, to those above. Rafael decided that, should he ever find himself in a position of authority, he would model himself on Jacob Rothstein.

*

On a stiflingly hot day in August the streets of Whitechapel filled with the unexpected sounds of music, chanting and cheering. A brass band appeared, heading a huge procession. People hurried out to see what it was all about.

The procession took a long time to go past. At its centre came an enormous model ship on wheels, big enough to carry twenty men, adorned with flags and notices, pulled by horses.

The dockers were on strike.

When the last strikers had passed, and with the sounds of the march fading into the distance, people returned to their homes or workplaces, chattering excitedly.

Over the next few days the marches not only continued, they became ever larger. The docks employed a vast number of men and soon almost all of them had joined the strike. The docks fell silent and the great Port of London, engine room of the mighty British Empire, was paralysed.

Yossel was thrilled to the bone. On Sunday, he and Rafael walked to Tower Hill to listen to the rousing speeches of the union leaders.

'It'll be us on strike next,' said Yossel. 'The garment workers. Everyone's whispering about it at work.'

'Are you sure? I mean, the Empire needs the Port of London, so the dockers have a lot of power. No disrespect, Yoss, but if the tailors go on strike won't the bosses just sit back and wait for them to starve?'

'I don't know, maybe. But I think if we stick together we can win. Remember the match girls.'

'You may have a point. I do think things are changing — the unions are getting more organised and there is quite a bit of public sympathy for the workers. Look, the police are just calmly watching this protest; I don't feel like they have been ordered to disrupt it.'

Yossel was right about the tailors; they came out on strike two weeks after the dockers. Their demands included a twelve-hour working day, with an hour for lunch. Like the dockers' strike, the tailors' strike was well supported, well run and, most surprisingly, well funded.

The Empire couldn't stand the cost of having the docks out of action and, predictably, the dockers won their battle.

There was, as expected, an attempt to starve the tailors back to work, but, to Rafael's surprise and delight, after five weeks their demands were met. Yossel and his workmates celebrated the unions' victories long into the night.

16

The Yacobsohn brothers now had enough money to be able a move out of the Goldsteins' apartment in Brick Lane to a larger lodging in Great Alie Street, south of Whitechapel High Street.

Now he felt more financially secure, and the English language felt more familiar in his ears and on his tongue, Rafael began to explore further afield. He liked to ride the city's trains which connected the East End to the West End and he loved visiting the National Gallery in Trafalgar Square, where he wandered for hours, lost in the beauty of the artworks. It was Rosa, of course, who had awoken in him an appreciation of art; he had never seen a painting, or given any real thought to art before he met her.

He soon settled on which painting in the gallery was his favourite, and he always visited it last, as a final treat. He knew very little about it, other than what the information label told him. It was apparently called Rain, Steam and Speed, by an artist called Turner. It depicted a train, rushing towards him across a bridge, but there were no hard outlines in the picture; everything was hinted at, suggested, obscure. He wondered where the train had come from, where it was going. Who were the people riding on it and what were they doing? Were they hurrying towards somewhere, or were they running away from something? Perhaps both. Maybe everyone was always doing both at once.

What would Rosa have said about it? He tried to recapture in his imagination some of the times they had spent together, something he did more infrequently these days, but he found it difficult. He realised he was, in general, thinking less and less about his life before he came to London. Like the back of the train in the painting, his own past was obscured, smothered by the fog and the rain of London.

Who was he, now? He wasn't sure any more. He was still a Jew; he knew that would never change, but what did it mean, to be a Jew in England? Inevitably, as time passed he was becoming more and more English. Did that mean he was becoming less Jewish? He couldn't answer that question, and he wasn't sure he wanted to. He knew that he spoke Yiddish rarely now, even with Yossel, and instead of measuring out each year by the passing of the Hebrew months — Nisan, Iyar, Sivan, he started to think more in terms of the English ones — January, February, March.

Shabbos was still of great importance to him, though, and the thoughts of Shabbos were inextricably linked in his mind with thoughts of family. He longed to reunite his family and to have one of his own. He wondered if he would ever find a wife, someone who would light the Shabbos candles and bless the flame. Someone who could share his dreams and his troubles. Someone who would give him children.

It was during this period that he received a letter from his father containing several important items of information. After the usual greetings, and questions about how they were getting on, the letter plunged straight into the first piece of news.

> *I don't know if you have heard about the new illness that we have here?' he read. 'It is a very severe type of influenza. It has been very bad in Riga and now, unfortunately, it has come to Tukum. Many people here are getting sick and sadly not everyone gets better.*

Of course he knew about the sickness, everyone was very worried about it. They called it Russian Flu, because it had started in Petropavlovsk. He knew it was bad in the Pale, but he was distressed to find it had spread as far as Kurland. He read on.

> *Perhaps you have already guessed why I am telling you this? I am very sorry to be the bearer of bad news yet again, but I have to inform you that Zeide is one of those who has passed away. He caught the illness a few days ago and he died earlier today. I will sit shiva for him.*

Rafael stopped reading while he examined his feelings. He and Yossel had never been particularly close to their grandfather. He was a cantankerous man, difficult to love. But it was still a great sadness to think they would never see him again — apart from anything else, he was a tangible link to their mother. Now he was gone she seemed even more distant. He wondered if his aunts, Feige and Blume, long estranged from their father, would attend the funeral. He thought probably not.

Nobody knew how the disease spread, whether it was from miasmas in the air or people infecting each other, but either way he prayed his father would not catch it. He couldn't bear the thought he might die and he might never see him again. He also worried about his friends in Riga; who else did he know who had caught it?

He dreaded to think what would happen if it spread to London. He read on.

> *I'm afraid there is more. Leib Lipman is, sadly, another victim of this awful disease. He was a strong man, but he never fully recovered from what happened to him on that terrible day we all remember, and being out in the cold all the time must have weakened his system further, so that when he caught the flu he had no strength to fight it.'*

That was also sad. He remembered how Leib Lipman had entertained them at their *Seder*. Thinking further back he smiled at the recollection of how he used to salute him and Yossel when he saw them in the street.

That wasn't the end of the letter; there was one more piece of news to come.

Now for some much happier news. I am delighted to tell you that Hannah and I are expecting a baby.

The letter went on, but Rafael didn't take it in; he was too shocked.

When he relayed the contents of the letter to Yossel he watched him go through all the same reactions as he had felt in himself. When he got to the final piece of news Yossel burst out furiously: 'What on earth is he doing?'

'Calm down. We always knew it was a possibility.'

'Yes, I know, but that's not the same as it actually happening, is it? It doesn't feel right. It feels, ... oh I don't know, just weird.'

'I know it feels weird to us, but it obviously doesn't to him. He's happy. He's done so much for us, Yoss. We should try to be happy for him.'

'I always thought he loved *Mamele*.'

'Of course he did. I'm sure he still does. But she's gone for ever, Yoss. He has the right to love again, doesn't he?'

'I suppose so. I wonder what "Uncle Reuben" thinks about it?' said Yossel with a wicked grin.

'Please,' cried Rafael, covering his ears. 'Don't call him Uncle Reuben.'

*

The Russian Flu pandemic hit England in waves. The 1889 one was short lived, but the disease came back every year for three more years. It affected young and old and was no respecter of class; The Prime Minister, Lord Salisbury became ill with the flu in 1890, and then Queen Victoria's grandson, the Duke of Clarence caught it. The sixty-year-old Salisbury, although incapacitated for weeks, survived; the twenty-eight-year-old Duke of Clarence did not.

The spread of the disease was unstoppable.

Since arriving in London, Rafael and Yossel had not had any serious illness, for which they thanked their youth and vigour. But their luck was bound to run out eventually and, in the winter of 1891, Yossel caught Russian Flu.

The first thing he was aware of when he woke up was the headache. Then he realised he was sweating, and yet felt cold. There was no time to feel sorry for himself, though; it was time to go to work.

He swung his legs out of bed and tried to stand up. But his legs buckled beneath him and he found himself on the floor. Rafael, who had been asleep, woke with a start at the sound of his brother falling.

'Yoss!' he said in alarm. 'What's the matter?'

'I don't know. I feel terrible. I think it might be Russian Flu; lots of them at work are down with it.'

'Oh no!' Rafael sprang out of bed and rushed over to help Yossel up. 'Come on, let's get you back into bed.'

'I've got to go to work,' said Yossel weakly.

'Not like this, you haven't. Come on, back into bed.'

Yossel complied and lay down. He was shivering all over and sweat was pouring off him.

'Look, Yoss, I'll go to the tailors on my way to work and tell them you're not coming in.'

'I'll lose my place.'

'Never mind. We'll worry about that when you're well. All you have to do for now is get better. Look, Yoss, I'd like to stay and look after you, but I've got to go to work. I'll leave some water by the bed in case you get thirsty and I'll be back as soon as I can.'

He fretted about Yossel all day and wondered how he was managing, and at the end of his shift ran back to the apartment as fast as he could.

He found Yossel asleep, or unconscious; it was hard to tell which. He was alive, at any rate but he was breathing noisily and with difficulty. The water was gone and he had shrugged off the bedsheet. He was drenched in sweat again. Rafael refilled the water mug, soaked a cloth in water from the jug, wrung it out and laid it on Yossel's forehead to cool him. It became warm almost immediately; it was clear his fever was dangerously high.

'I shouldn't have left him,' he thought. 'Thank God he's still alive. What else can I do for him?' He racked his brains but could only think of two things. He reached inside his shirt and took off their mother's amulet. Lifting Yossel's head gently off the pillow he slipped the chain over his head so that the amulet rested on his chest.

Then he recited the *Mi Sheberach*, the prayer for the sick.

> *May the One who blessed our ancestors Abraham, Isaac, and Jacob bless and heal Yossel son of Itzhak. May the Holy Blessed One overflow with compassion upon him, to restore him, to heal him, to strengthen him, to enliven him. May He send him speedily a complete healing of the soul and of the body, along with all the sick among the people of Israel and all humankind, soon, speedily, and without delay.*
>
> *Amen.*

He pulled a chair up to the side of the bed and sat there, listening to his brother's laboured breathing, watching his chest rising and falling, rising and falling.

He realised he must have fallen asleep when he was woken by a gentle tapping at the door. 'That's strange,' he thought. 'Who could it be?' Slightly anxiously, he opened the door a crack. There was a girl outside. She looked about sixteen or seventeen years old, with large eyes and a head of dark curls framing a pale face. She was carrying a large, heavy looking bag and seemed anxious, or nervous.

'Hello. Can I help you?' he asked gently.

'I'm Rachel Lazarus,' she replied. Seeing the puzzled look on Rafael's face, she explained: 'I work with Joseph at the tailors. Joseph Jacobson.'

'Joseph?' repeated Rafael, still puzzled. 'Do you mean Yossel?'

'Maybe,' she said doubtfully. 'We call him Joseph at work.'

'I see. Well, I'm sorry, but I'm afraid he can't see you. He's very sick.'

'Yes, I know. That's why I've come. Please may I see him?'

Rafael hesitated. He wasn't sure what to do. In the end, she looked so anxious and so vulnerable standing there alone that he decided he had better let her in. When she saw Yossel she gave a gasp and dropped the bag, her hand flying to cover her mouth. She hurried over to him,

'Joe? Joe?' she called softly. 'Joseph. It's Rachel. I'm here. Can you hear me?' There was no response. She looked at Rafael, her eyes wide with fear. 'Why won't he wake up?' she asked, tearfully.

'I don't know, Rachel. He has a very high fever. I think perhaps his body has shut down to protect itself.'

'What can we do?' she wailed.

'Not much, I'm afraid. Try to keep him cool, and hope it burns itself out, I think. That's all.'

She looked as though she was going to faint. Rafael guided her to the chair and she sat next to Yossel, staring at him with desperate eyes. Rafael looked at her in bewilderment. What was she doing here?

'Rachel, forgive me, I ought to have said before; I'm Yossel's brother, Rafael.'

'Oh yes, I know all about you,' she said. 'Joe's always going on about you. He worships you, you know.'

'Does he?' said Rafael, genuinely surprised. 'That's lovely to hear. But, I'm afraid I don't know who you are.'

'Well, I suppose I'm his girl. We're sweethearts,' she replied, simply. 'That's funny, I've never said that out loud before.'

Rafael was a little stunned. 'I didn't know he was walking out with anyone. Although … wait a minute, I remember now. He said there was a "wonderful girl" at work after his first day there. That must be you.'

'Did he say that?' she said, colouring. 'Yes, I suppose we did hit it off straight away. I sit next to him at work.'

'I'm afraid that by the time he gets better he will have lost his job. He'll need to find another one somewhere else. He won't be able to work with you any more.'

'Oh no, that's wrong. That's why I'm here.'

'I don't understand.'

'They sent me here with this. Look.' She retrieved her bag and held it up.

'What's that?' asked Rafael, confused.

'It's work. For him to do at home. If he keeps working then he won't lose his job.'

'But Rachel, look at him. He can't work.'

'No, I know he can't. But I can. Let me stay, Rafi — may I call you Rafi? Let me stay and help you look after him. Then while I'm here I'll do the work and tell them he did it. That way, when he's better he'll still have a job. And we can still work together.'

'Rachel, no. You can't stay here. It's not right. And also, there's no sewing machine here. That pile of work is going to take all night. You can't work all day and all night too; it's too much.'

'I can. Really. Please let me stay. At least tonight. I can't bear to leave him like this.'

Despite his misgivings, Rafael was deeply touched by her devotion. Secretly, he was relieved there was someone else there to share the burden of helping Yossel through his illness and to be there if… if the worst happened. 'All right.' he said. 'You can stay. I wish I could help you with that work, but I have no skill with a needle.'

'Oh that's all right. I'm quick, it won't take me as long as you think. You sleep. I can watch him and work at the same time.'

'Thank you, Rachel. But please wake me up later so that you can sleep. Also wake me if anything changes, will you?'

'Yes. Don't worry, I will.'

Yossel's fever broke in the early hours of the morning. He woke and immediately began to cough, a dry cough which seemed to rack his whole body. Rafael was instantly awake and by his bedside. Rachel was tenderly supporting Yossel's head and offering him sips of water in-between his coughing spasms.

'He's coughing and coughing, but nothing's coming up,' she said. Is that good or bad?'

'I don't know, I'm afraid. But I think he looks less hot; he's not sweating as much, anyhow.'

The coughing subsided for the moment and Rachel gently lowered Yossel's head onto the bed. Rafael looked at the garments Rachel had brought with her.

'Are they all done?' he asked.

'Yes,' she said. 'You've had a good long sleep. It's almost morning.'

It was still pitch dark outside, but the night always seemed endless in winter. It was bitterly cold in the room but Rachel didn't seem to feel it.

'His fever is going,' said Rafael. 'I think I'll light the fire, it's freezing in here.' Once the fire was going he looked again at Rachel, lit by its glow. He could easily see what attracted Yossel to her, and she had already proved herself a staunch friend. 'Well done, Yoss,' he thought. 'She's a gem. Please don't die. She needs you to get better. So do I.'

Rachel's eyes closed and she nodded off in the chair, still holding tight to Yossel's hand.

Rafael went over to the bed. Yossel felt clammy, and he covered him with the bedsheet again. Then he stood by the window, looking out through the winter smog as the East End began, slowly, to come to life.

He let Rachel sleep for an hour and then gently shook her awake. She had been in a deep sleep. She looked up at him in confusion for a moment, then remembered where she was and looked at Yossel. He seemed to be sleeping more normally now.

'What day is it?' she asked.

'It's Friday.'

'Oh!' she cried, jumping up. 'I'll be late for work. Will you stay with him?'

'Yes. I can stay. I don't think they'll fire me for missing one day if I explain the reason when I get back. But you had better go.'

'Please may I come back this evening?'

'Well, look, Rachel. I'm not sure if it's really seemly.' He saw her bottom lip beginning to quiver. 'But yes. All right.'

She beamed at him and nodded. Then, with one final look back at Yossel, she picked up her work bag and hurried away.

Yossel woke up. He stared at the ceiling, blinking, trying to work out why he felt so terrible, and remembered. He turned his head and saw his brother sitting beside the bed.

'Hello, Yoss,' Rafael said, tenderly. 'Welcome back.'

Yossel tried to reply but found he couldn't make his voice work properly. 'Water,' he croaked. Rafael lifted his head and gave him a few sips. It reignited Yossel's dry, painful cough, but he managed to moisten his lips and get a few drops down between spams.

'I feel terrible,' he said, sinking back onto the bed.

'I bet you do. I'm so sorry, Yoss.'

'No, I'm sorry to be a nuisance. What day is it?'

'Friday.'

'Oh no! I'm missing work. I've got to get up.'

'No you haven't.' Rafael told Yossel what Rachel had done, and how she was saving him his job. A tear rolled down Yossel's face onto the bed.

He managed to eat a little porridge during the day, and seemed stronger. He no longer felt as shivery and hot as before, but his throat was very sore and his cough was worse; he was starting to bring up thick mucus when he coughed, and his lungs rattled painfully when he breathed. Rafael knew from what he had read in the newspapers that he was still very much in danger; most of those who had died had succumbed not to the original fever but to the congestion of the lungs that developed after the first symptoms had gone.

'What about your work?' Yossel asked suddenly in the afternoon. 'Will they fire you?'

'I think they'll understand. I hope they will. For some reason, Cohen seems to like me. They might just assume I've got the flu myself. They've been pretty good about other metalworkers when they've been ill with it, so it should be OK. I won't get paid, of course, that's the only thing.'

By the evening Yossel was strong enough to get out of bed, and was determined to be up when Rachel came back. She was so happy to see him sitting in a chair she burst into tears.

The cough continued to worsen, though, and by the middle of the night Yossel was exhausted with the effort of keeping his lungs clear. Rafael didn't share his fears with Rachel, but he knew what a serious development this was. He wondered if there was a medical professional of some kind he could get hold of, but had no idea how to go about finding one, at least not one that he could afford.

Throughout the weekend he and Rachel took it in turns to sit with the patient. Between frequent bouts of coughing Yossel slumbered, or just lay still, looking up at the ceiling and breathing wheezily. Very slowly, he began to regain his strength. By Monday he was able to hold short conversation and Rafael considered it fairly safe to leave him while he went to work.

As he knew he would be, Rafael was automatically docked a day's pay, but nothing worse. He explained the situation to Jacob Rothstein and received an understanding nod.

'Don't worry,' Rothstein said. 'I'll make it all right with Mister Cohen. I'd have done just the same if it was my brother. Terrible thing, this Russian flu. How's your brother doing now? Do you think he'll be all right?'

'I think so, sir. I hope so. He seems a little stronger today.'

'Good,' he said, clapping Rafael on the shoulder. 'Let me know how he gets on.'

The worst was past and Yossel began to rally. Over the next few days his lungs began to clear, and the colour started to return to his face. Rachel came every evening and worked while she watched over him, and the following week he was, although still weak, strong enough to return to work.

'Thank you, Rafi, for everything,' he said in the evening, after his first day back at work. 'It turns out you're not as bad a brother as I thought.'

'Rachel seems to think you worship me.'

'She's such a liar. I'll have to dump her.'

'Oh really? Come on, Yoss, she's one in a million, and she adores you. Why not marry her?'

'I know she is, and I would, like a shot. But no. Not now. Not until I have something more than my good looks and charm to offer her.'

'Well, don't leave it too long. Good looks and charm can wear off, you know.'

'Depends how much you have to start with. Oh by the way, this is yours.' He took off the amulet and placed it in Rafael's hand. 'Thank you. I really believe it saved my life.'

'Why do you say that?' asked Rafael, putting it on.

'The first night I was ill I saw *Mamele*. She bent over me and gave me water. She put her hand on my forehead and it cooled me. Then she said something which I couldn't hear, but she promised me I would get better. Do you think I'm *meshuggah*?'

'No. I believe you. She comes to me sometimes, too. I think she's still looking after us.'

'She is.'

17

When Jacob Rothstein retired in 1896, Rafael, at the age of twenty-five, was made foreman. This astonished him, but the other workers, who had long considered him Rothstein's natural successor, were not surprised at all. Even those who had been at the factory longer than him accepted it; they knew he understood the business as well as, or better than, they did.

The factory was prospering; its development of electrical engineering expertise was paying dividends as the demand for electric light gathered pace. At the same time, Rafael had heard, Smart's was floundering. Demand for its traditional products was down and it had been too slow to adapt. Pay was stagnant, George Draper was an inept foreman, and good workers were quitting or being laid off. He hoped Ike would be all right.

As Rafael had said, Samuel Cohen seemed to have developed a soft spot for him. When he had been foreman for about a year, Cohen invited him to his home to meet his family. Gratified, Rafael accepted with pleasure.

Cohen lived in a comfortable terraced town house at the edge of the elegant Thornhill Square in Islington, with his wife Sarah and their daughter, to whom they had given the resolutely English name of Elizabeth. It was a prosperous area inhabited by the well-to-do middle classes; doctors, lawyers and other successful businessmen. Even before he arrived at the Cohens' house, Rafael felt uncomfortably out of place.

The door was opened by a parlour-maid, who showed him into the drawing-room, where the family was waiting. The Cohens' house was the first Rafael had been in where there were servants, and it increased his sense of unease.

Cohen welcomed him warmly.

'My dear fellow, how good of you to come. Sarah, this is Rafael Yacobsohn, who has taken over from Jacob.'

Sarah Cohen was a tall, matronly woman wearing an uncomfortable-looking high-necked dress. Her grey hair was scraped back into a tight bun. She greeted Rafael appraisingly, inspecting him for flaws as if he was a cheap goose in a butcher's window.

'Elizabeth,' Cohen continued, 'this is Mister Yacobsohn.'

The daughter extended a limp hand; Rafael wasn't sure if he was expected to shake it or kiss it. As a compromise, he brushed her fingers with his own and hid his confusion by bowing slightly and saying 'Pleased to meet you, Miss Cohen.'

'How do you do? Mis-ter Ya-cob-sohn,' she replied slowly, peeling apart the syllables of his name as if it were an orange.

She was, he guessed, rather older than him, maybe a little over thirty, with a long face and bulging green eyes. Her light blue dress was gathered tightly in at the waist and tied around with a silky green bow. It was an expensive outfit, but the effect was uncomfortable rather than stylish.

There were no other guests. Cohen chattered on, keeping the conversation resolutely away from factory matters, while Rafael made occasional brief responses and the two women maintained a silent, statuesque presence.

At last it was dinner time.

In the dining room, the four sat round a large table made of a dark wood, polished to a high sheen. Samuel and Sarah sat at each end, with Elizabeth and Rafael facing each other across the table's width. Rafael looked with dismay at the array of cutlery and glasses in front of him and fervently wished he was somewhere else. He decided simply to copy everything Elizabeth did.

A servant brought in some clear soup and he watched to see which spoon she would pick up. Nobody said any blessings.

'Miss Cohen,' said Rafael, searching for a topic of conversation. 'Are you interested in art?'

'Art?' she echoed, as if trying to recall where she had heard the word before. 'I suppose portraits of people one knows can be interesting. The clothes, you know. An Italian gentleman painted my portrait once.'

'It is a fine portrait, Mister Yacobsohn,' said Mrs. Cohen. 'Perhaps you noticed it in the drawing-room? Perhaps you would care to study it after dinner?'

'Thank you, Mrs. Cohen. Yes, I would. And, Miss Cohen, do you enjoy other types of picture? Still life, perhaps, or landscape?'

'No, not really.'

'Elizabeth plays the piano very prettily, Yacobsohn,' put in Cohen. 'Will you sing for us after dinner, my dear?'

'If you wish, father.'

The empty soup bowls were removed and more courses followed; fish, lamb cutlets, dessert, petit fours. The meal seemed endless and Rafael felt uncomfortably full; he couldn't remember ever eating so much in a day, let alone at a sitting.

At last, Mrs. Cohen stood up and said: 'Elizabeth and I will leave you men to your port. Don't keep us waiting too long, Samuel.'

Once they had left, Cohen poured himself a glass of port and lit a cigar. He passed Rafael the port and offered him a cigar, which he declined. He had never acquired the smoking habit, although he didn't object to the smell. It reminded him of heder.

Now he was alone with his foreman, Cohen turned his attention to business. 'Now, look, Yacobsohn, tomorrow morning I'm expecting a group of visitors from BEAC.'

Rafael nodded, understanding the significance of what Cohen had said. The British Electrical Apparatus Company was a large firm currently investing heavily in their lighting division. A large order from them would be an important win. 'You would like me to *schmooze* with them?' he asked.

'No Yiddish, please, Yacobsohn. Do try to put that behind you. Lapses like that will hold you back, you know. I'd like you to show them round the factory, be friendly, show them our latest equipment, then bring them straight back to me; I'll take them to lunch.'

'I understand, sir. But don't they have their own works?'

'Yes, in Coventry. But when they don't have spare capacity they contract out. I want to make sure they always come to us first.'

'I will try to impress them.'

Cohen continued to talk for a while about the factory and finally said: 'Well, shall we join the ladies?'

Rafael was made to examine the lifeless, formal portrait of Elizabeth, and to listen to her accompanying herself badly on the piano while she breathily squeaked through a number of tedious parlour songs. Eventually it was time to go and, with effusive thanks to his hosts, he hurried to catch the train home.

*

He was summoned to the office around mid-morning the next day and introduced to the small delegation from BEAC.

They followed him on a tour of the factory, asking occasional questions and taking copious notes. Once Samuel Cohen had treated them to a good lunch they were ready to sign and the firm won the order. Rafael was hoping he might be rewarded with a financial bonus, but he was disappointed.

A few weeks later he was invited to dinner at the Cohens' again.

'Do you play cards, Mis-ter Ya-cob-sohn?' asked Elizabeth during the endless meal.

'I'm afraid not, Miss Cohen. I don't know anything about card games.'

'Oh, you are funny,' she said with an attempt at coquettishness. 'Well if you really don't play cards, what after-dinner amusements do you have?'

'Well, I talk to my brother, or I read. Sometimes I visit the pub; I'm trying to teach myself to like English beer.'

'Oh, you mustn't drink beer, Mis-ter Ya-cob-sohn. That's very working class, you know.'

'Well, I am working class, Miss Cohen.' She gave a little shriek and looked at him with a horrified expression.

'Oh Mis-ter Ya-cob-sohn, don't say that!'

Cohen intervened.

'Calm yourself, Elizabeth. You know, I was not so very different from Yacobsohn when I was his age. I also had my struggles. Yacobsohn has come from hardy working class stock; nothing wrong with that. But now he has ambitions to better himself, just as I did. Isn't that so, Yacobsohn?'

'Well, sir. I'm not sure what you mean by 'better myself'. I do hope to be financially secure, but I'm not sure that would make me 'better'.'

'You must admit, Mister Yacobsohn,' put in Mrs. Cohen, 'that crime and immorality go hand-in-hand with poverty. The denizens of the Whitechapel rookeries are hardly paragons of virtue.'

'Well, Missus Cohen, it's true that there is wickedness and meanness found in Whitechapel. But as *Maimonides* said, "It is impossible to understand and comprehend wisdom when one is hungry and ailing." I'm sure there is wickedness and meanness even in wealthy places.'

'Who is Mai-mo-ni-des?' asked Elizabeth. 'Is he a com-mu-nist?'

Mrs. Cohen did not like the turn the conversation had taken, and at the reference to communists she decided it had gone far enough. She stood up and, exactly as at the first evening, said: 'Elizabeth and I will leave you men to your port. Don't keep us waiting too long, Samuel.'

Again there was factory talk over the port, followed by laboured piano playing and shrill singing. Rafael decided if he was invited again he would ask to be taught to play cards; anything to avoid Elizabeth's singing.

Rafael harboured the faint hope that, having disgraced himself by betraying mild socialist leanings, he might be spared further evenings at the Cohens'. So it was with a mixture of surprise and dismay that he received another invitation a few weeks later. Try as he might, he could not think of a polite way to decline, so back to Thornhill Square he went. This time the topics of class and the morals of the poor were sedulously avoided.

After the dinner, and the port and cigars and factory talk, he found a card table had been set up in the drawing-room. Mr. and Mrs. Cohen sat by the fire while Elizabeth tried to explain to him the rules of Bezique. Since she got rather muddled, and her slow drawling voice was tiring to listen to, Rafael found it hard going, and the card lesson was not a success. They played a couple of hands but Rafael made so many mistakes, and they both became so confused, that they gave it up.

Next time, they were back to the singing.

*

Being a foreman was in some ways easier, and in some ways much harder, than Rafael had expected. Organising the rotas and schedules was the easy part; dealing with people was much more complicated, and he found it hard to separate his emotions from the practical business of running an efficient workforce.

He enjoyed taking on new staff, and as the firm was thriving there was almost continuous recruitment. He loved the look in the eyes of someone when he was able to offer them a job. But he hated it when he had to turn someone away.

What he hated most was firing people, which unfortunately he did have to do from time to time. Bullies, thieves, or men who forced their attentions on the women deserved it, he felt. But the look of anguish in the eyes of the people he had to fire for contraventions such as drunkenness or lateness was hard to live with, and he was determined to do everything he could to prevent it happening.

He saw the signs of a potential problem of this sort one day when he was inspecting the timesheets. One of the women, a polisher called Mary Bell, had been late three times in a week. On further enquiry it transpired that she had left her place and been found an hour later asleep in a storeroom. This was clearly a sackable offence.

But Rafael remembered his conversation with the foreman in Gozinsky's the day he appeared at work covered in cuts and bruises and how grateful he was to be given a second chance. He decided to give her an opportunity to explain so, the next day, he called her over. 'Good morning, Miss Bell,' he said.

'Good morning, sir,' she replied, nervously.

'Do you know why I wanted to speak to you?'

'Yes sir. I was late.'

'Three times. Yes. And…?'

'And I fell asleep.'

'Yes. Can you explain why that happened?'

She hesitated for a long time. Then she said 'No, sir.'

'You have broken the factory rules. Do you understand that?'

'Yes, sir.'

'Mary, I don't want to fire you, but unless you can explain this to me I will have to.'

'I need this job, sir. Please don't fire me.'

'Then, for goodness sake, give me a reason not to.'

'I can't sir. I'm very sorry, sir. It won't happen again.'

Rafael felt sure there was something she wouldn't, or couldn't say. He thought he might look into her home life and see if there was an explanation there. 'What's your address, Mary?' he asked.

Mary looked surprised at the question, but replied 'Brick Lane, sir. Forty–eight.'

Rafael stared at her. 'Forty–eight Brick Lane? Which floor?'

'First floor, sir.'

He had a vivid picture of a scene he had almost forgotten. The frightened, exhausted eyes staring at him from a filthy apartment filled with children. He looked at Mary more closely. 'Yes,' he thought, 'it's the same girl.'

'How many brothers and sisters do you have, Mary?' he asked, gently.

'Seven, sir.'

'And you're responsible for all of them?' She looked terrified. 'Don't be frightened. You're worried they'll be sent to an orphanage, aren't you?'

She nodded miserably. 'How did you know, Mister Yacobsohn, sir?'

'I'm not going to betray you, Mary. Look, I don't know what you've been through, but if you've managed to look after your brothers and sisters all this time then you've shown yourself to be a remarkable young woman. Still, it's clearly too much for you. You can't carry on like this; you're exhausted. Perhaps you should consider whether the orphanage …'

Mary interrupted, greatly distressed. 'We're all right, sir. Really we are. Please don't tell anyone about us.'

Rafael hurried to reassure her. 'It's all right, Mary. I've said I won't betray you and I won't. But if it gets too much for you, come to me. I don't know what I can do, but I'll help if I can.' He saw Cohen coming within earshot so, raising his voice a little louder, he said 'All right, Mary. Back to your work now. Be on time in future, please.'

Mary curtseyed, tears of relief springing to the eyes. 'Yes sir. Thank you sir,' she said, and ran back to her place.

From then on, Mary found a basket of food outside her door once a week when she got home.

*

Rafael was invited to the Cohens' again. He was flattered to be asked, but he didn't think he could stand it many more times. He decided that, come what may, this time would be the last.

As it turned out, he was right, but not for the reason he expected.

In previous visits, as soon as Sarah and Elizabeth Cohen had left the table after dinner, the talk had been all about the factory. This time, however, his host sat back, puffing his cigar contentedly, glancing at Rafael from time to time but saying nothing.

Rafael became acutely aware of the ticking of the clock on the mantlepiece. Eventually, when the silence had become almost unendurable, Mr. Cohen beamed benevolently at him and said: 'Well, Yacobsohn, you're quite a familiar face round here now.'

'Yes, Mister Cohen.'

'You know, Yacobsohn — or perhaps I should start calling you Rafael? — it's always been a great sadness to me that I never had a son to pass the business onto when the time comes.'

Rafael wasn't sure how to respond to this and there was another uncomfortable silence before Mr. Cohen continued. 'Well? Don't you have anything to say to me, Rafael?'

'About what, sir?'

'About my daughter, of course.'

'Elizabeth? No, sir, nothing that I can think of.'

Cohen became brusque. 'You don't mean to say you've been coming here, eating my food, drinking my port and smoking my cigars all this time for no reason?'

'Sir I...'

'Are you the sort of man who toys with a woman's affections, Yacobsohn?'

'Sir, I protest, I...'

'Mister Yacobsohn, let me clarify my position. You came to me a few years ago as a penniless, unemployed immigrant. I gave you a job because I could see you were ambitious, and I wanted to give you a leg up, and, yes all right, because you had useful skills. I even made you foreman when Jacob Rothstein retired because you are clever, hard-working and popular with the men. I don't regret it, I admit you have been a good foreman. I have chosen to overlook your humble beginnings because, to be frank, I had humble beginnings myself. I have introduced you to respectable middle-class life and I suppose you have made a reasonable start. I have even overlooked your socialist tendencies because I was also once young and idealistic. In short, look at where you've come from, and what I'm offering you. Is this how you repay me?'

'Sir, I …'

'Dammit, man, I know Elizabeth isn't everyone's cup of tea, but she's not that bad, is she? She needs a husband, and I need a dependable man to run the factory when I'm gone. Surely that's not so hard to understand?'

Rafael sat in stunned silence for a few moments. Then he dabbed the corners of his mouth with his starched linen napkin and, pushing his chair back, stood up. 'Mister Cohen. Thank you for giving me a job when I needed one, and for your confidence in me. I have thoroughly enjoyed the work and I am glad you feel I have done it well. Thank you also for your hospitality and for your offer. I find after all that I do have something to say to you.'

'Ah, that's more like it. Out with it, then.'

'With the greatest of respect to you and your daughter, I must resign my position at your factory.'

Sarah and Elizabeth were surprised when, a few minutes later, Samuel joined them in the drawing room alone. 'Well? How did it go? Where is he?' whispered Sarah.

'No need to whisper,' said Cohen, slumping into an armchair. 'The damn fool's gone.'

Elizabeth began to cry.

*

Yossel was asleep when Rafael got back to Great Alie Street but the boys held a council the next evening. He listened, open-mouthed, to Rafael's story.

'The devious old man,' he mused. 'But, Rafi, why did you turn it down?'

'Elizabeth's five years older than me, she's boring as hell, she's a terrible snob, she has a voice like a rusty gate, she hates art and she looks like a frog. She's a nightmare.'

'And she comes with a factory, so what's your point?'

'Stop it, Yoss. It's done. Forget it. It's time to move on.'

'But what are you going to do now? Will you be able to find another job?'

'I'm not going to try. I'm going to open my own works, just like Cohen did. If he can do it, so can I.'

'A works? Making what?'

'Lamps, lanterns. The things I really understand.'

'But how?'

'I don't know yet. But I'll figure it out.'

The first thing Rafael needed was a premises. When exploring the streets of Whitechapel in the early days he had seen many small workshops and rooms, and he knew exactly where to look. He found a suitable space in a quiet side-street which he thought would make an excellent workshop and, with money he had saved over the years, was able to pay a month's rent in advance. He ordered a quantity of timber and nails, bought himself a wood saw, and by the end of the next day had constructed a sturdy workbench.

Now he needed some equipment; at minimum, a treadle guillotine for cutting the metal and a machine for folding it. Thinking about this problem, and following a hunch, he walked up Commercial

Street until he came to Smart's workshop. It was open, but empty. The cutting and folding machines stood idle; it was a world away from the thriving, busy workplace it had been when Rafael first saw it.

'Hello?' he called. From the office at the back stepped the familiar figure of George Draper.

'Yes?' he said. Then he looked again. 'Oh, it's you. If you've come to beg for your old job back, you're out of luck, mate,' he sniggered.

'Hello Draper. No, I haven't come looking for a job. Where is everyone?'

'Laid off.'

'Sorry to hear that. What about Isaac Klein?'

'They're all gone, I tell you. It's just me and the boss here. And as soon as I get my wages it'll be just him.'

'So where is he?'

Draper jerked his head towards the office door. 'In the back room, clearing out files.'

'Can I talk to him?'

Draper shrugged. 'I'm not stopping you.'

Rafael knocked on the office door and, without waiting for a reply, went in. John Smart was sitting at his desk sorting through a large pile of papers, as Draper had said.

'Hello, Mister Smart. Sorry to bother you, I can see you're busy.'

Smart looked up. He had a tired and defeated air. 'Don't I know you?'

'Yes. I used to work here.'

He shook his head. 'There's no jobs here any more. We're closing down.'

'I know, sir. That's why I'm here. What's going to happen to all the machines?'

Smart shrugged. 'We'll sell them if we can.'

'Would you sell some to me? I need a guillotine and a folding machine.'

'How much?'

Rafael named a price he knew would be rejected. They haggled for a while, for form's sake, until they settled on an amount much less than the machines were worth.

On his way out, Rafael went to shake Draper's hand.

'Good luck to you, Draper,' he said.

Draper turned away. 'Go to hell.'

In Spitalfields market Rafael found a costermonger willing to transport the machines for him for a small fee. By the end of the day he had them set up on the workbench in his room.

Now he just needed some customers.

*

Now that he had seen what had become of Smart's he was worried about Ike, so he looked for him in the only place he could think of, the Ten Bells. He wasn't there.

Leaving the pub, he found himself walking along Fournier Street, thinking about Ike, and also worrying about how he was going to find customers. Halfway along the road he was arrested by a sign for Schwartz' dairy. He stopped in puzzlement — why did that ring a bell? Then he remembered. Simon Schwartz the milkman was the first person they had met when they got off the boat.

Immediately opposite the dairy was a path into the graveyard of Christ Church, where they had found the Shusters on the first day. The memories came flooding back. There had been so many struggles since then, and they had come so far. Was he really back to square one?

He carried on to the end of the road, and turned right into Brick Lane. There was number fifty–two where the Goldsteins lived, and there was number forty–eight where Mary Bell struggled bravely to look after her brothers and sisters. And there were the pubs. The Three Cranes on one corner, and the George and Guy, with its enormous lantern, on the other.

Its enormous lantern.

The Three Cranes had no lantern, he realised. He looked into the George and Guy; it was packed. Then he looked into the Three Cranes; it was much quieter. He went up to the bar and ordered a pint of Truman's beer. When he had paid, he looked round the half-empty pub and said to the Landlord: 'A bit dead in here, isn't it?'

'It's always quiet midweek, sir.'

'The George and Guy's not quiet. It's heaving in there. You know why that is, don't you?'

'Go on, then.'

'It's their lantern; you can see it for miles. You've only got a painted sign.'

'I don't know if that makes any difference.'

'Oh it definitely does. I should know; I work for a company that makes pub lanterns.'

'Oh, I get it. Touting for business, are you?'

'Me? No, no, on the contrary; we've got more business than we can manage. Booked up for months. All the pubs round here that didn't already have lanterns are putting them up.'

'Is that right?'

'Absolutely. They've realised they pay for themselves in about a month; they push sales through the roof.'

'Really? Huh. What did you say your firm was called?'

'Strauss and Co.' But as I say, we're booked up solid for the next twelve months.'

'*Hmm*. Pity.'

'Sorry we can't help. Oh well, cheerio. Best of luck. It was nice talking to you, er … ?'

'James.'

'Right. Nice talking to you, James. My name's Rafael. See you again.'

He left the pub feeling rather pleased with himself and decided to have similar conversations in as many pubs without lanterns as he could find, especially if they were close to a pub that had one.

The problem with the plan, he quickly realised, was that he had to buy a drink in every pub he went into, which not only cost him money he could ill afford, but also made it disturbingly difficult to speak or think clearly. After the first few pubs he decided to call it a night and go home.

The following day he lay in bed nursing a hangover until lunchtime, after which he felt a little better. He decided to leave it one more day before putting phase two of his plan into operation.

Going back into the Three Cranes, he was worried James wouldn't be there. But he was standing behind the bar just as before.

'Hello again,' said Rafael.

'Good evening, sir. Pint of Truman's, wasn't it?'

'That's right.' He took a long sip and said: 'Quiet in here again tonight, James.'

'Yes, sir. Always is, weekends.'

'I've been thinking about the lantern. I'm sorry we can't fit you in.'

'Well, I hadn't definitely decided to get one ...'

'You seemed so keen, I feel really bad about it, so here's what I thought we could do. I happen to be Strauss' chief designer and I would be willing to design you a lantern, which I will make in my own workshop in my spare time. It'll cost you less than half of what they'd charge you at Strauss and Co., even if they had time to do it — which they don't — and it'll be the same quality, or better.'

James scratched his chin.

'Well, I'm not sure...'

Rafael played his final card. 'If you don't like it, you don't pay. Can't say fairer than that.'

The landlord took a look around his half-empty pub.

'How much?'

Rafael knew then that it would be all right. He named a price and they haggled for a little bit but it ended with a handshake and an agreement.

It was still a risk, of course, because he had to make the lantern with no guarantee of payment. But even if the Three Cranes rejected it, which he didn't expect to happen, he would design it in such a way that it would be simple to change the pub name so he could sell it elsewhere.

There was one more major problem to be surmounted. He didn't have enough money for the materials.

But he had a plan for that.

Above the fireplace in his room was a small shelf, and on the shelf stood the second of the two miniature candlesticks that Salomon Strauss had given him eight years earlier.

'I'm sorry,' he said to the candlestick. 'It's only for a week. Or two at most.'

He hid it carefully in his travelling bag to minimise the chance of being robbed on the way, and went to the pawnbroker's. The amount they gave him was disappointing but it was enough. He could buy the materials for the lamp.

But he only had one shot; he couldn't take on any more jobs until he got paid for this one. It had to work.

He had already given a lot of thought to the design. The pub was on the corner of two streets so it had to be clearly visible from both directions and to cast an enticing glow that would encourage customers to choose the Three Cranes instead of the pub opposite. Its design needed to be unique and memorable, but it had to be instantly recognisable as belonging to a pub. Gradually, a clear picture began to form in his mind and he transferred his ideas into detailed drawings.

He began construction as soon as the materials arrived. He worked obsessively on the lantern and it was completed well ahead of the date he had agreed. He knew he'd made something exceptional but forced himself to be patient, and not deliver it early. He knew that people value something more if they have to wait for it.

When it was time, he paid a friendly costermonger a few pence for transport, scavenged an old packing crate, picked up some straw at the hay market in Whitechapel High Street and delivered the lantern to the pub safely, with as much fanfare as he could manage. He needn't have worried about the reaction; James the landlord was delighted. He considered the lamp superior in every way to the one outside his rival's pub, and he paid up promptly.

Just as Rafael had hoped, the new light prompted quite an upsurge in business for the pub. It was a great success.

The first thing he did when he received his fee was to redeem the candlestick.

'Bless you, Salomon Strauss, 'he thought. 'That's the second time your present has got me out of a tight spot.'

He had hated having to pawn it, but it was worth it. Even after redeeming it there was more than enough left over from the fee to purchase the materials he needed for another lantern. 'This could actually work,' he thought.

He was in business.

*

The strategy was a success, and more orders started coming in. But Rafael knew that, although there were a lot of pubs in London, the supply would give out at some point.

He needed to put the business on a more solid footing.

One of the pubs he wanted to establish as a customer was the Ten Bells, because it was one of the very best known in the area. He had spent a lot of time in there *schmoozing* the landlord but, so far, no business had materialised. He didn't mind too much; he liked going in the Ten Bells because he thought he might run into Ike.

Then, one day, he went into the pub and saw him. He was standing at the central bar nursing a small drink and looked very unhappy; Rafael's heart went out to him.

'Hello Ike,' he said. Ike's eyes widened when he saw the familiar face of his old friend.

'Rafi! How wonderful to see you!' They shook hands warmly. 'Look at you! You look fine.'

'Thank you. Ike. Listen, I went to Smart's a few weeks ago; I saw what had happened. Everyone's gone.'

'Yes. It's been going downhill for years. Ever since they lost Mister Brown, really. Demand for their products has collapsed and Draper's been an absolute disaster as foreman.

'When did you leave?'

'I was actually one of the first people they got rid of.'

'Have you found another job?'

'No, not yet.'

'Oh, Ike, I'm sorry. If you don't mind me asking, how do you manage?'

'I'll be honest with you, Rafi, I don't, really. I just about scrape by, doing odd bits and pieces; mending pots, pans, kettles, all that. I'm a tinker.'

'Where are you living?'

'Well, it's a good question. Here and there. The trouble with these slum clearances is, I keep finding a place and then discover it's about to be knocked down. I keep hoping to get an apartment in the Four-per-cents.'

'What, the Rothschild Buildings?'

'That's it. But there's no space. But I'm OK; I've got a place to lay my head at night.'

'Look, Ike, come away from the bar. I really need to talk to you privately.'

He steered his old friend over to the other side of the room and they sat down, facing each other across the table.

'What's all this about, Rafi?' asked Ike.

'Well, it's like this. I'm just starting my own business and I would absolutely love it if you came to work with me. It's early days and I won't be able to pay you a proper salary, not yet, but I can give you a share of the profits, when there are some. I need you, Ike. What do you say?'

Ike's eyes brightened.

'I say "when can I start?"'

'Fantastic. As a matter of fact you can start right now. You're a regular in here, right?'

'Well I don't spend a lot, if that's what you mean. I mostly come in to get warm. But yes, they know me here.'

'OK, then. Listen.'

He briefly explained to Ike about his business model. Ike understood at once. 'Right, pass me the money for a couple of whiskies and leave it with me,' he said, grinning.

Widening his smile, he walked over to the bar and slapped the money on the counter. The landlord came over. 'You've perked up a bit, Ike,' he said.

'Certainly I have. I've just got a job. Two whiskies, please, Sam.'

'Congratulations. How did you manage that? You've been in here all afternoon.'

'See that man over there?' he pointed to Rafael. 'That's my old friend Rafael Yacobsohn. He runs a firm that make lamps for pubs. I'm going to be working for him'

'Oh, I know him. But I thought he was a one-man-band.'

'So he was, when he started. But he's been such a roaring success that he's had to take on new staff. He's been going round signing up all the metalworkers he knows to try and keep up with orders.'

'Is that right?'

'Absolutely. This is about the only pub round here that hasn't ordered a lamp from him.'

'Well, I'll tell you, Ike, I was thinking about it. But seeing as I didn't know the bloke, and him being just a one-man-band, I didn't want to take the risk.'

'That's a shame, Sam. Six months ago you could have got one of his lamps pretty cheap. Now, though? He can name his price. People are willing to pay a lot of money to get one of his lamps.'

'Is that so? That's too bad.'

'Anyway, where are those drinks?'

'Oh, right, sorry. Here you go. You know, Ike, I don't suppose you could have a word with him? See if he would do me a special deal? Since you're working with him now?'

'Well, I'll try Sam. I can't promise anything.'

'Thanks Ike.'

Ike took the drinks back to Rafael and said, quietly: 'He's biting. I've got my back to him now. Is he watching?'

'Yes.'

'Right, well in a few moments, shake your head, like you're saying 'no', and then I'll keep talking like I'm trying to persuade you, and then, after a bit, start nodding reluctantly. OK?'

'This is fun, isn't it?' said Rafael, frowning hard and shaking his head vigorously. 'You're a natural at this Ike.'

'Thank you. You know, I think if we play this right we might get more than just an outside light. This place could actually do with new lights inside too.'

'You're right,' replied Rafael, scowling and shaking his head even more furiously. 'See if you can get him to agree to that.'

'Right, that's probably enough. Make a face like you're giving in.'

Rafael turned down the corners of his mouth, threw his hands up in the air, and sat back in his chair. Ike went back to the bar.

'Well?' said Sam anxiously.

'It's all right. He didn't want to do it, Sam, but in the end I persuaded him. He says he'll take twenty–five percent off the price. He also said he'd do lamps for inside at the same rate if you order them at the same time.'

'Thanks Ike. Well done. Here you go, have a drink on the house. Maybe I should have a word with him. Let me just serve this other gentleman and I'll be right over.'

Ike having done the hard work, Rafael was able to conclude a deal easily and the pair left the pub with a commission for a large outdoor lantern and a number of new smaller ones for inside.

Ike came to the workshop first thing the following morning. He wasn't used to making lanterns but he was a quick learner and, under Rafael's supervision, the lamps were finished ahead of schedule.

As with the other pubs, the Ten Bells' new lights were a great success. The increased business made Sam the landlord very happy, and he promised to give the firm a glowing testimonial to anyone who asked.

Now, Rafael thought, it was time to expand the business further.

*

Leaving Ike at the workshop, Rafael went to the BEAC offices near Holborn. Ever since hosting the company's delegation at Cohen's he had wondered if his connections there would be useful later on, and he decided it was time to find out.

He remembered that the delegation had been headed by a man named Charles Mason, and he hoped he was still working for them. He was in luck; not only was he still there, but, Rafael discovered, he had been promoted and was now in charge of the entire lighting division. After giving his name and waiting for some time in the entrance hall, he was eventually called upstairs to Mr. Mason's office.

'Sorry to keep you waiting,' said Mason, shaking his hand. 'Staff meeting. Let's see, Jacobson, isn't it?'

Rafael had noticed that English people almost invariably anglicised his name and had decided he might as well stop correcting them.

'It's good of you to see me without an appointment, Mister Mason.'

'Not at all. Always glad to see someone from Cohen's. How's the old boy doing?'

'As a matter of fact, I'm no longer at Cohens.'

'Oh. Then …?' Mason looked puzzled.

'Then why am I here? Well I wanted to let you know that I've gone into business for myself. I've set up a small firm specialising in lamps and lanterns. I thought I might be able to persuade you to put some work our way.'

'All right. I'll come and take a look. Give the secretary the address on the way out, would you? Good to see you again. Thanks for popping in, Jacobson.'

He stood up and politely, but resolutely, showed Rafael out.

One morning, about two weeks later, Mason appeared at Rafael's workshop along with one of his underlings.

'Morning, Jacobson,' he said brusquely. 'Oh. Is this it?'

'Yes, sir. As a I said, it's a small firm.'

'Small? It's practically invisible. This is no good at all. Waste of time.'

They were gone in under two minutes.

It was Rafael's biggest failure for some time. It was a bitter disappointment to find all his efforts dismissed so unceremoniously. He found it hard to look Ike in the eyes; he knew that the success of his enterprise was as important to Ike as it was to him.

That evening Yossel noticed immediately that Rafael was deflated.

'What's up, Rafi?' he asked.

'I'm almost thirty, Yossel. I always thought that by the time I was thirty I'd have got somewhere. But I've done nothing.' Yossel looked at him in amazement.

'Done nothing? What are you talking about. You've done so much. We're OK, aren't we? We're safe, we've got beds to sleep in, food to eat, coal to put on the fire. That's not nothing. You've done it, all of it. You should trust yourself more, Rafi. You're not done yet, I know it.'

'Thank you, Yoss. That means a lot to me. I haven't given up, not really. I'm just tired and fed up.'

'Why don't you take a day off tomorrow? Go to the National Gallery; you always come back smiling.'

'That's not a bad idea.'

'Oh, that reminds me. I heard they're planning to open an art gallery in Whitechapel soon. I thought that would interest you.'

'Really? I didn't know that. Yes it does, how exciting. First a library, now an art gallery. Whitechapel's looking up, isn't it?'

Wandering through the paintings in the gallery the next day, Rafael reflected that Yossel's advice had been sound; he felt his disappointment evaporating. Suddenly his attention was arrested by a new picture. He was certain it hadn't been there the last time he had come. He went to look at it more closely.

It was a picture of a young woman, staring straight out of the canvas, dressed in an old-fashioned silky dress with an almost provocatively low neckline. She was wearing a straw hat adorned with flowers and a huge curved feather. What had first drawn his attention, though, was what she was holding. It was a painter's palette and a bundle of brushes. She was an artist. She was outdoors, somewhere in the countryside. It might easily have been Lucavsala. He couldn't draw his gaze away from her face; it was something about the way she was looking, as if she was trying to memorise everything she saw. The woman looked nothing like Rosa; but her expression was one he had never seen on anyone, except her.

*

The weeks rolled by. Autumn turned to winter, and the nineteenth century became the twentieth. There was some work for the firm, but not enough; Ike divided his time between working with Rafael on lanterns and mending pots and pans as before.

Then everything changed. Rafael received a telegram; a thrilling occurrence in its own right. He was to come as soon as possible to Holborn. The British Electric Apparatus Company wanted to see him.

Hardly pausing to put on his coat, he was out of the door and on his way. On giving his name at the front desk, this time he was shown straight up to Mason's office.

'Thanks for coming. Good to see you again,' said Mason shamelessly, showing no recollection of how he had snubbed Rafael the last time they had met. 'Got a big rush job on. Need thirty-five exterior wall lights made to this design.' He passed a sheaf of design papers across the desk. 'Can you do it?'

Rafael looked at the design. It was a familiar square frame design like the gas lamps he trained on, but modified for electricity. The biggest complication was the ornate lid.

He took his time examining the drawings and specifications until he felt confident he understood them well enough, all bar one detail which didn't seem to make sense. He pointed to a place in the drawing.

'Why does the lid attach in that way? That seems like a weak point; that will cause problems.' Mason looked at the design again.

'Well, how would you do it?'

Rafael described the improvement he had in mind.

'*Hmm.* Well, we've never done it that way. But if you think that would work, as long as it doesn't change the appearance, go ahead. The point is, can you make them?'

'Yes, we can do it. But why aren't you sending it to your Coventry works?'

'We did. Weeks ago. Now they say they can't do it. Overstretched. Short staffed. Something or other.'

'I see. You said it was a rush job. When do you need them?'

'Three weeks.' Rafael's eyes widened and the colour drained from his face. It was an almost impossible challenge. He did some rapid calculations in his head. He couldn't work on *Shabbos,* so three weeks was eighteen working days. Minus at least a day for getting the materials and one for delivery. Sixteen. More than two a day. He hesitated.

'Well…'

'There's plenty more jobs we can send your way in the future. If you do a good job for us on this one.'

It would change everything. But this was too big for him. He should walk away now; that would be the sensible thing to do. But instead, he found himself saying 'Yes. No problem.'

Mason slapped him warmly on the back. 'Good man. Knew we could count on you. And the cost?'

Again, Rafael's brain worked furiously. If he went too high he might still lose the job. He quickly calculated the minimum he should accept, and then named a much higher figure. Mason looked at him steadily for a moment.

'Agreed.' Rafael couldn't believe it.

'There's a considerable amount of materials to buy in. So we'll need half the fee in advance, and the rest when we deliver.'

'Agreed.'

They stood up and shook hands.

Before letting go of Rafael's hand, Mason leaned forward and said emphatically: 'They must all be here, at these offices, three weeks from today. Not a day over. If you let us down, that's the end. No more work from us. Ever.'

Rafael also leaned forward. 'Agreed.'

*

'How many?' said Ike.

'Thirty-five. Two a day, or thereabouts, six days a week for three weeks.'

'You're mad. It would take at least a day to make one of these, and that's once we know how to do it. Look at those lids. We need more help.'

'I can't afford more help. And I don't have time to train anyone up. Let me worry about the lids and the electrics. Can you do the frames?'

'Yes I can do the frames. We'll need someone on painting and glazing, though. What about your brother?'

'He's at work all week too.'

'What's he earning, though, Rafi? Almost nothing. If we get this done in time it will change the fortunes of the firm for the better. Surely he'd prefer to work with us instead of slaving his guts out at the tailors? Ask him, Rafi. Please.'

'Yoss doesn't understand metal.'

'He doesn't need to, if he's assembling and painting. There's plenty of less skilled jobs to do. We'll need him if we're going to have a hope of getting this done in time.'

'You're right. I don't know why I feel so reluctant. I'll talk to him tonight. In the meantime, let's figure out what materials we need and get it all ordered.'

'Where are we going to put it all?'

'You're right, I can't order it all at once, there's no room. It will have to arrive in batches. What am I thinking?'

'Come on, Rafi, you know this stuff. You're panicking. Take a deep breath. It's going to be all right.'

'Thank you, Ike. I'm so glad you're here.'

Yossel listened to Rafael's story carefully, sat thoughtfully for a moment and said: 'I'm in.'

'Really?'

'Definitely.'

'It's risky, Yoss. You're the only one of us with a steady job right now. If you give it up to do this and we don't succeed, we could be back to square one.'

'But it will succeed, I know it. Listen, Rafi, you've done so much for me. This is my opportunity to repay you.'

'Well, that's very noble. I'm really touched. Is that really the reason?'

'No, of course not, that's not it at all. Sounded good, though, didn't it? The real reason is because I hate working in the sweatshop and also — actually mainly — because this could be my only chance to make some money so I can ask Rachel to marry me.'

'Ah, that's more like it. Now look, Yoss, there'll be assembling and painting and puttying, but we'll also have you doing things like packing and sweeping. Will you be all right with that?'

'Rafi, I'm not thirteen any more. I've been working in a garment sweatshop for years; I'm hardly likely to complain at a bit of sweeping. Give me some credit.'

'I'm sorry. You know, Yoss, with your help we might just pull this off.'

By the end of the second day they were already behind. 'The quality's good but we're not fast enough,' Rafael told the others. 'If we don't increase the pace we're going to get further and further behind.'

'We'll get faster, Rafi,' said Ike, confidently. 'Once we've got into a routine.'

'I hope so.'

Ike was right, they did increase the pace, and by the end of the fourth day they had almost caught up. But they were exhausted. 'Good job it's *Shabbos* tomorrow,' said Rafael. 'We all need a rest.'

'Rafi, instead of waiting until Sunday morning,' said Yossel, 'what if we start again tomorrow evening, after *Shabbos* goes out?'

Rafael narrowed his eyes as he looked at him. 'Are you sure?'

'Why not? Ike, what do you think?'

'Sure. Why not?'

Maybe it was the exhaustion, but Rafael found he had tears in his eyes at this display of loyalty. 'Thank you. Both of you. Tomorrow evening, then.'

After the rest day they found they were working faster and, because of the extra hours Yossel had come up with, by the middle of the second week they were on schedule.

An anxious telegram arrived from BEAC demanding a progress report. Rafael ignored it; there was simply no time to go to the post office to send a reply.

As they came nearer to the end, Rafael became, if anything, more anxious. There was so much that could go wrong; to take just a couple of examples, he had allowed for some glass breakages, but if they ran short of stock and there were breakages too near the end they might have no time to order more. Or what if they discovered completed lanterns which were below the quality needed and had to be redone?

When they came back to work after the second *Shabbos* break he began to believe it would be all right. They had a smooth routine going now, each of them knew what they were doing and trusted the other two to do their part. It was time to think about delivery.

'What's the plan, Rafi?' asked Ike. 'Costermonger, as usual?'

'Sure, why not? Except one barrow won't be enough; We may need a fleet of them.'

'It must be at least two miles to Holborn, along busy roads. They won't like doing it.'

'It's three, I looked into it. Don't worry. they'll do it if we pay them enough. Anyhow, there isn't really another way.'

'We'll need lots of straw for packing.'

'Yes I've allowed for that. I'm planning to go to the hay market on Tuesday to order it.'

The last twenty-four hours were the worst. Rafael was desperately worried they were going to come up one short when it came time to load them all onto the barrows the following morning. There came a point at which there was nothing more that Ike or Yossel could do and he sent them home to get some sleep, but he worked through the night to make sure that the order was complete and that there were no flaws in any of the lanterns.

As the sun came up on the final day he put the finishing touches to the final one and slumped onto the floor, utterly spent, to grab an hour's sleep.

*

The three weeks were up and the work was complete. Three costermongers, with their donkey–pulled barrows, pulled up outside the works. They helped the three exhausted lampmakers line the barrows with clean straw and lift the cases full of lamps, packed with plenty more straw, into position.

'Right, I'll see you when I get back,' said Rafael to the others.

'Oh no, you don't. We're coming with you. We want to see them safely delivered as much as you do.'

'Are you sure? It's a long way, and you look pretty tired.'

'Pretty tired?' repeated Yossel incredulously. 'We're absolutely *tsugelklappt*. But we're still coming.'

It was a slow and anxious procession along the uneven, cobbled streets. Rafael fervently hoped they had protected the glass with enough straw.

They made their way out of Whitechapel, through the City, past St. Paul's, along Fleet Street and finally up Kingsway to the BEAC offices.

Rafael went inside and marched up to the front desk. 'Please tell Mister Mason his lanterns have arrived,' he said.

After the lanterns had been unloaded and the costermongers had been paid, Rafael, Ike and Yossel went home to sleep.

Charles Mason and his colleagues examined the lanterns carefully and then he convened a meeting so they could share their thoughts.

'This craftsmanship is exquisite, Mason. It's better than we can do in Coventry.'

'I agree. I haven't seen this standard of folding before. And that innovation on the lid is a big improvement.'

'Did you say your people made these in a one-room workshop in three weeks?'

'Yes, that's right.'

'Well done, Mason. The client should be delighted.'

'Thank you. Yes, I think they will be. Walsh, get thirty-two of these packaged up and shipped off, would you?'

'Thirty-two? There's thirty-five here.'

'Yes there are, but the customer only wants thirty-two. I had them make a few extra just in case there were a few duds. Since they are all good, though, I thought we'd send the unwanted ones up to Coventry for copying. At least we'll have better lids from now on.'

There was laughter from the others.

'Good idea, Mason. Very sly.'

18

When Favel Gutman passed away during the Russian Flu pandemic, Itzhak inherited the bakery. He knew nothing about the making of selling or bread and didn't know what to do with it, so when Ester offered to take it over he willingly passed the running of it over to her in return for a share of the profits. Since her new husband owned the mill it made perfect sense. Both mill and bakery were thriving.

Reuben had left his job at the slaughterhouse, and now worked, and lived, at the mill, which he found a much more congenial life. Neither he nor his mother appeared to have given any thought to the question of finding him a wife, which Itzhak thought was strange. When he had mentioned it to Hannah, though, she had said mysteriously, and in a voice that discouraged further discussion, that he was not the marrying kind. So that was that.

The curse of Russian Flu had spread a gloomy pall over everyone's lives, so the birth of Hannah and Itzhak's first child, a daughter Leah, named in honour of Itzhak's mother, felt like a blessing from God. Leah was a strong, happy baby and the source of much joy to her parents and grandmother.

When Leah was still under two, Itzhak and Hannah's second child was born, this time a boy. Unlike his elder sister, who had been so easy, Meyer, named in honour of Hannah's father, was a fretful baby, poor at sleeping.

Itzhak adored his new family and simply couldn't believe his luck. Everybody had assumed that Itzhak and Hannah's marriage was more a marriage of convenience than anything else, but to their surprise they really did form a loving and committed partnership.

Motherhood had brought out hidden reserves of strength in Hannah and she developed a maturity that belied her relative youth.

When the third child, Benjamin, came along, the apartment started to feel cramped. He and Meyer couldn't share a bedroom with their sister Leah indefinitely; eventually they would need separate rooms.

The problem, as always, was money. Despite the numbers of Jews fleeing the Pale, Tukum's Jewish population had actually grown, and there was pressure on accommodation, pushing up the rents. They simply couldn't afford anywhere with more bedrooms.

One evening Itzhak came home from working at the haberdasher's to find that Hannah had prepared him a special meal. The children were in bed asleep, and she was being particularly affectionate.

'*Uh–oh*', he thought. 'I don't like the look of this. She wants something. I hope it's just a new dress. God forbid she wants another child.'

'Well this is very nice,' he said. 'Is it a special occasion?'

'No, not a special occasion.'

'Well, then, why this special feast?'

'Can't I treat my wonderful husband to a special treat now and again? You work so hard, you deserve it.'

'I do? Well, if you put it like that, why not? It certainly smells delicious.'

She placed the food on the table and they began to eat.

'What is all this in aid of?' he wondered. 'Oh well, she'll come out with it when she's ready. In the meantime, this is really a very nice dinner. She's a good cook.'

After they had eaten, they sat on companionably and Hannah said: 'You know, my dear, Leah is almost ten. She can't share a room with her brothers for ever.'

'I know, but what can we do? We've talked about the boys sleeping in the living–room, but that's not a great solution.'

'No, that won't work. I think we should move.'

'Move where?' We can't afford anywhere bigger, we've looked.'

'We can't afford anywhere in Tukum, it's true. I was thinking perhaps we might look further afield.'

'Further afield? What do you mean, further afield?'

Then he listened in amazement as she explained her idea.

*

The triumphant completion of the BEAC project marked a significant turning point in the lives of Rafael, Yossel and Ike. More contracts arrived from them, and other customers soon followed suit.

The work quickly overran the capacity of his single room, and Rafael took the lease on a much larger premises in Commercial Street. He made Ike foreman, and Yossel manager, and they began to take on additional staff. After a while, though, he started to perceive a strange new pattern emerging. When BEAC invited him to quote for a job they would demand a sample prototype along with the quote. He would provide the sample but, as often as not, the project would fail to materialise.

Discreet enquiries revealed what was actually going on. They were stealing his designs; Charles Mason was simply sending the samples to BEAC's Coventry factory for copying. When a furious Rafael went to his office to lodge a protest, Mason strongly denied that such a thing had ever occurred and there was an angry exchange. Rafael left the office deeply frustrated, feeling betrayed. He was angry with himself for his naivety as much as with Mason for his underhand behaviour. He had plenty of other customers now, though, and he vowed to do no more work for BEAC. He also decided to be more cautious, and less trusting, in the future.

One day, Yossel made a big announcement. He and Rachel were getting married.

'*Mazel tov!*' said Rafael, slapping him on the back. 'That is wonderful news. When can I see her again? I'd like to congratulate her in person.'

'Well, how about tonight? I'm taking her to the Pavilion Theatre. Why not come too, and we can go out for dinner afterwards?'

'Sounds wonderful. Are you sure I won't be in the way?'

'Of course not. No more than usual.'

'Very funny. Have you fixed a date for the wedding?'

'No. We thought sometime next year.'

'You know *Tatty* would love to be there, don't you?'

'Yes, I know. I would love that too. Even if it meant having Hannah and all those children. How many do they have now? Twenty?'

'As you know perfectly well, it's three.'

'If you say so. But is it possible?'

'Maybe. Who knows? I'll write to him.'

'And what about you, Rafi?'

'What do you mean?'

'Don't you have anyone special yet?'

'When have I had time to meet anyone? No, I think it's too late for me, Yoss.'

'What are you talking about? You're twenty-nine. It's nowhere near too late. You'll find someone, Rafi, I know you will. When you least expect it.'

'*Hmm.* Maybe.'

*

In January 1901, Queen Victoria died on the Isle of Wight. Her body was taken, via London, to Windsor. Rafael and Yossel watched the funeral procession make its stately way from Victoria, the railway station which bore her name, to Paddington. It felt to them, and to all the onlookers, like a significant moment in history. The nineteenth century was finally properly over.

They prayed the new century would be a good one for the world and for the Jewish people who had suffered so much in the old one.

'It's bound to be better,' thought Rafael. 'It could hardly be much worse.'

In the spring the Whitechapel Art Gallery finally opened to the public; an event Rafael had been looking forward to for a long time. His interest was more than just general; the inaugural event was to be an exhibition of nineteenth century paintings from Eastern Europe, a topic designed to be of particular interest to the borough's largely immigrant population. He wondered if there might be any works by Elise von Jung–Stilling, Rosa's teacher, although he knew it was unlikely.

He went along on the morning of the opening day, and was at first glad to see it had attracted a big crowd. He was less pleased when he realised it meant it was going to be a frustratingly slow shuffle through the galleries. He was even more disappointed to discover that the temporary exhibition he wanted to see was not yet actually open.

He thought he would try to sneak a quick look at it, even so, and ducked past the 'no entry' sign. After walking along a short corridor he entered another gallery almost empty of people.

There were paintings stacked against the walls and lying on the floor. A small team of young women were picking their way between the canvases, rifling through the stacks or hanging the paintings. One of the women hanging pictures turned away from the wall and noticed him watching them.

'I'm sorry, sir,' she said, 'but the exhibition is not open to the public yet.'

Rafael turned to reply.

'Oh, excuse me,' he began apologetically, 'I just wanted to ...'

The words dried up as he saw the painting the woman had just hung, and the colour drained from his face as he stared at it, open-mouthed. He had only seen the image once before, and then only in the flickering light of a pair of candles, but he knew it immediately.

'Where did you get that picture?' he asked, his voice shaking.

'Which one? This one?' She turned to look at it again, then back at him and gave a squeak of surprise. 'I say, it looks just like a younger version of you.'

'It is me.'

'Yes, there certainly is quite a similarity.'

'No, you don't understand. It's my portrait. What I want to know is; why is it here?'

'Oh! Goodness. I don't know. Wait a minute, where's Susan?' She beckoned to one of the other women, who put down the picture she was studying and came over. 'Susan is the exhibition curator. She'll be able to tell you all about it.'

The woman she had called Susan looked properly at Rafael for the first time and stopped dead in her tracks. Her head turned slowly to look at the picture and back again to Rafael.

'It's you,' she said.

'Yes. My name is Ralph Jacobson. That is a portrait of me made over ten years ago by…'

'By Rosa Krupp. I'm honoured to meet you, Mister Jacobson.'

'Honoured?'

'Yes. Rosa Krupp is a very well-known and well-respected name, and this is considered by many to be her best work. It's absolutely unexpected and wonderful to meet the sitter. I've spent a long time wondering…' She seemed almost flustered, which made Rafael look at her more carefully.

She was tall, with long chestnut-brown hair and large, gentle eyes. She had an elegant poise which reminded him of a Gainsborough countess.

'What I mean is,' she continued, tucking a strand of hair behind her ear, 'I am fascinated by this painting and I would love to know more about the circumstances around its creation. And I believe you'd like to know how it got here.'

'Yes, I really want to know about that. As to the creation, it was when I was…'

'Oh, I don't mean now. Sorry, but we have to get this hanging finished. But would it be possible for us to meet up again later today? Or tomorrow? Sorry, does that sound forward of me?'

'Not at all. I would like that. I'll come back later. Shall we say six o'clock?'

'That would be perfect. I look forward to it, Mister Jacobson.'

After Rafael had gone the girl who had first noticed him went up to Susan and raised an interrogatory eyebrow. By way of response Susan put her hands up to her face and squealed with suppressed excitement.

'Well at least that answers one question, Annie,' she said.

'What?'

'He *is* as good looking in real life.'

*

Rafael went to the factory but found that he was wishing the day away. Time seemed to have ground almost to a halt. Lunchtime took days to arrive and the afternoon stretched out before him like a desert.

At half past four an unexpected visitor appeared: Charles Mason from BEAC. He had come to admit what he had done, and to apologise. The reason was not a guilty conscience; they had another large, important order and Coventry had let them down again. He begged Rafael to take it on.

Reluctantly he eventually agreed, but at a price. He wanted financial compensation for the stolen designs and a guarantee it would never happen again. The two men shook hands, and the partnership resumed. Coventry received no more samples.

By the time Mason had left it was time to head back to the gallery. Rafael tried hard to walk at a normal pace but his legs had other ideas and kept hurrying him forward so that he arrived ten minutes too early and had to walk up and down the street several times before going in to avoid feeling foolish.

At one minute to six he went in through the main door and found Susan waiting for him with her coat on.

'Hello again,' he said. 'Oh, you've got your coat on; I thought we'd be staying here.'

'Hello. Well we can, if you'd rather, but there really isn't anywhere comfortable to sit. In any case, I could do with something to eat and drink. Would you mind if we went to a Lyons tea room? There's one further down the High Street if you don't mind walking?'

'Not at all, that sounds fine.'

They walked together along the bustling street. The wind was cold and the sky dark and threatening, but as they walked through the pools of light created by the gas lamps Rafael had the sensation of walking through the dappled shade of a sunlit forest. They chatted of this and that, nothing very consequential, but he barely noticed; he was listening more to the beating of his heart.

When they reached the Lyons, and had ordered, Susan put her elbows on the table and, resting her chin in her hands, stared into his face. It startled him; her eyes were piercing.

His alarm must have shown in his face because she sat up straight again, shook her head, and said: 'Oh goodness! Forgive me, Mister Jacobson. I'm used to you being a painting. I've stared at your face for so long it's rather hard to think of you as a real person.'

He smiled, and she felt she'd never seen such a gentle, kind smile in her life. 'Please don't worry, Miss... Oh! I don't know your last name.'

'Levy. Susan Levy. Or, rather, Shoshana Levy; that's what my parents call me. But my English name is Susan. Let's go with that.'

'I like the name Susan. In the old days I was Rafael Yacobsohn, but I've been Ralph Jacobson for a while now. Tell me about yourself Miss Levy.'

'Is this an interview? Well, I was born in Krakow but I've lived in England almost all my life. I've always loved art and my parents didn't know what else to do with me so they let me study at The Slade. I got interested in East European art history and, well, here are. And what about you, Mister Jacobson?'

'Please, call me Ralph.'

'Well, Ralph, tell me how you came to be the subject of one of the best known portraits of the last few decades.'

'Is it well known? I had no idea. Well, it's a long story. I… oh, wait a moment, here's our waitress.'

They waited for their order to be laid out and then he continued.

'Well, to begin with, I was good friends with David Krupp.'

'Rosa's brother,' interrupted Susan.

'Yes, her twin brother. He introduced me to Rosa and … then she painted a picture of me, for some reason.'

'Really? Can you remember how many sittings you did for it?'

'Sittings? Oh no, none, she did it from memory. I didn't even know she was doing my portrait until I saw the finished painting.'

'That's astonishing. She did it from memory? She must have known your face extremely well. So, that's the whole story? She painted you because you were friends with her brother?'

'That's it.' She narrowed her eyes suspiciously, and said: '*Hmm.* Well, that is very disappointing.'

'What do you mean?

'One of the reasons why I love this picture so much — I mean why everyone loves this picture so much — is the expression on the subject's face. Your face. Especially the eyes. People have speculated that the painter and the subject were having a love affair. Frankly, it's rather a let-down to be told that there was nothing in it.'

'I was just a friend of her brother, that's all.'

'All right. If you say so.'

'So, you haven't told me yet; how does the portrait come to be here?'

'Oh, that's easily told. It was first shown as part of an exhibition organised by Elise von Jung-Stilling.'

'Yes I know, that's where I saw it.'

'Ah. Well, what you seem not to know is that it caused an immediate sensation. It was the hit of the show. When the exhibition closed it was given on permanent loan to the Riga City Art Gallery, and they have very kindly lent it to me for this exhibition.'

'On loan? So Rosa still owns the painting?'

'Well, of course, after her death it formed part of her estate. Oh!'

She gasped as he dropped a full teacup onto the floor. It smashed into pieces and the tea spread across the floor in a wide pool, causing all the other customers to fall silent and stare.

The waitress rushed over and began to clear away the mess. They apologised to her and then sat in an awkward silence until she had finished.

When the waitress had gone at last, Susan was the first to speak.

'I'm so terribly sorry. You obviously didn't know. I should have thought. Please forgive me.'

'That's all right. It was just a bit of a shock, that's all. When did she...?'

'She died in 1890.'

'So young. Do you know why?'

'Russian Flu, I think'

He found he was unable to speak, or to think clearly for a few moments. He closed his eyes and waited for the dizziness to subside. When he opened them he looked at Susan, who was staring at him with a look of such tender compassion that he felt he wanted to put his head on her shoulder and let her comfort him.

'Do you mind if we leave?' he asked. 'I'm feeling a little... shaken up.'

'It's all my fault. I'm so sorry.'

'Not at all. I think maybe some fresh air...' With shaking hands he fished some coins out of his pocket to cover the bill and left them on the table.

Once in the open air he did feel a little better, although the sense of unreality stayed with him. They strolled slowly back the way they had come, she gently steering him towards the station where she would need to catch the train home.

When they reached the station, she said: 'This is where I leave you. Will you be all right?'

'Leave me?' he said in alarm.

'To catch my train,' she explained, gently. 'Not for ever, I hope.'

'Oh yes, I see. I'm so sorry for my behaviour this evening. It was just the shock. I hope we do meet again.'

'Look, I wanted to say; the exhibition will be open tomorrow — invited guests only. Of course we'd be delighted if you were there.'

'That's kind. I'm… I'm not sure.'

'Well, look, I don't know what you think about this but — David Krupp will be there.'

'What! David is in London?'

'Yes. He escorted the picture here.'

'I'll be there.' Her face lit up into one of the most breathtaking smiles he had ever seen. Suppressing the strong desire to kiss her, he shook her hand. 'Thank you for the invitation, Susan. Goodnight.'

'Goodnight, Ralph. It was lovely to meet you. I'm so glad you're coming tomorrow.'

The next day seemed, if anything, stranger and more surreal than the previous one, and Rafael struggled to keep track of the number of emotions swirling around inside him.

He loved watching Susan mingling with the invited guests, plying them with drinks and canapés and exchanging easy pleasantries. 'How elegantly she moves,' he thought.

He loved the way she smiled, and the way she tucked her long hair behind her ear.

Every now and then she would look over and catch his eye and smile, and then he would feel an electric spark fly up his spine.

It was wonderful to see David again, and it was obvious that he was equally delighted. He looked older, of course, but in a few moments the years seemed to fall away and it was as if they had never been apart.

There were many people who wanted to speak to David about his famous sister, and, once they discovered to their astonishment that the portrait's subject was present Rafael quickly found himself the centre of attention.

He quickly tired of all the fuss, and he steered David away from the crowd to a quieter corner.

'Can't we get out of here, David? I'm fed up with this. I would love to be able to talk to you properly.'

'I feel the same way. But I think we might be unpopular if we left now, everyone wants to talk to us. Look Rafi, there's plenty of time later — I'll be in London for quite a while. I'm hoping to get some drawing work here.'

'Ah, I was going to ask you about that. So you're a professional architect now?'

'I certainly am. And a busy and well respected one back home, I'll have you know. But nobody here knows me from Adam; I'm hoping to change that.'

'Well, good luck.'

'So, where can I find you?'

'In my factory, most days.'

'YOUR factory?'

David's mouth fell open and Rafael smiled at his old friend's astonished expression.

'You're not the only one whose been busy since we last met, David. Wait, I've got a card somewhere. Here it is.'

'A card? Well, look at you, that's smart. I'm so pleased. Let's see. "Ralph Jacobson, Electrical Engineer. Shoe Lane, Farringdon." Ralph Jacobson is it, now? And look at that! There's even a telephone number.'

'Funny to think that the last time I saw you I'd never used a telephone. These days, it seems I'm seldom off it.'

'Well done, Rafi' said David smilingly, tucking the card into his pocketbook. 'I can't wait to see it. The factory, I mean, not just the telephone.'

'Well, don't get too excited. It's not quite there yet; it urgently needs some modifications. Listen David, after we went to that worker's meeting outside the Dom Cathedral I said to you: 'As soon as my metalworks needs an architect I'll call you.' Do you remember?'

'I remember.'

'Well, my metalworks needs an architect. Will you help me?'

'Rafi, I've been waiting for the call for fifteen years. I'll be there first thing in the morning.'

*

The following day Rafael proudly showed David around the factory. He explained exactly what modifications were needed, which David understood at once, promising he would set to work on the designs straight away.

While he was in the factory David took the opportunity to watch how Rafael interacted with his staff. He observed with great pleasure that Rafael really was the benevolent and thoughtful employer he had always hoped he would be.

He also noticed that Rafael's secretary, Mary Bell, although rather young, was efficient, energetic, intelligent and seemed to be especially devoted to Rafael.

After the tour Rafael and David sat in the office and Rafael was at last able to say what was on his mind.

'David, I was so sorry to hear about Rosa. If it's not too painful, can you tell me what happened?'

'It was ten years ago, Rafi, so I can talk about it more easily than

I used to be able to. It was Russian Flu. Like lots of people who caught it, she initially just felt a bit rough and carried on working. Then, just when we thought she was getting better, it went to her lungs, she got pneumonia and died. The whole thing was over in a few days. They say a million people died of it. Everyone in Russia knows somebody who was affected.'

'And it was only two years after Yoss and I left. That's so very sad. And all the art she could have made. Should have made.'

'I know. She achieved a lot in a very short time, but she could have done so much more if she had been spared.'

They sat in silence for a few moments, thinking about Rosa. At length, David said: 'She really loved you, you know.'

'Thank you David, but I don't think she did.

'What makes you say that?'

'I asked her directly if she loved me and she said "Yes. But not enough". I'll never forget that moment.'

'What do you think she meant?'

'Well, I suppose just that she didn't love me enough to want to marry me.'

'Not that it can change anything now, but for what it's worth, Rafi, I don't think that was quite what she meant. You see, Rosa was very ambitious. Her career meant everything to her. She thought if she had any chance of making it in the art world she had to renounce her Judaism thoroughly — and unfortunately I think she was probably right about that. Eventually she realised that also meant renouncing you. It broke her in half. I think that's what she meant by "Yes, but not enough." Not enough to renounce her career and her future.'

Rafael heaved up a long, deep sigh.

'I adored her, David. It broke my heart when she sent me away. I'm not sure if I have quite got over it even now.'

'Oh, Rafi. You know, she kept the metal rose you made for her. It was with her when she died.'

He waited a few moments, as Rafael brushed away a tear, and

then, with a deliberate change of mood, said: 'I'm truly sorry that things didn't work out. But do I detect there might be a little light at the end of this long dark tunnel?'

'You mean Susan?' He smiled. 'No, no, we've only just met.'

'It took you about fifteen seconds to fall in love with my sister. You forget how well I know you. I saw you looking at her at the party. If you ask me I think you may have knocked a couple of seconds off your record.'

In spite of himself, Rafael laughed. When it comes to telling you the truth about yourself, there's nothing like old friends, he reflected.

*

Urgent business at the factory prevented him from visiting the gallery for a few days and it wasn't until the following week that he had a chance to go back.

He went straight to the exhibition and saw her immediately. She was standing with her back to him, studying his portrait. Silently he went and stood next to her. She sensed his presence but didn't say anything, or move her eyes from the picture. After a few moments he realised she was waiting for him to speak. 'I may not have been entirely frank with you about Rosa,' he began.

'Go on,' she prompted.

'I was desperately in love with her. But it didn't work out. Until a few days ago I believed she simply didn't love me back.'

She turned to face him. 'Oh, no, you can tell by the way she painted you. She loved you.'

'I'm sorry I didn't tell you the truth at once. I'm not sure why I did that. Let me make it up to you. Lyons again?'

'Well, it is lunch time. Annie, will you hold the fort? I'm just going for lunch.'

Annie looked at them and smiled.

'Off you go, then. Don't hurry back.'

*

As soon as Yossel had told him about his forthcoming marriage, Rafael had written to their father as he had promised. He received a reply within two weeks which surprised and delighted him. Itzhak and Hannah had applied for passports and visas, and would be leaving Tukum as soon as they received them, bound for London. They were emigrating.

They planned to follow what was by now a well-trodden path: they would travel by train to Libau on the coast and then take a steamship all the way to London. By selling their furniture and using their savings they could afford the fare. The only problem was to find accommodation, but they assumed in a large city like London that would be easy; please could Rafael find them somewhere inexpensive with three bedrooms, near a good Jewish school for the children, and with a *shul* nearby?

Rafael and Yossel smiled at their father's naivety, but set to work. Eventually they found something they thought would suit the family's needs; a comfortable apartment in a clean, quiet Spitalfields lane called Duke Street, within easy walking distance of the Jews Free School in Bell Lane and the little *shul* in Princes Street (now known as Princelet Street) that Rafael loved.

When the day arrived, the brothers were at the docks well before the ship was due in. They stood impatiently, straining for the first sight of the vessel, and when they finally glimpsed it steaming up the Thames they found it difficult to grasp that it contained their father. After what seemed an impossibly long time the ship docked, the gangplank was lowered and, after yet another wait, the passengers eventually began streaming off.

Suddenly, there they were. The father they hadn't seen for fourteen years, his young wife, and their three half-siblings, whom they had never met.

It was a very different scene from their own furtive arrival thirteen years earlier. This time there were customs and immigration officials checking passports, asking questions, opening suitcases. There were representatives from the shelter, offering advice and trying to protect the new arrivals from those who, like the rat-faced man who had robbed the Shusters, were hoping to take advantage of them.

And, most importantly, there were Rafael and Yossel, beaming all over their faces, thrilled to be reunited with their father and the others and to steer them safely to their new home.

Their excited anticipation had been mingled with trepidation; what would Hannah be like, now that she was their step-mother instead of just Reuben's older sister? They were prepared to bristle at the first sign of haughtiness or condescension on her part but in the event she behaved with such delicacy, gentleness and tact that they were instantly disarmed. Their father had spoken the truth in his letter when he said that she had blossomed into a charming and beautiful young woman. Their half-sister Leah and her two younger brothers were enchanting; impish and delightful. Yossel couldn't have been more proud and happy when the youngest, Benjamin, put his little hand in his.

As for Itzhak, he looked older of course — he was fifty-one, after all — and somewhat stooped. But he seemed fit and well otherwise. The boys watched him fussing with the bags, asking Hannah where such-and-such an item was, helping with the children, looking around him in wonderment.

Hannah was a serene presence in the centre of the chaotic scene. She helped little Meyer to do up his coat, and straightened his cap, then licked the corner of a handkerchief and knelt to wipe a dirty mark from Benjamin's face. Then she linked her arm in Itzhak's and he looked at with pride and devotion. 'Yes,' thought Rafael. 'It's a real marriage after all.'

The brothers had a cab waiting, which was hugely exciting for the children, and on the way to Duke Street they talked about the journey, about Rachel, and about the factory.

*

There was plenty for Rafael to think about. Almost too much. There was the task of getting Itzhak and Hannah and the children settled in to their new home, and Yossel and Rachel's wedding to plan.

There were the modifications to the factory, which David was going to oversee, as well as all the normal day-to-day issues connected with the factory.

But for now, all that would have to wait. All Rafael could think about was Susan.

One warm Sunday afternoon in summer they went for a stroll under the trees in St. James' Park. They talked about art and politics. They teased each other and laughed. He told her stories about the early days in London; the feeling of despair when he and Yossel thought they had found their uncle and aunt only to be told they had left. The story of how he got his job at Smart's. She talked about her student days and her current job at the new gallery.

When they got tired of walking they sat on a bench by the lake enjoying the feeling of the sun on their faces and the pleasure of each other's company. 'It's very strange,' Rafael said, 'but I feel as if I've known you for years.'

'I feel the same way, Ralph. But then, I have actually known you for years — sort of.'

'How do you mean?'

'Don't forget, I've been studying your face for a long time.'

'Oh, I see what you mean. It's a wonderful thing that it should be that portrait which has brought us together.'

'Together. *Are* we "together"?'

'I think so. Don't you?'

Instead of replying directly, she turned the full force of her smile on him. He reached out and they held hands. 'There's something I want to ask you,' he said. 'I hope you won't mind.'

'Yes?' she said, a little breathlessly.

'Would it be all right if I called you by your Hebrew name, Shoshana, instead of Susan?'

'Oh.' She looked rather disappointed.

'Is something the matter?' he asked.

'No, It's just — that wasn't quite what I was expecting you to say.'

'You see, I find 'Susan' quite difficult to say, with my accent. All those esses.'

'Yes, I noticed that. Everybody does call me Susan — except my parents — but, to be honest, I've never particularly liked it. On the other hand, my Hebrew name, Shoshana, well, it doesn't sound very English, does it? No, I don't really want to go back to that, either.'

'Well, what can I call you then?'

'I don't know. How about "Hey you"?'

'It's tempting.' He was silent for a few seconds. 'I do have another idea,' he said, thoughtfully at last. 'The name Shoshana — it's in the Song of Songs, isn't it?'

'Yes, that's right.'

'It's the name of a flower. But I don't know what it's called in English. I remember Ibn Ezra calls it a "white flower of sweet, intoxicating perfume."'

'Oh I actually didn't know that. That's nice.'

'And very appropriate, if I may say so. What would you call that flower in English?'

'It's called a lily. It's actually quite a popular name.'

'Lily.' He thought about the sound for a moment. 'It's a lovely name. No esses. How would it be if I called you Lily?'

'Lily,' she repeated. Then she smiled. 'I like it. I actually like it better than Susan. Do you know? I think I could get used to it.'

A few more moments went by while they thought about the idea. 'Oh!' she exclaimed suddenly. 'Lily Levy. I don't like that so much. It makes me sound like a music-hall singer. "Miss Lily Levy". And it's hard to say, too.'

'Oh, I wouldn't worry too much about that. You might not be "Miss Lily Levy" for ever.'

'Whatever do you mean?' she said mischievously, although she knew exactly what he meant. The breathlessness seemed to have come back.

'Well, isn't it traditional for a woman to adopt her husband's name when she gets married?'

'Do you know, Ralph, I believe it is. Go on.'

'Well then, let's say, for the sake of argument, that you did decide to change your last name at some point.' He leaned in a little closer and looked deep into her eyes. 'Do you have any thoughts about what you might decide to change it *to?*'

'Well, Mister Jacobson,' she replied, her eyes sparkling like the sunlight on the lake. 'That is a very interesting question. I suppose we shall see what we shall see.'

ACKNOWLEDGEMENTS

A lot of the research on the historical background to this story was conducted online. I have spent hours on *Wikipedia* and found a great deal of useful information there, so I would like to acknowledge my debt to all those who have contributed articles.

Jewishgen, the "global home for Jewish genealogy on the web" has provided me with a wealth of detail, so I would like to thank whoever runs it, particularly the Latvia & Estonia Research Division and its director Arlene Beare.

The websites of the *Jewish Museum* in London the *Yivo Institute for Jewish Research* in America (particularly its online *Encyclopaedia of Jews in Eastern Europe*), and the *Jewish Historical Society of England* have also been invaluable.

Some of the incidents in my story, along with a lot of background information, are drawn from the reminiscences of my father, Jerrold Assersohn, and in particular the stories he wrote down in his book *As It Was* (published privately).

Some information about Tukums and Bauska comes from the *Encyclopedia of Jewish Communities: Latvia and Estonia*, edited by Dov Levin, published by Yad Vashem, Jerusalem.

For information about Yiddish folksong I consulted Ruth Rubin's seminal *Voices of a People,* which is where I found the lyrics to the folk songs sung by Yossel in Part Two.

For background I have consulted a number of books, including *Yiddish Civilisation* by Paul Kiwaczek, *The Shtetl Book* by Diana K. Roskies and David G. Roskies, *On Brick Lane* by Rachel Lichtenstein,

Journey Through a Small Planet by Emanuel Litvinoff and *Rothschild Buildings* by Jerry White.

Inevitably I have been inspired and influenced by some of the classics of Jewish fiction, including (of course) Sholem Aleichem's *Tevye the Dairyman* and Israel Zangwill's *Children of the Ghetto*.

Many thanks to Lucy Quinnell, who runs the amazing Fire and Iron gallery in Leatherhead, for her helpful insights into lamp making. Also my engineer father-in-law Dennis Hewitt for his invaluable advice on Rafael's apprenticeship.

Thank you also to Madeleine Humphrey and the other volunteers at The Spitalfields Centre charity. They work to preserve the synagogue at 19 Princelet Street and kindly let me look around this amazing building.

I would like to acknowledge the contributions of my brothers David and John and my sister Maureen. Despite the fact that none of us knows very much about our ancestors, we've had a lot of fun speculating on their lives and coming up with competing theories. Theirs are definitely wrong.

My grateful thanks to our lovely friend Georgia Scott for reviewing the finished book.

And finally, thank you to my wonderful wife Jan, without whom nothing would be worth doing, for all her help, support and wonderful suggestions. She has improved the book as she improves everything in my life.

GLOSSARY

Aleph–beys. The alphabet, named after the first two letters of the Hebrew alphabet.

Ark. The ornamental chamber in the synagogue which houses the *Sifrei Torah* scrolls.

Bar mitzvah. Coming–of age ceremony for boys at thirteen.

Bentching. Reciting the grace after meals.

Bimah. A raised platform at the front of a Synagogue.

Bubbe. Grandma.

Challah. Plaited bread made for to accompany the Sabbath evening meal.

Chazzan. The Synagogue cantor, a singer who leads the congregation in songful prayers.

Chutzpah. Nerve; cheek; Audacity; impudence.

Ganef. Thief.

Goy. (Plural *goyim*) A non–jew.

Gut yomtov. A holiday greeting. "Happy holidays".

Haggadah. The text describing the order of the Passover Seder.

Hanukkah. Jewish Festival of lights, lasting eight days, which commemorates the recovery of Jerusalem and the dedication of the Second Temple in the 2nd century BCE.

Hasidim. Members of the orthodox Jewish Hasidic sect.

Haskalah. A movement, or ideological worldview amongst Jewry in Central Eastern Europe in the 18th and 19th centuries, often termed The Jewish Enlightenment.

Heder. A type of elementary school, widespread amongst Eastern European Jewry from the Middle Ages.

Kaddishel. Baby son, or endearing term for a boy or man.

Kashrut. The dietary laws that govern what food Jews may eat and how it should be prepared.

Kiddush. Blessings said at the start of the Sabbath evening meal.

Kol Nidre. Kol Nidre ("All vows") is the name of a ritual performed on the eve of *Yom Kippur* (Day of Atonement), and by extension, the name of the evening service on that day.

Koppel. A Jewish skullcap, worn by orthodox Jews at all times except when sleeping or bathing, and by the less devout only for praying or when in a sacred building. Also called a yarmulke or kippah.

Kvetch. To moan and complain.

L'chaim. A traditional toast. Literally, 'to life'.

Lilith. A primordial she-demon in Mesopotamian and Jewish mythology, supposedly the first wife of Adam. She was said to intend harm to children and babies, and charms against her power were common in Eastern European Jewry.

Lokshen. Jewish egg noodles.

Luftmensch. A beggar — a man of the air, someone with no means of support.

Maimonides. Moses ben Maimon, more commonly known as Maimonides, was a medieval *Torah* scholar.

Mame. (Pronounced "mah-muh") Mother.

Mamele. (Pronounced "mah-muh-leh") Diminutive of *Mame*. An informal word for mother, used among family and friends.

Maoz Tzur. A prayer sung as part of the lighting of a Menorah, an eight-branched candelabra, each evening during *Hanukkah*.

Matzo. A wafer of unleavened bread eaten by observant Jews during Passover.

Mazel tov. Congratulations!

Melamed. (Plural *melamdin*) A school teacher or tutor.

Mensch. An admirable person.

Meshuggener. Madman, lunatic. (**adj.** meshuggah)

Mezuzah. A small piece of parchment inscribed with Hebrew letters which is fixed, in a small case, on the doorpost of Jewish homes and other buildings.

Minyan. A quorum of ten male adults required for certain religious obligations.

Mishnah. An early written collection of Jewish oral traditions.

Momzer. Bastard.

Nu?. So?

Pale of Settlement. Region of the Russian Empire that existed between 1791 and 1917 in which permanent residency of Jews was allowed. Only certain Jews were allowed to live outside the Pale.

Pentateuch. The first five books of the Hebrew Bible (The "Old Testament").

Pesach. Jewish festival of Passover.

Rashi. An acronym, the common name for the Mediaeval *Torah* scholar Rabbi Shlomo Yitzchaki.

Reb. Mister.

Rebe. (Pronounced "reh–buh") A respectful title for a learned man or teacher.

Rosh Hashanah. Jewish New Year festival.

Shiva. A week–long mourning period beginning after the burial, following the death of a close relative. The ritual is known in English as "sitting *shiva*".

Schlemiel. A dolt, or fool.

Schlep. To slog, or to drag or carry something with difficulty.

Schlorem. Cheap trinket, piece of rubbish.

Schmaltz. Chicken or duck fat used as a spread.

Schmooze. To talk in a friendly way, but insincere way; to 'butter someone one up'.

Schmutter. Cheap clothes, rags.

Schnorrer. A semi–respectable type of beggar.

Seder. A ritual feast on the first night of Passover (*Pesach*).

Shabbat shalom. Good Sabbath.

Shabbos. The Jewish Sabbath, beginning at dusk on Friday evening and ending at dusk on Saturday.

Shavuot. A Jewish Festival in the summer celebrating the giving of the Five Books of the *Torah* by God to Moses.

Shiksa. A non-Jewish girl.

Shochet. Someone who performs *shechita*, the ritual slaughtering of animals for food.

Shofar. A blown musical instrument, sounding a little like a bugle, made from a ram's horn.

Shtreimel. A fur hat worn by some Ashkenazi Jewish men.

Shul. Synagogue; Jewish house of prayer.

Siddur. A book containing daily prayers.

Sefer Torah. (Plural *Sifrei Torah*). A scroll of parchment, considered sacred, on which Bible verses are written, read during services in the Synagogue.

Spiel. A sales-pitch or speech intended to persuade.

Sukkos. Jewish harvest festival, also known as the Feast of Tabernacles.

Tallis. (Plural *tallitot*) A fringed garment worn in synagogue for prayer.

Talmud. After the *Torah*, the primary text of Jewish law and theology.

Talmud Torah. A publicly funded religious elementary school.

Tate. (Pronounced "tah-tuh") Father.

Tatty. Dad. Informal word for father, used among family and friends.

Tefillin. Small black leather boxes, attached to long leather straps, containing parchment scrolls inscribed with verses from the *Torah*, worn during prayers.

Tisha B'av. A Jewish fast day in late summer commemorating a number of calamities in Jewish History including the destruction of the Temples.

Torah. The Pentateuch, the first five books of the Hebrew Bible.

Tsugelklappt. Exhausted. Done in.

Tsum gezunt. Informal farewell. 'Take care'.

Tsuris. Problems, trouble, heartache.

Tush. Bottom.

Tzitzit. A fringed garment worn under the shirt.

Yashar koach!. Bravo! Well done!

Yom Kippur. Jewish fast day, The Day of Atonement, the holiest day of the Jewish calendar. It follows on ten days after *Rosh Hashanah*, the Jewish New Year.

Zay gezunt. Be well.

Zeide. Grandpa.

Ian Assersohn is descended from Latvian and Polish immigrants and was brought up by Jewish parents in North London. He was educated at Westminster School, the Royal College of Music in London and Koninklijk Conservatorium in The Hague.

He worked in the IT industry for twenty years and left in 2009 to pursue a career as a composer, choral director and piano teacher.

He is the author of a number of short stories, poems and song lyrics, and has composed extensively for choirs. His music is published by Oxford University Press and also by his own imprint, Apple Tree Music. The Lampmaker is his first novel.

Ian can be contacted through www.LimetreeBooks.net